Also by Robert Dugoni

Murder One
Bodily Harm
Wrongful Death
Damage Control
The Jury Master
The Cyanide Canary (nonfiction)

THE
CONVICTION

A Novel

ROBERT DUGONI

A TOUCHSTONE BOOK
Published by Simon & Schuster
New York London Toronto Sydney New Delhi

Touchstone
A Division of Simon & Schuster, Inc.
1230 Avenue of the Americas
New York, NY 10020

First Touchstone hardcover edition June 2012

TOUCHSTONE and colophon are registered trademarks of Simon & Schuster, Inc.

For information about special discounts for bulk purchases, please contact
Simon & Schuster Special Sales at 1-866-506-1949
or business@simonandschuster.com.

The Simon & Schuster Speakers Bureau can bring authors to your live event. For more
information or to book an event contact the Simon & Schuster Speakers Bureau at
1-866-248-3049 or visit our website at www.simonspeakers.com.

Manufactured in the United States of America

10   9   8   7   6   5   4   3   2   1

Library of Congress Cataloging-in-Publication Data
Dugoni, Robert.
    The conviction : a novel / Robert Dugoni.—1st Touchstone hardcover ed.
        p. cm.
    I. Title.
    PS3604.U385C66 2012
    813'.6—dc23

                                                2012013923

ISBN 978-1-4516-0672-0
ISBN 978-1-4516-0674-4 (ebook)

To my son, Joe, and my daughter, Catherine.
You both make me so proud.
God blessed me and your mother the day each of you was born.

THE
CONVICTION

ONE

David Sloane stepped through the metal detector, grabbed his briefcase, and put on his coat while running toward a staircase, ignoring the elevators. On the second floor he slowed his pace, considering the letters above the tall wooden doors and the names on the clear plaques mounted to the wall. He entered the courtroom for the Hon. Irene Glazier as Judge Glazier scribbled final notes in a file and set it aside on her elevated desk. He had never met Lisa Lynch, a partner in Foster & Bane's San Jose office—the law firm didn't have a San Jose office when Sloane worked there, but he quickly deduced Lynch to be the blonde in a black suit standing and approaching counsel table as Judge Glazier called out the final case of the morning and the prosecutor shuffled through a stack of files at the adjacent table.

Sloane met Lynch as she set down her legal pad. "Good timing," she said.

Ordinarily relaxed in the courtroom, today Sloane's stomach churned. Lynch had sounded both competent and knowledgeable on the phone, but Sloane knew she too was working on the fly; neither of them had been provided with much in the way of details.

"Counsel." Judge Glazier acknowledged them in a flat tone, face devoid of expression. African American, she pulled her hair back in a severe bun, accentuating high cheekbones.

"Marsha Gutierrez for the State," the prosecutor said with a slight Hispanic accent.

"Good morning, Your Honor, Lisa Lynch for the defendant. Also present at counsel table is Mr. Carter's stepfather, David Sloane."

Glazier stopped the busy work and raised her eyes. The prosecutor had also turned in Sloane's direction. After a series of high-profile legal cases, Sloane's reputation preceded him.

"Mr. Sloane. Are you here this morning as an attorney or as a parent?" Glazier asked.

"A parent, Your Honor. And Jake's biological father, Frank Carter, will also be joining us," Sloane said. "He's parking the car." As if on cue, Frank Carter pulled open the courtroom door, fixing his hair as he made his way to Sloane's side.

Judge Glazier folded her hands atop the legal file. "I want to talk with you before we bring in your son. This is Jake's second arrest for public intoxication in less than six months, and this time it was accompanied by violent acts and significant property damage."

All Sloane knew was Jake had been arrested stumbling down a street in Concord not far from the home of a friend where he had requested to spend the night.

"Jake's file indicates his mother is deceased?"

Sloane answered. "That's correct, Your Honor."

"She was murdered?"

"Yes," Sloane said, voice falling.

"And I understand from the counselor's report that Jake witnessed that event."

"He did."

Glazier sat back, index finger sawing across her lower lip. "He's no longer in counseling?"

Sloane looked to Frank. "He was, for about a year, but the counselor felt he didn't need it anymore."

"I'd say it's time for a new counselor," Glazier said.

"He was doing okay up until about nine months ago."

"What happened nine months ago?"

"Nothing I can pinpoint," Carter said. "Adolescence, I guess."

"Nothing? Change of schools? New friends? Some change in the home?"

Carter shook his head. "No. None of those things."

Glazier leaned forward and propped her elbows on her desk. "I'm concerned, gentlemen. Your son's offending behavior is escalating. According to the police reports he was drinking vodka with a stimulant called Red Bull. Are you familiar with it?"

"Not in any detail, Your Honor," Sloane said.

"The stimulant acts to impede the body's natural ability to shut down and pass out when intoxicated. It can increase a person's normal tolerance. Jake's blood alcohol level was two and a half times the legal limit. Point two-five. He wasn't far from an overdose."

Lynch spoke. "Your Honor, we would certainly abide by any court recommendation that Jake enter a substance abuse program and that he also restart his grief counseling."

Gutierrez jumped in. "Your Honor, completion of a substance abuse program was a condition of Mr. Carter's *prior* release," she said, holding up a multipage document. "According to his caseworker, he failed to complete that program, was frequently absent, and displayed disdain when he did attend."

"Mr. Sloane, you reside in Seattle, do you not?" Glazier asked.

"I do, Judge."

"So, Mr. Carter, you have primary care of Jake?"

"Sole care," he said. "But I work. I thought he was going. When I found out, I talked to him about it. I grounded him. I took away the car, his iPod, Xbox. He told me he was going."

"That's a problem," Glazier said. "If I release him pending successful completion of the program and he does not attend, and you have no ability to ensure he does, I'm left with little choice but to incarcerate him and have him complete an in-detention program."

Sloane had thought much of this through on the plane from Seattle and he and Frank discussed it on the car ride from the airport. "Your Honor, I'd be willing to take Jake back to Seattle with me and ensure he attends both grief counseling and a substance abuse program."

Glazier's brow furrowed. "And what about your career, Mr. Sloane; how would you manage that?"

"I'd take a leave of absence, if necessary," Sloane said.

Glazier folded her hands, thumbs twirling.

Gutierrez spoke. "Judge, releasing Mr. Carter might very well be enabling him, in a sense sending him a message that no matter what he does he can get away with it."

"That's an extreme statement," Lynch said. "We don't discount that the charges here are very serious, but under the prosecutor's rationale the court would be enabling any child it did not confine. Jake has a substance abuse problem. The violence evolved out of that problem. He needs help."

"Not every child has 'the lawyer who does not lose' as a step-father," Gutierrez said with noticeable bite. Before anyone could respond she added, "Your Honor, the officer's report indicates Mr. Carter had an aluminum baseball bat in hand, and had left a trail of broken taillights and smashed headlights in his wake, along with landscape lights strewn across lawns. He then resisted arrest and when the officers finally subdued him, he spewed forth a string of profanities and taunted them that Mr. Sloane would, quote, 'make them look like assholes when he got through with them.'"

"The boy was severely intoxicated," Lynch said. "It's unlikely he had any idea what he was saying or the gravity of his circumstances. His record does not warrant placement in a juvenile facility. We would again suggest Jake be given home confinement pending successful completion of a substance abuse program and grief counseling."

"And you would be willing to take personal responsibility to ensure Jake completes both programs, Mr. Sloane?" Glazier asked.

"I would, Your Honor."

"And what about you, Mr. Carter, would you be agreeable to Jake living with Mr. Sloane?"

"If that would be the best thing for Jake, sure, I'd do it."

"It's summer," Lynch said. "The court could reschedule a hearing for early September."

Glazier sat back, poker-faced, lips pursed. She spoke to her bailiff. "Bring him in."

The bailiff returned with Jake. The boy's appearance surprised Sloane. His hair had grown, nearly shoulder length, and he looked two to three inches taller, approaching Sloane's height. He also looked to have filled out since his wrestling season concluded. He'd been good enough to finish second in the state in his weight class, and his coach had told Sloane that Jake was naturally strong and could be even better if he were to apply himself. Sloane did the math in his head. It had been nine months since he'd flown to California to watch that final match—his last visit.

As Jake entered the courtroom the right side of his mouth pulled back in what was, under the circumstances, a most inappropriate smirk.

"Mr. Carter," Judge Glazier said, "these are very serious charges I have before me. I'd suggest you lose that smug expression."

Jake did.

"We were just discussing what to do about you; you were ordered to undergo a substance abuse program but I'm told you never completed it. Why not?"

Jake shrugged, a sixteen-year-old boy's response to just about any question. "I couldn't always get there after school."

"So what option does that leave me now? If I can't trust you to commit to an out-of-detention program my only option is to incarcerate you to make sure you complete the program. Is that what you want?"

"No," Jake said.

"Do you think you have a problem with alcohol, Mr. Carter?"

"I don't know. I guess so."

"You guess so?"

"No, I mean . . . yes."

"Do you realize, Mr. Carter, that you were about that far from possibly killing yourself?" Glazier held her thumb and index finger an inch apart. "Are you aware of what happens to your body when you mix an over-the-counter stimulant like Red Bull with alcohol?"

"Not really."

"It allows you to drink more than you should. That's how people overdose, Mr. Carter, by taking more of a drug—and alcohol is a drug—than their body can physically handle. Do you understand me?"

He nodded.

"Do you want to die?"

Jake shrugged. "No."

Glazier glanced at Sloane before returning her attention to Jake. "What are we going to do about the damage to all those people's cars and property? How do you intend to pay for that?"

"I don't know."

"Are you in any sports?"

"Not anymore."

"Any activities? Drama? Band? Journalism? Debate?"

"No."

She looked again to Sloane and Frank Carter. "Then there should be nothing to prevent you from completing a substance abuse program and getting a job to pay for all the damage you've caused. Do I make myself clear?"

"Yes."

"Good. Because there will not be a third chance, Mr. Carter. You mess up again and I *will* incarcerate you. And let me make this perfectly clear. If I do, there is not a lawyer in this world"—her eyes again shifted to Sloane, two black pinpoints—"not even one who never loses, who will prevent me from doing just that."

TWO

Sloane parked the Cadillac diagonal to the laurel hedge beside Charles Jenkins's Buick. If Jake recognized the car it did not elicit any response. Not much had. Jake didn't utter a word on the flight back to Seattle, slipping on headphones and tuning out, eyes closed. Even on takeoff and landing, when the flight attendant instructed him to turn off the music, he kept the earphones in place, eyes closed. Sloane gave up trying and put his head back against the seat, but he did not sleep. It evaded him as it had the prior evening, his mind flooded with thoughts of Tina and how she had done such a great job raising Jake. Sloane had always been apprehensive about his ability to be a father, but each time he'd expressed doubt Tina had reassured him, serving as his parenting docent. Without her, he felt like a man at an art gallery pretending to understand all the nuances that had gone into a painting's creation, but really not having a clue.

Robotically, Jake stepped from the car. A light breeze blew his hair off his face. The mist held the briny smell of the Puget Sound. Sloane popped the trunk and Jake retrieved his suitcase and lugged it up the porch steps. A lemony ammonia smell greeted Sloane as he stepped into the kitchen. Alex had cleaned while waiting, the blue marble counters spotless. Sloane asked her and Charlie to drive down from Camano Island and clear his house of alcohol, but the truth was he wanted them there for support when he brought Jake home.

At the sight of Jake, little CJ Jenkins wiggled from his father's arms and ran on tiptoes from the living room into the kitchen, laughing and jabbering. The sight of the three-year-old boy brought the first genuine smile to Jake's face. He slipped the headphones from his ears and picked him up as Charlie and Alex stood watching.

"Hey, CJ."

CJ held up a purple stuffed animal. "I have a dragon."

"I see that."

"But he's not real. What are those?"

"Headphones. You want to listen?"

Jake placed one of the headphones near CJ's ear. CJ pulled away and pressed a palm to his ear. "Too loud."

Jake gave Charlie a one-arm hug, which was like trying to wrap an arm around a refrigerator. He matched Alex in height, five feet ten.

"What are you doing here?" Jake asked.

"Your dad told us you were coming home, so we wanted to come visit," Alex said.

Jake glanced back at Sloane. "He's not my dad and this isn't my home."

"We just wanted to see you," Alex said, touching Jake's shoulder. "You've grown. I think you might have me." She touched his head. "I like your hair."

Jake let CJ slide to the ground.

"You want to play Legos?" CJ asked, apparently recalling Jake's stash in his closet.

"You go ahead," Jake said. "You can have them if you want."

CJ raced across the living room and up the stairs.

Jake looked around. "What am I supposed to do here?"

Sloane did not have video games or an Xbox and had only basic cable. "We can take the boat out and do some fishing later."

"It's freaking raining out. It's always raining here."

"It's supposed to clear up," Charlie said.

"Yeah," Jake scoffed. "Like in August . . . for a week."

Jake started to put his earphones back over his ears. "Uh-uh," Sloane said.

"What?" Jake looked and sounded incredulous.

"In your room or outside you can listen to your music. When you're down here it stays off."

"Whatever." Jake stepped past him, pulling open the Dutch door, and shoving the screen with enough force to bounce it off the side of the house. Halfway down the lawn he reached inside his pocket and produced a pack of cigarettes, shaking one out and turning his back to the wind to flick a lighter.

Sloane started for the door but Alex interceded. "David, don't. You have bigger issues to deal with than his music and smoking."

"Tina said a boy needed rules."

"He also needs room to grow and make his own decisions."

Sloane looked to the window. Jake sat on the picnic table with his back to them, facing the gray landscape and smoking his cigarette. The wind had caused small whitecaps. "Yeah, well, we can all see how well he's doing so far."

"The more you push him the more he's going to push back."

"So what do I do?"

"Give him his space. And love him."

They went into the living room and sat.

"I've made a few telephone calls," Alex said. "One of the best substance abuse programs is right at Virginia Mason." Sloane had asked her to try to find something close to his office downtown where he could take Jake during the day. "And I'm looking into a grief counselor here in Burien, for both of you."

"What are you going to do with him while you're at work?" Jenkins asked.

Sloane had given the matter more thought on the plane. "Carolyn is always complaining she has too much filing, and John has a big criminal matter with a lot of documents that need organizing. This way I can keep an eye on him and maybe we can interact in a manner other than father and son."

Jake walked in the kitchen door and slipped the headphones from his ears. "You trying to figure out what to do with me?"

"We're just visiting, Jake," Alex said. "I was going to make dinner. Any special requests?"

"Yeah, Enrico's Pizza; it's in California." He retrieved his suit-case and started up the stairs, stopping on the step where he had watched his mother bleed to death.

Sloane started toward him. "Jake," he said.

"I don't need a bunch of freaking babysitters," he said and continued up the flight.

THE TIN ROOM
BURIEN, WASHINGTON

The following morning Sloane felt punch drunk, physically and emotionally spent. He hadn't slept. When he closed his eyes he had a vision of a smiling Tina reaching out to him, but as he reached for her a trickle of blood escaped the corner of her mouth, the trickle becoming a torrent of red that spewed down the front of her white robe. He got up early. Alex too was awake, getting a bottle for CJ. She suggested exercise to relieve his stress.

Sloane ran up the steep hill from Three Tree Point to Burien, and by the time he reached The Tin Room he was gasping for air and perspiring profusely. Father Allen sat on a barstool with his back to the plate-glass window, alternately sipping a mug of tea and picking at a bran muffin in a stream of morning sun. When Sloane walked in Allen slid off the seat to shake hands, and Sloane thought Allen looked like a college kid home from school on summer break with his head of unkempt blond curls, baggy shorts with pockets to the knees, brown sandals, and a T-shirt that said ZEPPELIN LIVES. In actuality Allen was thirty-seven with degrees in theology and psychology. Along the way he had acquired a heavy dose of common sense. Sloane took a minute to greet Dan House, the Tin Room owner, and his mother, Chirlee, before sliding onto the stool beside Allen. Kelly brought him a hot tea and a tall glass of ice water.

"I thought you were ducking me because I kicked your butt in our last game of one-on-one," Allen said.

"You played well," Sloane said.

The priest considered him over the sound of a soccer game on the television and the rattle of plates in the kitchen. "No response? No comeback? No quip?"

"Sorry to bother you so early," Sloane said.

"I'm a priest; if someone isn't bothering me at an odd hour of the day or night I'm not doing my job."

Sloane sipped his tea. One of the bartenders peeled lemons. Kelly carried a stack of glasses from the kitchen to arrange on the shelf beneath the hanging sheet metal roller. "I need some advice, Allen. It involves Jake." Allen waited. "He's back living with me."

"I don't sense a lot of joy in that statement."

Sloane explained what had transpired. Finishing, he asked, "Any words of wisdom?"

"Such as Jake is crying out for help? I think you know that already."

"He doesn't want my help; he doesn't want to be here."

"That's what he's saying; it isn't likely what he's feeling. Violent outbursts and mood swings can be associated with the alcohol or drug abuse, but the real question is what is driving Jake to the alcohol and drugs."

"Pain," Sloane said, knowing well the agony of a child who witnesses the brutal murder of his mother.

"The problem with you is you're always stealing my diagnosis." Allen was equally familiar with Sloane's background, and knew that Sloane had also witnessed the murder of his mother. "One of the characteristic symptoms of post-traumatic stress disorder is the person reexperiencing a trauma either through nightmares, flashbacks, or intrusive thoughts—you can't get an image out of your head."

"I was afraid of that."

"Another is avoidance. The person will avoid the activities, places, and people he associates with the trauma. You said Jake seemed tired to you, listless, that he's constantly wearing his headphones, listening to music."

"He's trying to tune out these intrusive thoughts," Sloane said, feeling more guilt for making Jake shut off the music.

"When he should be sleeping he's likely up late, listening to music, trying to avoid whatever it is that comes in the night. A prolonged lack of sleep can have a pronounced effect on a person's ability to function and to concentrate, and on his mood. The alcohol and drugs became a means to escape."

"So it isn't just an act of defiance," Sloane said.

"It's an act of self-preservation. So is pushing you away."

"Because he associates me with Tina's death."

Allen nodded. "You were there. You're part of his nightmare. He sees you and he recalls that night and what happened. You also have to consider this from Jake's perspective. Where were you the last nine months? What interest did you take in his life, his studies, his friends, in his schoolwork?"

Sloane didn't answer.

"Is it a difficult question to answer or just to hear?" Allen raised his voice.

"I had that trial and then the aftermath with Barklay."

"Uh-huh. And now you want to gallop back into Jake's life and take on the role of 'Dad' again. Here comes David Sloane, the knight in shining armor to save another day."

The bartender stopped peeling the lemon. Sloane leaned closer. "What else was I supposed to do, leave him there?"

"Why not? You left him there for nearly two years and didn't care what happened to him."

"That's uncalled for, Allen."

"What? This isn't the reaction you expected? Did I disappoint you?"

Sloane paused. "Touché."

Allen offered a sympathetic grin. "Now you know how Jake felt. You're drawn to people who need your help; we've talked about this before. Well, now you have someone telling you to fuck off. He doesn't want your help. You weren't there when he needed you, so why should he accept your help now?"

"It isn't what I wanted, Allen. I thought it best for Jake, and Frank never said there was anything wrong."

"So when did you start trusting Frank? From what I know of him he's immature and narcissistic."

"He said he wanted a second chance at being Jake's father. Things seemed to be going okay."

"He abandoned Jake when he was a child; he wanted nothing to do with him. You don't think Jake remembers that?"

Sloane massaged his forehead. He had a headache. "And I did the same thing, didn't I?"

"In Jake's mind, yes, that's exactly what you did. You gave him up. Then you abandoned him."

"I thought it was the right thing. I would have had to destroy Frank on the witness stand. Jake had already lost his mother. I didn't want to take his father."

"He'd already lost his father, years before you were ever in the picture. Maybe you thought you were doing the right thing. Maybe it was noble, perhaps even Solomon-esque, but do you think a twelve- or thirteen-year-old boy saw it that way?"

"No."

"And then he gets a call from a strange woman who invites him to come back to Seattle for an unexpected visit, and he sees the man he considers his father seemingly moving forward with his life without him, seemingly happy. Was it not shortly after he returned to California from that visit that Frank says the changes began?"

Sloane had done the time line in his own head when Judge Glazier asked about changes in Jake's life that could have caused his behavior. "Nine months." Sloane said.

"What happens after the summer is over, David? Do you ship him back to Frank?"

Sloane looked out the window. "He said I wasn't his father."

"You're not his father—not biologically and not practically."

For a while neither man spoke, the sound of the soccer game and the clatter of dishes and voices in the kitchen filling the dead air.

"And now you have another problem," Allen finally said.

"I brought him back to the place he watched her die."

"There you go, stealing my diagnosis again."

"I need to get him out of there."

"You need to ease him back into the environment, just as you need to ease back into the role of parent. Your friend Alex is right; you can't start laying down a bunch of rules and start telling Jake what he can and can't do. He doesn't see you in the role of parent.

You're just another authority figure telling him what he can't do, and it is authority he is rebelling against. Until you tackle the bigger issues, fighting him on his music or his smoking is just something for him to fight with you about."

"Has anyone ever accused you of being subtle, Allen?"

"Catholic priests major in guilt, you know that." Allen put his hand on Sloane's shoulder. "This is going to take significant time and effort, not to mention a great deal of patience. You know that, don't you? You know this is not a problem you're going to be able to fix by marching into court and outsmarting everybody."

"Whatever it takes to make this right, Allen; I promised Tina I'd take care of him."

"Forget what you promised Tina. Guilt is never as good a motivator as love, David. Act out of love. Do it because you love your son."

THREE

Back at Three Tree Sloane did not go immediately inside. He sat on the picnic table, staring out at the snow-capped peaks of the Olympic Mountain range. Allen was, as usual, right. Sloane might have had the best intentions when he conceded custody to Frank, but that was from the perspective of an adult. It was doubtful Jake saw it that way. The boy had just lost his mother. That day in the courtroom he also lost his father.

When his cell phone rang Sloane initially ignored it, but checked caller ID and wondered whether there was some truth to the belief that people could sense when you were thinking of them. The last time he had seen Detective Tom Molia was when Molia came out from West Virginia after Tina's murder.

"Tom?" he answered. He wondered if Jenkins had called to advise Molia of Sloane's situation.

"I hope I'm not interrupting some great legal thinking," Molia said.

"Not much thinking going on here, Tom, legal or otherwise. How've you been?"

"I've been better, actually. I'm in California. My mom passed last week."

"I'm sorry."

"I appreciate the condolences, but she lived to the ripe young age of ninety-three and had a great life. We should all be so lucky, huh?"

Sloane thought of Jake, just sixteen, and how the boy had

hesitated when Judge Glazier asked him if he wanted to die. "We should all be so lucky," he agreed.

"You sure I didn't catch you at a bad time? If you have something else going on . . ."

"No, Tom, it's fine. Things are a bit out of whack here at the moment."

"Anything I can do to help?"

"Thanks but no, just stuff, you know. What's up?"

"I'm having a little problem with the probate of my mother's estate here in Oakland. It's not a huge issue, but it involves a life insurance policy my parents took out many years ago. The company's no longer in business and the successor is balking. I was hoping a strongly worded letter on your stationery might catch their attention better than my feeble threats to drive out to Rhode Island and start shooting like John Wayne in *True Grit*."

Sloane didn't want to turn Molia down, but he also didn't have the time. "I'm heading out for a few days with Jake, Tom. But I could have Tom Pendergrass handle it for you if that would be okay."

"That would be fine. I'm betting they're bluffing and will fold quicker than a shirt in a Chinese Laundromat."

"I'll call the office and have Tom get in touch with you directly."

"Much obliged. Where are you and Jake headed?"

"Don't know," Sloane said. "Haven't made any plans yet."

"You feel like doing a little hiking?"

Sloane sat up straighter. "Maybe."

"I brought T.J. with me. After I get things settled with the estate we're heading up into the Sierras above the gold country to do a little hiking and fishing. I used to go with my dad. He said sleeping in a tent and breathing fresh air cleared the soul and the body. T.J. and I pick different spots around the country every year. This year we had the choice made for us when Mom died."

The offer was tempting, but Sloane was reluctant to get anyone else involved in Jake's problems. "It's not that simple, Tom. Jake's having some real issues."

"Tell me about it. What boy his age doesn't?"

"This goes beyond the normal problems, I'm afraid."

"So shoot, what's going on?"

"I don't want to burden you with this while you're handling your mother's affairs."

"Now you're just insulting me."

Sloane took a breath and started. For the next several minutes he laid out the situation as best he could.

"Okay," Molia said when Sloane had finished. "So it sounds like hiking and camping are just what you both need, get him away from there and give you two a chance to spend some time together."

Sloane was tempted. "He's unpredictable. I'm worried he could be volatile."

"Like I said, what boy his age isn't? Listen, the invitation is extended. If you change your mind just call and we'll pick you up at the airport. We're planning on heading out Wednesday and spending the night in a town my dad and I used to stay at, get a wilderness permit, and start out early Thursday morning. You're welcome to join us, and I know having another boy his age would thrill T.J."

"Thanks, Tom. I'll think about it." Sloane disconnected and looked out again at the mountain range. Maybe it was fate Tom Molia had called. Maybe the mountains were just the thing he and Jake needed. They'd be miles from other people and from temptation and in an environment over which Sloane would have complete control.

FOUR

Sloane didn't know if the unusual spelling had been deliberate, or just a mistake by settlers delirious with gold fever. Truluck's block-long Main Street sprang up as suddenly and unexpectedly as the other small towns through which they had driven. Sloane guessed no more than two dozen buildings bordered a county road a mile or so off the highway, itself nothing more than two lanes of black asphalt winding through barren hills of sunburned grass and gnarled oak trees.

They drove past the Truluck Hotel, E. E. Werner's Drugstore, Milt's General Store, a tannery, and a bakery, with Molia providing commentary of how the town sprang to life in 1848 and swelled to a population of nearly eighteen thousand during the gold rush peak. While the other towns they had driven through appeared worn and tired, Truluck looked and felt like one of those tourist towns in a wild west theme park with the freshly painted storefront facades, fake cowboys staging shoot-outs in the streets, and stuntmen tumbling off roofs into hidden cushions to the delight of audiences. But Truluck wasn't a Hollywood re-creation. Molia explained that the fresh paint and otherwise well-kept appearance was likely the result of the town being named a California Historical Landmark.

"After we get settled we'll have dinner at Whistling Pete's Saloon. How's that sound?" Molia asked.

T.J. had the window down, head sticking out like a dog, delighted by it all. "Is that the place with the bullet holes in the ceiling?"

"Came from the gun of none other than Billy the Kid, they say." Molia gave Sloane a shrug. "And I'll show you the table at which President Theodore Roosevelt ate dinner."

"Cool," T.J. said.

Jake offered no response. He'd abided by Sloane's request that he not listen to his headphones in the car, but that didn't mean he'd participate in the conversation. He had largely ignored T.J. who, at fourteen, was significantly smaller and maintained a boyish appearance and enthusiasm. T.J.'s attempts to engage Jake in conversation had been met with either snide remarks or silence, much to Sloane's embarrassment.

Just outside of town, past the White Oak Cemetery, Molia turned onto a dirt and gravel lot and parked in front of a horse hitching post. The Mule Deer Lodge was a single-story log structure, the rooms accessed off a wood porch shaded by an overhang likely added after the original construction. Several rocking chairs sat motionless on the porch.

"This looks great," Sloane said, stepping out to a dry heat and the sound of water trickling over rocks. A bank behind the lodge looked down on a creek so clear the water ran nearly invisible.

"Seemed a lot bigger when I was a boy," Molia said, admiring the lodge. "And the creek seemed a lot smaller. It's running high this summer from the snowmelt. I caught a trout right off that bank."

"Can we fish, Dad?" T.J. asked.

"We can try," he said before turning to Sloane to add, "But I'm not convinced my dad didn't buy the fish and hook it to my line when I wasn't looking."

Inside the lodge, antlered deer heads hung beside gold leaf paintings on red wallpaper. A glass bead chandelier dangled over red velour couches and wingback chairs. Molia tapped the bell on a wood counter, a single *ting* and a man appeared from a doorway behind the counter, still chewing what he'd bit into and wiping the corners of his mouth with a dish towel.

"Sorry to interrupt," Molia asked.

"Just finishing up; how can I help you?"

"Looking for a place to rest the dogs," Molia said.

The man shook his head. "We don't allow pets."

"That would be my feet." Molia gave Sloane a sideways glance. "Reservation is under Molia. Two rooms."

The clerk considered an old-fashioned hotel register. Sloane didn't see a computer screen anywhere on the desk. Behind the man, on shelves above mailbox slots labeled for each of the twelve rooms, Sloane read the spines for registers dating as far back as 1847. "Wow. Are those authentic?" he asked.

The clerk didn't bother to look up. "That's what they tell me."

Sloane heard the bells above the door jingle and turned in time to watch Jake leave.

"Why don't you help Jake get the stuff out of the car," Molia said to T.J., though Sloane doubted Jake had left to be of help.

"Sorry about Jake."

"No worries. I explained to T.J. that Jake's going through a rough patch. He'll loosen up when we get on the trail. Give him time."

"I appreciate this, Tom. I know we're intruding on some fond memories."

Molia sighed. "The thing about memories is they're rarely as good as you remember them. We'll make our own this week."

The clerk handed them old-fashioned keys attached to wooden doorknobs. "Put that in your pocket and the whole town will think you're happy to see them," Molia said.

The clerk didn't smile. "It keeps people from wandering off with them."

Outside Molia said, "The man has the sense of humor of a turnip."

T.J. unloaded their backpacks from the rental and Jake picked up his and started up the porch.

"Can Jake and I share a room?" T.J. asked.

Molia looked to Sloane. "That okay with you?"

Sloane wasn't so sure. "I don't want to take you away from your dad," he said.

But T.J. persisted. "Is it okay, Dad? It's only for the night; we'll be hiking tomorrow."

Molia nodded. "It's okay with me."

"That all right with you, Jake?" Sloane asked.

Jake shrugged. "Whatever."

T.J. stepped onto the porch. "We'll take seven. That's my lucky number."

They dined at Whistling Pete's, and the ambiance was everything Molia said it would be with barmaids in low-cut hoop dresses and a man in a bowler hat and bow tie banging the keys of an upright piano. Afterward Molia led the way back to the Mule Deer Lodge, and Sloane thought they resembled four outlaws walking the deserted streets of Tombstone in the blue light of a spectacular full moon, the music from the stand-up piano competing with crickets.

"Can T.J. and I go to the general store?" Jake asked. It was the first complete sentence he'd uttered all day.

They stopped in the road. "What do you need?" Sloane asked.

"I just want to get some candy . . . for me and T.J. to eat in our room while we're watching TV." Jake didn't wait for a response. "We can meet you back at the lodge."

"We'll go with you," Sloane said.

Molia grabbed his arm. "Don't be long. We have an early start in the morning."

"No, we won't be," Jake said. "Come on, T.J."

T.J. looked thrilled at the invitation, which Jake had expected. He was like one of those annoying little dogs bouncing around every time someone tossed a stick. "Can we go fishing?" "Can we see the bullet holes?" "Can we have our own room? Huh? Can we? Can we?"

The bullet holes turned out to be two holes in the ceiling. Big freaking deal. You couldn't even tell a bullet made them. And T.J. made an even bigger deal about the table and chair where Roosevelt supposedly got drunk. The saloon hung a black-and-white picture on the wall of Roosevelt sitting with a group of people and strung a red rope around the table and chairs like it was in some museum. Who gave a shit? It was just a freaking table and chair.

And look here, the toilet that Roosevelt sat on!

The general store smelled like a basement cellar, and the pickings on the shelves were slim, mostly fishing tackle and the stupid souvenirs tourists buy, like refrigerator magnets and hats and T-shirts with TRULUCK on them. Jake made his way to a standing freezer at the back of the store.

"Jake, the candy's over here," T.J. said.

"Yippee," Jake muttered. He found what he wanted: beer. He chose two cans of Pabst Blue Ribbon, which was the cheapest. The key was not to hesitate, but when T.J. caught sight of what Jake held, his eyes grew to the size of saucers, totally blowing it.

"What are you doing?"

"Shut up." Jake looked over his shoulder. Luckily the cashier was waiting on other customers.

"You can't buy that; you're not old enough."

"Why don't you broadcast it," Jake said. "Just shut up. Don't say anything." Jake turned toward the counter and spoke in a normal tone. "Come on, T.J., make up your mind. Dad wants me to get you home before it gets too late." He made his way to the register and put the two cans of beer on the counter. "My brother can never decide what candy he wants. Takes him forever. Pack of Marlboro Gold please."

He fished his money out of his front pocket and peeled off a twenty, putting it on the counter. The cashier had one of those thin and craggy faces, like the freaks they find to play the undertaker in horror movies. Bells chimed. Jake looked over his shoulder at another couple walking into the store. T.J. put a single candy bar on the counter.

"Is that all?" Jake chuckled. "You were whining about getting candy all evening. Go get some more."

"I don't want any more."

The cashier picked up the candy bar and pressed the keys on an old-fashioned cash register. "Dollar fifty," he said.

Jake looked up at him. "You didn't ring up my beer and cigarettes."

"No I didn't."

Jake opened his wallet and slapped his fake ID on the counter. "It's okay. I know I look young, but I'm twenty-one."

The man picked up the license and studied it. Then he put it down and slid it back across the counter. "Maybe in Washington. Not in California."

"What are you talking about? That's an official Washington license."

"You want the candy bar or you want me to call the police? If you're twenty-one, I'll buy you the damn beer myself."

Jake glared at him. Ordinarily he'd have called the man's bluff. If he actually called the police Jake could run and be long gone before they arrived, but there wasn't anyplace to run in this shithole of a town, and Jake was already on parole. Better to cut his losses and just leave. Then the man took back the license.

"On second thought, I think I'll hold on to this and call first thing tomorrow morning to see if the Washington DMV has any record of a Jim Peterson."

"Hey, give me it back; you have no right to take it."

"I do if I suspect it's a fake. And I suspect it's a fake." He hit the cash register. Bells rang and the tray door popped open. The man slid the license in the drawer and slammed it closed. "Now get out of my store, punk."

"What did you call me?"

"I said get out. We don't like your type here in Truluck."

"What type is that, someone with a brain?"

The man started from behind the counter. "Get out."

"Not until you give me back my license."

"Forget it, Jake, let's just leave," T.J. said.

"Not without my license," Jake said. Others in the store stood watching. "It's mine and I want it back."

The man stepped up to him. "Get out, or I'm going to throw your ass out into the street."

Jake took a step back. "You touch me and my father will sue the shit out of you and I'll own this store and the whole crappy town."

The man took another step toward them. "Why don't you go and get him and we can discuss that license of yours."

T.J. grabbed his sleeve. "Jake, let's go."

Jake pulled his arm free. "Maybe I will get him."

"I'd listen to your friend."

"He's not my friend and I'm not leaving until you give me back my license."

"Last warning, kid."

"Jake, come on."

"You're walking out of here or you're flying out. Take your choice."

"Give me back—"

The man's hand shot out, grabbed a bunch of Jake's shirt beneath his chin, and spun him. The next thing Jake knew he was being shoved toward the door, the man gripping him by the collar, the way someone lifts a cat off the ground. Caught unaware, Jake's feet shuffled forward before he had time to dig in his heels.

"Get your hands off me. Let go of me. I'm going to sue you for assault and battery."

Jake grabbed the doorframe, used it for leverage, and spun behind the man. He brought his arms up and under the man's armpits, locking his fingers behind the man's head. It wasn't easy, because the man was tall, but Jake had perfected the wrestling move over three years and it caught the man completely off guard. "T.J., get my license!"

T.J. stood stunned.

"T.J.!"

The man reached back, grabbed Jake's wrist, and bent suddenly forward at the waist. Jake felt his feet lift from the ground, his body going heels over head. He landed on his back on the boardwalk. The next thing he knew he was tumbling into the street. He got to his feet in time to see T.J. running from the store.

"You come back and I'll call the police and have your ass put in jail," the cashier said. Then he turned and walked back inside.

T.J. stood on the boardwalk, mouth agape. "Nice going," Jake growled. He started down the street, T.J. jogging to catch up. Jake wheeled on him. "I told you to get candy. You get one candy bar? Don't you know anything? Are you that stupid?"

"I didn't know you were going to do that."

"You don't get *one* thing. You get a bunch of stuff so the guy doesn't pay attention to the beer. He just wants the money. You made it too obvious."

"I didn't know."

"Now I lost my license. Do you know what it cost me to get that? And I have to spend the entire night with you without anything to drink or smoke." He imitated T.J.'s voice, an octave higher. "I know. Maybe we can grab our fishing poles and pretend there are fish in the creek, or look for footprints where Joe Blow Bad Guy once stepped."

"I'm sorry."

"Sorry won't get my license back." Jake walked faster. "Just shut up. Don't talk to me. It's bad enough I have to spend the night with you."

T.J. startled awake. The silhouette stood in the frame of the open door, a shadow backlit by the light of the moon. He nearly screamed, thinking it the cashier, or maybe the police, but the shadow did not walk into the room. It walked out, closing the door. When T.J. looked to his left he saw Jake's empty bed.

He threw off the covers, slipped his feet inside his high-top tennis shoes, leaving the laces untied, and grabbed his fleece. By the time he pulled open the door Jake had reached the end of the parking lot, a shadow turning left, toward town. T.J. looked for the key to the room, but it was not on the dresser where he had put it that night. He left the door open a crack and stepped down onto the porch. His shoes crunched the gravel despite his attempts to step lightly. At the edge of the parking lot he paused and looked around the corner. Jake continued toward town, twenty yards ahead. T.J. contemplated going back, waking his father and David, but that would get Jake in trouble, and Jake already hated him. When they returned from the store he'd spent the rest of the night lying on his bed with his earphones on, eyes closed. T.J. tried to talk to him, but Jake had shut him out. He finally gave up and pulled out the paperback he'd brought, reading with the television on.

T.J. kept enough distance so Jake wouldn't hear his footsteps. At one point Jake turned and looked back down the road, but T.J. slipped into the shadows of the trees and tall grass, waiting until Jake walked on.

The streets of Truluck had gone to bed, the town blanketed by a night sky overflowing with stars. Jake stopped outside the general store and T.J. moved behind one of the posts holding up a wooden awning over Candy's Ice Cream & Treats, watching. Jake looked around before pulling something from his pocket, holding it by his side as he walked up the steps onto the boardwalk. T.J. crept closer, squatting. Whatever Jake had in his hand, he used it to smash one of the windowpanes in the door. The glass crunched and clinked as it hit the wood boardwalk, the sound carrying. T.J. looked about but the streets remained deserted. Jake reached through the hole, then pushed the door open and stepped inside.

He'd come back to get his license.

T.J. ran farther down the street to the alley between the pharmacy and the general store, fear making him sick. He again considered going back to the lodge but instead crept up the wooden steps onto the boardwalk and looked inside the storefront window but did not see Jake at the cash register. When he pulled back he noticed the sticker in the lower corner, the kind people put in their windows or on a sign staked in the lawn to let robbers know their home is protected by a security system. The realization came at the same time he saw the headlights of the car moving swiftly down Main Street.

Silent alarm.

He contemplated running. Instead, he went inside the store. "Jake? Jake?"

Jake materialized out of the darkness, holding a six-pack of beer and a bottle of vodka. "What are you doing here?"

"The police are outside; this place has a silent alarm."

Jake moved to the window, looking out into the street. "Let's go." He hurried down a narrow hall at the back of the store into a room with a desk squeezed amid stocked shelves and an old-fashioned sink with exposed pipes running along brick walls. Jake pulled open the back door but hesitated when something else caught his attention.

"What are you doing?"

Jake shoved the vodka bottle and six-pack against T.J.'s chest. He had no alternative but to take them or have them crash to the floor. Floorboards creaked inside the store. A light swept across the darkness at the end of the hall.

Jake returned, holding a rifle and a box of shells.

T.J.'s knees weakened.

Jake smiled. "Come on, we'll have some fun."

"No, Jake, put it back."

"Don't be such a pussy."

Footsteps approached. The beam of light crept farther down the hall. When T.J. turned back Jake had already fled out the door into the alley.

They ran into the foothills, high stepping through waist-tall brown grass and scrub. T.J.'s ankles turned on the uneven ground and his chest burned, but panic spurred him on, following until Jake stopped in a grove of oak trees with bent and gnarled limbs. The moon shone through the gaps in the branches in strips of light. Jake fell back against a trunk, chest heaving, gasping for air. He looked at T.J. and started to laugh. "Damn, that was fun."

T.J. thought he must be crazy. "Fun? How was that fun?"

Jake pushed away from the tree, threw out his arms, making a cross in the blue light, the rifle still in hand, and screamed. "Ahhhh!"

T.J. felt his heart leap into his throat. "What is wrong with you? They're going to hear you!"

"Relax," he said. "No one is coming." He set the gun against the trunk and walked to where T.J. stood, relieving him of the beer and vodka. Up until that moment, T.J. had forgotten he still carried it. Jake tossed a can to T.J. and sat in the grass. He nearly dropped it.

"I don't want one."

Jake popped the top on a second can, beer foam spraying, and covered the opening with his mouth, drinking in gulps. He sat back wiping the foam dripping from his chin with the sleeve of his jacket. "Just drink it," he said. "We earned it."

T.J. didn't open the beer. "You shouldn't have done it, Jake. You shouldn't have broken in."

"He shouldn't have taken my license."

T.J. paced. "We should go back."

"We'll be gone before they figure it out. You heard your dad. We're leaving at the crack of dawn."

"What about the police officer?"

"That? That wasn't a cop. It was a rent-a-cop, a security guard with a flashlight. They can't do anything."

T.J. looked about. "I don't know, Jake."

"Just drink it. One beer isn't going to kill you."

"You broke into that store. You stole this stuff."

Jake reached into his pocket and produced his license. "But I got this back." He took another drink. "Look, it's not like I stole money."

"You stole a gun."

"He deserved it for taking my license." He lay back in the grass. The crickets chirped and the insects buzzed. "Peace and quiet," he said. "I sure do like camping."

"We should go back."

"Just drink your beer." Jake got up and took the can, popping it open, and handing it back. He held out his own can until T.J. tapped it. "Thanks for not running off and leaving me. I owe you."

It was the first decent thing Jake had said to him all day. T.J. nodded and took a sip.

Jake frowned. "Not like that. Drink it like a man." He put his can to his mouth and tilted it up, throwing back his head, drinking until beer trickled down his chin onto his shirt. When he had finished he crushed the can in his hand and belched loud and long.

T.J. raised the can to his mouth and Jake put his hand on the bottom, tilting it up as T.J. drank. "Chug! Chug! Chug!"

Not able to keep up with the flow of beer, T.J. began to cough and sputter, choking. He pulled back, beer frothing down his chin.

Jake laughed. "Damn, you really are a rookie. I am going to have to teach you some things on this trip."

He untwisted the top of the vodka bottle, took two gulps, and grimaced. "Wow, this is rotgut shit." He handed the bottle to T.J.

Not wanting to be called a pussy again, T.J. took a sip. The vodka felt like sandpaper sliding down his throat.

"Drink the beer now. It will help."

T.J. did as instructed.

"Now take another drink." When T.J. hesitated Jake said, "Might as well. We can't bring it back to the room with us."

T.J. drank vodka and chugged beer. Jake popped open two more beers and handed him one. They got to talking, Jake telling him how school sucked big time and how he'd had a girlfriend, but he dumped her because she was too needy. T.J. didn't have a lot to say but he listened and tried not to say anything to make Jake call him a pussy again. Before T.J. knew it, he had crushed his third can. The vodka bottle was nearly empty.

His legs felt unsteady and the trees kept shifting. "I'm dizzy," he said.

Jake laughed. "You're buzzed, dude."

"I feel sick."

"No, man, you're just buzzed."

"You're blurry."

Jake stumbled, laughing so hard he fell into the grass. "Wasted, man. You are totally wasted. Isn't this more fun than sitting in the damn room?"

"Hell, yeah," T.J. said, his outlook brightening.

"You know what's even more fun?" Jake held up the rifle and got to his feet. "Shooting targets."

"You've done it?"

"Lots of times. My uncle Charlie takes me to the driving range."

T.J. laughed in a burst.

"What?"

"You said driving range."

"I did?" Jake laughed and patted him on the back. "You're all right, you know. I thought you were a dork, but you're all right."

"Thanks—"

"For a pussy!" Jake shoved him in the back. "Come on."

He led them higher up into the foothills where the oak trees and scrub became more dense. He stopped in a small clearing. "Look at that!"

"What is it?"

They walked closer. It was the frame of an abandoned car, rusted and riddled with bullet holes. It had no tires or glass, the headlights like hollow eye sockets on a skull.

"Target practice!" Jake said. He turned and paced, counting to ten. "Okay," he said. "Me first. Then you. Then me." He leveled the gun, put the stock against his shoulder, and pulled the trigger. The kick caused the barrel to jump, the shot echoing like a canon blast.

"Damn, I think I missed." He handed T.J. the gun.

T.J. mimicked Jake's movements but when he pulled the trigger nothing happened.

"You have to cock it, like in the movies. Cock the handle." T.J. cocked the handle of the rifle and snapped it back. "Try it now," Jake said.

T.J. took aim, pulled the trigger. The gun kicked so hard it flew from his hands and landed in the grass, but a metallic ping rang out.

"I hit it," he said, turning to Jake. "Jake, I hit it."

But Jake was not looking at the car or at T.J. He was looking straight ahead, slowly raising his hands.

FIVE

Sloane awoke to the sound of running water, Molia in the shower. Molia said he wanted to get an early start, and he wasn't kidding. Judging by the light outside the curtained window, it was just after dawn. Sloane swung his legs over the side of the bed and gave his body a moment to wake. The cool air brought goose bumps to his bare skin but helped revive him. He hadn't slept much, and in those brief periods when he had drifted off, sleep had been more fitful than sound. If he was having trouble waking, he could only imagine how difficult it would be getting Jake out of bed. He'd need a crane. T.J., on the other hand, was likely up, showered, and packed, anxious to get going.

Sloane had checked on the boys after they returned from the general store, but whatever spark had lit Jake earlier in the evening had extinguished. He returned surly as ever, and T.J. also did not seem happy. When Sloane asked what candy they had bought Jake muttered, "The store was closed."

Sloane padded barefoot across the room and out onto the porch. The temperature was brisk. When he knocked on the door to room 7 it popped free from the jamb, confirming his suspicion that T.J. was up and eager to set out. "Jake? T.J.?" Even in the dark, with the shades pulled over the windows, he could see the two empty and unmade beds. He flipped the light switch. The two candle sconces above each bed flickered on. Two backpacks remained against the wall. He checked the bathroom and also found it empty. Exiting the room, he walked to the end of the covered porch and looked down to the bank of the creek but did not see either boy.

Reentering his room, Sloane found Tom Molia in his shorts, using a towel to dry his hair.

"You get the boys up?"

Sloane sat on the edge of the bed and worked socks over his feet. "They're not in their room."

"Did they go out to the creek?"

Sloane shook his head as he slipped on a hiking boot, tying the laces. "I looked."

"So maybe they went into town?" Molia did not sound confident.

"No way Jake got up this early on his own." He tied the laces. "Something's wrong."

"What could have gone wrong?"

Sloane tied his second shoe. "I don't know, but I'm going into town."

Molia dropped the towel on the bed. "Hold on. I'm going with you."

Truluck looked like a town waking, most of the shops not yet open, the boardwalks clear except for a man sweeping outside the general store. Sloane saw no sign of either boy. When he looked back to the general store he noted a piece of cardboard over one of the panes in the door and realized the man was sweeping up bits of glass. Sloane crossed the street with a feeling of trepidation.

"Excuse me."

The man stopped sweeping, looking down at them.

"Sorry to bother you. Have you seen two teenage boys?" Sloane asked. "One's about—"

"Yeah, I seen 'em," the man said, voice unfriendly. "Came in last night trying to buy beer and cigarettes."

"Beer and cigarettes?" Molia asked.

"One of them had a fake ID from Washington State. I confiscated it and put it in the cash register. Last night I get a call in the middle of the night telling me the alarm here at the store went off, that someone broke in. I had a hunch who it was. When I looked in the cash register and saw that the license was gone I knew."

"Those are our boys," Sloane said.

"They might have been your boys last night," the man said. "This morning I'm betting their butts belong to Judge Earl."

HARRY N. MORSE JAIL
TRULUCK, CALIFORNIA

A sharp pain woke him. When he opened his eyes, the pain spread across the top of his skull, which felt as though someone was using a saw to cut through the bone, about to crack it straight down the middle. Jake was looking at a brick wall with a tiny window, both foreign at first, but as the cobwebs cleared his recollection of the night returned. Sitting up, the jail cell spun and twisted, and he collapsed back onto the mattress, nauseated.

"You going to throw up, you get yourself to that toilet because I ain't cleaning it up." The police officer spoke through the bars, remaining seated at a desk in a small cluttered room. "Wake your friend. The two of you have an appointment this morning."

T.J. lay sprawled across another cot in the same cell, his right arm hanging limp over the side, head back, mouth open, snoring. Jake pushed off his cot to his feet, the ground unsteady. He walked over and kicked the bottom of T.J.'s tennis shoe. T.J. startled, momentarily resisted, then bolted upright. The sudden movement caused the blood to rush from his face, leaving him pale as a sheet. He fell back, hit the edge of the cot, and rolled hard onto the floor. Had Jake not felt so awful himself he would have found it funny.

"Got to wake up," he said.

T.J. lifted his head from the floor and considered their accommodations—a single metal sink and toilet, the two cots. Jake watched as the stark reality of where they were pushed past the fog of alcohol and T.J. started to cry.

"Don't cry," Jake said, the pain in his head now pulsing. "You'll get out of here. I might not, but you will. I'll take the blame. I'm going to jail anyway."

"My dad's going to kill me," T.J. sobbed.

"He's not going to kill you. I'll tell him it was my fault, that you tried to stop me, that I forced you."

T.J. sat up and took a deep breath, a heaving sigh before he managed to make it to the edge of the cot and sit. "I think I'm going to puke."

The officer rapped on the bars with a baton. It felt as though he'd rapped on Jake's head. "You boys have a nice evening last night?"

"I want to call my dad," T.J. said, and the mention of a phone made Jake check his pockets for his cell phone. It was gone.

"You had that chance last night. You declined."

"Can I call him now?"

"Nope. You're going to see Judge Earl now. He decides what you get to do. You got two minutes to make yourself presentable, and I'd suggest you do. Judge Earl does not like to be kept waiting, and we have a twenty-minute ride ahead of us."

WINCHESTER COUNTY COURTHOUSE
WINCHESTER, CALIFORNIA

Thirty minutes later Jake stepped from the backseat of the police car, feeling worse after the winding ride. The windows did not lower and the air inside the car had been stifling hot. Throughout the ride Jake suffered alternating hot flashes followed by cold sweats and a burning sensation scratched the back of his throat. Several times he had to resist the urge to vomit, pushing the bile taste back down. T.J. looked as bad as Jake felt, his face the color of ashes in a fire pit, with dark circles under his eyes.

Handcuffed at the waist, Jake squinted up at the bright sun as the officer led them across the parking lot toward a three-story stone-and-brick building surrounded by a manicured yard that looked more like a mansion than a courthouse. The hedges were perfect rectangles, and despite the heat the grass was lush and green. Brilliant-colored flowers filled flower beds and overflowed baskets hanging from old-fashioned lampposts. At the top of the incline the courthouse rose atop a foundation of unfinished blocks of granite, orange brick with white, terra-cotta trim. Fixed atop the third story, like the top tier of a massive wedding cake, shone an impressive bell tower, the sun glinting off its metal dome. Pediments and pillars adorned a massive entrance at the top of a steep and wide staircase, but the officer led them toward a glass door entry at ground level. Jake noted a bronze plaque embedded in a corner foundation stone chiseled with the year 1898 but didn't get the chance to read anything more than one word, BOYKIN.

Inside, the officer unlocked an elevator and pressed the button for the third floor. Exiting, they walked down a sterile corridor past framed portraits of bearded men in black robes to another locked door. The officer ushered them inside a windowless room, instructed them to sit on benches, and removed their handcuffs and belly chains. Jake rubbed at his wrists. T.J. lowered his head in his hands, moaning and looking even worse.

Jake leaned over. "Everything is going to be fine. Just—"

The officer tapped Jake's shoulder with a billy club as he passed to a door on the opposite side of the room. "Shut it."

When the officer opened the door a man's voice filtered in. The officer pulled back his head and carefully closed the door. "When we go in you go straight to the table in front of the judge's bench. You stay on the left side and you remain standing. Keep your mouths shut. You got it?"

Jake and T.J. nodded.

"Let's go."

The officer opened the door, waited a beat, and nodded for Jake and T.J. to enter. As they did, another boy walked past in the opposite direction. Maybe fourteen, the boy considered them with red, swollen eyes before he looked down, shaking his head.

Walking to their designated spot at the long oak table, Jake took a moment to survey the courtroom hoping to see David and Tom Molia sitting behind them. It looked like something out of a western, nothing like Judge Glazier's modern courtroom in Martinez. Wooden folding seats, like the kind in an old movie theater, faced a railing with decorative metal screens that separated the seats from the single, sturdy table. A man in a three-piece suit stood at the opposite end directing his comments to an enormous man in a black robe with a bald pate and full, soot-colored beard. At first Jake thought the judge was standing, but realized he was seated behind the elevated bench. The hand-carved name plate read HON. EARL J. BOYKIN.

Boykin ended the conversation and glanced at Jake and T.J. over the top of half-lens reading glasses perched on the tip of his nose before lowering his head, licking his finger and flipping pages, reading.

T.J. wobbled, put a hand on the table to momentarily steady himself, then collapsed into one of the burgundy leather chairs. The officer started forward, but Jake grabbed T.J.'s elbow, speaking into his ear. "Get up," he said.

T.J. reluctantly rose.

"Hold on to the edge of the table," Jake whispered, keeping a hand on T.J.'s elbow. When he looked up, the judge was staring at him but resumed reading. For the next few minutes, the only sound in the courtroom was the ticking of a grandfather clock mounted on the wall. When he had finished the judge let the pages drop, removed his reading glasses, and sat back, rocking with his elbow propped on the chair arm, his index and middle finger extended to his temple. He considered Jake and T.J. for what seemed like forever, the squeaking chair blending with the sound of the ticking clock. A red velvet curtain hanging from a ceiling curtain rod framed the judge between two arched windows that admitted enough morning light to make the artificial gas lamps hanging from the ornate ceiling unnecessary.

"It sounds like you boys had yourself quite a night last night," he said.

HIGHWAY 89
WINCHESTER COUNTY, CALIFORNIA

Sloane sat in the passenger seat with one hand gripping the handle above the window as Tom Molia punched the accelerator and the tires squealed, fighting to grip the asphalt. Sloane shoved his feet into the floor mat each time Molia passed a car with seemingly too little space before the next blind hill or turn.

The store owner didn't have the full story, or didn't want to give it, but the facts he did provide were more than enough for Sloane to fill in the blanks. Jake's sudden change in attitude after dinner had been a ploy to use a fake driver's license to buy beer and cigarettes. The man refused and confiscated the license. This apparently led to a confrontation, with the man forcibly removing Jake from the store. Sometime later that night, Jake broke into the store to retrieve his license and in the process he decided to take a six-pack of beer and a fifth of vodka. What Jake didn't know was that apparently every store in Truluck had been wired with a silent alarm. What was less clear was T.J.'s role in the affair. According to the store owner T.J. had been intent to buy candy and had tried to convince Jake to leave, which meant T.J. had likely been an unwitting participant. Why the boy had gone back to the store with Jake, however, remained an unanswered question.

Molia approached the bumper of a minivan, veered left into the oncoming lane, but had to brake and return when a car crested a hill in the opposite direction. Though his stomach was in his throat, Sloane wasn't about to tell Molia to slow down. He had a bad feeling, and for reasons that went beyond the obvious. Something about the tone of the store owner's voice when he referred to "Judge Earl" had set off bells and whistles.

A short blast of a police siren drew both their attention. Sloane turned to see flashing lights atop a blue and gray Mustang.

"Damn! Where the hell was he hiding?"

"Didn't see him," Sloane said.

Molia drove onto a rare patch of dirt and gravel. "I'll handle this." He pulled out the card that identified him as a West Virginia police detective from his wallet and pushed open the door. The amplified voice greeted him instantly.

"Return to your vehicle. Now."

Molia held up his identification. He had not brought his badge or his gun. He got one step farther.

"Sir, I repeat. Return to your vehicle now."

Molia slid back in, swearing under his breath. "It's always the young ones who want to act like the bull screw moose."

When the officer did not immediately approach, Sloane looked back again. "What's he waiting for?"

"He's probably calling in the license plate to find out if there are any outstanding warrants. Some of these guys can't think outside the box to save their ass."

The digital clock on the dash changed to 8:10. Sloane looked back again and this time the driver's door of the patrol car pushed open and the officer stepped out, pausing to fasten a Smokey the Bear hat on the crown of his head. He looked young, but then again it was difficult to tell with the hat and dark reflector sunglasses. He hitched up his utility belt as he made his way alongside the car, stopping a foot back from the lowered window.

"License and registration, please."

Molia handed him his police identification. "I'm a West Virginia police detective."

The officer considered it. "You're a long way from home, Detective Molia."

"Yes and no. I was born in Oakland. We're up here to do a little backpacking but our sons got in some trouble last night. We're headed over to Winchester to find out what's going on."

"What kind of trouble?"

"Not sure, exactly," Molia said.

"They the two boys who broke into the general store in Truluck?"

"Listen, I know I was driving fast—"

"Reckless is more like it," the officer said. "You could have killed somebody, passing that close to a blind turn back there."

"I apologize. I'm worried about my son is all. I'll be more careful." Molia reached for his identification, but the officer did not hand it back. "Can we go?" he asked.

"Go? Go where?"

"To get our sons."

"I suppose so. Right after you hand me your license and registration."

When the officer said nothing further Molia asked, "Are you kidding?"

"Do I look like I'm kidding?"

Molia started to push open the car door. The officer shoved it closed. "I told you to stay in your vehicle."

Molia looked at Sloane before looking back to the window. "What type of treatment is this for a fellow law enforcement officer?"

"Oh, I'm sorry. Are you on duty, Detective Molia?"

Molia didn't answer.

"I don't know how they do things in West Virginia, but here in Winchester County we have laws that *all* citizens are obligated to keep, and that includes driving on the right side of the road."

"Do you have a supervisor, Officer"—Molia paused, reading the man's name tag—"Wade?"

The officer stepped closer to the door, bending so that the edge of his hat made contact with the top of the door. "I sure do."

"What's his name?" Molia asked.

"Wade. Carl Wade. You're looking at him."

WINCHESTER COUNTY COURTHOUSE
WINCHESTER, CALIFORNIA

Judge Boykin folded his hands on the desk and leaned over them. "Do you not feel well, son?"

T.J. looked up. "No, sir."

"Well I can certainly understand why. The report here says you boys did a little drinking last night."

"Yes, sir," T.J. said.

"Would you prefer to sit down?"

T.J. nodded.

"Well, then, go ahead."

T.J. sat; Jake remained standing. Something felt wrong to him. The judge's attitude did not seem normal.

"What about you?" Boykin asked. "You feel sick too?"

"No, I'm okay."

Boykin stared. When Jake said nothing further the judge said, "You're okay . . . what?"

"I'm okay. I don't need to sit."

Boykin smiled, pushed back his chair, and stood. Jake guessed the judge was at least six feet six. "You see this robe I'm wearing, son?"

"Yes, I see it."

Boykin's lips disappeared in his beard. "Now I understand that your friend there, I'm assuming that's Mr. Molia," he said, mispronouncing it as "Mole-ee-a" instead of "Mol-ya." "Am I right?"

Jake nodded.

"I'm assuming that maybe Mr. Molia doesn't understand court procedure, but the file I have in front of me indicates you are all too familiar with it, Mr. Carter." Boykin let the ticking of the grandfather clock fill a brief silence. "So you should know that you need to address me as 'Your Honor.'"

"Yes, Your Honor," Jake said.

"Let's try it again to be sure. You're okay, what?"

"I'm okay, I don't need to sit, Your Honor," Jake said.

"Much better." Boykin sat. "Now, Mr. Molia, why don't you explain to me what you boys are doing in Truluck, other than breaking into Mr. Willingham's general store and doing a little underage drinking?"

"We're going hiking, and backpacking," T.J. said, his voice croaking.

"This is the time of year for it." Boykin nodded. "A little fishing, too?"

T.J. nodded. "Yes. Yes, Your Honor."

"Good man," Boykin said. "When were you planning to leave?"

"This morning," T.J. said. He wiped a hand beneath his nose.

Boykin looked over at the grandfather clock. "You're going to get a late start, I'm afraid." He flipped through the pages in front of him.

Jake started to speak. "Your Honor, we'd like—"

Boykin raised one of his meaty hands but did not look up, reading. The ticking clock continued to fill the void. Boykin lowered the hand, one eyebrow arched. "What were you about to say, son?"

"We'd like to call our fathers."

Boykin looked to the officer who had brought them in. "They had the opportunity last night, Judge, but declined that invitation."

"We'd like to call them now," Jake said. Boykin shifted his gaze, waiting. ". . . Your Honor."

"Well the problem with that, Mr. Carter, is I am on a schedule here and I am already well behind. And I'm sure you boys would like to get on out of here as well, wouldn't you?"

T.J. stood. "Yes, Your Honor; we're real sorry about what we did."

Jake grabbed T.J.'s arm to keep him from saying anything more. Boykin's eyes followed Jake's hand, before returning to T.J. "Something you wanted to say, Mr. Molia?" he asked.

Jake leaned over to whisper. "Don't say anything."

T.J. glanced at him. Boykin sat waiting. "Just that we're sorry."

"Sorry for what you did?"

Jake whispered again. "Shut up."

"Something *you* wanted to say, Mr. Carter?"

"We want a lawyer . . . Your Honor."

"Is that so? Do you know any here in Winchester County?"

"My father," Jake said.

Boykin nodded, as if giving the request due consideration. "And I suppose you'd want a trial with witnesses and exhibits as well . . . the whole shebang. Is that right?" He looked down at a woman sitting to his right. "Ms. Valdez, when do I have a free day on my calendar to conduct a trial?"

Ms. Valdez played with the keys on a keyboard, staring at her computer terminal. "First available day would be the last week of June, first week of July, Judge."

"Okay. Officer Langston, will you escort these two gentlemen back to their cells."

"No," T.J. said.

"What was that, Mr. Molia?" Boykin asked.

"I don't want to go back to jail. I want to get this over with."

"T.J., be quiet," Jake said.

T.J. shot Jake a glance. "No. I'm not going to be quiet. I wouldn't be here if it wasn't for you. This is your fault." He turned back to the bench. "I want to go now."

"You want to cooperate with the court?"

"Yes."

"You admit that the statements by the general store owner and by the police officers in the reports I have before me are true?"

"Yes."

"T.J., no," Jake said.

"You did all these things?"

"Yes."

"But you're sorry for what you've done."

"Yes, Your Honor."

"And you won't do it again."

"No, Your Honor."

"I won't see you back here in my courtroom again?"

T.J. became more adamant. "No, Judge, I swear. Never."

"I'm glad to hear you say that, Mr. Molia. Good man." He shifted his gaze to Jake. "What about you, Mr. Carter. Are you sorry for what you've done?"

Jake hesitated, careful with his choice of words. "Yes, I'm sorry."

Boykin looked across the room to where the prosecutor stood silent. "Mr. Pike, did you hear Mr. Molia indicate his willingness to cooperate with the court?"

"I did, Your Honor."

"And did you hear him admit to the charges brought against him."

"I did as well, Judge."

Jake started to speak. Judge Boykin cut him off. "It's important to take responsibility for our actions, gentlemen. It is the first step in rehabilitation. Let's get on with this and get you boys out of here. Mr. Molia, would you walk to that window over there and look out on that ledge?" When T.J. hesitated, Judge Boykin pointed to a tall window next to a huge painting of a lone oak tree in a gold leaf frame hanging over the jury box. "That window right over there."

T.J. left the table and pushed through the swinging gate in the wooden railing, looking back as he walked to the window. Boykin pointed again. At the window T.J. looked out, then back to the bench.

"Do you see anything out there on the ledge?"

T.J. looked again. "Pigeons?"

Boykin nodded. "Pigeons. And do you see the sharp wire on the ledge as well?"

T.J. nodded. "Yes, Judge."

"How many pigeons are out there on that ledge?"

T.J. took a moment to count. "Six."

Boykin motioned for him to return to the table and waited to speak until T.J. had done so. "Do you know what pigeons are?"

"Birds?" T.J. said.

Boykin smiled. So too did the prosecutor. "Birds, I like that. No, Mr. Molia, pigeons are pests. They come into your town and they have no regard for anyone or anything. They deface buildings and statues, sidewalks, store awnings. And no matter what one does, even putting up spiked fences, somehow they find their way back."

The sick feeling in Jake's stomach returned.

"But pigeons are just dumb, stupid birds with brains about the size of the tip of my finger here. They don't do the things they do on purpose; it's just instinct. You understand that?"

"Yes," T.J. said, sounding hesitant.

"That's what separates us from pigeons. We also have instincts, but as humans we are obligated to control those instincts so we do not become pests for the rest of society. When a person fails to control his instincts, it's my job to put up those spiked fences to try to protect society. Do you understand that also?"

T.J. swallowed hard. "I think so."

"So here's the thing about 'sorry.' I know you boys are sorry, but what I'm not convinced of is whether you're sorry that you committed your crimes, or just sorry you got caught."

"I'm sorry, I did it," T.J. said.

Boykin pointed to a tall painting hanging just to the right of the grandfather clock. "You see that man?"

Jake initially thought it to be a portrait of the judge in his black robe, his ash-colored beard extending to his chest, like a bib. But upon closer inspection, Jake realized the portrait was not Judge Earl, only someone who looked like him.

"They named this courthouse after my great-grandfather. I am the fourth generation to sit in this chair. During that time I've had a lot of people—boys, girls, men, and women—stand right where you're standing now. They come into my courtroom, my courthouse, the courthouse named after my great-grandfather, and tell me they're 'sorry.' They're sorry for what they did. The thing is they're always sorry after they got caught. I can't recall a single person coming in here and confessing to their crime and telling me they were sorry before they got caught. Have we ever had that happen, Mr. Pike?"

"No, Your Honor, I can't recall that we have," the prosecutor said.

"Officer Langston?"

"No, Judge."

"Ms. Valdez?"

"No, Judge."

Boykin sat back, smiling. "Just once I'd like to have that happen so I could go home and tell my wife, 'Dear, you're not going to believe what happened in my courtroom today.'" He shook his head. Then he looked down at them. "This is your lucky day, Mr. Molia. There are days we can have a dozen or more pigeons on that ledge. But today I am sentencing you to just six months detention in the Fresh Start Youth Training Facility here in Winchester County."

"What?" T.J. said, bursting into tears. "But you said I could go home."

Boykin's voice hardened. "I said I'd get you out of here and I'm going to do just that." He motioned and the officer approached from behind and grabbed T.J. by the shoulder, steering him toward the door.

"You said I could go fishing," T.J. sobbed. "I said I was sorry."

Boykin waited until the officer had escorted T.J. from the courtroom before turning his attention to Jake. "Mr. Carter, what I have here before me are sworn statements by the store owner and by the officers who arrested you. And now I have a confession from your cohort admitting to the crimes. I'd say that about does it for you. I'm finding you guilty based upon the evidence presented here before me. And I am not feeling as charitable toward you as I did toward Mr. Molia."

HIGHWAY 89
WINCHESTER COUNTY, CALIFORNIA

Officer Carl Wade strolled back to his police cruiser and pulled open the driver's-side door but paused to look about, as if to admire the view, though there wasn't much to see but the rolling hills of bleached grass and scrub. He removed his hat, revealing a head of rust-colored hair, and ducked inside, presumably to write Tom Molia several tickets.

"I've never seen anything like this," Molia said. "Cops do not give tickets to other cops; I'll have this guy's ass, I promise you that."

Unfortunately that would not get them moving, though Sloane knew better than to say it. Foremost on Sloane's mind remained the statement by the owner of the general store concerning Judge Earl, as well as a nagging question that had apparently also been bothering Molia.

"Why haven't they called?" Molia asked.

Given the status of his relationship with Jake, Sloane could rationalize the lack of a phone call, but T.J. would have called if given the opportunity, and if able. And if T.J. had not been able to call, for whatever the reason, then why hadn't someone within the jail system called? They were juveniles. Shouldn't someone be trying to contact their parents?

The clock on the dash glowed 8:23.

"Courthouse wouldn't open 'til nine, would it?" Molia asked, catching Sloane's gaze.

"I wouldn't expect any hearings before then," Sloane said, but he was feeling less and less confident with each minute of delay.

When the digits read 8:26 Molia slapped the steering wheel hard enough to shake the car. "I'm going to go find out this guy's problem."

Sloane grabbed his arm. "Don't. It will only delay things further."

"He doesn't get here soon, I'm going to start this car and leave. He can arrest my ass if he has the balls and I'll have his badge."

Sloane looked through the back window and saw Wade push out of his car. "He's coming."

Wade reapplied the hat and sauntered forward, handing Molia back his license, police ID, and the registration for the rental car. "Okay, Detective, looks like everything checks out."

"What?" Molia asked, turning his head, as if he hadn't heard him.

"We're all good." Wade spoke in a conversational tone, like they were old friends who had just bumped into each other in the supermarket and were catching up.

Molia's eyes narrowed. "So, you're *not* writing me a ticket."

"Do you want me to?" Wade smiled. Molia did not answer. "I'm in a charitable mood this morning, Detective. I'm going to let you off with a warning."

The back of Molia's neck turned a crimson shade of red and Sloane thought the detective might grab Wade by the collar and pull him headfirst into the car. Before Molia could do so Sloane leaned across the seat. "So we can go?"

Wade lowered to make eye contact, though with the sunglasses Sloane only saw Molia's reflection in each lens. "You can if you follow the speed limit and obey the rules of the road." Wade smiled. "Can I be of any help with directions?"

Ten minutes later, Sloane beat Molia to the glass doors of the Winchester County Sheriff's Department. Inside, Sloane attempted to explain their circumstances to a female officer seated behind the desk, but the woman stopped him in midsentence. "Did you say Truluck?"

"Yes," Sloane said.

"If they were arrested in Truluck they weren't brought here. Truluck has its own jail. Did you check with them?"

Not knowing, they hadn't. "We were told they'd be brought before Judge Earl?"

"That would be Judge Earl Boykin." The woman looked at her watch. "You're late though. Judge Earl's an early riser. He likes to get started at eight."

"Where?" Molia asked. "Where's the courthouse?"

The woman gave them directions. "Court Street," she said. "It's in Old Town. You won't miss it."

They didn't. The courthouse sat atop a hill overlooking Winchester.

"They wouldn't have a hearing without us, would they?" Molia asked as he turned into the parking lot.

Sloane's only experience with juvenile law had been through Lisa Lynch, but he recalled her telling him that a juvenile in custody was to be given a preliminary appearance to assure the kid's well-being, to allow the court to obtain preliminary information, and to call parents, but he was no longer certain about anything. He wiped sweat dripping down the side of his face as he and Molia shuffled quickly up steep steps to a columned entrance only to find a wooden sign with an arrow redirecting them back down and around the side of the building.

Once inside, they were both huffing and puffing as they emptied their pockets onto a conveyor belt and stepped through the metal detector. Molia asked the correctional officer operating the machine for directions to Judge Boykin's courtroom, and the man pointed to an elevator beneath a large clock, the hands of which now indicated it was a quarter to nine. "Third floor. It'll be on your right."

Sloane and Molia raced across the terra-cotta floor. When the elevator doors didn't immediately open Molia started up the staircase to the right. Sloane followed. Atop the third floor they pulled open tall wooden doors and stepped back in time to a courtroom straight out of the Old West. The judge had risen from his chair and started down from his raised dais. A woman in the well beneath the bench stood talking with a man in a three-piece suit shoving files into a leather satchel. Court had ended.

"Excuse me!" Sloane and Molia stopped at the wooden railing. "Judge Boykin?"

The judge considered them.

Out of breath, Sloane said, "Our sons were arrested last night in Truluck; we were told they would be brought here before you this morning."

Boykin walked back up to the bench and put his files on the edge of the railing. "Your sons are Jake and T.J.?"

"Yes," Sloane said, relieved to know that, at the very least, they had located them.

"They got themselves in a lot of trouble last night," Boykin said. "Serious trouble."

"We got here as quickly as we could," Sloane said.

Boykin looked at the grandfather clock on the wall. "Not quickly enough. Juvenile proceedings just ended."

"We're sorry; we came as soon as we heard."

"Funny, that's what your sons said this morning."

Sloane didn't understand the comment. "Excuse me?"

"Do you know the two easiest words to say in the English language and not mean?" When neither Sloane nor Molia answered Boykin finished his own riddle. "'I'm sorry.' Well, now I'm sorry, gentlemen. But my courtroom runs on time. We've finished that matter and I have a full calendar to attend to this afternoon."

"Finished?" Molia asked. "You mean we can bail them out?"

Boykin, who had again started down the steps, stopped. "I mean finished as in concluded."

"Concluded how?" Molia asked. "Where is my son?"

Boykin glared. "Do not raise your voice in my courtroom, sir." He paused. "I assume your sons are being processed and awaiting transport."

Sloane felt the floor coming out from under his feet. "Transport where?" he and Molia asked almost in unison.

"To a juvenile detention facility," Boykin said.

"What?" Sloane asked, voice rising. Boykin's eyes narrowed.

Sloane put up a hand and took a moment to calm. "Your Honor, you can imagine we've had quite a shock this morning and we've received very little information. We're concerned about our sons. Why are they being transported to a detention facility before they've had a hearing on the merits?"

"We had a hearing on the merits, this morning, at eight, when my courtroom begins. We had a full hearing. Isn't that correct, Prosecutor Pike?"

Boykin addressed his comment to the man in the three-piece suit. Thin and bald with round wire-framed glasses, he stood with a bemused smile. "That's correct, Judge."

"But they were just arrested a couple of hours ago," Sloane said.

"Drunk as skunks I might add and having a grand time of it, shooting off a rifle and with enough shells to do some serious harm."

"A rifle? Where'd they get a rifle?" Molia asked.

"They stole it. They broke into another man's store and they stole his property, along with alcohol. They broke the law, gentlemen. And in Winchester County, if you break the law you go to jail."

"Without a trial?" Sloane was unable to keep the anger from creeping back into his voice. The officer approached.

Boykin's finger shot out from under the robe. "I am cautioning you for the last time. Watch your tone in my courtroom."

"Watch my tone? I just found out my son was arrested, tried, and convicted in a matter of hours and you're telling me to watch my tone? What type of tone would you expect? What sort of hearing did you conduct? What sort of trial were they given? What sort of legal assistance? What sort of court are you running?"

The officer pinched the microphone clipped to his shoulder and turned his head to speak into it as Boykin approached the railing. "I'll tell you exactly what type of courtroom I'm running. My type. Fair, impartial, and efficient. Your sons waived their right to an attorney and to a trial, and they admitted to their crimes. Mr. Pike, did they or did they not waive their rights?"

"They did, Your Honor."

"Officer Langston?"

"They did, Judge."

"They're kids," Molia said. "T.J. is fourteen years old. He wouldn't even know he had rights to waive."

"Now I told you where to find your sons. I'd suggest you do just that. I have a courtroom to run and you are delaying me." Boykin started toward a door.

"Are you for real?" Sloane asked.

"Last warning," Boykin said. "Do not try my patience."

"You have the nerve to talk to me about patience." Sloane could no longer control his anger. "This is blatant misconduct; I'm going to take you up on charges with the judicial board. How could you conduct a trial without a parent or an attorney present?"

The correctional officer stepped in front of Boykin, but the judge shouted over the top of him.

"Present? Present!" he roared. "You have the nerve to talk to me about being present? Where were you last night when Truluck police arrested your sons? Where were you when your sons broke into another man's store and stole his possessions? Where were you when your sons were out drinking themselves unconscious and firing a loaded weapon in the vicinity of a populated area? I spend my day sentencing kids like yours because parents like you are *not* present. Well let me tell you, you fail your kids, that's your business; but when they break the laws of this county, *my county,* it becomes my business. And the good people of Winchester County have decreed it to be so for seventeen years."

"Then the good people of Winchester County have gotten it wrong for seventeen years," Sloane shot back.

"You're in contempt."

"And you're a clown. I should hold you and this entire circus you run in contempt."

Sloane heard footsteps, two additional correctional officers hurrying into the room. The one behind the railing removed a pair of handcuffs from his utility belt.

"We'll see who got it wrong," Boykin said.

SIX

They weren't at the jail long before the same police officer reapplied their handcuffs and belly belts and led Jake and T.J. back out the door, this time with the third kid sentenced that morning, whose name they learned was Aaron. They walked single file, T.J. first, Jake in the middle, Aaron bringing up the rear. T.J. continued to whimper, and nothing Jake could say consoled him. The officer had placed them in separate cells and Jake had heard T.J. throw up twice, but when he tried talking to him T.J. did not answer.

When the door to the building slammed shut behind them a flock of birds burst from the trees, black arrowheads against a pale blue sky. Jake squinted into a bright sun, watching the birds bank and turn in military precision before disappearing again into the safety of the shimmering leaves. As the morning progressed so had Jake's headache, now pounding a steady beat, and without any food or water to help settle his stomach he felt nauseated. As Jake watched the last of the birds flitter back to the trees, he nearly walked up the back of T.J.'s heels.

T.J. had come to a stop, eyes fixed on a yellow bus parked at the back of the dirt and gravel lot. Spotted with patches of rust, cages covered the windows above black, block letters stenciled on the side.

FRESH START YOUTH TRAINING FACILITY

Two men dressed in multipocket khaki shirts, shorts cut above the knees, boots laced up their ankles, and eyes hidden behind reflector sunglasses waited outside the open bus door.

T.J. burst out crying, shoulders shuddering. The police officer encouraged him forward with a shove. The sight of the bus also hit Jake in the gut, but he would not cry. That's what they wanted; they wanted him to cry, to be scared. He wasn't about to give them the satisfaction. He continued telling himself they would not be there long, wherever they were going. David would get them both out.

As they approached, the bigger of the two guards held out his hand for the clipboard, and scribbled the pen across the paperwork without removing his sunglasses or looking down, a mere formality.

"All yours," the police officer said, taking back the paperwork. "Happy trails, boys."

As the officer left, the guard stepped forward, hands on hips. Huge pectoral muscles flattened and widened the pockets of his shirt. Bulging veins traversed his biceps and forearms. "You will proceed onto the bus one at a time," he said, his voice surprisingly calm and soft. "You will sit one to a seat. You will not talk to me. You will not talk to Officer Bradley. You will not talk to each other. Is that clear?" Getting no response, he turned his head and cupped a hand behind his ear. "I asked, is that clear?"

The three mumbled an acknowledgment.

"You will address me as Officer Atkins—"

"I thought you said not to talk to you," Jake said.

Atkins paused. Jake noticed a grin before the guard turned and spoke to the guard by the bus door. "That didn't take long, did it?"

Turning back, Atkins stepped so close Jake's face reflected in the man's sunglasses. "Did you just interrupt me while I was speaking?" He was taller by an inch or two, but he outweighed Jake by a significant amount.

Realizing his error, Jake did not respond.

Now Atkins barked, "I said, do not ask me any questions; you will, however, answer my questions. Did you just interrupt me while I was speaking?"

When Jake still did not answer, Atkins grinned. "I can wait all day, son. I love the sunshine."

"Yes," Jake said. Atkins inched both eyebrows above the silver rims of his sunglasses but did not otherwise move. His voice softened again. "Did I or did I not just tell you to address me as Officer Atkins?"

"Yes."

"Then you will address me as Officer Atkins."

"Yes, Officer Atkins," Jake said.

Atkins smiled. "Are we now clear?"

"Yes, Officer Atkins."

Atkins repositioned himself beside the bus door. Bradley climbed on board, waiting at the top step. T.J. entered first. Since he could not use his hands to grab a railing with them handcuffed to the belt Atkins put a hand under his elbow to steady him. Jake lifted his leg to follow, but Atkins blocked the doorway with his arm. "Wait behind the yellow line until you're told to proceed," he said.

When Atkins removed his arm Jake stepped up three steps and waited behind a yellow line painted on the bus floor while Bradley directed T.J. to sit on the bench seat third from the front.

"Wrists on the bar," Bradley instructed.

T.J. placed his wrists atop a bar running across the back of the seat in front of him, and Bradley slid a chain through the center of the cuffs and locked it to the bar. It had just enough slack for T.J. to sit back with his hands in his lap. Bradley then directed Jake to the bench seat two behind T.J. and repeated the process. After situating Aaron on the right side, Bradley slid behind the wheel. Atkins did not immediately board.

Jake leaned forward, speaking in a hushed voice. "T.J.? T.J.?"

T.J. glanced over his shoulder. "Just shut up before you get me in more trouble."

"What? I'm the one who told you not to say anything in court; I told you to ask for an attorney. You got six months; he gave me a freaking year."

The bus shook. Jake looked up to see Atkins coming fast down the aisle. The guard cracked a baton across the bar to which Jake had been chained and a heavy metallic *ting* rang out, causing Jake to jump back against the seat. "Am I going to have a problem with you following rules?"

"No, Officer Atkins."

"You got two strikes. Don't make it three. Three strikes and . . ."

When Atkins didn't finish, Jake said, "I'm out, Officer Atkins."

"Wrong. We aren't playing baseball, boy. Three strikes and you're mine."

WINCHESTER COUNTY JAIL
WINCHESTER, CALIFORNIA

Sloane and Molia sat on bunks in adjacent cells, bars between them. The sheriff's deputy who processed them did a double take when he flipped open Molia's wallet and saw his police identification. "You're a police officer?" he asked.

"I'm a detective, son. If you had spoken to your compadre, Wade, you would have known that."

The deputy called over the female deputy who Sloane had spoken with earlier that morning and the two had a brief conversation before he left. Forty-five minutes later a uniformed sheriff's officer with more gray in his hair hustled in, stopping to give the deputy at the desk a look. The woman pointed to where Tom Molia sat.

"Detective Molia?" Molia stood and came to the bars. "I'm Sheriff Matt Barnes." Barnes looked to be early to midfifties, hair cut short on the sides, longer on top, and darkened with some gel product. Molia hoped the additional worry lines on a well-tanned face and the few more pounds on Barnes's frame meant he had more experience and common sense than his deputies. Maybe even someone to reason with. "One of my deputies called and told me about your circumstances. I took the morning off to get in a little fishing with my son."

"I'm sorry if you had to cut short your fishing trip," Molia said, hoping it meant Barnes was sympathetic to their plight. "And any assistance you might be able to provide would be appreciated."

"Well, the fish weren't biting all that much this morning anyway." He looked to Sloane, who had come to the bars and introduced himself. "First thing we can do is get you both something to eat while I walk over to the courthouse and find out the lay of the land."

"I can tell you the lay of the land," Molia said. "They arrested, tried, and convicted our sons, and when we questioned it, Judge Earl held us in contempt. What kind of judicial system are you running around here, Matt? I've never seen anything like this in my life."

Barnes scratched an itch at the back of his neck and grimaced. "Yeah, Judge Earl has a short fuse."

"Judge Earl is a megalomaniac," Molia said.

"What about our sons?" Sloane asked. "Boykin said he sentenced them to some juvenile facility."

"That would be Fresh Start," Barnes said.

"Fresh what?" Molia asked.

"Fresh Start. It's a juvenile detention camp about an hour from here up in the mountains."

"You mean a boot camp?" Molia asked, familiar with the facilities that used drill sergeants and scared-straight tactics on juvenile offenders.

Barnes seemed to be considering his answer. "Fresh Start has certain military-style elements to it, but it also has year-round educational programs and counseling; it's for teens convicted of nonviolent offenses or referred by their parents."

"Voluntarily?" Sloane asked.

Barnes nodded. "Parents can't control their sons; they pay to have them sent to Fresh Start to get straightened out. I know it's not much consolation, but as far as these kinds of places go, it's not a bad situation for your boys."

"Not a bad situation? They had to be in and out of there in less than twenty minutes. That's not justice."

"Yeah, Earl doesn't like to waste time."

Sloane scoffed. "God forbid someone should slow him down with minor inconveniences like constitutional rights."

"I hope you didn't make that suggestion to Judge Earl."

"He said they waived their right to a trial and to an attorney," Molia said, giving Sloane a look intended to convey that they needed Barnes as an ally.

"And you don't think so?"

"Whether we think they did or not is irrelevant, Matt. These are boys."

"Pretty serious crimes though."

"Which is why it was even more important for us to be there in the courtroom with them," Molia said. "And we would have been if one of your officers hadn't pulled us over. If you got a complaint department point me in the direction because I have a list at the moment." Molia said it with a smile.

"Who pulled you over?"

"The name was Wade, Carl Wade."

Barnes gave a small shake of the head and his face pinched, like he'd just smelled something distasteful. "Wade is an ass, and he's not one of mine. Truluck has its own private police force. They have no jurisdiction outside the city limits."

"Yeah? Well, somebody might want to remind him because he pulled us over on the way to the courthouse," Molia said, the situation becoming more clear.

"What's a private police force?" Sloane asked.

Molia turned to explain. "Just what it sounds like. They're hired, sometimes by a company, sometimes a private homeowners' association. Other times it can be the citizens of an entire town."

"Security guards?" Sloane asked.

"Not always," Molia said. "They can be granted official police powers in the particular jurisdiction they serve and do things like patrol city streets, respond to 911 calls, and hand out parking and speeding tickets."

"So they're police officers?" Sloane asked.

"Hardly," Molia said, looking to Barnes for confirmation. "My understanding is they don't attend the academy."

Barnes chipped in. "They haven't had any formal training, but inside the Truluck city limits, they're empowered to enforce the laws. With California on the verge of bankruptcy and budget cuts in the police and fire departments I suspect we're going to see more of this type of thing. Word out of Sacramento is that all of Winchester County is on the chopping block. They're calling it a consolidation of resources, but what it means in practical terms is fewer police and firefighters covering a whole lot more territory. The alternative is private police forces and volunteer fire departments."

"Who pays for it if the state is bankrupt?" Sloane asked. "It's got to cost money."

"It does. In this case it's the citizens of Truluck through a business tax, though Victor Dillon subsidizes the expense," Barnes said.

"Who's Victor Dillon?" Molia asked.

"Sorry," Barnes said. "I take some things for granted around here. Dillon owns the Gold Rush Brewery just outside Truluck. You might have seen signs for it driving in. He bought it about twenty years ago when it was failing and built it back up. Made a fortune. Since then he's pretty much bought up all the land around it to grow his hops, including Truluck."

"He owns the whole town?" Sloane asked.

"Every building."

"I thought it was a historical landmark?" Molia asked.

"That was Dillon's doing." Barnes pointed to his temple. "You get the state to make the town a historical landmark, slap a coat of paint on the buildings, and it increases the tourists. More tourists means more business. Everyone in Truluck either leases space from or works directly for Victor Dillon, and they pay a tax to support a private police force."

Molia rubbed the back of his neck. "That's why they didn't make a phone call," Molia said. "How T.J. and Jake could be brought before a judge so quickly. Wade and his pals don't work for the citizens of the state, so those small things you mentioned like due process and civil rights don't concern them like they do the rest of us."

"Technically they aren't public servants," Barnes added.

"So constitutional safeguards just get tossed out the window?" Sloane asked.

"Pretty much," Molia said. "They can't be sued for civil rights violations." Another thought came to him and he turned his attention back to Barnes. "Why would a town like Truluck need its own police force? I can't imagine it has much crime."

"Ordinarily, it doesn't," Barnes said. "Just makes everyone feel better, I guess. Dillon likes things run orderly."

"Sounds like a common trait around here," Molia said.

Barnes nodded. "Between us girls, I hear you. And I don't much care for the way Judge Earl does things at times, but he's the law in Winchester County, has been for seventeen years, and that's not likely to end before I either put in my thirty and retire or the state goes through with their consolidation and puts me out to pasture. So we deal with it best we can."

"I intend to deal with it," Sloane said, "as soon as I get out."

Barnes grimaced, as if the bad smell had returned. "Can I make a suggestion? Hold off a bit longer on that kind of talk. Judge Earl's got a short fuse, but it tends to burn down just as quick. After he's had a chance to simmer a while he calms and I can usually talk sense to him. If he thinks he's getting pushed you'll only relight his fuse. Let me have one of my deputies get you something to eat and drink and I'll take a walk over and assess the situation, like I said. I'll talk to Archibald Pike. He's the county prosecutor and a reasonable enough fellow. I doubt seriously he wants to prosecute an officer of the law on a contempt charge, and between the two of us, I think we'll be able to convince Judge Earl to let this one go."

Molia looked to Sloane, who gave a resigned shrug. Under the circumstances they didn't have much choice.

FRESH START YOUTH TRAINING FACILITY
SIERRA NEVADA MOUNTAINS

Jake's head bounced against the window. He opened his eyes and sat up, fighting to stay awake. Officer Bradley ground the gears and the bus lurched as it slowed into another bend in the road. Coming out of the turn, Bradley shifted again, this time the engine revving as the bus ascended a steep grade, continuing to pitch and bounce up the mountain. Jake estimated the ride to have been forty-five minutes, maybe an hour, when Bradley came to a complete stop to make a hard left and the bus left the asphalt for dirt. The new road wasn't nearly as steep, but the tires kicked up a cloud of reddish orange dust that penetrated the grates and left a fine layer of soot on the windows.

Jake had fought to stay awake and to pay attention to the drive in case he needed to tell David where they'd been taken, but as uncomfortable as the ride had been, the suffocating heat made it near impossible to keep his eyes open. Perspiration dripped down his face and neck and beaded on his forearms until the droplets trickled off his skin. When he sat forward he felt his shirt peel away from the vinyl seat. The stale air held the bitter odor of perspiring bodies that had ridden the bus before them and was as thick as a sauna. Two seats in front of him, T.J.'s head pitched and rolled about his shoulders. Aaron had his head back, asleep. Atkins, however, sat ramrod straight in his front seat, like a mannequin anchored in place, impervious to the conditions.

After what Jake estimated to be another ten minutes on the dirt road, the bus came to a complete stop. Through the dust-covered windows and diamond-shaped holes in the grate Jake read a bronze plaque mounted to a large boulder.

FRESH START
YOUTH TRAINING FACILITY
2009

A ten-foot-high chain-link fence rose above the boulder and extended as far as Jake could see down the road, barbed wire spiraling across the top. Behind it, in the distance, Jake saw a rectangular patch of dirt about the size of a football field and the metal roofs of buildings glinting in the sun. Bradley had the side window open, in conversation with a guard in a booth. After a moment the gate opened, Bradley ground the gearshift, and the bus lurched forward. The buildings became more distinct—squat, one-story cement block structures with green corrugated tin roofs along the southern perimeter of the dirt field. Some of the buildings were larger than others, likely to hold group activities. Jake had spent two weeks at a soccer camp in Washington State at what had been a former military base. The open field and barracks had been similarly situated, though the field had been green grass, and no fence caged them in. To the east he noted basketball hoops that looked reasonably new, chain nets hanging from orange rims, and in the northeast corner sat a series of wooden walls, cargo nets and poles he quickly deduced to be an obstacle course of some kind. He'd been expecting the worst but now didn't think the camp would be so bad, at least not so bad he couldn't handle it until David got them out.

When the bus came to a stop Atkins walked down the aisle, unlocking their chains and removing their handcuffs, issuing instructions. "When the doors open you will exit the bus single file. You will not speak. You will proceed to the front of the bus and await further orders."

Jake rubbed where the handcuffs had cut into his skin and flexed his wrists to encourage the flow of blood to his fingers. When he stood his legs felt weak. T.J. stumbled ahead of him. Stepping from the bus Jake lifted a hand to deflect the harsh glare of the sun. He did not see anyone else in the camp.

"Eyes front." Atkins stood with his hands behind his back, as if considering Jake and T.J. for the first time. Officer Bradley had disappeared inside the nearest building, taking Aaron with him.

"Inside this gated facility you have no rights. You have forfeited your rights. The Constitution does not apply here. Every right, every privilege must be earned. You will adhere to a strict schedule. You will wake when you are told to wake, eat when you are told to eat, go to school when you are directed, exercise when you are told to exercise, and piss, shit, and shave when told to piss, shit, and shave. Am I making myself clear?"

Jake and T.J. acknowledged him in unison. "Yes, Officer Atkins."

He cupped his ear and leaned in, waiting like some wannabe drill sergeant, but Jake told himself he'd play along. They repeated the mantra, only louder. "Yes, Officer Atkins." Jake's voice cracked, his throat raw and dry.

Atkins straightened. "You will receive daily work assignments. Points will be earned when you complete your task on time. Demerits will be given when you fail. When you earn points you earn privileges. When you earn demerits you earn punishment. You own nothing, possess nothing, and have rights to nothing." Atkins took two steps toward them. "Those clothes no longer belong to you. They are mine." He waited, though for what Jake had no idea. T.J. turned and glanced at him, equally puzzled. Then Atkins rushed at them, yelling, "What are you doing wearing my clothes? Remove them! Get them off!"

Jake and T.J. stumbled to remove their shoes and socks, hopping from leg to leg to remove their pants, Atkins yelling a stream of instructions at them. They pulled their shirts over their heads and tossed them also onto the dirt, standing in their underwear.

Atkins shouted, "When an order is given you will follow it without hesitation or question. Plank."

Again, Jake had no idea what Atkins had just ordered him to do. Given that T.J. also remained standing he did not either.

"I said 'plank'! When I say 'plank' you will assume the push-up position. Now. Drop."

Jake and T.J. dropped.

"Count them out."

Pebbles pressed into the flesh of Jake's palms as his elbows bent and straightened. By ten his arms already felt weak from the lack of food and sleep. T.J. collapsed at fifteen. Atkins dropped to a plank, holding his body as rigid as a two-by-four, his face inches from the ground. "Do not quit. Do not quit!"

T.J. groaned and attempted to lift his body from the dirt, but his arms would not straighten. By twenty Jake too was struggling. By thirty he had to pause at the top, butt raised, arms trembling. Atkins circled, continuing to scream. "Get your ass down. Why are you sticking your ass in the air? Am I your boyfriend, Inmate Carter? Do not bend your back."

During wrestling season Jake could do three sets of fifty, but that was with food and sleep and not being hung over. At thirty-seven, his arms felt like cooked spaghetti.

"Well look what we have," Atkins said. "A showboat." He dropped to his hands, body again rigid, face parallel with Jake's. "Are you a showboat, Carter? You trying to humiliate your friend?"

"Thirty-nine," Jake grunted. "Forty." He paused at the top, elbows locked, snorting like a bull, spittle spewing between clenched teeth. "Forty-one." The pauses became longer. Bile burned his throat. His shoulders ached, and he could no longer keep his back straight. His body looked like an inverted V.

Atkins sprang to his feet and used the sole of his boot to shove him in the ass. Jake pitched forward, the side of his face impacting the ground.

"On your feet. Get up. Get up."

Jake struggled to lift his chest from the ground and made it to his knees. He laced his fingers behind his head and sucked the searing, thin air into his lungs. Perspiration dripped down his chest.

"I said, stand up!" Atkins ordered.

Jake rose to his feet.

"Now remove all of your clothes."

Jake and T.J. struggled to lift their legs but managed to remove their undershorts and discard them onto the piles. They stood naked as Atkins circled. "What do you own?" he asked.

"Nothing, Officer Atkins." T.J.'s voice croaked, tears streaming down his face.

Atkins leaned between them, voice soft. "Then what are those clothes doing on *my* ground?" He yelled, "Get those clothes off *my* ground."

SEVEN

T rue to his word, Sherriff Matt Barnes fed them and somehow secured their release. After doing so, he arranged a
consultation with a woman in the Winchester County
Office of Youth Services at city hall, introducing Sloane and Molia
to Lynne Buchman, who identified herself as a "parent liaison."
Barnes left them alone to talk.

"You're a parole officer?" Molia asked. He and Sloane sat in two
chairs across from Buchman's desk in a small, utilitarian office.
Sloane estimated the woman to be midforties, but she wore a lot
of makeup, making it difficult to be certain. From the two pictures
on the shelves behind her desk, Buchman was married and had two
sandy-headed boys. One apparently played high school football.

"My job is to assist you during your child's transition to the juvenile justice system and to answer any questions you may have."
Buchman's smile and tone looked and sounded well rehearsed, like
the employees for one of those companies that lures people to a
no-strings-attached breakfast then tries to convince them to spend
their life savings on a time-share in Cancun. She even had a series of
brochures spread across her desk with pictures of teenage boys in
red coveralls sitting at a picnic table, playing basketball, and listening attentively in a classroom.

"Let's call a spade a spade, shall we, Ms. Buchman," Molia said.
"Fresh Start is a boot camp in a pretty wrapper and you're a parole
officer."

Buchman's tone turned condescending. "Fresh Start is not a boot camp. Physical and emotional punishment is strictly forbidden. The camp believes in a system of positive reinforcement through the use of a rewards-based incentive program."

The speech, like the smile, sounded rehearsed.

"Fresh Start removes the juvenile from the negative environment that led to the inappropriate behavior and puts them in a positive environment with the focus on physical challenges and improving interpersonal skills. Studies have revealed the root of most juvenile offenses to be poor self-esteem that causes poor interpersonal skills."

"What types of physical challenges?" Sloane asked, not drinking the Kool-Aid but seeking as much information as he could get.

"Individual and group challenges such as completing a hike, building a campfire without matches, or demonstrating an ability to complete a task on time. The system is designed to account for each juvenile's physical conditioning so they can experience success. Studies show that physical fitness helps build self-esteem and confidence, and that translates into success in the classroom."

And Sloane bet she had another study to prove that as well. "You said 'classroom.' So they attend class?"

"Five days a week." She slid another piece of paper across the desk. Sloane studied it as Buchman continued.

7:00–7:05 AM Wake-ups
7:05–7:30 AM Morning calisthenics/exercise
7:30–7:55 AM Showers/room & cleaning jobs/meds
7:55–8:10 AM Room inspections/finish cleaning
8:10–8:25 AM Breakfast meeting/hygiene inspection
8:25–8:55 AM Breakfast
8:55–9:10 AM Morning meeting
9:10–2:15 PM School

"Fresh Start adheres to a strict schedule to help the juvenile remain focused. Initially every minute of their day and night will be scheduled for them. As they move toward graduation from the program they earn free time, as well as the right to choose electives."

Sloane didn't finish reading the afternoon schedule. "What kind of training do the people running this place have?"

"The staff includes licensed educators, therapists, counselors, and military personnel, along with support staff—office managers, medical coordinators, kitchen staff, and persons such as myself."

"And what's your background?" Sloane asked.

She folded her hands on her calendar pad and tilted her head. "I have a PhD in child psychology and twenty years working with troubled youth."

"But you're here," Molia said. "Who ensures the safety of those kids at the facility?"

"Fresh Start only accepts nonviolent offenders. If an attendee demonstrates any form of physical aggression toward another attendee or staff, he is immediately removed from the facility. Weapons of any kind are strictly prohibited. No weapons are maintained anywhere at the facility. And the facility is fully enclosed. Any excursions outside the gates are led by experienced personnel trained in both first aid and wilderness survival. Inside the facility state-of-the-art surveillance equipment provides security in every hallway, dorm, and common area twenty-four/seven. Bedroom checks are completed by staff members every half hour, seven days a week from lights out at ten to lights on at seven."

"Why do they need military personnel if it's not a boot camp?" Sloane asked.

"Fresh Start adopts certain military-style practices. Attendees are given a uniform and assigned to a communal bunkhouse within a supervised unit. Each attendee is treated equally. Their drill sergeant is responsible for their physical training and seeing that they maintain their daily schedule. Again, however, I can assure you there is no physical or verbal abuse tolerated, if that is your concern. The emphasis is on promoting self-esteem through positive reinforcement."

A former marine, Sloane knew well the emphasis on breaking down the individual and building up the unit. He had been seventeen, not much older than Jake, when he walked away from his final foster home and signed on the bottom line at the Marine

Corps Recruitment Center. Boot camp had been the most physically demanding and mentally difficult challenge he'd ever endured. He had not remembered a lot of positive reinforcement, and something about employing similar tactics to juveniles as young as thirteen did not sit well with him. Tired of the sales pitch, Sloane cut to the chase. "When can we see them?"

Buchman responded by handing them another form. "Each attendee is allowed one phone call upon arrival and one outgoing letter per week."

Sloane read the next sentence out loud. "'There are no visitations during the attendees initial thirty days.' Are you kidding me?"

"What?" Molia snatched the brochure from Sloane's hand.

"Are you telling me we can't see our sons for thirty days?" Sloane asked.

"They are allowed a phone call—"

"I don't care about a damn phone call. I want to see my son," Molia said, standing. "Do you have any idea the size of the new one my wife is about to rip me when I call to tell her that our son is in prison?"

"Fresh Start is not—"

"I heard the spiel. It's a regular summer camp. I should be jumping for joy T.J. is so lucky to be one of the chosen few. I'll tell her he's going to be sitting around the campfire roasting marshmallows and singing Kumbaya."

"Why are we not allowed to visit them?" Sloane asked. "Why can't we see this facility?"

"It is important for the program to establish a system of authority, for the attendee to understand that he is responsible for himself. Studies—"

"Enough with the studies," Molia said. "I know about studies and how remarkable it is that most studies prove the premise the person conducting the study sets out to prove. I also served in the military and I have been a police officer for more than thirty years, and I am having a very difficult time understanding how that concept can be applied to a fourteen-year-old boy who has never even been to an overnight summer camp."

"As your son progresses through the program he earns an increase in visitations from one a month to one per week," Buchman said, undeterred. "It is intended to ease the juvenile back into the familial living environment while maintaining a system of discipline and authority. It reduces the chance that a juvenile will slip back to his old habits once he leaves the program."

"I don't need to establish a system of authority and discipline in my home," Molia said.

Buchman folded her hands; her silence intended to convey that she had heard more than one parent make the same statement. "I will make sure your sons call each of you after they are processed." Her tone conveyed it was the best she could do and all she could offer.

Seeing they were getting nowhere, Sloane slid back his chair. "Thank you for your time."

Buchman reached for another form. "Before you leave we'll need to discuss payment."

Molia turned his head, as if he had not heard her. "Payment? Payment for what?"

She looked up from the forms. "For the cost of the program."

"We didn't volunteer our kids for this," Molia said. "Judge Earl sentenced them."

"That doesn't matter," Buchman said. "Fresh Start is a private facility."

"Private?" Sloane asked. "Someone owns it?"

"The county leases the facility. Now, most insurance companies cover the cost because it is considered therapeutic. You will likely only be personally responsible for any copayment and portion not covered . . ."

Sloane couldn't believe what he was hearing. He took the forms, reviewing them as he spoke. "How much is it?"

"The cost is six thousand dollars a month, but as I said, insurance covers a large percentage, and we can bill you in equal installments over a twelve-month period."

Molia used a finger as if cleaning out an ear. "I'm sorry. Did she say *six thousand dollars a month*?" He looked to Sloane. "Did I miss the part about them earning a college degree while attending this fine institution?"

"And if we refuse to pay?" Sloane asked. "Then what?"

Buchman finally lost the smile. "Then your sons will be removed from the program and assigned to a county juvenile detention facility."

Sloane set the forms on the desk, leaning into Buchman's personal space. She leaned back. "Let me ask you a question, not as a 'parent liaison' but as a parent of those two young men in the pictures on the shelf behind you. I assume those are your boys?"

"Yes," she said, sounding off routine.

"So I'm asking you, parent to parent, do we need to be concerned about the safety of our sons at this facility?"

FRESH START YOUTH TRAINING FACILITY
SIERRA NEVADA MOUNTAINS

The barber had said one word: "Sit." Jake sat. The man hit a button and the clippers buzzed to life, blades vibrating over Jake's skull, great clumps of hair tumbling to the ground. His head freshly shaved, Jake was issued red coveralls that he slipped over white boxer shorts, a white tank-top T-shirt, and white socks. The boots he was issued were worn and a half size too big for his feet.

Atkins and Bradley met them outside what Jake learned was the "Administration Building." Jake suspected this would be a recurring nightmare. Atkins wasted no time barking more orders, directing them to zip up the fronts of their coveralls and to move quickly down a dirt path behind the corrugated block buildings. When they reached a small amphitheater with split-log benches on three sides of a firepit and facing a wood plank stage he separated them, T.J. to Jake's right, and ordered them to sit. Rays of sunlight slid through the canopy, dust motes dancing in the light. The shade offered little relief from the oppressive heat, and with each passing minute Jake did not eat or drink he felt more and more weak. It made it next to impossible to comply with Atkins's next order.

"Do not slouch. Slouching is a sign of physical weakness. Physical weakness is a sign of mental weakness. Are you mentally weak, Inmate Carter?" Atkins had commenced calling them "Inmate Carter" and "Inmate Molia" after they had been processed.

Jake sat up, but it was with effort and he could not maintain the posture long. When he slumped Atkins tapped his lower back with the baton. Otherwise Atkins and Bradley stood with hands clasped behind their backs, staring at the stage, as if awaiting some show. A flicker of light through the trees caught Jake's attention. Diamonds of light reflected off the surface of a distant body of water.

Atkins voice drew him back to the amphitheater. "Eyes front."

The man standing on the stage wore the same khaki shirt and shorts, as well as the dark sunglasses, but that was where the similarity with Atkins and Bradley ended. Pear-shaped and pale-skinned, the man had straw-colored hair that appeared to emerge from a single spot on the crown of his head, cut in a bowl shape. Methodically, the man removed his sunglasses, revealing eyes so pale they were nearly clear, and slipped the glasses into the front pocket of his shirt.

"I am Captain Overbay," he said, his voice higher pitched than Jake had expected. "You will address me as such. I am the chief operating officer here at Fresh Start. That means I am in charge of this facility. But I do not just work here. I eat here. I sleep here. I live here. This is my home as well as my place of business. My *home*." He emphasized his words. Then he paced left. "You are neither a resident of my home nor an invited guest. You have been discarded, left on my front porch by others who could not raise you. You have demonstrated an inability to adhere to and live by the laws that govern society. Therefore, that task now falls to me. I make the rules in my home. Disregard those rules and you will be disregarding me." He stepped to the edge of the stage, into one of the rays of light, as if finding his mark in the spotlight to deliver his next line in a near whisper. "It is impolite to disregard a man in his own home."

It was all very dramatic, but having just heard a similar spiel from Atkins it no longer held Jake's interest, and the lack of food and sleep and the oppressive heat continued to chip away at his reservoir of energy. His body began to shut down, without the resources to even lift his hand to swat at the fly rubbing its legs against the hairs of his arm. His eyelids rolled shut, opened, closed again. He shook his head, sat up straighter, but each reprieve was brief. Captain Overbay continued to talk, something about the need to instill discipline, about a rigid daily schedule, privileges and punishment. His voice faded to a hollow echo.

The noise of the baton against the log brought Jake back to attention. Atkins stood over him. "Are you having a good nap, Inmate Carter?"

"I'm trying," Jake said, "but it isn't easy with Captain Kangaroo going on and on up there." Jake had stumbled upon the show one night while flicking through the television channels and finding a station showing reruns from the 1970s and 1980s.

Atkins appeared momentarily taken aback, uncertain what to do. He looked to the stage.

Captain Overbay moved so that he stood in front of where Jake sat. He was grinning. "Was that a joke, Inmate Carter?"

Jake did not answer.

"Officer Atkins," Overbay said, "I think we have a comedian in our midst."

"I think you might be right, Captain."

"Are you a comedian, Inmate Carter?" Overbay asked. "Because I have always enjoyed a good joke. Do you wish to tell me another joke?"

"Not really."

Overbay looked offended. "Why not? You don't think I have a good sense of humor, Inmate Carter?"

"I don't think you'd find my jokes funny."

"How would you know? People tell me I have a marvelous sense of humor."

"I can't think of any."

"Maybe it's because you're sitting. Maybe what we have, Officer Atkins, is a stand-up comedian."

"Maybe we do, Captain."

"Stand up, Inmate Carter."

Jake stood.

"Now, tell us all another joke." Overbay spread his arms then folded his hands at his waist.

"I don't know any."

Overbay looked to Atkins. "Inmate Stand-up does not appear to have any more jokes, Guard Atkins. Maybe there are other interests we could cultivate."

"Maybe there are, Captain."

"Do you have other interests, Inmate Stand-up?" Overbay asked.

"Not really."

"None? No outdoor interests?"

"I used to like to fish."

"Did you? But not any longer?"

"Not really."

Overbay looked troubled. "Inmate Stand-up has no other interests, Officer Atkins. We should rectify that. A boy without interests is a boy with too much time on his hands, and a boy with too much time on his hands is a boy who gets in trouble."

"I was thinking the same thing, Captain."

Overbay looked down at the first row of empty benches, pacing left, right, back to center. He raised a finger. "I'm betting a young man like Inmate Stand-up would enjoy hunting. Would you enjoy hunting, Inmate Stand-up?"

Jake shook his head. "I don't think so."

"No? Have you ever been hunting?"

Jake shook his head. "No."

"Well then don't be so quick to judge. You need to be receptive to trying new things. How would you like to go hunting with Officer Atkins and me?"

Jake shook his head. "I don't think so."

"But you haven't even asked what we'd be hunting."

Atkins smiled. Overbay waited. Jake shifted from one leg to the other. "What would you be hunting?"

"Not 'you,' Inmate Stand-up. 'We.' This would be a group excursion. A team-building exercise. What would *we* be hunting."

"What would *we* be hunting?" Jake asked.

Overbay nodded to Bradley, and with no further words Bradley disappeared behind the stage walls. When he reappeared he carried a wired cage and a rifle. Inside the cage a rabbit hopped about, nose and whiskers twitching. Bradley handed Overbay the rifle, walked across the stage and stepped off, placing the cage about twenty feet to the right. Then he bent and opened the front flap, clipping it to the top.

The rabbit did not immediately dart at its sudden and unexpected chance at freedom. Whiskers twitching, it cautiously inched forward until its nose protruded out the open door, sniffing at the air to assess danger. It hopped a third time, half its body now outside of the cage. Atkins cracked the baton against the bench. Jake flinched. The rabbit darted with a burst of speed as if shot from a cannon, powerful hind legs propelling it toward the underbrush. Seemingly just as quickly, Overbay spun the rifle to his shoulder, aimed, and pulled the trigger. The rabbit flipped in midair, its back legs having pushed off the ground and its front paws reaching forward at the moment of impact, spinning 180 degrees, dead before it hit the ground.

Overbay lowered the rifle, turned, and directed his attention to Jake, the diminishing echo of the rifle's retort still carrying on the thin mountain air.

"Anything that runs," he said.

EIGHT

HIGHWAY 89
WINCHESTER COUNTY, CALIFORNIA

Sloane tried to keep his mind moving forward as Molia drove the winding road from Winchester back to Truluck. He'd had trials that had gone completely offtrack, witnesses changing testimony or disappearing the day they were to appear in court. He felt now as he did then, off balance, struggling to keep his feet planted firmly on the ground. He needed to think of options even while hearing Father Allen's admonition that saving Jake was not a problem Sloane could solve by walking into a courtroom and out-smarting everyone.

And yet the law was all he knew, all he ever had.

He had placed a call to Lisa Lynch, and now relayed the substance of that conversation to Tom Molia. "We'll file a motion for a new trial tomorrow and ask to have it heard on shortened notice."

Molia did not respond.

"If that doesn't work, we'll file an appeal."

Molia shook his head.

"We'll seek to expedite it."

Molia slammed his hand against the steering well. "Enough!"

The outburst startled Sloan.

"Enough, okay? Enough with the motions and the appeals. I'm not one of your clients you can placate with some bullshit legal jargon, all right? I know the chances of a motion for a new trial being granted and I know how long it will take to get an appeal filed and heard."

"I didn't mean to treat you like a client, Tom. I'm just trying—"

"What? You're trying to what, raise my spirits? Give me hope?" Molia exhaled. His words came with a slight tremor. "What do I tell her?" he asked. "What do I tell Maggie? That's her baby. That's her boy. So you tell me. What do I tell her? That we're filing a motion? Huh? That we're going to appeal?"

Sloane did not have an answer and knew Molia did not seek one. They drove back to Truluck in silence.

When they reached the Mule Deer Lodge, Molia turned off the engine but did not immediately get out of the car.

"I'm sorry," Sloane said, and it sounded as futile as it felt. "I never should have brought you and T.J. into this."

Molia cleared his throat. "I'm not buying that whole camp Fresh Start crap," he said. "Are you?"

Sloane shook his head.

"Something stinks," Molia said. "It's why I became a cop; I can feel when things aren't right and I can smell bullshit better than a hound."

"Lynch already has someone working on the motion. She's on her way here."

"But it's going to take time," Molia said, voice soft. He glanced at Sloane. "It's going to take time."

"You tell Maggie the truth," Sloane said. "You tell her this was not T.J.'s doing, and you tell her I'm going to get him out. No bullshit, Tom. I'm going to get them both out."

Molia shifted his gaze. Though he did not speak, his drawn face spoke volumes.

Don't make promises you can't keep.

The man who had checked them into the lodge emerged from the back room, alerted to their presence by the bells hanging above the door. "I thought you'd skipped out on me," he said

Music filtered in from the back room.

"We'll need the room for another night, possibly longer," Sloane said, reaching for his wallet.

The man shook his head. "Can't. We're full."

Sloane looked past him to the mailbox slots. He counted the knobs of six keys. "What are you talking about? There are keys right behind you."

The man didn't bother to turn. "Those rooms are reserved. We're busy summers here in Truluck. It's tourist season."

Sloane sensed the man was angling for more money. "How much do you want?"

"Don't want your money."

"Listen, I don't know—"

Molia stepped in. "Okay, partner. Just give us the keys to our rooms. We'll grab our stuff and get out of your hair."

"Can't do that either," the man said.

"Why not?" Molia asked.

"Your stuff's not here."

"What do you mean it's not here; we left it in the room." Sloane said. "Where is it?"

The man looked at a grandfather clock hanging on the wall amid framed period photographs—the people depicted sharing the same solemn expression and coal-black eyes. "Checkout's eleven o'clock."

"So?" Sloane asked.

"So when I heard you'd been thrown in jail by Judge Earl I figured you wouldn't be making checkout. Your stuff's at the police impound."

Sloane bit his tongue. "Where might that be?"

"Down the road. Look for the foundry. You'll see signs. You'll need to settle our bill first, though."

"We already paid for the room," Sloane said.

"You paid for one night. You missed checkout. I had to charge you a penalty."

Sloane sensed what was coming. "And how much is the penalty?"

"Four hundred dollars. Two hundred a room."

"That's more than the rental rate."

The man shrugged. "Like I said, it's a penalty."

Sloane leaned across the counter. "I'm not paying you four hundred dollars. I'm not paying you a dollar. And if you try to charge our credit cards I'll call and have the charges removed, tell the company they're fraudulent, just like you." He turned from the counter, Molia with him.

"I could call the police," the man said.

Molia spun so hard and fast the man stepped away from the counter. "You do that. And you make sure it's that wannabe rent-a-cop, Wade, who comes looking for us because I am just itching to see him again."

SIERRA NEVADA MOUNTAINS

The sun beat mercilessly, the heat seeming to attack not only from above but to also rise up from the ground, penetrating the soles of his boots. Bent over, Jake's body convulsed, stomach muscles wracked by pain, throat burning from the acidic phlegm that made him continue to gag uncontrollably.

"Not much for the great outdoors, are you, Jake?" Atkins held two leashes, the dogs attached to them no longer pulling them taut. The animals, some type of hound, though sleek in build, had sat as instructed, tongues hanging out the sides of their mouths, chests panting, eyes darting from Jake to their master, eager to get started again.

Jake had no idea how long or far they had hiked. Wrists cuffed to the chain around his waist, he used the shoulder of his red coveralls to wipe his mouth. "Are we done?"

Captain Overbay got up from the boulder on which he sat, rifle in hand, barrel pointing at the cloudless sky. "Done? We haven't even started hunting yet." Eyes again hidden behind sunglasses, his face revealed no expression. "And the dogs have to be run, Stand-up. Dogs are trained to behave through repetition. When you take dogs from their pens and put a leash on them, take them into the mountains, they expect to hunt. It's bred into them. We're going to train you the same way." Overbay looked about the landscape of boulders and trees while wiping a red bandanna across his neck and chest. "You see a rabbit, Stand-up?"

Jake didn't bother to look. He just wanted to get the hike over with. "No."

"Well, I guess we have two options. Your choice. One, we continue on until we see one, or two, we find something else for the dogs to hunt." The corners of Overbay's mouth lifted slightly. "What'll it be, Stand-up?"

"I don't care," Jake said.

"Well then, I'll decide for you. You got a ten-minute head start."

Jake's reflection stared back at him in the lenses of the captain's sunglasses. "What?"

"Start running, son."

"You can't shoot me."

Overbay smiled. "I told you, Stand-up. I can shoot *anything* that runs." He considered his watch. "And the clock's ticking."

TRULUCK FOUNDRY
TRULUCK, CALIFORNIA

Sloane did not see signs indicating a police impound. The hand-painted wooden sign above the canopy of the building at the eastern edge of Truluck identified it to be a foundry, but that was likely 160 years earlier, when the town had been flush with residents in need of metal tools for digging the gold out of the hillsides and to pan the river. With that no longer the case, the present renter had turned the building into an antique store. The porch overflowed with period furniture, metal bed frames, light fixtures, and trinkets tourists would buy to commemorate their visit. Inside, clutter filled the shelves and spilled onto nearly every square inch of the wood plank floor. The shop had the same musty odor as damp wood that never quite dries out, despite the efforts of an oscillating fan near a glass countertop displaying rings, necklaces, and metal bracelets. A man behind the counter wore a white T-shirt with a Harley-Davidson motorcycle above the words HOG WILD, gold and silver bracelets like the ones on display, and rings wrapping every finger.

"We're looking for the police impound," Molia said. "Someone directed us here."

"Yeah, I got the call you'd be coming." The man hooked one thumb behind a brass belt buckle bearing the image of a miner

carrying a lantern, a pickax over his other shoulder and the words
UNITED MINE WORKERS OF AMERICA circumventing the oval. "I have it
out back. Four backpacks."

Molia looked about. "This is the impound?"

"Today it is."

"What's that mean?" Sloane asked.

"It means, today it's the police impound."

"So how much do we owe you?" Sloane asked, again sensing
where the conversation was heading.

"Five hundred dollars."

"Five hundred dollars," Sloane said, unable to keep from chuckling. "You've had the stuff for less than an hour."

"It's a flat fee."

"Today anyway?" Sloane asked.

"That's right," the man said.

Molia pounded a fist on the counter, rattling the glass. The man
jumped. "You listen to me and you listen good," Molia said. The
veins in his neck bulged.

Sloane stepped between Molia and the counter. "Hang on. Hang
on."

"I'm calling the police," the man said.

"Just hang on," Sloane said. "You don't need to call the police."
Sloane walked Molia away from the counter, lowering his voice.
"Neither of us is going to do our sons any good in jail," he said.

Molia did not respond. He was breathing heavily, and his focus
remained on the man behind the counter.

"Let me handle this. Tom?"

Molia's gaze shifted to Sloane.

"Let me handle this."

Sloane walked back to the counter. The man adjusted his glasses.
"I don't like being threatened," he said, trying to sound tough
though his words came out tentative and he looked unnerved.

"Okay, fine. Five hundred dollars," Sloane started.

Molia stepped forward. "What? You're not honestly—"

Sloane put up a hand. Molia stepped back. "If you'll just show
me your California license authorizing your establishment to impound possessions, we'll be happy to pay and get on our way."

"What's that?"

"You do have a license, don't you?" When the man didn't immediately respond Sloane said, "You need a license to impound another person's possessions in the State of California. Otherwise it's just extortion, and that's a serious crime. The newspapers and television people would love to get ahold of a story like that, tourists being exploited. You'd likely lose your business license as well as go to jail."

"Funny you should bring up the subject of crimes, seeing as how you just skipped out on a hotel bill."

Sloane shrugged. "You can explain that to the state officials when they come to discuss the complaint I'll be filing against you."

"Wait." The man glared, but the game of chicken didn't last long. "Like I said, stuff's out back."

They found the four backpacks on a cluttered patio. "An impound license?" Molia asked, eyebrows arched and unable to suppress a grin.

Sloane smiled. "I figured they have departments for just about everything in California, don't they?"

SIERRA NEVADA MOUNTAINS

The dogs gained ground. Jake could not see them, but the rabidity and volume of their wailing and bawling had increased as they neared, sensing him, perhaps smelling his scent. Their barking echoed across the canyons and reverberated off the mountains, sounding as if the two had become many, a pack encircling him, closing in.

He climbed over fallen trees and boulders, the altitude causing his lungs to ache. The back of his throat burned. He had fled at too quick a pace, fueled by adrenaline and fear. The lactic acid burned deep in his muscles and he now ran on fumes. He'd unzipped the upper half of his coveralls and folded them to his waist, but as the dogs neared, the echo of their yowls made him pull the fabric back over his bare skin.

He followed no discernible path, his only goal to climb higher. A steep pitch, his legs labored as the rock and shale gave way with each step, dirt and gravel avalanches leaving a trail of dust down the mountain. When he fell he scrambled like a bear on all fours.

Reaching the peak, he turned and looked down, hands on thighs, emitting great gasps and moans. The muscles of his legs and feet cramped, and his chest felt as if someone had reached inside and gripped his heart. Light-headed, his vision spotted black and white, but he could still make out the dogs, tethered together, pulling Atkins up the mountain. The captain trudged behind them not looking at all pleased, his khaki shirt darkened with sweat. Something told Jake this was not what they had expected.

He plunged down the other side, an equally steep pitch, leaning back, fighting gravity, using a hop and a slide in the loose terrain. The descent would slow the dogs' pursuit, but they'd never quit. He remembered that from the movie his uncle Charlie liked so much, *Cool Hand Luke*. The dogs would run themselves to death before they quit.

He stumbled and lost his balance, pitching over like a tired skier on a steep run leaning too far forward and unable to correct his weight distribution. He had the presence of mind to tuck and roll as he fell, using his arms to protect his head. The ground slammed hard against his back and shoulders, the loose rock scraping and tearing at his forearms and biceps. He managed to swing his legs in front and dig in with the heels of his boots, skidding and sliding, splinters of pain shimmying up his legs. He came to a stop in a cloud of dust.

His tumult had increased the distance between him and his pursuers, but it would be a short reprieve. Only the human at the end of the leash prevented the dogs from already overtaking him. He rose in pain but continued to where the ground flattened at the tree line, picking and weaving his own path through the brush and twisted wood. He heard the roar of water, like the din of rush-hour traffic on a freeway, and moved toward it. The water would be cold, winter snowmelt, but it would quench his thirst and might provide him a means to escape.

He pushed through brush and abruptly stopped, standing at the edge of a sharp drop above a swollen river of white water crashing into and over large boulders. Nowhere to go. "Shit." He turned from the edge and pushed back through the brush, continuing into a forest of mature trees. The canopy prevented heavy undergrowth, which left the ground a bed of pine needles and boulders. It was easier to maneuver, but left no place to hide.

The dogs bellowed, drawing near.

He looked back over his shoulder and saw the dogs come out of the brush, tugging and straining their leashes, fighting to be set loose with their prey now in sight. Atkins held the end of the leash; the veins in his arm as swollen as the river. Overbay materialized behind them.

Atkins smiled. Then he bent, and unleashed the dogs.

Overbay raised the rifle.

Jake fled.

The blunt pain struck him between the shoulder blades, a piercing blow his weakened leg muscles could not absorb. He fell, rose to a knee, turned. The dogs bounded forward, each stride eating up huge chunks of ground. Ears pinned back, mouths open, they advanced with menacing grins.

Overbay reshouldered the rifle.

The second shot hit Jake square in the chest.

NINE

T he green and white highway sign marking Tristan listed
to the side, and the town didn't seem far from toppling
into extinction itself. The sign indicated a population of
just 565, but even that was hard to believe. As far as Sloane could
tell, Tristan consisted of a Valero gas station with an attached
minimart, a stock and feed store, and a tired-looking, single-story
stucco strip mall, the windows mostly vacant. A headless mannequin in a bridal gown stood out in front of one of the shops.
Another in its window faced the parking lot. Two doors down a
sign advertised a real estate office. Both seemed equally unlikely to
attract much business.

Molia likened the town to the rural towns in West Virginia. The
population, he surmised, lived down the dirt tributaries off the asphalt road, beyond where the eye could see, past the gnarled black
and white oaks and sunburned grass hills. He pointed out barbed
wire and split rail fences, which he said would have had no use if
there wasn't livestock to keep from meandering onto the road, and
livestock meant people.

The Tristan Motel sat kitty-corner from the gas station. A one-
story, corrugated block building, it had been cut into the hillside,
the dirt and shale beneath the grass a rust color. When Sloane
pushed out of the comfort of the air-conditioned car the blistering
air buzzed with swarms of hidden insects, and high overhead buz-
zards circled against a cloudless, pale blue sky.

The woman in the manager's office gave them the keys to rooms 5 and 6, which she said would be cooler, since the sun did not beat on them directly during the heat of the day. You could have fooled Sloane. When he pushed open the door to room 5 he felt as if he had stepped inside an oven, the air stale and reeking of cigarettes and the antiseptic smell of whatever chemical had been used to clean the bathroom.

Molia tinkered with the knobs on a portable air conditioner framed into the window, his eyes puffy and red. He'd called Maggie, and Sloane deduced from his solemn demeanor that the call had been an emotional one and had not gone well, though Molia had offered no specifics. Sloane had also called Frank Carter. He provided the facts with as much patience and as many details as he could, as well as explaining the efforts he would undertake to get Jake out. To his credit, Frank had offered to drive to Tristan, but Sloane advised against it, telling Frank there was nothing he could do, and they couldn't even visit Jake for the first thirty days.

When Sloane stepped outside to open the door to room 6 his cell phone rang.

"How far are you?" he asked.

Lisa Lynch had spent the late morning and early afternoon obtaining equipment and supplies they would need to set up a portable office to create and file pleadings. He also asked her to send an associate out to buy him appropriate courtroom attire: a sport coat and slacks, dress shirts, a tie, and shoes.

Lynch said she had been delayed in traffic getting out of Oakland and again on the outskirts of Sacramento, but the line of cars was now moving and she expected to arrive within the hour. Sloane provided her the address for the motel to plug into her GPS.

"Tristan isn't coming up," she said. "What's the next biggest town?"

"Big is relative," he said. "Try Truluck. It has a post office, so it's probably on some map." He spelled it for her.

"Got it."

"Tristan is about fifteen minutes before Truluck. Look for a Valero gas station. The motel is across the highway."

"That nice, huh?"

Sloane had stepped inside what would be Lynch's room to turn on the air conditioner. It emitted only a trickle of cool air. "Think the Four Seasons of Winchester County," he said.

An hour later, Sloane and Molia carried laptop computers, a seventeen-inch flat-screen monitor, a high-speed printer, and a portable fax machine and scanner from the back of Lynch's car into room 6. At least Lynch had maintained a sense of humor.

"I see you took the suite with the Jacuzzi tub and wet bar for yourselves," she said upon entering.

The air conditioner had cooled the room to sweltering, which was a notch below oven. After unloading the supplies, Molia went across the street to the convenience store and returned with cold drinks. Lynch pressed a can against her forehead and cheeks while fanning her sleeveless cotton shirt in front of the air conditioner. With her hair in a ponytail and dressed in shorts and flip-flops she looked ten years younger than she did in court.

Lynch linked the computer to her iPhone and pulled up a satellite image using a search engine to point out the location of the Fresh Start Youth Training Facility on the edge of the Eldorado National Forest. "It's rugged country," she said, which Sloane could deduce from the heavy green canopy surrounding the facility. Fresh Start looked to be half a dozen buildings surrounding a rectangular plot of dirt. "There's nothing up there, which is usually where these types of camps get put. The remote location deters thoughts of escape and allows for excursions outside the facility without encountering the general public."

"What did you find out about this one in particular?" Sloane asked.

Lynch opened another file on the computer. "Not much. It's flown pretty much under the radar since it opened." She clicked on several icons. Newspaper articles appeared on the screen. "It's a former Conservation Corps Camp. California sold it off to help alleviate its financial crises, and Winchester had it converted to a juvenile detention facility to replace an outdated county facility, but not everyone was in favor of the switch."

"Who opposed it?" Sloane asked.

"The correctional officers union, for one, but maybe that was to be expected, since closing the old facility put them out of jobs. They said there was nothing wrong with the old facility, that it met all state regulations and applicable codes."

"Did it?"

"I don't know."

"Let's find out. Anyone else?"

She scribbled a note. "In general there's been increased opposition to the idea of boot camps. I don't want to alarm either of you . . ."

Molia shook his head. "Trust me, after the day we've had, not much else would register on the alarming scale."

"I found some articles of physical and emotional abuse at some of these facilities. The most egregious was the death of a sixteen-year-old boy in Utah who had been branded a malingerer when in reality he had a serious medical condition."

"And people commit their children willingly to this," Molia said.

"Not like they once did," Lynch offered. "These camps were much more popular in the 1980s and 1990s when a perception developed that juvenile crime was the product of too much coddling, that society needed to get tougher on juvenile offenders before they became hardened criminals. The thought of using military type boot camps to accomplish this was almost romantic: taking the ragged edges off troubled teens and shaping them into sharp lines of marching cadets."

"That's not how I remember boot camp," Sloane said.

"After the reports of emotional and physical abuse, critics began to question the propriety of using military techniques to instill discipline in kids, not to mention the ethical dilemma associated with a system that allows private individuals to make a profit off the incarceration of those kids."

Lynch pulled up another article she'd downloaded. The headline said everything Sloane needed to know.

Selling Justice for a Profit
The dilemma of privatizing the criminal justice system

"Fresh Start is owned by a limited liability company, Fresh Start LLC." She clicked open a file and clicked through documents she'd downloaded from the California secretary of state's office.

"Stop," Sloane said. "Go back. That one. Scroll down." He read the names of the individual members of the liability company and pointed to the screen while looking up at Molia. "Victor Dillon."

"The same guy who owns Truluck?" Molia asked.

"And the brewery," Sloane said.

The road meandered along the South Fork of the Cosumnes River, a roller coaster of asphalt barely wide enough to accommodate a car traveling in each direction. The sun had not yet set, but it had descended low enough that the rolling hills and trees cast shadows across the road, making it even more difficult for Molia to judge the proximity and degree of approaching turns. More than once he had to hit the brakes hard to keep from ending up in the ditch.

Back at the motel, Sloane and Lynch had dug in, preparing the motion for a new trial, which they would file in the morning, as well as a second motion to have it heard on shortened notice, which meant asking the court to forsake the lengthy time delay usually associated with anything that has to do with the legal system. Wanting to keep busy, Molia volunteered to find them something to eat, though he had no appetite himself. The task had proven easier said than done. He tried Dillon, the closest town to Tristan, but struck out, though a gas station attendant offered a recommendation. The young man said he lived in Dry Creek and that his mother and father owned a diner there that stayed open later than most. He'd even agreed to call ahead and let them know Molia was coming. It was further evidence that businesses in the small towns were hurting.

Not long after the road sign announcing the town of Dry Creek's existence, Molia came upon the string of brick and rock buildings the gas attendant had described. The Dry Creek Diner, just past the Dry Creek Theater, reminded Molia of Merle's Coffee Shop, his favorite diner back in Charles Town, West Virginia, and that made him melancholy for home.

The woman behind the counter had already set to work on the order, but said it would be a few more minutes. She offered Molia a cup of coffee and a seat at the window. He picked up a copy of the *Dry Creek Reporter* and read without much interest, but hoping anything would take his mind off the conversation he'd had earlier that afternoon with Maggie. It had been the single most difficult call he'd ever made. Maggie had answered with a bright tone, but she knew him too well for him to sugarcoat the news. He told her straight out that T.J. had gotten himself in some trouble with the law.

"T.J.? What kind of trouble?"

As he set out the details of what had transpired Maggie listened in stunned silence, whispering little more than "Oh my God" until Molia told her T.J. had been incarcerated and that he might not be getting out anytime soon.

"What?" she exploded, anger and fear fueling a string of difficult questions for which Molia had no answers.

"How did this happen, Tom? How could this happen?"

"I don't know."

"Where were you?"

"The boys wanted to share a room. We were in the room right next door; we never heard them get up."

"This isn't like him. Why would he do this?"

"I don't know."

"You haven't spoken to him?"

"They sentenced him without us present."

She grew more upset with each answer, crying now, "Where the hell were you?"

"A police officer pulled us over. He wouldn't let me go."

"But you're a cop."

"I explained that to him. He—"

"Can you visit him?"

"Not for thirty days."

"Thirty days! That's a month."

"I know."

Then she'd asked the most difficult question of all. "How long is the sentence?"

"Six months."

And the string of "Oh my God"s began again.

"David is working on getting them both a new trial; he's filing a motion tomorrow morning."

"What are the chances?"

Molia suspected she knew the answer. "If we lose we'll file an immediate appeal. He's also filing a motion to have them transferred to facilities closer to home."

"An appeal? How long will that take?"

Too long. "I don't know."

"My God, Tom, he's just a boy. How could you let this happen?"

"I'm sorry."

"How could you let this happen?"

"I don't know."

The tone of her voice hardened, a mother's resolve. "You get him out, Tom Molia. Do you hear me? You get my boy out. You do what you have to do, but you get him out."

"I will."

"Don't you come home, Tom; don't you come home without my boy. Don't you dare." Then she hung up. She had never hung up on him. She'd rarely ended a conversation without saying "I love you."

When he'd disconnected, Molia felt as if he'd been run through with a spear. He knew Maggie had spoken out of anger, but he also knew she'd spoken the truth.

He set the paper on the table and turned toward the window, wiping the tears that leaked from his eyes, and caught a blurry glimpse of what appeared to be the back end of a two-tone, blue-and-gray car driving down the street. He spilled his coffee getting up, and stepped out onto the boardwalk but only in time to catch red taillights ascend a hill and disappear around the bend.

* * *

Molia set the two bags of food and the cardboard tray with three chocolate milk shakes on the passenger seat and set out for the drive back to the Tristan Taj Mahal. The switchback, black asphalt, had become even more difficult to navigate with the blanket of darkness. Molia straddled the center of the road, finding a rhythm to the turns and trying to focus, but his thoughts continued to drift back to his conversation with Maggie and the question he could not answer. *How could he have let this happen?* He'd told her he didn't know, but he did know. He knew exactly how it had happened. He'd been so eager to help Sloane with Jake that he'd forgotten to consider what was best for his own son. Sloane had warned him of Jake's problems, but Molia had downplayed it, trying to minimize Sloane's concern. When T.J. asked if the two boys could share a room together, Sloane had known it was not a good idea and tried to say so, but again Molia had not listened. He was trying so damn hard to be a good friend he'd forgotten to be a good father. Had he been thinking about T.J., had he listened to Sloane's admonitions, none of this would have happened.

He'd been wrong to explode at Sloane, his anger born from his concern for T.J., his frustration with the parent liaison's rigid adherence to her bullshit spiel, and his own guilt. What had happened wasn't David's fault, and his attempts to explain the next steps in the legal process had simply been his way of trying to focus their attention on things they could do, rather than obsess and despair about all the things they could not.

Headlights in the rearview mirror refocused Molia's attention on the road. The car had approached at a high rate of speed and did not stop until it was just feet from the Jeep's bumper. Molia flipped the mirror to cut the glare and saw the metal grill and the lights. Police car. He hadn't imagined it.

Wade. Had to be. The son of a bitch was following him.

Molia contemplated taking Wade on a wild-goose chase, but just as he thought it the flashing lights atop the car spun to life and Wade's voice echoed through the speaker. "Pull over."

"No thanks," Molia said. "Been there, done that. No jurisdiction outside Disneyland, Carl."

Wade punched the accelerator, and the police car shot forward, the metal grill impacting against the Jeep's back bumper.

"Son of a bitch," Molia said through clenched teeth. He decelerated, contemplating coming to a complete stop and confronting Wade right there, but Wade was armed and Molia wasn't, and along a deserted stretch of road who knew what the crazy SOB was capable of? He sped up, then slowed, deliberately changing speeds, a herky-jerky pattern intended to keep Wade just off balance enough to make him think twice about giving Molia's bumper another love tap.

It didn't work.

The force of the second attack could have been a result of Wade misjudging Molia's tactics, or intentional. Either way it jarred Molia's head back and nearly spilled the cardboard box with the shakes off the seat. And that gave Molia his idea.

He hated to do it. Chocolate was his favorite flavor.

He reached across the seat and lifted one of the cups from the tray, removing the straw and waiting until he saw what he needed, a short length of straight road. He slowed.

"Stay with me, Carl," he said, alternately considering the rearview mirror and the distance before the next turn. "Just a little longer."

Wade tapped the bumper, and in the rearview mirror Molia saw him gesticulating through the windshield for Molia to pull over.

"Not this time, Carl." Molia lowered the driver's window.

As he approached the turn he let fly. He couldn't judge the trajectory of his toss, but he could see Wade's reaction in the rearview mirror.

Wade swerved and hit the brakes. Too late. The cup exploded against the glass, its thick contents splattering the windshield in a broad swath of chocolate.

Molia braked, made the turn, and punched the accelerator. The last thing he saw was the back end of the police car fishtail, the tire sliding from the asphalt and into the ditch.

TEN

T he bright light blinded him. Jake raised an arm to deflect the glare, surprised that it came from four fluorescent tubes in fixtures mounted to a pitched ceiling. Disoriented, he struggled to his elbows, but felt lightheaded and lay back again.

The last thing he recalled was assuming a fetal position, using his forearms and elbows to protect his head and face. The dogs attacked his limbs, pulling and tugging at the coveralls, but Jake resisted the urge to kick out and remained curled in a ball, hearing the snarls, feeling the saliva wet on his skin.

Only Atkins's command had ended the attack. "Off!"

The dogs continued to bark and lunge at him, paws digging at the ground, until Atkins reattached their leashes. Even then, still amped from the hunt, they sprang up and down on their front legs, tongues hanging out the sides of their mouths, ears perked and attentive.

Jake sat up again and this time remained upright long enough to consider his surroundings. He lay atop a bunk bed, apparently in one of the corrugated block buildings he'd seen out the bus window. He ran his tongue over his lips and felt the jagged edges of cracked skin and tasted blood, which made him remember the two bullets. One hit him in the back and one in his chest. He looked down at the dark red spot that had flowered in the center of his coveralls, which was sticky to the touch. When he brought his fingers closer he saw that the remnants had stained his fingers and hands, making the cracks look like hundreds of intersecting rivers and tributaries run red. But it wasn't blood. It was paint.

He closed his eyes again and this time saw Captain Overbay standing over him, the corner of his mouth twitching, the movement almost imperceptible but just enough to signify enjoyment, bemusement, perverse satisfaction. Then Overbay flipped the rifle, the barrel twirling, and aimed it directly between Jake's eyes.

"No second chances," he'd said.

The room began to tilt and twirl but Jake held the edge of the metal frame to steady himself. Perhaps forty feet in length and half the width, the room looked like the dormitory at the soccer camp he'd attended in Washington. A series of bunks were positioned perpendicular to unblemished walls with a pale green linoleum floor down the center. Whereas the thin mattress on which Jake sat remained unmade, the other beds were identical in their perfection—white sheet folded back six inches over a forest green blanket tucked so tight Jake could not detect a single wrinkle. No pictures or posters adorned the walls and he did not see any dressers or nightstands or articles of clothing of any kind. He thought maybe he had the dorm to himself. Then he saw the plastic bins beneath each of the lower bunks, like the bins the guard had given him and T.J. for their extra set of coveralls, white socks, T-shirts, and boxer shorts.

A clock high on the wall, its face protected by a metal cage, indicated it was just after eight, and judging by the darkness outside the row of rectangular shaped windows above the top bunks, it was night, not morning. In the corner of the room, mounted to the ceiling, a camera continuously rotated left to right and back.

At the end of the bunk on which he sat, Jake found a plastic water bottle resting atop a neatly folded white sheet, green blanket, and thin pillow, but the simple task of reaching for the bottle brought pain pulsing through every inch of his body and it took three tries to reach it. The knuckles of his hand ached when he twisted off the top, and the lukewarm water stung his lips and burned his throat but he drank greedily, until he felt a hollow pang in his stomach and thought he might heave. He fell back, one leg dangling over the edge of the bed, forearm covering his eyes. Another image came to him, this one of him being pulled down the mountain by a chain, stumbling and falling frequently.

Mercifully the images faded and his mind drifted. His aching body, craving sleep more than even food, gave in to fatigue. He did not know whether five minutes or five hours passed when he heard the first voice.

"Hey, who's that?"

"Fuck if I know. He's a newbie."

Too tired to care, Jake tuned the voices out, pretending to be asleep.

The bunk shook, someone standing on the bottom bed frame to get a closer look. "What happened to his face?"

"He looks like shit."

Jake ignored them.

Someone tugged on his leg. "You're on my bunk." The voice, high pitched, sounded almost girlish. The person shoved Jake's shoulder. "I said you're on my bunk."

Jake wasn't in the mood to make friends. He kicked out, striking something solid. "Fuck off. It was empty."

The response was a blow to the chest that hit him like a jackhammer and knocked the wind out of him. Before Jake could react the hand that hit him grabbed his coveralls and lifted him as if the bunk were spring-loaded and ejected him. Jake had the sensation of flying, but it was brief. His shoulders and the back of his head hit the block wall, bringing stars. When they cleared Jake was looking at a head as big and round as a pumpkin, the face acne pocked with a jagged red scar that extended from the left eye to the corner of the mouth and caused the eyelid to appear half-closed.

"I said, this is my bunk." The behemoth discarded Jake like a rag doll, tossing him across the room and throwing the neatly folded bedding on top of him. "You sleep on the floor."

The others in the room, each dressed in the same red coveralls, stood watching. Some smiled, as if this were part of the camp entertainment, but most looked equally terrified. Then one of them shouted.

"Officer in the barracks!" They scurried to the ends of their bunks and snapped to rigid attention.

Atkins walked the aisle between the beds, stopping at the bunk beside which the man-child had taken position. He dwarfed even Atkins, a foot taller and a good hundred pounds heavier.

"Any problems, Clarence?"

"No sir, Officer Atkins." The boy spoke with a pronounced lisp.

Atkins's sunglasses were clipped to the front pocket of his shirt. Jake was surprised the man's eyes were green; he'd expected them to be pitch-black or something equally demonic, yellow or red.

Atkins considered the bedding on the floor before raising his eyes to Jake. "Inmate Stand-up, I see you've made friends with Big Baby."

THE TRISTAN MOTEL
TRISTAN, CALIFORNIA

Tom Molia entered the room carrying two bags and balancing a tray with two Styrofoam cups. "We have company."

Sloane took the tray and looked out the door but did not see anyone or any suspicious vehicles in the parking lot or parked along the highway.

"Wade," Molia said, placing the bags on the bed closest to the door. The other bed had papers scattered across it. "He followed me to Dry Creek. I didn't see him, but he was there."

"How do you know it was Wade if you didn't see him?" Sloane asked.

"Because we played bumper cars on the drive back. I was the bumpee."

Lynch sat at the computer. "Who's Wade?"

"Friendly Truluck police officer," Molia said. "He likes us so much he's trying to convince us to leave."

"Why?" she asked, concern creeping into her tone.

"It's just a power play," Sloane said, then to Molia, "But it sure seems like overkill, doesn't it?"

"I had to waste a perfectly good chocolate shake, but I bought us time if we want to move; it will take an hour or more before the tow truck pulls his car from the ditch."

Sloane looked at the two remaining Styrofoam containers and deduced the rest of the story.

"You think this guy is dangerous?" Lynch asked, standing now.

Sloane shook his head, though after what Molia had just told them he was no longer certain. "He's just testing the waters." He addressed Molia. "We're set up here. And remember what Barnes said. Wade has no jurisdiction outside of Truluck."

"Yeah, I keep hearing that," Molia said. "And he keeps ignoring it." He opened a bag and removed one of the food containers, handing it to Lynch. She didn't open it. Molia picked up the small stack of papers from the bed and glanced through them. "So what do you think? Should I get my hopes up?"

Sloane shrugged. "We're swinging in the dark a little bit without a transcript of the hearing. Without it we can't be certain exactly what Jake and T.J. said in court."

"Can we get it?"

Lynch handed him a second document. "That's the next motion, to get a copy of the transcript. The proceedings are supposed to be recorded."

"Should we wait to file the motion for a new trial until we do?" Molia asked.

Sloane shook his head. "Better to file the motion tomorrow and have it heard as soon as possible. Otherwise we'd have to wait until Monday. And if Boykin is going to deny it, the sooner he does the sooner we can file the appeal."

Molia sighed, frustrated. "What does it matter what they said? They're kids. T.J. wouldn't even know he had rights to waive."

"A juvenile can confess and waive his right to counsel just like an adult," Lynch said, "but it has to be done knowingly and intelligently. We need the transcript to determine if that was the case."

"He's a fourteen-year-old boy; fourteen-year-old boys don't do anything intelligently."

"You're preaching to the choir," Lynch said. "I have two, sixteen and eighteen."

"So who decides if it was intelligent?"

Sloane answered. "The judge."

Molia dropped the papers. "Oh, that's just great."

Lynch continued, undeterred. "Boykin still has to show he considered the totality of the circumstances: Jake and T.J.'s ages, their intelligence, and the circumstances under which they made their confession and waived counsel. We know they were likely hung over and hadn't slept much and that they were rushed to court early on the morning of their arrest without counsel, or the chance to speak to either of you. Those are some strong circumstances and no judge wants to be overturned on appeal."

Molia shook his head. "It still leaves an awful lot of discretion for a guy we already know plays fast and loose with the rules."

"No doubt," Lynch said. "But in this instance we have a real case of piling on. The failure to accord Jake and T.J. an attorney calls into question the validity of their confessions, especially because Boykin proceeded without a parent or guardian present. It makes it that much more difficult for the prosecution to meet the knowing and intelligent standard."

Sloane knew Lynch was doing what any lawyer would, focusing on her strongest legal arguments, trying to be an advocate, but he also knew that too often in the judicial system the law got ignored. So did common sense.

Molia knew it, too. "Maybe so," he said. "But I don't get the impression Boykin lets a little thing like the law get in the way of what he does. He'll do what he wants and then find a way to justify it."

FRESH START YOUTH TRAINING FACILITY
SIERRA NEVADA MOUNTAINS

Jake followed Atkins across the dirt yard to the Administration Building. Atkins had not explained the purpose of this visit, just told him to move, and Jake wasn't about to ask the guard any questions. He struggled to keep up.

Entering the building Atkins knocked on a Plexiglas wall to gain the attention of a civilian seated at a desk behind the wall. The lock buzzed. Atkins pushed in the door and escorted Jake down a sterile corridor past two doors with narrow windows. Jake slowed to look in and saw a kid in red coveralls sitting alone on a bunk.

"Eyes front," Atkins ordered.

At the end of the hall Atkins used a key to open another door and led Jake into a room with nothing but two blue plastic chairs. He directed him to sit and exited the opposite side of the room, leaving Jake alone. His imagination provided any number of scenarios as to what awaited him.

After several minutes the interior door opened and T.J. walked out, tears streaming down his cheeks, his eyes puffy and red. Officer Bradley stepped out after him.

"Hey," Jake said, but T.J. turned his shoulder and continued past, not uttering a word.

"Stand-up!" Atkins motioned Jake inside. He took a tentative step forward. Atkins shoved him the rest of the way in. "Move, I don't have all night."

The room contained a single chair and a metal table. On the table was a black, old-fashioned telephone except it did not have either a number keypad or a rotary dial. A window separated the room from a smaller room, the setup like a recording studio.

"You get one phone call."

Jake sighed in relief. Then he asked, "How do I dial?"

"You don't. I place the call. Before I do, let's get a few things straight. I'll be sitting in that room listening to every word you say. Understood?"

Jake nodded.

"There's a time delay between the time you speak and when the words are transmitted. The person on the other end won't know it, and you don't tell them. I have a button. I press it any time you say something I consider inappropriate. Understood?"

Another nod.

"So unless you want to go hunting again in the morning I'd suggest you think real hard about what you intend to say." He glared. "You get three minutes. At two minutes and forty-five seconds you'll hear a buzz. That means it's time to wrap it up. If you go over your allotted time you lose your next phone privilege. Is that understood?"

"Understood."

"Who do you want to call?"

"My father."

"Give me the number."

THE TRISTAN MOTEL

TRISTAN, CALIFORNIA

Tom Molia disconnected the call and wiped his eyes, taking a moment to compose himself before he opened the interior door connecting the rooms to rejoin Sloane and Lynch. When he did, Lynch stood.

"I'll be in my room if you need me." She placed a comforting hand on Molia's shoulder but offered no words before closing the door.

"He's okay," Molia said, still gathering himself. "He's scared, but he says he's okay."

Sloane knew Molia well enough to know from his restrained tone that he didn't fully believe that to be the case.

"I did fine until I had to hang up," Molia said. He blew out a breath. "That was the hardest part."

"Did he mention Jake?" Sloane had still not received a phone call, and given the status of his relationship with Jake he wasn't sure he would. If, as the parent liaison said, Jake only got one call he might choose to call Frank.

Molia shook his head. "He said he's not allowed to talk about anyone else."

"What about the confession or the waiver of his right to an attorney?"

Molia shook his head. "He couldn't discuss those either."

"What could he say?"

Molia slumped on the edge of the bed, voice soft. "He has a bed in a dorm. They've fed him. They're treating him okay."

"You didn't say anything about us filing a motion for a new trial."

Molia shook his head. They had discussed it and decided not to tell either boy and get their hopes up unnecessarily. "They've obviously coached them on what they can and can't talk about, and most jails monitor phone calls and incoming and outgoing mail. I'd suspect this place does the same. There's a pause. At first I thought T.J. was being hesitant, but it's too consistent. It's a time delay to allow someone listening in to edit what's said and heard. I'd keep anything you don't want broadcast under your hat."

Sloane nodded. "I am sorry, Tom."

Molia raised a hand and let it fall. "This isn't your fault, David. I shouldn't have said what I said earlier. I was tired and frustrated. I took it out on you. When I talked to Maggie she told me not to come home without T.J. It's just that . . . I'll never forgive myself if something happens to him, but I don't know what I'd do if I ever lost her."

"We're going to get them out."

Molia didn't comment.

"Jake's all I got left, Tom. Tina's gone. I don't have anyone else. I'm not leaving here without him. I'm going to get them out. And no judge with an overinflated ego or security guard masquerading as a cop is going to keep me from doing so. A day. A month. A year. I don't care how long it takes. They're going to get to know me around here. They're going to get to know me real well."

Sloane's cell phone rang. No numbers appeared on the screen, just the word "Private."

"Blocked call," he said.

"That's Jake," Molia said.

FRESH START YOUTH TRAINING FACILITY
SIERRA NEVADA MOUNTAINS

David answered before the third ring.

"Jake?"

"Dad?"

"How are you, son?"

David's voice had a strange, amplified tone. Jake looked to the glass behind which Atkins sat wearing headphones. Atkins pointed to his wristwatch and smiled.

"I'm okay. How are you?"

"What's wrong with your voice? It sounds hoarse."

"I, uh, I don't know. I think maybe I caught a cold or something."

"I'm sorry, Jake. We tried to get there. Tom and I tried to get to court but—"

The words stopped. Jake looked to Atkins. He had pressed the button.

"—anyway for the first thirty days."

Jake had no idea what David had just said. "I'm sorry, too, Dad. I guess I deserved this, but I'm real sorry about T.J. I think he's having a harder time." Jake looked to the window. Atkins shook his head and pressed the button.

"Could you tell Mr. Molia I'm sorry?"

"I'll tell him. But he doesn't blame you, Jake. Are they treating you okay?"

Atkins held up his finger to indicate he would depress the button. "Yeah. Yeah, they're treating me real good, Dad. This is a real nice place. It's like a camp, you know? Remember that soccer camp I went to that I loved so much?" Jake had not liked the camp and hoped David recalled as much. "They have basketball courts and a lake and one of those outdoor theaters. What are they called?"

"An amphitheater?"

"I think maybe they put on plays or something. I don't know yet. And we get to go on hikes." Jake looked to Atkins. "I went on a hike this afternoon."

"How was that?"

Atkins sat poised to depress the button. "It was hard, but I think this place is going to help me do better, you know?"

Jake heard three beeps. He looked to Atkins, who made a slashing gesture across his throat. "I have to go now, Dad."

"I love you, Jake. You take care of yourself."

Jake spoke more quickly. "Could you do me a favor, Dad?"

"Anything."

Jake looked to the glass. Another three beeps. "Could you tell Mom I love her? And tell her I miss her, and I hope she comes to visit." Atkins tapped on the glass.

Time was up.

Jake hung up the phone and stood from his chair as Atkins re-entered the room. "You did real good, Stand-up. I was sure you'd screw up again, but you actually stuck to the rules. Maybe there's hope for your sorry ass."

"Maybe," Jake said, "I just needed the right motivation."

THE TRISTAN MOTEL
TRISTAN, CALIFORNIA

When Tom Molia reentered the room Sloane had his head down, eyes closed.

"What is it? What's the matter?" Molia asked.

Sloane couldn't get his jaw to work, couldn't speak. His mind continued to go over Jake's request. "He asked me to tell his mother he loved her. He asked me to bring her for a visit."

Molia stood mute.

Sloane stood. "He also talked about a soccer camp he attended and how much he loved it. He said Fresh Start was like that camp."

Sloane looked to Molia. "Jake hated that camp. He hated the bunkhouse and the food and said the older boys bullied the younger ones. He wanted to come home after a day. He was sending me a message. They're in trouble, Tom. They're in a lot of trouble."

Big Baby lay on his lower bunk, a hand down the front of his white boxers, nursing a boner as if he were the only person in the room. Jake had removed his mattress from the top bunk and shoved it against the far wall, as far from the man-child as he could get. At just minutes before "lights out" some in the dorm were screwing around, hurling insults at one another. Others were rushing to get things into their plastic bins. A guard stood at the front of the room watching.

When the first bell rang everyone dutifully climbed into their beds. A minute later the clock on the wall buzzed and the lights shut off, plunging the room into darkness but for elongated rectangles of light on the floor, moonlight streaming through the overhead windows. Jake heard the guard leave, the door shutting. His eyes adjusted quickly. He noted a green blinking light atop the camera in the corner of the room and three red lights, evenly spaced across the ceiling, marking the locations of the smoke alarms. Though exhausted, he fought to stay awake, alternately counting to himself or singing the words to songs in his head, but his body could not hold out. His eyes fluttered open and shut and he felt himself drifting off.

The sound of metal springs creaking woke him. Big Baby rose from his bed, a huge black shape. He seemed to hover for a moment, staring down at Jake. Fear pulsed through him, and he clenched his fists, determined to fight if Big Baby came for him, but Big Baby turned and walked down the aisle, toward the door, likely headed to the bathroom to relieve his boner.

Halfway down the aisle, however, Big Baby stopped.

Jake sat up and looked to the corner of the room. The light above the camera no longer blinked, and it was no longer green. It was solid red.

He looked back to the center aisle and watched Big Baby move to one of the bunks. He heard another bed creak, then a muffled protest followed by a frightening silence that seemed eternal. The ensuing sounds, however, were even more horrifying: whimpers of pain, the rhythmic creaking of the metal bed, and Big Baby's escalating, hedonistic grunts.

ELEVEN

The spray hit him in the face, startling him awake.

Jake jerked to a sitting position and instinctively raised a hand to deflect the stream. Big Baby stood over him, urinating.

Jake jumped to his feet but with the block wall at his back he had no place to escape. The yellow stream became an arc, and Big Baby laughed as he redirected his aim, finishing with a shot to Jake's mattress.

"Time to wake up," he said. "You don't follow the rules, we all get punished."

Big Baby gave Jake a final inane laugh before walking to where the others had already formed a line for the door. A guard stood waiting but if he saw Big Baby's wake-up call he didn't care. Jake, dead tired, had not heard the alarm. He trudged to the back of the line, assessing his condition. He felt as though he'd been run over by a truck, his legs and arms leaden and his head heavy. He followed the others, looking up at the camera as he approached the door. The blinking green light pulsed, but the camera no longer rotated left and right. It remained stationary, the lens pointing directly at him.

The following morning, Sloane and Lynch filed the motion for a new trial along with their motion that it be heard on shortened notice as soon as the Winchester County clerk's office opened at 8:00 AM. They also filed a separate motion to obtain a transcription of the record of the prior day's hearing. The Winchester County clerk, Evelyn Newcomber, handled the papers herself and said she would hand deliver copies of the pleadings to the prosecutor's office, also located on the first floor of the courthouse, as well as to Judge Boykin's chambers on the third floor. She suggested Sloane and Lynch wait in the lobby and she would bring them file-stamped copies of the pleadings, as well as Boykin's order either granting or denying the motion to hear the matter on shortened notice.

Sloane paced the terra-cotta tiles, alternately adjusting the knot of his tie and tugging on the sleeve of the sport coat. The clothes Lynch brought were not a bad fit, but his left arm was slightly longer than his right, and he usually had to have his pants hemmed. Molia also paced. Neither of them had slept, not after the phone call from Jake, and the detective had pronounced bags under his eyes.

Sloane knew it possible Boykin would refuse to accommodate them, refuse to hear their motion that morning and instead set the motion to be heard at some future date on the court's calendar just to make their lives difficult and to send his own message reaffirming who was in charge. But Sloane didn't think so. He hoped that the ego and temper Boykin flashed the prior morning was not an aberration but a reflection of the man's personality and that it would again get the better of him. Sloane pegged Judge Earl to be the type who did not like to have his authority challenged, and in Sloane's experience those were the types who usually went out of their way to look for a fight and rarely had enough common sense to back down gracefully. The motion for a new trial was a direct challenge to Judge Boykin's decision to incarcerate T.J. and Jake, and Sloane and Lynch had deliberately not pulled any punches drafting it. If anything they chose words intended to inflame, calling the sentencing "a gross miscarriage of justice" and Boykin's decision "woefully lacking in both legal support and equity." Their request that Boykin hear their motion on shortened notice, that very morning, was also a direct shot at the judge's compulsive need to run his courtroom on schedule.

Just fifteen minutes after filing their motion Newcomber pushed open the smoked glass door and stepped into the rotunda. She wore colorful beads that matched the color of her long, decorated purple fingernails and handed Sloane the file-stamped copies. "Judge Boykin will hear the motion first thing this morning," she said.

Sloane flipped to the second page and saw Boykin's flowing signature in black ink.

Challenge accepted. The fight was on.

They made their way to Judge Earl's ornate eighteenth-century courtroom on the third floor and took seats in the gallery.

"Like stepping back a hundred and fifty years," Lynch said, looking about.

"Wait until you meet Judge Earl," Molia said. "You'll think Judge Roy Bean was cryogenically preserved and brought back to life, without his brain."

Not long after they sat, the courtroom door opened and the prosecutor from the prior morning walked in. Balding, with wire spectacles and a thick mustache, Archibald Pike apparently favored three-piece suits, this one brown. The gold chain of a pocket watch draped from a button on his vest and looped to a pocket.

"Looks like everyone is in costume," Lynch said.

Pike carried a stack of files, a loose pleading on top, no doubt Sloane's motion for a new trial. He used a leg to push through the swinging gate and set up in the location he had taken the prior day, at the end of the table closest to the jury box. Once settled he picked up the loose pleading and flipped through it, occasionally adjusting his glasses while reading.

Lynch and Sloane made their way to the rail when Pike lowered the pleading. He turned to shake their hands. "I understand Judge Earl has granted your motion for shortened time."

"We're sorry we were unable to provide you with more notice," Lynch said, ever gracious. "Given the urgency of the matter we felt it necessary to file it first thing this morning."

Pike nodded. "Would you consider a continuance to allow the court clerk to transcribe the recording of yesterday's proceedings?"

"How long would that take?" Sloane asked.

"I could ask that it be expedited. I would think we could get a copy early this afternoon and hold the hearing first thing Monday morning."

It wasn't an unreasonable request, but Sloane didn't want to wait three days.

"Do you plan to oppose the motion?" Lynch asked Pike.

"I stipulated to the motion for shortened time; I will oppose the motion for a new trial. Both boys waived their right to counsel and confessed. I was here in court when they did."

"We don't believe the waivers or the confessions were made intelligently and with full knowledge of the consequences," Lynch said. "They didn't have counsel to advise them, or a guardian present."

"Judge Earl spelled it out pretty clearly," Pike said, a smirk to this tone.

"We also don't believe Judge Boykin should have sentenced them without holding a separate hearing with parents present. This entire thing was rushed."

"A gross miscarriage of justice?" Pike asked with a bemused smile.

"And if it was your son what would you think?" Sloane asked.

Pike looked from Sloane to Molia, who had joined them at the rail. "I don't have anything personal against either of your sons, gentlemen. We get juveniles through here regularly, but this wasn't some penny-ante crime they committed either. They broke into an establishment, stole alcohol and a firearm, and discharged that firearm within range of a populated area."

"They're boys; they made a mistake," Molia said.

Pike shook his head. "Mistakes are accidents. This was no accident. It was a premeditated act of vandalism. We're just lucky no one was seriously hurt, or worse." He turned to Sloane. "And it isn't the first time for your son, Mr. Carter. He's developing quite a file, and it reveals a continuing pattern of progressively worse criminal conduct. Maybe this is what he needed, to get him back on track."

Lynch stepped in before Sloane could speak, like a referee separating two boxers. "What about getting the transcript and having the hearing this afternoon?" Lynch asked. "We'd be amenable to that."

"If the clerk can get it transcribed that quickly, I wouldn't oppose it."

The woman who had been in the well beneath Boykins's elevated bench the prior day entered the courtroom through the door leading to the Judge's chambers and retook her seat. The courtroom bailiff followed, with Judge Boykin fast on his heels. Boykin strode past a brass spittoon, an old wooden box, and what looked like an antique stenographer's machine, and took the three steps to his bench in one bound. Once there he wasted no time.

"Ms. Valdez, call the first case."

Valdez stood. "The People of the State of California versus Jake Andrew Carter and Thomas James Molia," she said.

Lynch pushed open the swinging gate and stepped to her left. Sloane caught the gate and followed. Boykin looked up and raised a meaty palm. "Mr. Carter, you may remain in the gallery. Only attorneys and defendants at counsel table."

Lynch spoke. "Your Honor, this is David Sloane; he's a licensed attorney in the State of California and cocounsel in this matter."

Pike turned his head at the mention of Sloane's name then picked up the pleading, flipping to the last page with the signatures.

"I thought you told me yesterday you're the boy's father," Boykin said.

"His stepfather," Sloane said.

Boykin stroked his beard, no doubt considering this another power play, but he had no basis to keep Sloane from appearing at counsel table. Recognizing this, Boykin motioned Sloane forward to join Lynch.

"I have granted a motion for shortened time to hear defendants' motion for a new trial this morning. Mr. Pike, the State stipulates to the motion for shortened time? Mr. Pike?"

Pike looked up from the pleading, the bemused smile gone. "Uh, yes, the State does, Your Honor."

"Are we going too fast for you, Mr. Pike?"

"No, Judge. My apologies."

"Then what I have before me is a motion for a new trial and a motion to have a transcript made of yesterday's proceedings."

Lynch spoke. "Your Honor, we spoke with the prosecutor this morning and discussed the possibility of putting this matter over until this afternoon, after we have obtained the transcript and had the chance to consider it."

Boykin cut her off. "The prosecutor is very generous with my time, but does not keep my calendar."

"I apologize, Judge," Pike said.

"I have a criminal trial continuing this afternoon. Besides, the issue is moot. I had Ms. Valdez check with the clerk's office this morning and she has advised that the recording of yesterday's proceedings is not available. Is that a correct statement, Ms. Valdez."

The woman in the well spoke. "That's correct, Judge."

"What does that mean?" Sloane asked. "When will it be available?"

"It means, Mr. Sloane, that the recording was inadvertently erased. The clerk's office made a mistake and did not retain it."

"A mistake?" Sloane asked. Evelyn Newcomber had not said a word to them about it. He turned to Pike. "As opposed to a deliberate, premeditated act?"

Boykin leaned forward. "You will watch your tone, Counselor, or you will again find yourself a guest of Sherriff Barnes, and this time I will not be as lenient."

"So we have no record of the proceeding?" Lynch asked.

"I believe that's what I just got through explaining, counsel. Now—"

"Then we would request that the court grant the motion for a new trial," Sloane said.

Lynch looked caught off guard. So too did Pike. Boykin leaned forward. "Excuse me?"

"The defense requests that the court grant the motion for a new trial."

Boykin looked bemused. "I heard you the first time, Counselor. Perhaps you would care to educate me on what basis the court would do that?"

"Without the transcript the State has no evidence to meet its burden that either the confessions, or the waivers of counsel, by either defendant, were made knowingly and intelligently. Unable to meet that burden the court must grant the motion."

"Must? Did you just say 'must'? Let's get something straight, Mr. Sloane. I am a superior court judge of Winchester County. Duly elected. The only things I must do are pay taxes and die. Do not presume to tell me what I must do in my courtroom." He turned his head. "Does the State wish to add anything, Mr. Pike?"

Pike did not immediately respond, an indication he had been unaware of this development or, if he had been, hadn't considered this potential ramification. "The State opposes, Your Honor."

Boykin shook his head. "Would the State care to enunciate the basis for its opposition?"

"Uh, yes, it would," Pike stammered. "We, uh, the State has witnesses. I was here, as was Deputy Langston and Ms. Valdez. I can have another attorney from my office examine me if necessary."

Sloane responded. "It's extremely prejudicial to the defense, Your Honor. We should not have to take the word of the county prosecutor and a peace officer."

"You're suggesting they would lie?"

"Lying has nothing to do with this. Without a transcript of the hearings, the defense can't conduct a proper cross-examination of the witnesses. We have no way to corroborate that what they might testify to is an accurate recollection of what was and was not said."

Boykin sat forward. "I disagree. I was also present in court and can make that determination."

"Then the defense requests that Your Honor recuse himself if he intends to be a witness for the State," Sloane countered.

"Don't be insolent, Counselor. I have no intention of recusing myself or becoming a witness. I was merely attempting to alleviate your concern that Mr. Pike, Deputy Langston, or Ms. Valdez would lie, under oath, in my presence."

"Begging Your Honor's pardon," Sloane said. "But it's your presence that concerns us."

Boykin flushed and took a moment to adjust his glasses. "Are you suggesting, Counselor, that I would subordinate perjury?"

"Not at all, Judge," Sloane said, "Only that it is your ruling that these fine citizens of Winchester County would be trying to uphold. With all due respect, it's not the same as having a transcribed record."

"Maybe not, but it is what it is. Do you wish to proceed or not?"

Lynch looked to Sloane with hopeless resignation. They both knew the witnesses weren't about to say anything but that the confessions and waivers were knowing and intelligent. In fact, Sloane and Lynch's motion now provided a road map of what they needed to say to meet that legal standard. Without a record, Sloane and Lynch had no way to challenge their testimony.

"We'd like to examine someone in the clerk's office concerning this mysterious disappearance of the recording of yesterday's hearing," Sloane said.

"So now you're suggesting the loss of that recording was the result of something untoward?" Boykin asked.

"I am merely trying to create a full record, Your Honor," Sloane said, meaning a complete record to be submitted to the court of appeals.

Boykin looked to his clerk. "If you wish to conduct a full hearing with the testimony of witnesses we will have to place this on my regular hearing calendar. Ms. Valdez, when do I have an afternoon free?"

Valdez played with the keys on her computer screen, studying it. "Two weeks from next Wednesday, Judge."

Lynch stepped in. "Your Honor, if the court is unable to hear this matter this morning we are prepared to stipulate, without conceding the accuracy of their recollection, that the witnesses for the State will testify that Jake and T.J. waived their right to counsel and confessed if the prosecution will stipulate that the defendants did not have counsel present, no counsel was offered, and each appeared in court without a parent or legal guardian within six hours of their arrest."

Boykin looked to Pike.

"The State will so stipulate," Pike said.

"Then we would request that you deny the motion and issue your order," Lynch said.

Though it pained Sloane to hear it, he knew Lynch's strategy was correct. It made no sense to wait more than two weeks for a hearing that would most certainly result in the witnesses testifying as had been represented and Boykin denying their motion for a new trial. To go forward with a full hearing would only be wasting time, and after his conversation with Jake, Sloane felt even more compelled to get the boys freed quickly. By pushing Boykin to issue his order they could now move immediately to file an appeal and seek to have that appeal expedited. The suspicious lack of a transcribed record only strengthened their case. It wasn't great. An appeal, too, would take time, but they were not going to get anything better, not in Winchester County, not from Judge Earl.

"Fine," Boykin said. "Defendants' motion for a new trial is denied. Mr. Pike, you will prepare an order for my signature. Counsel may obtain a copy of that order from the clerk's office."

"Your Honor, may we ask to have the order faxed to my office," Lynch said. She would waste no time drafting her appeal.

"Leave your business cards with Ms. Valdez and she will see that it is taken care of."

Sloane and Lynch left their business cards on the oak railing.

Boykin never even dismissed them. He just shifted files. "Ms. Valdez, call the next matter."

Turning from the railing, Sloane watched a correctional officer escort two boys into the courtroom. The door had nearly closed when a hand emerged, grabbing the edge and pushing the door open. Carl Wade stepped in wearing his Truluck police uniform, pausing when he caught sight of Sloane and Molia.

"State of California versus Griffin Knight," Ms. Valdez said.

Molia timed his walk with Wade's approach to the swinging gate and spoke into the police officer's ear. "I hope you liked chocolate," he said before following Lynch to the exit.

In the corridor outside the courtroom, Molia said, "That was a waste of time."

Lynch tried to sound optimistic. "We had to go through this step to file the appeal. Now we've gained a stipulation that Jake and T.J. were tried without counsel and without a parent."

"We already had that," Molia said.

"And that they were tried and convicted within six hours of their arrest. I'll get a toxicologist's opinion, but I suspect he'll conclude from the amount of alcohol the police report states they consumed that Jake and T.J. were still legally drunk when they appeared before Judge Earl."

"That's got to help," Molia said, brightening.

"And the loss of the record is just one more thing for the court to look at and conclude something untoward occurred. I'll have someone working on the appeal while I'm driving back. We'll get it filed first thing Monday morning and seek to have it expedited."

"You think it was an accident, David?"

Sloane turned and looked at Molia but did not answer. His mind remained in the courtroom. He had seen no attorneys or other adults seated in the gallery. "He's going to do the same thing to those two boys," he said. "Boykin's going to railroad them." Before Lynch or Molia could respond Sloane pulled open the door and stepped back into the courtroom. Archibald Pike had been reading the complaint, making reference to violations of the California Penal Code section when Sloane pushed through the swinging gate. Pike stopped in midsentence.

FRESH START YOUTH TRAINING FACILITY
SIERRA NEVADA MOUNTAINS

The morning had not started with a shower, it started with twenty-five minutes of calisthenics in the yard, though Jake noticed that Big Baby went directly to the bathhouse. The workout wasn't particularly rigorous—push-ups and sit-ups and jumping jacks. Jake's wrestling practices had been much more arduous, but in his weakened physical condition he had trouble keeping up and Atkins took every opportunity to berate him. He felt light-headed, like when he would crash diet to make wrestling weight, and at one point thought he'd throw up, though there was nothing in his stomach to vomit. After calisthenics they proceeded to the showers, five minutes in lukewarm water. Still, it felt refreshing to be clean for the first time in days. When Jake entered the dorm he found clean bedding on his mattress. The other inmates moved with robotic precision, remaking their beds to military standards. One of them, the blond-haired boy who Jake suspected had been Big Baby's victim the prior night, saw Jake struggling with the sheet and quickly approached.

"Like this." He took an end, shook the sheet out and let it fall so that the top was six inches longer than the mattress. "Tuck it in," he said. He repeated the process with the blanket until Jake's bed looked the same as the others. When they had finished he said, "Atkins likes to drop a quarter and see it bounce."

They'd find out quickly enough. At precisely 7:55 AM Atkins appeared in the dorm, greeted again by the shout of "Officer in the barracks."

As they had the previous night, each boy snapped to attention at the foot of his bed. Jake did the same, not out of any respect for Atkins, but because he had vowed not to do anything to jeopardize his chance to eat his first meal since the dinner at Whistling Pete's in Truluck, nearly forty hours ago. He needed to regain his strength, suspecting he would likely have more encounters with Atkins.

Atkins inspected each bed, pulling on corners to ensure snug fits. He also considered each inmate's appearance, telling one to zip his coveralls, another to retie his shoelaces. He didn't like the way one had shaved. Each responded without hesitation. When Atkins reached the foot of Jake's mattress his eyes narrowed. Jake suspected Atkins had hoped to find the bed unmade, another reason to punish him. He turned without comment.

After Atkins released the dorm they walked single file to the mess hall. Jake was salivating by the time they entered the building, but to his bitter disappointment they did not get in line for food. They took seats at one of the tables closest to the plate-glass windows. Streams of pale light shone on administrators in civilian clothing who stood to discuss a wide range of topics, from their classroom work to structured recreation time, group therapy, and assigned afternoon chores. As if to further taunt him, each person spoke while standing in front of the serving counter, where wisps of steam from water boiling beneath the food pans filled the room with the aroma of eggs and bacon.

After the final announcement Atkins ordered the guards to release the tables one at a time. They released Jake's table last. When he finally grabbed one of the yellow trays and a plate he feared he'd reach the front of the line only to be told they had run out of food. He anxiously watched as the servers dished out helpings of eggs and potatoes, two strips of bacon, and a small carton of milk. When he reached the front they filled his plate full and he felt a great sense of relief. He searched for a place to sit among the inmates who were engaged in excited chatter about the morning menu. From their comments Jake deduced bacon to be a rare treat. Jake spotted an opening at the table with the kid who helped him with the mattress and started in that direction. Halfway there he heard a loud bang and turned to see one of the servers kneeling to pick up a stack of dropped trays. Big Baby sat close by, smiling at Jake.

Turning quickly, Jake never saw the leg.

It stuck out as he passed the corner of the table, hitting him across the shins and knocking him off balance, too much for Jake to recover. The tray pitched forward, and the plate and utensils slid off the edge, hitting the concrete floor with a clatter. Jake landed face-first, grimacing in pain.

After the initial shock, he got to a knee and turned toward the perpetrator, a big kid sitting at the end of the row. Had there been any doubt the act was deliberate, the shit-eating grin erased it. Tired, hungry, and frustrated, Jake saw black. He went at the kid in a blind rage, bull rushing him as the kid started to get up from the bench. The look of shock indicated this was not what the kid had expected. Jake hit him full force, bodies, plates, and trays flying. The kid was bigger than Jake and, because of Jake's weakened condition, stronger. But Jake remained quick. He grabbed a wrist, and managed to get it behind the perpetrator's back, his other hand pressing the face against the concrete floor.

"You son of a bitch. You did it on purpose."

Jake felt arms grabbing him, pulling him off. He continued to struggle, managed to free an arm, and was in the process of bringing his fist forward when Atkins's face appeared in his line of sight. The guard caught Jake's fist before impact and two other guards sandwiched him, interlocking his arms, immobilizing him.

"You just can't seem to get along, can you, Stand-up?"

"He tripped me," Jake said, spitting with anger. "He did it on purpose."

The perpetrator stood, touching a bloody lip, grinning but out of breath. "You tripped on your own feet."

"You're a fucking liar." Jake lunged, but the guards weren't about to let him go.

"Captain Overbay has a strict view about the use of vulgarity in his home, Inmate Stand-up, as well as fighting. He did bring that to your attention, though you might have been sleeping during that part of the orientation." Atkins smiled. "It seems you are in need of a lesson in both."

"He tripped me. He made me spill it."

Atkins looked at the upended tray and food splattered on the floor. He addressed the kid who had tripped Jake. "What about it, Inmate McCarthy, did you trip Inmate Stand-up?"

"No sir, Officer Atkins."

"Well then, how do you explain this waste of food on my kitchen floor?"

"He dropped it, sir. He tripped over his own feet and dropped it."

Atkins turned back to Jake. "Captain Overbay also has a strict rule about not wasting food. You take it, you eat it."

Jake looked down at the lump of food on the cement floor. Then back at Atkins.

"I'm not eating that."

"Then you will go hungry," Atkins said. He raised his voice, addressing the others. "Inmates! Lower your forks."

An audible groan and hushed profanities accompanied the sound of silverware hitting the tables.

"Inmate Stand-up has refused a direct order from an officer, and he has wasted food." The response was another collective groan. "If Inmate Stand-up will not eat, then neither shall any of you."

Atkins looked to Jake. "Inmate Stand-up, you'll find what you need to clean up this mess in that closet. And Captain Overbay expects his kitchen floor to shine." Atkins pivoted and made his way to the exit. Reaching it, he turned back, raising his voice. "Inmates, I expect Inmate Stand-up to have your full cooperation this morning," he said before leaving.

The inmates stood from their seats, eyes fixed on Jake. One by one they lifted their trays and, in near unison, turned them over, scraping the remaining contents onto the floor.

WINCHESTER COUNTY SUPERIOR COURT
WINCHESTER, CALIFORNIA

Boykin looked up from what he'd been reading. "Mr. Sloane, what are you doing interrupting my courtroom?"

Sloane stepped to counsel table. "David Sloane appearing on behalf of Griffin . . ." He looked down at the kid, maybe fourteen. "What did you say your last name was, son?"

The kid looked confused, eyebrows arched. "Uh, Knight."

"David Sloane appearing on behalf of Griffin Knight."

"You can't do that," Pike said, then addressing the bench and sounding less sure. "He can't do that."

Sloane looked down at Griffin Knight. "You want an attorney to represent you, don't you, son?"

The kid's brow furrowed. "I don't know. Are you any good?"

Sloane couldn't hold back a smile. He put a hand on the kid's shoulder. "They tell me I'm pretty good."

Knight shrugged. "Okay."

Sloane turned to the bench. "David Sloane appearing on behalf of Griffin Knight."

If Boykin had been angry before, he was livid now. The portion of his face not covered by the beard flushed red. "Mr. Pike, call your first witness."

"Your Honor?"

"I said call your first witness, Mr. Pike."

A flustered Pike fumbled through his stack of files, which had apparently been more for show than utility. He pulled out one and quickly opened it, reading and flipping pages, making it even more apparent he was not familiar with the circumstances warranting the charges against Griffin Knight. "The State calls . . ."

"Why don't you call the arresting officer," Boykin offered.

"Yes. The State calls Officer Carl Wade to the stand."

Wade stood from his seat in the gallery and made his way to the witness stand. Without his hat and sunglasses he looked decidedly younger and far less intimidating, with freckles and red hair tamed with some gel product.

"Good morning, Officer Wade," Pike said, continuing to stall. He read the file while approaching the witness stand. "Can you state your name and occupation for the record?"

Sloane interjected. "Your Honor, the defense would request that these proceedings be recorded and would further request a transcription of that recording."

Boykin's lips pinched. "So noted, Counselor, at your expense."

For the next ten minutes Wade took Pike through the circumstances leading to the arrest of Griffin Knight. The boy had been walking the streets of Truluck after curfew when Wade stopped him. Wade reported smelling marijuana, conducted a search, and found a metal pipe concealed in Knight's hoody.

"No further questions." Pike turned to Sloane. "Your witness."

Sloane pointed to the police report on Pike's side of the table. "May I?" Pike handed it to him. Sloane approached the witness stand reading. "Officer Wade, what time is it?"

Pike shot out of his chair. "Uh. Objection. Irrelevant."

"Sustained."

"Officer Wade, what time was it when you first approached the defendant?"

Wade flipped through a copy of his report, which Pike had provided during his direct examination. "My report indicates Mr. Knight was arrested at ten-twelve in the evening."

Sloane pointed. "And did you note the time on that shiny wristwatch?"

Wade flashed his watch. "Mostly likely. I probably did. Yeah."

"And you first observed the defendant walking down the street sometime before you arrested him, did you not?"

Wade smirked and sat back folding his hands in his lap. "I had to observe him to arrest him, Counselor."

"Did you stop him right away?"

"What do you mean?"

"I mean did you see him and arrest him Johnny-on-the-spot, or did you first observe whether Mr. Knight was engaged in criminal activity."

Another smirk. "I observed the suspect to determine if he had any criminal intent."

Sloane nodded, continuing to read, asking the question without looking at Wade. "And how long did it take for you to make that determination?"

"How long?"

"You didn't just rush to judgment, did you?"

Wade shrugged. "I never rush to judgment."

"So how long did it take you to determine that Mr. Knight had criminal intent?"

"Five or six minutes, maybe."

"And what did you see the defendant doing during that five to six minutes that indicated to you a criminal intent?"

"He appeared to pull something from his pocket and throw it in the bushes."

"That's not true," Knight interjected.

Boykin rapped his gavel. "Counselor, you will keep *your* client under control or I'll hold you both in contempt."

Sloane winked at Knight. "Let me handle this," he whispered. He returned his attention to Wade. "What did you do after observing this behavior?"

"I called it in, said I was going to be making an arrest, waited to be advised that backup was on its way, and left my vehicle."

"Another couple minutes there?"

"Probably."

"Three or four?"

"Yeah, I'd estimate that to be about right.

"And I assume you and the defendant spoke."

"I asked him what he was doing out past the Truluck curfew, if that's what you mean."

"That's what I mean. What is the Truluck curfew, by the way?"

"Ten o'clock sharp for any person under the age of eighteen."

"And what did the defendant tell you he was doing after you engaged him?"

"He said he was walking home after work."

"Did he say where he worked?"

"I know where he works."

"You and the defendant are acquainted?"

"He's been arrested before."

"So where does the defendant work?"

"At the Truluck Hotel. He washes dishes. It's part of his aftercare program."

"Where was the defendant when you arrested him?"

Wade considered his report. "Heading south on Magnolia, three blocks east of Main Street."

"The hotel, his place of employment, is it on Main Street?"

"Yes."

"And where does Mr. Knight live?"

"He lives with his mother on Magnolia."

"So he *was* walking to his home after work?"

"That's what he said."

"And all of the facts would lead an experienced police officer such as yourself to reach the same conclusion, would they not?"

"I suppose so, yeah."

"And where on Magnolia in relation to the defendant's place of residence did you stop him?"

"He was two doors south."

"Of his home?"

"That's right."

"Forty feet?"

"I suppose that's about right."

"And you proceeded to interrogate him, to ask him where he'd been and what he'd been doing. Questions such as that?"

"Not necessarily."

"Well, you did speak to him long enough to conclude that he was under the influence of marijuana, didn't you? I mean you didn't just slap the cuffs on him and put him in the car, did you?"

"Of course not."

"So how much time did you speak to the defendant before you did slap the cuffs on him?"

"A few minutes."

"Four or five?"

"Something like that."

Sloane tossed the report back on the table in front of Pike and walked to the stand. "Officer Wade, I ask again, what time is it?"

Pike quickly rose. "Objection, Your Honor, it's irrelevant."

Before Boykin could rule on the objection, Sloane said, "Let me rephrase the question to alleviate the prosecutor's objection. Officer Wade, what time is it on *your* wristwatch?"

Wade looked past Sloane to Pike, but this time Sloane did not hear an objection. He suspected Pike was either trying to figure out what was happening, or already had.

Wade hesitated. "It's eight twenty-two."

Sloane looked at the grandfather clock on the wall. "Let the record reflect that the clock on the wall in this courtroom has the time as eight-nineteen. Let the record reflect that the time on my cell phone, which, it is common knowledge, is set to the nation's official atomic clock in Colorado, is eight-eighteen."

Pike pulled the pocket watch from his vest and clicked it open. "You wish to contribute, Mr. Pike?" Sloane said. Pike snapped shut his watch and slid it back in his vest pocket.

Sloane turned to Wade. "Officer Wade, you testified, and you wrote in your report, that you arrested the defendant at ten-twelve in the evening. But you spent five to six minutes observing him before the arrest, another three to four minutes calling for backup, and four to five additional minutes observing his demeanor before placing him in custody, correct?"

"Well . . ."

"That was your testimony wasn't it?"

"I suppose, yes."

"Which would mean that when you first observed the suspect it was between nine fifty-seven and one minute after ten, according to your watch, which we now know is four minutes fast. That would put the time that you first observed the defendant, forty feet from his front door, at nine fifty-three to nine fifty-seven. Which means, if you hadn't stopped him, he wouldn't have been out past the Truluck ten o'clock curfew, would he?"

Wade cocked his head, hands still folded in his lap, but the smug, confident grin was no longer present. Boykin massaged his forehead, eyes closed, as if fighting a migraine. Griffin Knight sat at counsel table, smiling from ear to ear.

That was when the second kid, sitting on the bench off to the side, suddenly stood and thrust out his arm, pointing at Sloane.

"I want him," he said.

TWELVE

FRESH START YOUTH TRAINING FACILITY
SIERRA NEVADA MOUNTAINS

A guard remained in the mess hall while Jake cleaned the floor, and Jake deduced the man's presence was in case the temptation to eat something off the floor became too great to resist. It didn't.

By the time Jake had finished cleaning, morning classes had recessed. Some of the inmates headed back to their dorms, others hurried to the basketball courts. Jake took a seat on a bench at one of the picnic tables in the yard, staring at the ground, hungrier than he'd ever been.

He sensed someone drawing near and lifted his head, expecting either Atkins, Big Baby, or the kid who had tripped him. Instead a thin black kid stepped onto the bench seat and sat beside him. The kid didn't say a word, just stared out at the yard, eyes scanning left and right. After a minute he reached inside his coveralls and produced a napkin, using his other arm to conceal the motion as he set it on the table.

"Don't eat it here," His eyes remained focused across the yard.

"What is it?" Jake asked.

The kid's eyebrows pinched together and he glanced at Jake. "Do you care? It's food."

Jake was so hungry he would have eaten just about anything, but he also didn't exactly trust anyone at the moment.

"Why are you doing this?"

"Don't look at me when you talk." Jake faced forward. "Find

someplace where the guards can't see you. And stay away from T-Mac and Big Baby."

"T-Mac?"

"The kid who tripped you. They're the resident psychopaths."

"Yeah, well, that could be a little difficult, seeing that I'm supposed to share a bunk with Big Baby."

"You look like you can handle yourself okay; I'm just saying don't get caught alone. And *never* go into the bathroom if they're in there."

"Why do the guards let them get away with it?"

"Because they act as the guards' eyes and ears around here. In exchange they get to do pretty much whatever they want. Plus the guards aren't supposed to inflict physical punishment . . ." He let that thought hang.

"Why does everybody around here take it? They can't beat everyone up."

"They don't have to beat up everyone. They just have to catch one of us alone. And trust me; you don't want to be the one. Like I said, stay out of the bathroom unless there are others with you."

"What did they do? Why are they here?"

The kid shrugged. "I've heard rape, murder, arson. Who knows what's the truth? What I do know is they're crazy. So is Atkins. That boy is the poster child for roid rage. I don't know what you did, but you pissed him off good, that's for sure, the captain, too. You want to avoid that in the future."

"What's with that guy's hair?"

"The captain? It's a wig. Rumor has it he was involved in some accident as a kid and had his scalp pulled off."

"So how do I get them off my ass?"

"Let them think they broke you. That's what they want."

"How do I do that?"

"Start by doing what they tell you. Just don't make it obvious. They always pick the bigger kids and make an example out of them."

A bell sounded. The kid rose. "Break's over."

"Why are you doing this?" Jake asked again.

"Most people would say 'thanks.'"

"Thanks," Jake said.

"Not everybody in here needs to be your enemy. I saw them bring you in the other day. You were in bad shape." The kid started across the yard. "Come on. More classes. I'll show you."

Jake stuffed the napkin inside his coveralls and ran to catch up. "Hey? What's your name anyway?"

"Just call me Bee Dee."

"Bee Dee? What's that stand for?"

"Big Dick. Remember, do not get caught with that sandwich. You do and I don't know you. And if you tell them where you got it Big Baby and T-Mac aren't going to be your only enemies."

THE LAST STOP
WINCHESTER COUNTY, CALIFORNIA

Sloane had secured Griffin Knight's full release, exposing his arrest as a trumped-up charge by Carl Wade and his Truluck band of brothers. He also had every charge but one dismissed against the second boy. Boykin sentenced him to a month at Fresh Start. If there had been any doubt before, there was none now: Sloane had made himself an enemy in Judge Earl Boykin. Boykin had left the bench "hotter than a wool sweater in hell" according to Molia.

In the courthouse parking lot Sloane tried to explain his actions to Molia and Lynch. "I just couldn't stand there and let it happen without doing something."

"That's all well and good," Lynch said, "but do you intend on sitting in Judge Earl's courtroom every morning."

Sloane had considered doing just that. He was staying in town after all, and if for no other reason than to be a burr in Boykin's and Archibald Pike's collective butts. But he also knew it got them no closer to getting Jake and T.J. released. In that regard, the morning had been a hollow victory, an act born from frustration. For the first time in his career Sloane felt utterly paralyzed by the judicial system.

"I'll tell you what," Lynch said. "I've worked with our Sacramento office on a couple of matters, and I know they have a group of bright young associates who'd love to get some spontaneous trial experience. They can rotate the assignment to cover the juvenile calendar. I'll make a call on the drive back and I'll keep you posted on the appeal. We'll get it filed Monday."

After Lynch departed Sloane and Molia walked down the hill into Old Town in search of a place to regroup rather than drive back to their sauna at the Tristan Motel. On a sunny Friday morning The Last Stop diner was doing a brisk business, the dozen tables full. According to the plaque on the wall the building had at one time been the Winchester post office, the last stop west for the famed Pony Express. Inside, waitresses shouted orders and cooks in white hats snatched slips from a spinning rack, deftly working pots and pans. The hostess led them to a table beside a window that looked out on a small patio.

Sloane loosened his tie while surveying the menu, but he had little appetite. Molia hadn't bothered to pick up his menu. He looked deep in thought.

"You all right?" Sloane asked.

"Just wondering if maybe we're going about this the wrong way."

"How so?"

"No offense. I know the courtroom is your domain, and I don't mean to imply anything by what I'm about to say."

"Just say it, Tom; we've been friends a long time."

"You figure what, two to three weeks before we can get an appeal heard?"

"Unfortunately, Lisa seems to think so, even if it's expedited."

"So in the interim, what? We sit on our thumbs and do nothing? I'm not built that way, and I know you're not either."

"What'd you have in mind?"

"A contingency plan."

"Such as?"

"What's his deal in this?"

"Who?"

"Boykin. He could be a hard-ass within the law. A lot of judges are, and remember Barnes said Boykin is no dummy. Why is he stepping outside the lines?"

"Maybe it's like you said last night—a guy like Boykin doesn't pay much attention to things like rules. He doesn't believe they apply to him."

Molia nodded, sipped his coffee. "Maybe, but in my line of work people are usually motivated to do stupid things by something more tangible than ego."

"Money?"

"That's usually atop the list." He put down his cup. "Think about it. Boykin can't be sentencing these kids without others being complicit. The correctional officers have to make the arrests and the prosecutor has to convict. Even someone like the court reporter, Ms. Valdez, has to know this isn't right. And where are the defense attorneys? Does no one in this county give a shit that kids are being unfairly sentenced?"

It was a good point. Pike had been completely unprepared to put on evidence in either case that morning. It was as if he didn't expect he'd have to. "Keep going," Sloane said.

"Okay. And now a recording gets conveniently erased?" Molia arched his eyebrows. "I'm beginning to think nothing in this scenario has been a coincidence, and that includes Wade stopping us on the way into town."

"Agreed," Sloane said. "I don't think we can discount anything around here. But what did you have in mind? We can't very well storm Fresh Start."

"Boykin's playing outside the law. I think we should do the same. I'm thinking you get that big friend of yours and his wife with the computer skills to start digging around, see what they can come up with on old Judge Earl and Archibald Pike."

"Maybe Carl Wade while they're at it?"

"Might as well invite them all to the party."

"Okay. But what do *we* do until then?"

"We go back into friendly neighborhood Truluck and start asking questions, see what the locals have to say about Carl Wade arresting their kids and Judge Earl locking them up."

"Speak of the devil." Sloane nodded to the door.

Carl Wade removed his hat, holding the brim. His sunglasses were clipped to his shirt. He looked around, made eye contact, and walked over.

"You two seem to be having trouble finding your way out of town."

Molia sipped his coffee. "What town would that be, Carl, that Disneyland recreation you work for? You might want to run on back there before that plastic badge melts in the heat and ruins your costume."

Wade smiled, though he did not look amused. "You're a funny man, Detective. They teach you that back in West Virginia, did they?"

Molia looked up from his coffee. "They taught me a lot of things, Carl."

Wade looked to Sloane. "And I bet you think you're real slick after that show you put on this morning. You both think you can come in here and upset the apple cart, that you're better than us dumb country-folk, that the law doesn't apply to you or your boys."

"Actually, it's the law we're trying to have applied," Sloane said. "Seems to us it's you and that circus of a court that's forgotten how to apply it. You made it too easy for me this morning."

"I got news for you, you're going to lose. A month from now you'll be gone and I'll still be here. So will your sons."

Molia looked to Sloane. "Are we leaving, David?"

"Not me," Sloane said. "I'm beginning to like it here. I'm thinking of hanging a shingle right there in Truluck, specializing in juvenile defense. How about you?"

"They say California is the land of opportunity, and it sure looks like they need a real law enforcement officer around here."

Wade leaned forward, palms flat on the table. The weight caused the water in the glasses to spill over the rims. "Take a little friendly advice? Give up the Bob Hope and Bing Crosby routine. It isn't funny. Move on. Let your boys do their time. Don't keep poking the stick in the hornets' nest. That's how you get stung."

Molia stood, knocking the coffee cups and water glasses over completely. The conversations in the diner came to an abrupt stop.

"Do we have a problem here, gentlemen?" The voice was deep, a smoker's edge to it. Matt Barnes stood just to the right of the table. Sloane hadn't even seen him enter.

Wade didn't take his eyes off Molia. "This isn't your problem, Sheriff."

"My jurisdiction, Carl. That makes it my problem. I'd suggest you get on back to Truluck where you belong."

Wade took a moment before he straightened. "You think about what I said." Then he turned for the door.

"Carl?" Wade turned back. Molia tossed his hat like a Frisbee, hitting Wade in the chest. "Don't want you to get in trouble for losing part of your costume."

After Wade departed, Barnes looked around the restaurant. "Sorry to disrupt your meals, folks. Everything is under control."

The hostess used a towel to absorb the water and coffee and refilled their cups. She brought a cup and saucer for Barnes, who sat silently considering Sloane and Molia. When she left he spoke over the rim of his cup. "You want to tell me exactly what you were hoping to accomplish?"

"At the moment, breakfast," Molia said.

"I'm talking about what went on this morning in Judge Earl's courtroom." He looked at Sloane. "My deputy gave me the highlights."

"Is there something against kids being represented by an attorney in Winchester County, Sheriff?" Sloane asked.

"You going to move here, take up the cause?"

"I'm thinking about it."

Barnes lowered his cup. "Like I told you, Wade is a buffoon. Judge Earl is not."

"Something stinks in his courtroom, Matt," Molia said.

Barnes considered them with pitch-black eyes beneath silver eyebrows showing traces of black hairs. "You have evidence of that, Detective? Something I can take to the attorney general, maybe the judicial board of conduct?" His voice conveyed doubt. "What, you don't think I've thought the same thing, felt the same way? You don't think I've questioned a thing or two around here? Or do you think I'm just looking the other way, hoping to put in my time and leave it for someone else? This isn't just Judge Earl's town. This is my town. I was born and raised in this county. So while I may not like the prospect of the State doing a magic act and making Winchester and me disappear because of the legislature's fiscal irresponsibility, until it does, I still have a job to do, and I'm going to do it. As I already mentioned, I may not like the way things are run around here all the time, but I'm elected to enforce the laws. Judge Earl decides the consequences. And as long as the good citizens of Winchester County continue to put him in office, there's not a lot that I or anybody else can do about it. You come up with something, something I can use, you let me know, and then we'll both have something worth fighting over."

WINCHESTER COUNTY SUPERIOR COURT
JUDGE EARL BOYKIN'S CHAMBERS

Judge Boykin beat his staff into his chambers and closed the smoked beveled glass door with the words HONORABLE EARL J. BOYKIN stenciled in block letters. Those letters had been on that glass since the ceremony dedicating the reopening of the courthouse on July 4, 1898, three years after a fire destroyed the original building. His great-grandfather had chosen the site of the new county courthouse not for the spectacular 360-degree view, as most people now suspected, but for convenience. The old oak tree had been a short walk from the jail in the building's basement, and that's where the public hangings occurred. Even those citizens who didn't come up the hill could watch the festivities and receive the message loud and clear: break the law in Winchester County and the law in Winchester County will break your neck.

The hanging tree did its job until a blight killed it in the 1920s. The stenciled letters on the door, however, remained, going on 114 years.

A knock drew Boykin's attention. It wasn't the interior door, but the door to the private staircase leading to the secure parking area.

"Come in," he said.

Archibald Pike leaned in, looking tentative. "You busy, Judge?"

"I'm always busy. I've been busy for seventeen years." He drew Pike in with a crooked finger, removed his robe, and hung it carefully on the wooden hanger, returning it to the knob on the inside of his closet door. He started for his desk, stopping to run a hand over the mantel of the fireplace.

"I wanted to—"

"Did you know, Archibald, that my great-grandfather and grandfather used this fireplace to heat the office in the winters?" Boykin asked.

"Yes, Judge. You mentioned that once—"

"My father fought against having it sealed when the building was retrofitted with central heating. He said there was something comforting about working by the warmth of a crackling fire, but really he just didn't see the need to change something that had worked fine for half a century."

Pike carried a stack of documents. "I've been on the computer."

"Studying the law, I hope."

The comment stopped Pike in his tracks. Boykin left the fireplace for the arched window behind his desk that provided natural lighting and accorded him a magnificent view, like a crow's nest atop the mast of a grand schooner.

Pike adjusted his classes. "Actually the Internet, Judge. I thought I—"

"When I was a boy I remember the view of the valley being nothing but orchards of fruit trees and farmland. Now it's rooftops stretching as far south as the eye can see. And people complain that the price of produce has skyrocketed." He shook his head at the irony. "I can still look down on the same two dozen buildings as my grandfather and his father once did, but it wasn't called 'Old Town' back then. It was just Winchester. Then some people thought we needed to build a new city center, and so we built one." He paused. "And the economy crashed and vacancies soared. But do you know what the one constant has been, Archibald, what has not changed?"

"The law, Judge."

Boykin glanced over at him. "The law. Everything except the law. And do you know why?"

"Because the people of Winchester County have voted that way for four generations, Judge."

"That's right, Archibald. They have done just that. And do you know why the good people of Winchester County have seen fit to do that?"

Pike had run out of answers. "I suppose it's because—"

"Respect, Archibald. They have voted a Boykin to serve on that bench in that courtroom for more than a century out of respect. And we have returned their show of loyalty by administering justice with a strong and unwavering hand." Boykin pointed. "When I slip on that robe I am not just a judge, Archibald. No, I am much more than that. I am the keeper of a great legacy of justice, a legacy that my family has gone to great lengths to preserve. It's the reason my great-grandfather commissioned a painting of the old oak tree before it was cut down, and why that painting has hung in that courtroom for all to see. It was not just a tree, Archibald. It was a symbol of justice. Just like me. I am a symbol of justice. The Boykin name is symbolic of justice." Boykin's eyes narrowed. "And you let David Sloane thumb his nose at it in front of my entire court staff."

"I'm sorry, Judge."

"So am I, Archibald, but don't you for a minute think you were the intended target; don't you dare flatter yourself that way."

"No, Judge."

"Mr. Sloane was taking aim directly at me. Yes he was."

Pike paused. "That's why I was on the Internet, Judge, because I thought I'd heard that name somewhere."

"What name?" Boykin asked.

"David Sloane."

"And?"

"He's that big shot lawyer from Seattle."

"I thought they said he's licensed in California."

"He is. He's the lawyer that's always in the news." Pike started handing Boykin documents. "The one that had that murder case last year, the one in which that female lawyer was accused of killing a drug dealer."

Boykin shook his head. He hadn't heard of it. "So he's a defense attorney?"

"Not always," Pike said. He handed Boykin another document. "The year before he had that big verdict against a toy company using magnets in its toys that were killing kids. They changed the legislation because of him."

Still wasn't ringing any bells with Boykin. He set that article aside.

"And he had that case against the military on behalf of the family of that National Guardsman, the one that made Defense Secretary Northrup resign."

Boykin looked up from the document. That case had been all over the national news. "That's him?"

"He's the lawyer who doesn't lose," Pike said.

Boykin grunted, annoyed. "You sound like a damned Harry Potter movie." Boykin hadn't read the books but he'd taken his granddaughters to see one of the movies. "So he's a good lawyer. It's no excuse for what happened in my courtroom this morning."

"He's more than a good lawyer, Earl . . . Judge. He's, he's not going to go away. He *won't* go away."

"No kidding. I got that impression this morning, in my courtroom."

"So what are we going to do?"

"What do you mean, what are *we* going to do?"

"I mean about his kid."

"What would you have me do, release him?"

"Well, I was thinking that maybe that wouldn't be such a bad thing." Before Boykin could respond Pike raised a hand. "Hear me out. The loss of the recording gives you a legitimate reason. I mean, Sloane's right about it making it more difficult to meet our burden, and he's got a good argument of inherent prejudice. The court of appeals could grant the motion and send it back to us, and we'll be right back where we started. This way, you have someone to blame, the clerk's office."

"So I just call him up, tell him I've reconsidered my decision and, in light of the lost evidence, I'm going to grant his son a new trial. We bring them back here and we have ourselves a trial. And then what?"

Pike smiled, indicating he'd thought this through. "You sentence them to detention centers in Washington and West Virginia and get them out of our hair."

Boykin stroked his beard, appearing to give the plan due thought. "Let me ask you, Archibald, in light of what you've just told me about Sloane's reputation, what do you think are the odds he'll stop with the release of his own son?"

The question erased Pike's smile.

Boykin's mood darkened. "I don't give a good God damn who he is. This is my courtroom. *My* courtroom, and I am not about to cede it to anyone, not even the 'lawyer who does not lose.' If the court of appeals grants his motion, weeks from now, then we will have ourselves a trial, Archibald, yes we will. And if we do I am going to expect a far better showing than the one you gave this morning. Until that time, his son will remain a ward of the Winchester County Juvenile Detention Department."

Pike reached to take back the documents.

"Leave them," Boykin said.

After Pike shut the door, Boykin spun his chair and returned his gaze to the window, but his thoughts did not slip back into history. He gathered the documents Pike had left and walked to the shelves lining the wall, removing the four volumes of antique California Reporters that had been bound together at the spines, revealing the hidden wall safe his great-grandfather had asked be embedded when the building was constructed. The combination had never changed, the date the building had been dedicated. Opening the wall safe, Boykin reached past the .44 caliber Colt revolver and retrieved a cell phone. He hit the button for the preprogrammed number and waited three rings until the person answered.

"We have a situation," he said, considering the articles. "And I don't want that situation to become a problem."

THE TRISTAN MOTEL
TRISTAN, CALIFORNIA

Someone had gone through their things, and they hadn't been subtle about it.

"It was a police officer." The owner stood in the doorway, his blue jeans hanging well below an ample stomach, arms crossed over his short-sleeve cotton T-shirt. He'd apparently been waiting for Sloane and Molia to return. "He said it was police business."

"Was he wearing a Truluck uniform, blue and gray?" Molia asked.

The man nodded. "He was a police officer. Showed me his badge."

"Name of Wade . . . Carl Wade?"

A shake of the head. "No, sir. It wasn't Wade. My wife wrote it down." The owner looked from Sloane to Molia and back again, something clearly on his mind. "Listen," he said. "We run a quiet place here."

"We're not going to cause you any trouble," Sloane said.

"Just the same. It's just me and my wife. We're retired, and well, it's nothing personal. I like you fellas, but she'd feel a whole lot better if you moved on."

"Can you recommend someplace?" Molia asked, resigned.

"Down the road maybe in Dillon. You could check there. They have a couple places. I'll refund your money."

"No reason to do that," Sloane said. "How about you let us stay long enough to get things reorganized and packed and we'll be out of your hair."

The man nodded. "I'll check with the missus, but I think that'd be fine."

After the man had left, Sloane pulled out his cell phone. With the room sweltering, they stepped outside to a wedge of shade along the side of the building, but it offered only minimal relief. Sloane put the call on speaker when Alex answered. He'd kept her and Jenkins apprised of the situation. Jenkins had wanted to get on a plane and fly out to California, but Sloane had convinced him that, short of breaching the walls of Fresh Start, there wasn't much Jenkins could do. They had to let the legal system play out, as frustrating as that continued to be. That was before Molia broached the subject of taking a different approach.

"What happened with the motion?" Alex asked.

Sloane took a few minutes to explain what had transpired. Then he asked, "Is Charlie there?"

"No. He had to get on a plane to New Jersey yesterday afternoon. His sister called. His mother isn't doing well."

"Her heart again?"

"Looks like it. He's going to call if he thinks we need to be there. We've been through this a few times now."

Sloane knew. "Listen, I hate to ask for a favor under the circumstances."

"Anything."

"Wonder if you can do a couple of background checks for me."

"I can try. Who are you interested in?"

A judge for starters. Name's Earl Boykin, middle initial 'J.'"

"What am I looking for?"

That was the sixty-four-thousand-dollar question wasn't it? Sloane didn't really know. "Not sure at this point," he said.

Molia chimed in. "Anything that looks interesting. Check out his finances, real estate holdings, history on the bench. His legal career." He thought for a moment. "See if you can find any connection to a guy named Victor Dillon." He spelled the last name.

"Who's Dillon?" Alex asked.

"A guy with a lot of money," Molia said. "He owns Fresh Start."

"What do you mean *owns* it?" Alex asked.

"Fresh Start is privately owned through a limited liability company," Sloane said.

"You can do that?"

"Apparently."

"Well that's grounds for interest right there, isn't it?" she said.

Sloane watched a lizard lift its head from a rock. Before it did, Sloane hadn't seen it sunning itself. "Look up the other members of the LLC and see if any of them have any connection to Boykin. Oh, and Dillon apparently owns the Gold Rush Brewery near Winchester."

"Don't forget Wade," Molia reminded him.

"And see what you can find out about a guy named Carl Wade. He's a Truluck police officer."

"And a royal pain in the ass," Molia said, leaning toward the phone.

"Do you have access to a computer?" Alex asked.

"I will," Sloane said. "We're on the move again. I'll call and give you the name of the motel and a number when we touch down."

* * *

Sloane changed into a pair of shorts with multiple pockets and a lightweight blue cotton shirt. He exchanged the dress shoes for a pair of Denali sandals. As he and Molia repacked the car he could feel the heat of the asphalt seeping through the soles and burning the back of his neck. His cell phone buzzed. Lisa Lynch.

"Tell me the court of appeals granted the motion *sua sponte*."

"Don't I wish," Lynch said. "We'll get it filed Monday."

"How do you feel about it so far?"

"We have solid grounds. The lack of a transcribed record could have put us over the top."

"So what's the bad news?" Sloane could hear it in Lynch's voice.

"My assistant called the clerk at the court of appeals. Even if we file Monday we can't get it heard for two weeks."

"What about moving to expedite the hearing?"

"That is expedited."

Sloane sighed.

"If anything changes, I'll let you know. But, hey listen, I have a question for you. You didn't write any notes on the copy of the motion to have the record of yesterday's proceedings transcribed, did you?"

"Notes? What kind of notes?"

"There's a handwritten note scribbled on our file copy, just to the right of your signature."

"What does it say?"

"Best I can make out it says 'Knock - Me - Stiff. Eight, colon, zero-zero.'"

"Eight o'clock?" Sloane asked.

"Looks like it," she said.

"What's 'knock me stiff' mean?"

"That's what I was wondering."

"No idea," Sloane said.

"Okay. Just checking. I'll get you a copy of the appeal first thing."

Sloane disconnected.

"Who was that?" Molia asked as Sloane stepped back into the room to finish packing.

"Lisa. She says it's going to take two weeks for the appeal, even expedited."

"Well, we figured that, didn't we?"

Sloane started to gather more things, stopped, pulled out his iPhone and opened the browser.

"What are you doing?" Molia asked.

Sloane hit a search engine, typed in the three words, and waited for the Internet. "Just checking on something else Lisa said."

Molia walked over as Sloane typed in the words: Knock-Me-Stiff.

"What is that?"

Sloane got just over seven thousand hits. "I don't know. Lynch says it was scribbled on one of our pleadings by my signature. She thought I wrote it." Sloane typed in Winchester.

"Bingo," Molia said, reading an entry halfway down the first page. "Knock-Me-Stiff Saloon. Gold Creek, California."

Sloane copied the address and pasted it into a different search engine. "It's twenty-two miles down Highway 88."

"What else did the note say?" Molia asked.

"Eight o'clock."

"As in tonight?"

"I don't know." He looked to Molia.

Molia shrugged. "It's not like we have any other dinner plans."

FRESH START YOUTH TRAINING FACILITY
SIERRA NEVADA MOUNTAINS

It hadn't been much, just two pieces of bacon between dry toast, but Jake wolfed the food down in between classes. It wasn't easy with his lips still chapped and cracked. He had to chew until he'd worked up enough saliva so that he could swallow, and after the last bite his jaw hurt, but he didn't care. He hurried off to a class on math, which was basic algebra.

Situated near a dirt parking lot with boulders as parking curbs and separated by the chain-link and barbed wire fence, the school building allowed the teachers and other personnel a separate door into and out of the facility. The residents filed into the classrooms through one long corridor, and the teachers entered and exited the classrooms from doors on the opposite side of the room. From what Jake could tell the teachers and counselors spent no time with the inmates other than in class and had no access to the rest of the facilities.

In class the inmates were grouped by age, and the teachers provided a daily lesson, with each student working at his own pace in workbooks. Jack had learned the algebra equations his freshman year. His other classes—American history, language arts, science, and a class on reading comprehension—were conducted in the same manner. After school, from three thirty to four fifteen, they had study hall. Since Jake had finished his work in class he had nothing to do, but heeding Bee Dee's advice, he kept his head down. Atkins seemed ever present, like a shark waiting for that drop of blood to hit the water.

After study hall the guards released them into the yard for fifty minutes of structured recreation time, in this instance, dodgeball. What followed recreation time was something called Life Skills Group, fifty minutes of sitting in a circle discussing social settings and how they might properly react to unexpected situations. Jake tried to appear interested though he was bored to tears and starving. When the counselor, a man with a head of curly hair and a bushy beard, asked for a volunteer to discuss something he would like to change about himself no one raised a hand. Jake wasn't about to raise his either until he saw Atkins step quietly into the back of the room.

"I guess if I had to change something," Jake started, but the counselor stopped him and asked that an eight-inch carved stick be passed around the circle.

"That's the talking stick, Jake. If you wish to share with the group you raise your hand. Only the person with the stick can talk."

"Sorry," Jake said. "I didn't know."

"That's okay. What is it you wanted to share?"

"Well, you asked what we would want to change about ourselves, and I was thinking that . . . I don't know, maybe I'd like to not be so angry all the time."

The man leaned forward, notepad in his lap. "What makes you angry, Jake?"

"Everything."

"And what happens when you get angry?"

"I usually get in trouble."

The others laughed.

The counselor asked, "Can you be more specific? What types of conduct do you engage in when you get angry?"

"Well, I drink too much and I smoke pot. And I don't like people telling me what to do. So I guess I also say shit—I mean, stuff—that I shouldn't."

"And do you see how this behavior can be self-destructive?"

"I usually end up in trouble."

"And does it make you feel any less angry?"

"No, usually I'm angrier."

"So can you see how getting angry is counterproductive?"

"I guess so."

"What is it that makes you angry?"

"People don't listen to me. They assume they know what's best for me, but they never ask me. Like when my father sent me to California to live with my other father after my moth—" Jake caught himself.

"What about your mother, Jake?"

"After my mother and father got divorced."

"And that made you angry that no one asked you where you wanted to live?"

"Yeah."

"Can you think of some behavior that might be more productive than taking drugs or alcohol?"

"Maybe asking them to ask me what I want instead of just assuming they know what I want. Maybe talking to someone about it."

The counselor nodded. "It's a good start, Jake. Something concrete we can work on." He directed his gaze to the others. "Who else can think of self-destructive behavior we engage in when we get angry?"

Another kid raised his hand and Jake passed the stick. "I fucking swear a lot," the kid said, which caused everyone, including the counselor, to laugh.

Out of the corner of his eye Jake watched Atkins slip silently from the room.

After Life Skills they had ten minutes to clean up before dinner.

On the walk to the mess hall Jake noticed a dramatic change in the weather. The temperature, which had hovered near a hundred, had dropped significantly, and a strong wind rustled branches and caused the tops of the pines to sway. Ominous dark clouds rolled over the mountaintops, banding together and eliminating more and more of the blue sky.

"Thunderheads," Bee Dee said, walking beside Jake. "We get them when it gets really hot down in the valley. One minute it's baking and the next it's pouring rain."

Inside the cafeteria, Jake and Bee Dee got in line. With each step Jake expected Atkins to appear and find some excuse to keep him from eating, but he reached the serving station without interruption. He slid his tray along the metal bars and the servers handed him a bowl of salad with a single red cherry tomato and a sprinkling of carrot shavings, and slopped macaroni and cheese on his plate. At the end of the line he chose a banana, a carton of milk, and a square of white cake with chocolate frosting.

As much as he wanted to rush to the first available seat, Jake took a moment to make note of Big Baby and T-Mac sitting together at one of the tables. He gave their table a wide berth and picked a table on the other side of the room, sitting across from Bee Dee. When he set down his tray the conversation quieted. The others at the table gave him furtive glances, apparently still upset over the morning breakfast they didn't get to eat.

"This is Jake," Bee Dee said. "He's cool."

It seemed to break some invisible seal. The others introduced themselves in between bites of food and bits of conversation. Jake's focus, however, was drawn to the food on his tray, his first real meal in forty-eight hours.

"They do that," a boy named Jose said with a Spanish accent. "They keep you awake and don't let you eat. It fucks with your mind."

Jake grunted his responses, eating greedily, using a spoon instead of a fork to scoop up the starchy noodles swimming in melted orange cheese. Try as he might, he could not force himself to slow down. When another kid joined their table complaining about macaroni and cheese, Jake offered to trade his banana and ate a second helping. His stomach cramped, but the only time he stopped eating was when a pulse of blue light lit up the room and a clap of thunder shook the windows and rattled the silverware.

"Shit," Jose said.

"It's just a storm." Jake said.

"The rain messes up the yard; now we'll have to stay in."

Jake didn't care. He shoved the last bit of cake into his mouth and washed it down with his milk. The yard sparked with another blue flash, and a second blast of thunder sounded, this one so loud he thought it might rip the metal roof off the building. Everyone looked to the windows at the first sounds of rain splattering the glass. When Jake returned his attention to the table he noticed everyone had grown silent.

"What, haven't you guys been in a thunderstorm before?"

Bee Dee's eyes shifted. Jake glanced to his right and saw the khaki uniform.

"You get yourself a good meal, Inmate Stand-up?" Atkins stood with hands clasped behind his back, a crooked grin hanging from the corner of his mouth.

The bench, attached to the table, did not slide back, preventing Jake from standing. "Yes, sir, Officer Atkins."

"Well that's good, because you're going to need your strength."

"Sir?"

"You will meet me on the obstacle course in precisely three minutes."

"My schedule says I have group therapy at seven, sir."

Atkins placed his palms flat on the table, bending down so that his face was inches from Jake's. "Schedules are subject to change without notice, Inmate Stand-up. Yours changed after I received an interesting bit of personal information about you today."

Jake's eyes shifted. "Interesting, sir?"

"It seems, Inmate Stand-up, that you have not one, but two fathers."

"Yes, sir," Jake said feeling flush.

"Two fathers," Atkins said.

"That's right, sir."

"But no mother."

THIRTEEN

Tom Molia circled the block a third time, alternately glancing in the rearview and side mirrors. Sloane focused on the cars parked along the sidewalk and the few tourists hurrying to get out of the unexpected rain splattering the boardwalk along Gold Creek's Main Street. As far as Sloane could determine, they hadn't been followed, and the way Molia had driven from Tristan they would have known if they had been. Molia set out in the opposite direction for a good three minutes then made an unexpected U-turn on a straight patch of road. He made a few other random turns before reaching Gold Creek then drove through the town twice.

They had a lot in common, Sloane and Molia. They had been trained to question people's motives, to look for holes in their explanations and to consider everything that could possibly go wrong. It was a hell of a way to go through life, thinking the worst of people, but if a lawyer made a mistake the worst that could happen was he lost a case. If a detective made a mistake, people could end up dead.

Neither wanted to take a chance.

Molia parked across the street from swinging shuttered doors and watched people enter and exit the Knock-Me-Stiff Saloon, which was adjacent to the Gold Creek Restaurant and across the street from the Gold Creek Hotel, an ornate three-story structure with two carved balcony railings draped by red, white, and blue bunting. Old-fashioned street lamps lit the boardwalks, though lightbulbs replaced flames.

On the drive they had decided it best for Sloane to enter the bar alone, with Molia watching the door from the car. If the handwritten note was a setup, Molia did not want both of them vulnerable. Sloane had a different concern. If the person who scribbled the note had intended it to be a message for Sloane alone, bringing someone with him could make the person reticent to follow through.

"Okay," Molia said. "Punch in my number."

Sloane entered Molia's ten-digit number.

"If you get in trouble, just hit the send button, and if you can't use your hands lean up against something. If I hear it ring, I won't wait to answer it."

Sloane slid the phone back in his pocket, stepped out, and hurried across the street using an arm to keep the rain out of his eyes. He ascended the steps to the boardwalk and pushed through the swinging doors. Much like the Winchester Courtroom, the next step was back a century, to a place with brick walls, round wood tables, spoke-back chairs, and a polished wood bar with a brass foot railing that ran the length of the south wall. Liquor bottles behind the bar reflected in mirrors that also caught the light from an ornate, glass bead chandelier. Wood paddle ceiling fans stirred the warm summer night. Only flat-screen televisions, one mounted on each side of the bar, broadcasting motocross broke the ambiance.

Sloane took a spot at the bar and considered the faces of the patrons eating and drinking at the tables and sitting on the other bar stools. No one looked familiar. No one made eye contact. No one looked poised to approach. He checked his watch. When he looked back the bartender was placing a beer with a head of foam on a coaster in front of him.

"We're serving two specialty brews tonight," the man said before Sloane had time to tell him he hadn't ordered. He pushed the frames of his glasses back onto the bridge of his nose. "The second beer is on the other side of your coaster. Just flip it over."

The coaster advertised a beer called "Gold Digger." Sloane flipped it over and read the reverse side. When he looked up the bartender had gone about his business, serving a young couple seated a few stools to Sloane's left. "Can you point me in the direction of the bathroom?" Sloane asked.

The bartender nodded to a hallway at the end of the bar. "End of the hall."

The door to the ladies' room was first, the men's room beside it. Both doors were unlocked, both rooms were empty. The third door, at the end of the hall, was not marked. Sloane turned the door handle, his other hand on the phone in his pocket, pushed the door open, and stepped into muted light.

Tom Molia bit the nail of his index finger, a nervous habit he'd never quite conquered. Like a reformed smoker, the temptation never went away, and when he got anxious the temptation became harder to resist. Unlike a smoker, he didn't have to drive to a store to buy a pack of cigarettes. The fingernail was readily available and all too easy to gnaw on. Most times Molia didn't even realize he was doing it. Maggie usually scolded him.

Their conversation that afternoon had gone better than the one the day before. Maggie continued to sound distant, but it was born more from a mother's worry and fatigue than from anger. She asked how Molia was holding up, if he was doing okay. He told her he had moments when the loss felt crushing, but he pushed through those to focus on doing everything he could to get T.J. released. He explained what had happened in court that morning, refrained from telling her about the appeal taking two weeks, and said they were taking another tack, looking into Judge Boykin's background to see if there might be something more motivating his actions. He knew it didn't sound like much, but it was something for Maggie to hold on to, which was better than the alternative. An awkward pause followed. Then Maggie said, "I'm sorry, Tom, for what I said about you not coming home."

"Don't be. I have no intention of leaving here without him," Molia had replied.

The cell phone rang in his hand, drawing him back to the

present—Molia didn't pause to answer it. He pushed out of the car and hurried across the road just as the skies let loose a torrent of water.

FRESH START YOUTH TRAINING FACILITY
SIERRA NEVADA MOUNTAINS

His fingers slipped from the rung; his blistered hands and tired arms not able to hold his weight long enough for him to reach and grip the next rung. His legs folded upon impact, and he dropped into the mud, the rain having reduced the yard to an inch-deep brown pool of muck.

He vomited the macaroni and cheese, salad, and cake in a lump of yellow bile that mixed with the ever expanding puddles. The rain cascaded thick as a gray sheet, pounding the ground with such force it splattered and rebounded, and the clouds had brought a darkness that reduced the light fixtures atop the stanchions to small glowing rings.

Lightning pulsed, revealing Atkins's contorted face beneath a wide-brimmed hat. Water sleeted down his green poncho and the wind and thunder devoured his voice, though the strain on his face and neck indicated he continued to yell at the top of his lungs.

"You think you can lie to me? You think you are smarter than me?"

"No, sir, Officer Atkins," Jake said.

"I know everything about you, Stand-up. I said, stand up. Get on your feet. Get on your feet."

Jake struggled to rise, slipping in the sludge. The ground had become the consistency of wet cement, and his legs felt as if encased in blocks. The coveralls too had sucked up the moisture, further weighing him down.

"Stand up straight when I'm talking to you."

But Jake could not stand up straight. His stomach felt like a balled knot that refused to uncoil.

"You're a punk! You're never going to be anything but a punk. You're going to spend the rest of your life in a jail cell. Twenty-three hours of the day, seven days a week, three hundred and sixty-five days a year. And it won't be half as bad as the time you spend here with me. When we're finished you'll be begging for that cell. You will beg to be locked up."

Water flowed unimpeded down Jake's shaved head, blurring his vision. He blinked and shook it from his eyes, but did not dare raise his hands to wipe away the water.

"Do you think you can lie to me and get away with it?"

"No, sir," Jake yelled, barely able to hear his own voice.

"Do you think you are smarter than me?"

A blast of thunder shook the ground.

"No, sir," Jake shouted.

"Start again," Atkins said. "Move when I tell you, Stand-up! Move!"

Jake slogged to the start of the obstacle course, Atkins screaming incoherently in his left ear. He raised a foot onto the rope ladder and stepped up. It swayed and pitched. He reached for the next rung and willed himself up. His foot slipped through the net, but he held on, like a sailor climbing the mast of an old schooner in a storm. Blood and water trickled pink down his wrists from the cracked blisters of his palms.

"We're going to be out here all night, Stand-up. You got all night in you?"

KNOCK-ME-STIFF SALOON
GOLD CREEK, CALIFORNIA

Molia's eyes worked the room. Sloane wasn't there. He noted an exit at the back of the bar and a hallway to his left. He moved to the exit and pushed the door open, considering a narrow alley with a blue Dumpster. Shutting it, he saw that he'd gained the bartender's sudden interest.

"Can I help you?" the man asked.

"Looking for a friend." Molia moved toward the hallway.

The bartender became more animated. "Hey. Hey!"

Molia slipped down the hall, the bartender's voice trailing him.

He opened the door to the ladies' room to his left, then the men's room, calling out. "David?"

Sensing movement from behind, Molia turned. The bartender was moving quickly down the hallway, carrying a wooden ax handle.

Sloane cut off midsentence when he heard what sounded like Tom Molia's voice calling his name. He pulled open the door to find Molia cornered.

"No!" Sloane said.

The bartender's eyes shifted from Molia to Sloane, then beyond Sloane to the woman in the office. Sloane raised a hand. "It's okay. He's with me."

The bartender's chest expanded and deflated. He looked back down the hall before motioning for them to enter the office. When he closed the door his hands shook and he took a moment to collect himself.

Sloane looked to Molia. "What is it? What's the matter?"

"I was about to ask you the same thing." Molia held up his cell phone.

Sloane pulled the phone from his pocket and checked the call log. "Damn. I'm sorry, Tom. I must have hit the send button by accident."

Molia shook his head. "You know, accidents are mistakes, as opposed to deliberate acts that can have a tendency to induce heart attacks."

"I'm sorry," Sloane repeated. He introduced the woman. "Eileen Harper. She works in the Winchester County clerk's office."

Molia had not entered the clerk's office when Sloane and Lynch filed the pleadings. He had waited outside in the marbled rotunda. He looked from Harper to the bartender. "Who are you, Paul Bunyon?"

"Dave Bennett. I'm real sorry about that. I thought maybe . . ." He held up the ax handle. "My dad kept it under the bar when he owned it. I've never had to use it. It's really more for intimidation."

"Yeah? Well, it works."

No longer flush with adrenaline, Bennett had a gentle face with a reddish brown goatee graying at the chin. "I didn't know what to think. I thought maybe . . . I don't know. I better get back out there," he said to Harper. "You call if you need me."

They took a moment to settle in after Bennett left. Harper sat behind the desk. Sloane offered the only other chair in the room to Molia, but the detective declined. "I'll stand," he said. "My heart's still racing." He leaned against a green, three-drawer file cabinet.

The only light in the windowless room came from an antique, stained-glass desk lamp. The shadows it cast made the bags under Harper's eyes more pronounced. She tucked light brown hair behind each earlobe then picked up a paper clip, fidgeting with it.

"You wrote the note?" Molia asked.

Harper glanced at Molia then shifted focus back to Sloane. "I thought I recognized the name from the news. I looked it up on the Internet."

"Eileen's son is at Fresh Start," Sloane said, as if to explain.

"I'm sorry," Molia said. "What did your son do?"

"What did he do, or what do they say he did?"

"What did they say he did?"

"We live in Truluck," she said. "They said he had pot on him."

"But you don't believe that."

She shook her head.

"No attorney," Sloane said. Molia nodded. "Did you know he'd been arrested?" Sloane asked.

"It wouldn't have mattered. You don't challenge Judge Earl; it only makes it worse."

"What do you mean, makes it worse?" Sloane asked.

She sat back. "I've worked at the court for fifteen years. I thought maybe there might be—" Her voice choked. She paused to collect herself. "I asked if Tommy could go to one of those programs."

"An outpatient program," Sloane said.

"They have some in Sacramento. I asked if Tommy could go there instead."

"You asked who, Judge Earl?" Sloane asked.

Harper nodded.

"And he wasn't willing to do that," Sloane said.

She looked away but not before Sloane saw a tear leak from the corner of her eye. She unclenched her other hand, revealing a wad of tissue, and dabbed at the tear the way women do when trying not to smudge their mascara.

"He might have been." She let her statement linger.

"But he wanted something in return?" Molia asked.

She nodded.

"Money?"

She dabbed the tissue again. "I know his wife and kids."

Molia looked to Sloane.

Sloane said, "He wanted to sleep with you?"

"He didn't say it in so many words, but it was pretty clear that's what it would take. When I didn't show any interest he said he couldn't help me. He said that if I had done a better job raising Tommy, Winchester County wouldn't have to do it for me. He said that it would be best if I didn't make waves. He said it would be better for Tommy."

"And that's why you didn't hire a lawyer." Sloane said.

She nodded. "He sentenced Tommy to four months. He's been there two." She blew her nose, threw the tissue into a wastebasket under the desk and pulled more from a box on the desk. "I heard about what you did in court, about how you helped those two kids. Everyone's heard about it; people want to know if you're going to help."

"Help how?"

She shrugged. "I don't know. Help us get our kids out of there."

Sloane didn't want to go there. Not yet. His focus was on Jake and T.J.

"Let's take a step back; why all the cloak and dagger with the note, meeting here in this office?"

"No one can know I'm talking to you."

"Because you're worried about losing your job?"

"Because of what could happen to Tommy."

Sloane looked to Molia. "Why? What exactly are you worried about?"

"When I call or visit Tommy says everything is fine, but I know it's not."

"How?" Sloane asked, recalling his conversation with Jake. He hoped Harper could provide specifics about Fresh Start.

"I just know. I can hear it in his voice and I can see it in his face when I visit. He's lost weight. He looks tired and he speaks in a monotone. He's afraid, Mr. Sloane. They're all afraid. Even the ones who get released won't say much."

"Do they say what they're afraid of?"

"I know what they're afraid of. Everything. The guards, the police, Judge Earl. Mostly they're afraid of being sent back."

"How long have things been like this?" Molia asked.

"Ever since they built Fresh Start."

"And nobody's filed a complaint; nobody's challenged Judge Earl?" Sloane asked.

"One woman did. She filed a complaint with the board of judicial conduct and started talking to a reporter." Harper shook her head at the recollection. "After that, her life became hell. She got parking and speeding tickets and they garnished her wages to cover the cost of her son's incarceration. If she didn't pay they threatened to throw her in jail. Stores in Truluck wouldn't serve her. Fresh Start said her son lost his weekly visitation privileges. When she did finally visit him she said he looked horrible. She said he told her she had to stop what she was doing, that she was making it worse."

"What did she do?"

A shrug. "What any of us would have done. She stopped."

"Where is she now?"

"I don't know. When her son got released she moved away. I heard she had a sister in Texas."

"What about the reporter? Did she ever write an article?"

"As far as I know nothing came of that either. No one else would talk to her."

"Why not, Eileen? If nobody does anything how do they expect things to get better."

"People around here lead simple lives, Mr. Sloane. That's why we live here. It's a small town. Everyone knows everyone else's business. They're good people, but they're afraid. These are our kids. Nobody wants to sacrifice their son for the greater good. Most of us can't afford to sell our homes and move, especially not in this economy. Where would we go? Where would we find jobs? People don't know who to turn to." She paused. "People are asking if maybe you're going to sue Judge Earl."

Sloane took a moment to gather his thoughts. He wondered if his stunt in court would make things worse for Jake, and what could happen if they continued to push Judge Earl. "It isn't that simple, Eileen. A judge is immune from being sued for decisions he makes while sitting on the bench, no matter how bad those decisions might be."

"How can that be?" She nearly whispered her question.

"He may be wrong. He may be harsh, but that's what the court of appeals is for. Judge Earl can't be sued unless he's doing something illegal."

Harper seemed to give this some consideration, and as she sat in the shadows Sloane was suddenly struck with the image of a woman sitting at a poker table considering how best and when to show all of her cards. She was holding something back. She looked to Molia, then back to Sloane. "I know Thursday's proceedings were recorded," she said. "We use an audio recording system called 'For the Record.' The State has strict rules about keeping the recordings."

"That may be the procedure, Eileen, but that doesn't help prove someone erased the disk."

"Maybe not," she said. "But I can."

"And an accident," Tom Molia said, smiling, "is a mistake, as opposed to a deliberate, intentional act."

FRESH START YOUTH TRAINING FACILITY
SIERRA NEVADA MOUNTAINS

They had hurried from the cafeteria, leaping across the accumulating puddles to get to their dorm. T.J. ran with them and soon realized their hurry wasn't just to avoid the rain. It was to witness the spectacle.

They pushed two of the bunk beds sideways against the wall and sat across the top bunks like kids in the front row of a movie theater, though the show this night would not play out on a big screen. This was live theater, and it would unfold outside their windows, in the mud-soaked recreation yard. The problem was the storm had cloaked the yard in an ink-black darkness that not even the high-powered lights atop the well-placed stanchions could pierce. Ordinarily capable of illuminating every square inch of Fresh Start, the lights had been reduced by the storm to small rings.

"Are they out there?" Cal asked.

"Move over. I can't see," Henry said.

They would have turned off the lights to reduce the glare but they had no switch to control them. Like everything else in their lives a central nervous system inside the Administration Building controlled when the lights came on and when they went black.

"Stop breathing so hard, you're fogging the window," Rafe said to no one in particular as he wiped at the window with the sleeve of his coveralls.

T.J. did not join them. Once he realized the reason for their hurry he lay in his lower bunk on the opposite side of the room. He had no interest in seeing what further trouble Jake could make for himself or what punishment Atkins's twisted mind could conceive. Jake had made enough trouble for them both. T.J. was determined to steer clear of him. He did not want Atkins to associate the two of them as friends. It had left him feeling alone and vulnerable, and though he had been tempted to talk to Jake, he had resisted the urge. He would only be doing so out of desperation, not because he thought the two of them could ever be friends. Jake was angry at everyone. When he hadn't totally ignored T.J. he'd treated him like an annoying little kid, and T.J., in his desire to make the best of the situation, as his father had requested, had followed Jake into town. Look where that had got him.

"There they are!" Tommy shouted.

"Where, I don't see them," Henry said.

Tommy pointed during a burst of lightning. "Right there. Right there. That's Atkins. See him?"

"His head looks huge," Henry said.

Rafe punched him in the thigh. "Because he's wearing one of those hats to keep the rain out of his face, you retard."

"How was I supposed to know? His head looks as big as Big Baby's."

"Better not let Big Baby hear you saying that," Rafe said.

"Where's Jake?" Bee Dee asked.

"Standing right there," Tommy said.

"Where?" Henry asked.

"What are you, blind *and* retarded? He's right there."

"How long you give him, Rafe?" someone asked.

"Eight minutes."

"Eight minutes?" Henry sounded skeptical. "Maybe in good weather. Not in this shit. I say five. What do you say, Bee Dee?"

Bee Dee didn't answer.

They turned in unison to check the clock on the wall. Lightning pulsed again, a blue strobe that momentarily illuminated their faces and again reminded T.J. of kids sitting in a darkened movie theater, the film flickering across their faces.

"Atkins is really screaming at him," Henry said. "I wish I could hear what he was saying."

"You know what he's saying." Rafe jumped down and clasped his hands behind his back, eyes bugging, neck thrust forward, muscles straining. "You worthless piece of shit, Stand-up! You vertical, standing turd. Do you think you are better than everyone else? Are you too good for the rules? I shit things worth more than you. When we are finished you will beg me to ship your worthless, no-good punk ass to juvenile detention."

"Push-ups," Tommy said.

Rafe climbed back to his spot. "That's to get his arms tired so he can't do the obstacle course."

"How many?" Tommy asked.

"That's fourteen. Fifteen, sixteen," Henry counted.

"Time?" someone asked.

"Four minutes," Henry replied.

"Fuck, it's raining hard."

T.J. looked up, almost expecting the roof to give way under the rush of water. It didn't sound like rain. It sounded like people running across the metal.

"He's on the obstacle course," Tommy said.

"Where?"

"The cargo netting," Rafe said.

"That shit cuts up your hands when it's wet," Tommy said.

"He's up top," Rafe said.

"No way he makes it across the rope ladder," Henry said.

"He's already halfway," Rafe said.

"Won't make it. See, he's stopping," Henry said, sounding like an announcer at a sporting event. "He's losing his grip. Ohhhh! He's in the mud."

"More push-ups."

Curiosity finally got the better of T.J. and he climbed up onto the bunk bed between Bee Dee and Henry. Bee Dee had been surprisingly quiet.

"Time?" Tommy asked.

Henry's head swiveled to the clock. "Seven minutes."

"He's done, man. He won't get up," Henry said, then, "fuck, he's getting up."

Lightning pulses provided snapshots of Jake getting to his feet, Atkins continuing to yell at him as Jake made his way back to the start of the obstacle course. He climbed the cargo net, started across the rope bridge, and reached for each successive overhead rung.

"Shit," Henry said, sounding in awe. "He made it across."

"That will just make Atkins madder," Jose said.

"More push-ups," Rafe said.

They paused, watching in silence.

"He's going back to the start," Tommy said, sounding astonished. "Why doesn't he quit, Bee Dee?"

But Bee Dee didn't answer. He continued to stare in silence, watching. And with each passing minute, the boys' enthusiasm and amusement dwindled until they all sat silent, faces blank, eyes without any glimmer of their initial enjoyment.

"Time?" someone asked, the voice a whisper.

Henry turned his head to the clock on the wall. "Fourteen minutes."

"Holy shit."

More silence.

"Why doesn't he quit?" Tommy asked again, his voice cracking. "Bee Dee, why doesn't he just quit?"

"I don't know," Bee Dee said. "Maybe he doesn't have any quit in him."

"Atkins gonna kill that boy," Rafe said. "Take his body out into the mountains and tell his momma he tried to escape."

"He doesn't have a momma," T.J. said.

"That's why Atkins has him out there. Who's the retard now?" Henry said.

"Both of you shut up," Jose said. He turned to T.J. "What'd he do anyway?"

The others looked to T.J. "I don't know," he said.

"Must have been something bad to piss off Atkins this much," Henry said. "I haven't seen him this mad in a long time. He's gone crazy."

Another flash of light revealed Jake at the start of the obstacle course.

"Yep," Rafe said. "Atkins going to kill him for sure if he don't quit."

Henry looked at the clock. "Sixteen minutes. Nobody's ever gone sixteen minutes."

"Nobody's gone fourteen minutes," Rafe said. "How long did you go, Bee Dee?"

Bee Dee looked down at red welts across both palms. "Twelve."

Tommy was first. He slid from the bunk and wiped his hand beneath his nose. Jose followed, looking embarrassed that he had rushed to witness Jake's torture. The others too began to get down, silently returning to their bunks.

"Twenty minutes," Rafe said, leaving the bunk. "Enough of this shit."

Only T.J., Henry, and Bee Dee remained. On it went, even after the thunder and lightning subsided and the rain eased to a steady mist.

"Where is he?" T.J. asked, no longer able to see without the bursts of light.

Bee Dee inched forward and wiped at the condensation. "I think he's on the ground."

The others came back, standing along the edge of the lower bunks to look out the windows. T.J. wiped more of the condensation. With the rain easing and the dark clouds separating, the lights on the towers began to retake the yard from the darkness, revealing a body lying in the mud.

"There he is," Henry said. "Time?"

Rafe hit him in the shoulder. "Shut up, Henry."

"He's not moving," T.J. said.

"Told you," Rafe said. "Atkins done killed that boy."

KNOCK-ME-STIFF SALOON
GOLD CREEK, CALIFORNIA

Dave Bennett pushed open the door to the office. "Everything okay?"

Harper nodded. Sloane and Molia had agreed to keep everything she told them between the three of them, at least for now. Harper could not afford to lose her job, particularly with her son at Fresh Start, and they didn't want to make things potentially worse for the boys until they were prepared to act. Besides, Sloane was not yet certain how he might use the information Harper had provided and he was learning that Winchester County was a small place and that word traveled fast, as news of his stunt in court that morning obviously already had.

"You have any good hotels here in town?" Molia asked Bennett.

Bennett shook his head. "Not really. The cost can add up pretty quick. They tend to gouge the tourists."

"Unfortunately we're running out of options; they're doing their best to push us as far out of Truluck as they can."

"I got a place you can use. It isn't much, but it's yours if you like."

"We don't want to impose," Sloane said.

"Does it have air-conditioning?" Molia asked.

"It's a bunkhouse. It used to be for the ranch hands back in the day. My father used it for storage. It got pretty run-down, but I've been cleaning it out and fixing it up for Eileen to use as a studio."

"A studio?" Sloane asked.

"It's nothing," she said, waving it off.

"It's not nothing," Bennett said. "Eileen designs and makes women's clothing, all kinds. She's very talented." Bennett looked to Molia. "Sorry, no air-conditioning."

"That's all right." Molia sighed. "I'm going to treat this as one long weight-reduction program."

"No indoor plumbing either, I'm afraid. But we fixed up the outhouse so it's presentable and you can run your wireless off my Internet if you need it."

Sloane turned to Harper. "We don't want to cause you any problems."

"It's fine," she said. "Dave and I keep our relationship quiet."

"Can we pay you something?" Sloane asked Bennett.

Bennett shook his head. "Like I said, it mostly sits unused. You're welcome to it."

"I'll find you the name of that reporter when I get home tonight," Harper said. "How should I get it to you?"

"Call him," Molia said, nodding to Bennett.

"You'll be all right getting home?" Bennett asked Harper.

"I'll be fine," she said.

After seeing Harper safely to her car, which she had parked in the back alley so she could use the emergency exit, Bennett instructed one of his employees to watch the bar, grabbed a set of keys and led Sloane and Molia out the swinging shutters. "Let me show you the way then," he said.

Carl Wade sat in his truck, watching the front entrance to the Knock-Me-Stiff. Sloane and Molia exited the swinging doors with a third man, who pointed up the street, apparently giving directions.

Then the man walked around the corner of the building as Sloane and Molia returned to their rental car. Minutes later a red truck emerged from the alley and turned right. Wade made note of the license plate. The detective, driving the rental car, pulled from the curb to follow.

Wade flipped open his cell phone. "I have a license plate I want you to run for me." He waited a beat then read the letters and numbers into the phone. "I don't know," he said in answer to a question. "But Sloane is not going away. He's still making inquiries." He listened a beat, fielding another question. "Maybe. But let everyone know that if I can't convince him to move along, we may have to move earlier than anticipated."

FOURTEEN

O utside the window a crow cawed. Disoriented, Jake tried
to sit up, felt pain all over his body, and fell back.

"The best thing is to start moving. It's going to hurt
like hell, but it will no matter how long you try to wait it out. Better to get it over with."

Bee Dee sat on the edge of an adjoining bed, elbows on his knees.

"Where am I?"

"In my dorm."

Jake looked about the dorm, a carbon copy of the other one.
"How did I get here?"

"We carried you." Bee Dee stood and came closer. "Come on.
Get up."

But Jake couldn't get up. His arms and legs wouldn't move. And
he had no will to face another day of Atkins's verbal and mental
abuse. He couldn't take it anymore. His body had quit, and so too
had his mind.

"Forget it."

"Can't forget it. They won't let you forget it. You got to get up or
they'll get you up."

Jake chuckled. "So what? What more can Atkins do to me if I
don't?"

"You don't have to worry about him. It's Saturday. Even an
asshole like Atkins takes a weekend off." Bee Dee reached down.
"Come on, get up."

"Just leave me alone."

"You don't get it, do you?"

"Get what?" Jake asked.

"Why do you think they put you in a bunk with Big Baby? Why do you think they picked you to punish?"

"You already told me. They pick on the bigger kids. Lucky me."

"But do you know why?"

"I don't give a shit why."

"They pick the ones they think will be the toughest to break, because then they don't have to break everyone else. Everyone else sees you're broke and they're broke."

"Well, they won. I'm broke."

Bee Dee smiled, just a hint. "No. They didn't break you. We all saw it."

Jake coughed. His stomach cramped. When the coughing subsided he grimaced, fighting back tears. "I can't take it anymore."

"You went twenty-four minutes. Nobody has ever gone twenty-four minutes. Nobody has ever gone past fourteen. And you did it in a freaking thunderstorm."

"What are you talking about?"

"I'm talking about last night. I'm talking about you and Atkins on the obstacle course. What, you think you're the first one Atkins ever did that to?" Bee Dee held up his hands so Jake could see the scar just below the pads at the base of the fingers. Jake lifted his own hands and examined the red and blistered welts running horizontally across the palm. The skin hung in flaps, pulled back to reveal raw, red meat. "He's done it a lot. But you're the first one to break Atkins. He gave up. *Atkins* gave up. He walked away." Bee Dee emphasized the words. "Atkins never gave up before."

Jake lowered his hands. "So what? Who gives a shit if I lasted one minute or twenty?"

"Twenty-four."

"Who cares?" Jake yelled. "It doesn't mean anything."

Bee Dee scowled. "Who cares? Who do you think dragged your sorry ass through the mud last night? Who do you think risked getting punished to bring you in here? You think I did it by myself? Everyone's in that cafeteria right now, and do you know what they're waiting for? They're waiting to see if you're going to walk through that door."

Jake wiped tears streaming down the side of his face. "I can't stand it here, Bee Dee. I can't stand thinking I'm going to spend a year here."

Bee Dee squatted. "You don't think about a year. You don't think about a month or a week. You don't even think about tomorrow. You think about today. Just make it through today."

"What if I can't? What if I can't make it through another day?"

Bee Dee stood. "Then I guess we wasted our time. I guess we should have just left you out there in the mud." He started for the door, stopped and looked back. "You know why we didn't? Because for those twenty-four minutes it wasn't just you out there. It was all of us. We were all out there."

"Really?" Jake spat. "'Cause I didn't see anybody out there but me."

For a moment Bee Dee didn't speak. Then he said, "They ain't gonna let you lie there. So, the way I see it you have two choices. Let them get you up and continue to punish you, or get up. You get your ass out of bed and you'll see. You'll see you're not alone.

KNOCK-ME-STIFF RANCH
GOLD CREEK, CALIFORNIA

Dave Bennett's home on the Knock-Me-Stiff Ranch was a two-story log cabin that looked like something out of the old western TV show *Bonanza*, with a circular drive leading to a portico and a tall, wide door beneath a hanging chow bell. The bunkhouse sat several hundred yards down a dirt road. Bennett hadn't oversold it. Longer than it was wide, the narrow structure had two doors beneath a rickety overhang that faced a field of black oaks and brush. The knotted pine siding had weathered nearly black and the building looked as if it would fall over in a stiff breeze. Inside, a third door at the back led to the outhouse, perhaps thirty yards across an open grass field.

"That could be an adventure in the middle of the night," Molia had said, holding up one of two propane camp lights Bennett had provided.

The four-paned windows still had the original silica glass and weren't constructed to open. Bennett propped open the doors to create a cross draft and let out the heat of the day while Sloane and Molia moved headless and limbless mannequins, which Harper used to design her clothing, along one wall. Before bunking down, Molia had dressed one in a long-sleeve shirt and fastened a baseball cap atop a stick, rigging it where the head would be. Then he positioned the mannequin near a window. "I saw it in *Home Alone,*" he said.

Molia and Sloane had slept in the lower bunks though neither slept much, if at all, and finally got up well before dawn. Sloane used Bennett's battery-operated hot plate to heat water for coffee. Later that morning Bennett stopped by to jerry-rig two plugs that allowed them to fire up the computer equipment, which they set on the table, a massive rectangular slab of wood. Bennett was working to get the wireless modem set up when Alex called Sloane's phone.

"I think I got your article," she said. Sloane had called her the night before and asked her to search for any articles on Fresh Start, hoping she'd find the one Eileen Harper had mentioned. "It's called 'The Selling of Youth Offenders.' I'll forward it when your computers are set up. It's strong on details but weak on quotes and provides no names."

"Any luck finding the reporter?"

"You got a pen and paper?"

"In hand."

"Then I have a name and a number."

SHANGHAI ALE HOUSE
WINCHESTER COUNTY, CALIFORNIA

Tamara Rizek rose from her chair as Sloane and Molia entered the brick ale house. Tall and athletic with a black ponytail, she waved them over to join her at a table far from the picture windows in the back near floor-to-ceiling glass enclosing stainless steel beer vats that prevented anyone from sitting close.

Sloane greeted Rizek over the guitar riffs of AC/DC's "Highway to Hell" and introduced Molia. "You indicated you might not have much time?"

Rizek had hesitated at Sloane's invitation when they spoke by phone, though not because she was reluctant to talk. She had a newborn son, three months, along with a three-year-old daughter. "Double trouble" she had called them on the phone. Sloane had offered to meet at her house, but that just made her laugh.

"I take it you don't have a toddler," she'd said. She told Sloane she'd make arrangements with her mother-in-law to help out and would call Sloane back with a time and a place to meet.

"I'm good for a couple hours," she said, retaking her seat.

A waiter refilled Rizek's coffee mug. Sloane opted for an iced tea and Molia joined Rizek with a cup of coffee. "And I'll have a Guinness," Rizek said.

"A woman after my own heart," Molia said.

"Doctor's orders."

"No kidding? Where can I find him? I'd like a prescription with a lifetime renewal."

"You'd have to give birth first."

"There's always some small catch."

"I'm anemic since my son's birth. Happened with my daughter too. Guinness is loaded with iron. Also helps with the milk production."

"Maybe two catches," Molia said.

Molia never ceased to impress Sloane with his ability to put a witness at ease. He'd seen the detective do it more than once. "Can I buy you breakfast?" Sloane asked Rizek.

Rizek declined. "The Last Stop is better for breakfast." She paused. "I thought there'd be fewer people in here this hour of the morning."

"You're concerned?" Sloane asked.

She shook her head. "Curious. I wrote that article two years ago and it didn't generate much interest then."

"Is that when you moved to Winchester County?"

"About six months before. My husband wanted to get out of the Bay Area after my daughter was born to get out of the traffic and congestion. He's a lawyer and he was looking to change careers, and we both wanted to be home more for the kids than either of our jobs would have allowed living in the Bay Area. He grew up not far from here. Country living sounded like a good thing at the time."

"So how did the article come about?" Sloane asked.

"I took a job part-time with the *Winchester Recorder* just to keep from going stir-crazy. Mostly fluff pieces, you know, the local Girl Scout troop raising money for a mission to Mexico. It was fine. I was burned-out. I'd spent ten years at the *Mercury* doing investigative pieces." She pulled her ponytail tight at the back of her head. "Then the phone rings one day. Aubrey Garzinni. I won't forget that name. She tells me she's filing a complaint against Judge Earl Boykin, that he's sent her son to someplace called Fresh Start without her knowledge and without any trial."

"At least he's consistent," Molia said.

"Honestly, I thought it was bullshit, you know. You get that a lot as a reporter, people wanting to use you for their personal vendettas. But I confirmed she'd filed the complaint and told her I'd look into it. When I tried to get a copy of the hearing, the clerk wouldn't release it. She said juvenile records are sealed. When I had Aubrey try to get a copy she got the runaround, and I got more interested."

"Funny how that works," Molia said.

"Are you a reporter?"

"Detective."

She nodded. "I made an FOIA request on her behalf to get copies of Judge Earl's sentences. It took awhile and I didn't get names, but I got a list of the offenses and the sentences. When I compared them with other counties I found them completely out of whack, kids being sent away for minor stuff that other counties were giving home confinement, and Boykin's sentences much longer than the average. That was all very interesting, but what really caught my attention was it seemed they were all being sent to this place Fresh Start."

"We know it," Molia said.

"So I shifted focus and I find out Fresh Start is a private detention facility, that the parents have to pay when their kids get sentenced there. Now I'm really interested. So I call up and ask if there is someone I can talk to. I tell them I want to do a feature article on the place. They put me in touch with a woman, I forget what they called her."

"Parent liaison," Sloane said.

"That's it. But really she's just a PR person."

"Felt like she was going to sell us a time-share," Molia said.

The waiter returned with Rizek's Guinness and Sloane's ice tea. Rizek sipped her beer and wiped the foam with a napkin. "I asked if I could tour the facility but she shined me on for a week or two then said the request had been denied because it could violate the privacy of the occupants. Now I'm just pissed. So I arranged to go with Aubrey when she went to visit her son. She said I was her sister."

"Did you get in?" Sloane asked.

She nodded. "We got in. They dress the place up nice enough, kids playing on the basketball courts, shooting pool and playing pinball in the recreation room, but there was something that made my skin crawl, you know? The guy who runs the place calls himself 'Captain' something, I can't remember his name. Freaky guy. Something not quite right, you know? Anyway, when Aubrey's kid enters the room and sees me with his mother he pauses like he's wondering what's up. When Aubrey tells him I'm a reporter the blood drains from the kid's face and he gets skittish. He tells her she has to stop whatever she's doing. He says she's making things worse but he won't say how. When I try to ask a question he leaves the table."

Sloane looked to Molia, an unspoken thought between them.

"I'll tell you, I worked the police desk at the *Mercury* for two years, and I'd met a lot of victims of crime. I'd seen fear etched on faces before, and this kid was scared, I'm talking genuinely terrified. And that's when I realized what was bothering me. The kids were all going through the motions, but not one was smiling."

FRESH START YOUTH TRAINING FACILITY
SIERRA NEVADA MOUNTAINS

Getting up had been agony, putting on clean clothes he found by
the side of the bunk worse. But Bee Dee had been right; the more
Jake moved, the more the initial pain and stiffness lessened. His
chest felt as if someone had stomped on it with a boot and he could
barely bend his fingers. When he did his blistered palms burned. He
forced himself to walk about the room before sitting on the edge
of Bee Dee's bed to carefully slip on socks and push his feet into
his boots. He didn't bother to tighten the laces and the boots made
a shuffling sound when he walked across the concrete floor. The
door to the dorm was open, but no breeze greeted Jake when he
stepped out. He saw no one in the yard.

Despite the torrential downpour the sun had already begun to
bake the ground dry, leaving the imprints of the soles of boots, like
molded clay dried in a kiln. The camp was eerily quiet as he made
his way across the yard to the mess hall. When he pulled open the
door he saw inmates seated at tables, others carrying their canary
yellow and orange trays, and others still waiting in line to be served.

As Jake stepped into the room, Henry looked up at him then
nudged the kid sitting beside him. It had a domino effect, elbows
and whispers spreading throughout the cafeteria until each pair of
eyes found him, including the guards stationed around the perimeter. Having stopped in the doorway, Jake's muscles and joints
felt as if they'd refrozen, and he grimaced when he started again,
the sound of his shoes sliding on the floor more pronounced. He
flinched when the tray pressed against his palm, and placed it on
the horizontal metal bars, adding a plate and utensils. As he made
his way down the line the first server heaped what appeared to be a
larger than usual stack of pancakes on his plate. The second added
two slabs of ham instead of one. At the end of the line Jake added a
milk and grimaced when he picked up his tray and turned in search
of a table.

He took a step and heard a knocking sound. Uncertain, he took
another and heard the knock again. A third step and the knock grew

louder. The guards, Atkins not among them, turned and looked at one another, an indication they too had heard but not expected the sound. Jake took another step, and when the knock again accompanied him he realized the source. Bee Dee held a spoon, and with each step Jake took he knocked the handle on the table. Henry had joined him, along with the others at his table, and the beat quickly spread, infectious, growing in both numbers and in volume.

SHANGHAI ALE HOUSE
WINCHESTER, CALIFORNIA

"But you wrote the article," Sloane said, sliding the copy Alex had sent to him that morning across the table.

"Not the article I originally intended," Rizek said. "When I went to Fresh Start that day I realized the story wasn't just one boy; it was the facility, and Judge Earl's sentences. That's the story I wanted to write but of course he wasn't about to comment, and the prosecutor gave me some bullshit quote about how getting tough on juvenile offenders reduces recidivism. I decided to find out for myself."

"Does it?" Molia asked.

"Depends on who you talk to and what you read. Most of the studies I read said these boot camps do little to decrease the rate of recidivism and some contend graduates have *higher* rates than more traditional detention facilities because the juveniles don't complete the aftercare programs once they're out."

"The notion of being 'scared straight' wears off when the immediate threat of punishment evaporates," Molia said.

"Exactly. The correctional and military experts I spoke to said most juveniles lack the maturity and self-control to succeed once they leave a disciplined military environment. A boot gets out of boot camp and he or she is still in the army, still in a highly structured, rule-oriented environment with a chain of command. The kid graduating from a boot camp is sent home to the same parents that couldn't control him in the first place. That's what the studies say, anyway. But I think there's a better explanation."

"Which is what?" Sloane asked.

"That a confrontational model using intimidation and humiliation is counterproductive with kids, some of whom may already have severe emotional or behavioral problems."

"You take a kid who has spent his life committing violent crimes—robbery, rape, assault—and you're basically just reinforcing that use of physical force," Molia said.

"*And* that using degrading tactics is appropriate to achieve your purpose." Rizek added. "You reinforce that in a kid who's bigger and stronger than the others, and you've created a potential Frankenstein."

FRESH START YOUTH TRAINING FACILITY
SIERRA NEVADA MOUNTAINS

The guards had put an end to the utensil salute, but they couldn't erase the smiles on the faces of the inmates, not completely anyway. Jake set his tray down across from Bee Dee, who was doing his best to conceal his own shit-eating grin. He knew he should be hungry, but he had little appetite. He sat staring at the mound of food on his plate.

"Just start slow," Bee Dee said.

Jake started with the eggs, which he figured would require minimal chewing. His jaw, like the rest of his body, hurt to move. The ham was a problem but for a different reason. He couldn't hold a knife and apply the pressure needed to cut the meat.

"I gotcha, man." The kid sitting next to him stabbed the two pieces, put them on his plate, and cut them up.

"Thanks," Jake said, realizing he didn't know the kid's name.

"Rafe," he said. "No problem."

The kid seated beside Bee Dee introduced himself as "Tommy" and the kid beside him was "Jose." Jake already knew Henry. T.J. sat at the far end, but unlike the others he kept his head down, picking at his food.

"Why is breakfast so late?" Jake's voice was hoarse from yelling over the sound of the storm.

"Saturday," Bee Dee said. "Everything gets pushed back for family visits at ten. If you don't have family, you have chores. You're working in the horse stables with me and Henry. Afternoon we get free time."

Jake looked around the room.

"I told you, he's not here," Bee Dee said.

"Even an asshole like Atkins gets a weekend off from torturing us," Rafe said.

"Probably why he gave up last night," Henry said. "Wanted to get home and beat his dog."

"Maybe the steroids wore off and he needed another shot to pump back up," Tommy said, puffing out his chest like a body-builder.

Rafe leaned forward for all to hear. "He gave up because our boy Jake beat him. That's why."

"How'd you do it?" Tommy asked. "How'd you last so long?"

Jake shook his head. "I don't know. I guess I didn't think I had a choice."

That brought chuckles, though not from T.J.

Jake ate most of his meal, though his stomach balked at times, cramping. When the bell clattered guards barked out orders and the inmates dutifully carried their plates to be cleaned, scraping the leftovers into large blue garbage cans before setting them down on the wash belt.

"Fifteen minutes to get cleaned up before we have to be at the horse stables," Henry said, getting up from the table. "Come on, I'll show you."

Jake looked to the end of the table. T.J. had picked up his tray, moving slower than the others. "You go ahead," he said. "I'll catch up."

"I got your tray." Rafe lifted Jake's tray. "And with Atkins gone you can bunk in our dorm. The weekend guards won't know. Cal went home yesterday, so we got an empty bunk. They don't bring in nobody on the weekend."

"Get moving," one of the guards said, approaching their table.

The table emptied. Jake started after T.J., about to call out his name when he overheard a conversation at another table where the inmates sat lingering.

"I don't know," a kid with a horse face said. "He was there arguing about something; I think his kid's in here. He left, but then he comes back in."

"And he just agreed to represent you?" another kid asked.

Jake's pulse quickened. He moved closer to the table.

"Like I said, he was walking out and then he just came back. He walked up to the kid and asked him, 'Hey kid, you want an attorney, don't you?' or something like that. He didn't even know the kid's name. He said it just like that. 'Hey kid, you want an attorney, don't you?'"

"What did the kid say?"

"At first he just stood there, like he didn't know what to say. Then he says, 'Are you any good?' Man, I about peed my freaking pants. 'Are you any good?' And the guy, this attorney, he just says, 'Yeah.' So the kid says 'okay.'"

"And he got him off?"

"I thought Judge Earl's head was going to explode."

Jake leaned closer. "What was his name?" The group stopped talking and pulled back. "The attorney," Jake said. "Did he tell you his name? Was it David? David Sloane?"

The kid nodded. "Yeah, that was it. Sloane."

"You said he was trying to get his kid out?"

"Him and a woman. They were asking for a new trial."

Jake remembered the lawyer with David in the Martinez courtroom though not her name. "The woman. Was she short with blond hair?"

"Yeah, that's her."

"What happened? What did the judge do?"

The kid shrugged. "Fucking Boykin does what he always does. He said no. So they said they were going to appeal it."

They were still close. They hadn't left. They were still trying to get him and T.J. out. Jake looked up but did not see T.J. at the table or in the line to scrape his plate. He hurried for the exit.

Outside Jake did not see T.J. He started across the yard, figuring T.J. would go back to his dorm before going to whatever chore he'd been assigned. He was halfway there when something weird caught his eye, a mass exodus of red coveralls from the bathhouse, like ants pouring out the top of their mound. Then T-Mac stepped out from behind the block wall that shielded the entrance, casually leaning against the edge as if waiting for someone.

Jake looked to his left and saw T.J. walking in the direction of the bathhouse with his head down. He had not seen the others fleeing. Jake was about to call out when a guard stopped in his path, blocking his view.

"Do you have someplace you're supposed to be, Inmate?"

"Uh, yes, sir."

"And where is that?"

"Horse stables, sir."

"Then I'd suggest you get moving before you're late."

"I need to use the bathroom."

"You should have thought of that before you stood here jerking off. You're just going to have to hold it until you get there."

"Yes, sir."

Jake started for the path leading to the horse stables. In his peripheral vision he watched as T.J. neared the bathhouse. T-Mac did not try to stop him. He stepped out of his way, as if about to walk off. But T-Mac didn't walk away. He walked to the side of the building. Jake could not see what T-Mac did next, but seconds later Big Baby lumbered around the corner of the building and entered. Jake's instincts made him want to change course, but when he looked back over his shoulder the guard remained rooted in place, watching him.

"They don't have to beat us all up," Bee Dee had said. "They just have to catch one of us alone. And trust me, you don't want to be the one."

FIFTEEN

Shanghai Ale House
Winchester, California

Rizek continued to explain what she had learned from her research into private detention facilities. "Fresh Start is a good example," she said. "It's remote. That's good in some respects but it also makes it expensive to operate. They have to truck in all the food and supplies."

"They need bodies," Sloane said. "They need a certain number of kids paying a certain amount to make a profit each month."

Rizek nodded. "They get some state and government subsidies, but yeah, the more bodies, the more money."

"And the longer the sentences, the longer the income stream," Sloane said.

"The selling of youth offenders," Rizek said, sliding her article beneath that headline back to Sloane.

"Did you find anything that could explain Judge Earl's sentences? Why he would do it?" Sloane asked.

Rizek smiled. "You mean like was he taking kickbacks?" She shook her head. "But Boykin was the reason they built it."

"What do you mean, he was the reason?" Sloane recalled Lynch telling them Fresh Start's construction was controversial.

"Boykin convinced two of the three county supervisors that the existing juvenile facility was outdated and a potential source of lawsuits. He convinced them to approve a land grant gifting the land to Victor Dillon. The trustee for the estate objected and sued the bank that held the deed in trust to recover the land."

"What was the basis for the suit, a noncomforming use?" Sloane guessed.

Rizek nodded. "The deed specified the land was to be used for a nonprofit camp for kids, you know, like a YMCA."

"How'd it come out?" Sloane asked.

"Dillon settled it. Reportedly he paid the estate a million dollars."

"No small change," Molia said.

"Dillon can afford it. The county supervisors gave him a twenty-year, fifty-nine-million-dollar lease. Add in what parents pay for each child, state subsidies, and what other counties pay if their facilities are full, and juvenile offenders stop being a problem and start being fungible commodities."

"Why didn't this cause more of a public outcry in the county?" Sloane asked.

"Because the *Winchester Recorder* wouldn't run the article. Boykin got word of my investigation and told the editor he would consider any insinuation that he was incarcerating kids for profit to be nothing short of slander. It was a mom and pop paper, they weren't about to take on Boykin or Victor Dillon. The *Sacramento Bee* also declined."

"Do you know why?"

"Not completely. I brought it to one of my former editors at the *Mercury*. She loved it but wanted a more personal angle. She wanted me to get a family to open up and talk. That wasn't going to happen in Winchester. *Nobody* would talk. The *Mercury* ran it, but severely edited." She shrugged. "And I had another bun in the oven to keep me busy."

The mention of the baby caused Sloane to consider his watch. He knew Rizek needed to leave. "What can you tell me about Victor Dillon?" he asked.

WILBER HOUSE
BLACK OAK WINERY
WINCHESTER, CALIFORNIA

Victor Dillon called it a Kodak Moment. With his left arm draped around the boy's shoulders and his right hand holding one end of the oversize check, the shot was worth more than gold, even at its current inflated prices.

PAY TO THE ORDER OF   **Joshua Aceves**   *$10,000*

Ten Thousand and 00/100 _____ DOLLARS.

The boy and his mother stood on each side of Dillon, each holding the prop with two hands, as if it were the check itself. After the photographers finished they stepped to the side and another boy and his mother, Caucasian, stepped into place. The process would be repeated a third time, for an African American boy. Three scholarships to underprivileged kids. Thirty thousand dollars. It was not an inconsequential sum, but it was a tax write-off, thanks to how Dillon's financial advisers had structured his nonprofit foundation, and it was a publicity bonanza. In addition to the local paper, which would run the article and photographs on the front page, the *Sacramento Bee* was also present, thanks to some well-placed phone calls, as were reporters from the local television stations, including the show *Good Day Sacramento*.

When the last photo op finished, Dillon returned to the elevated platform and took his seat just to the right of the podium, the place reserved for the guest of honor at this breakfast to promote opportunity, his publicist's idea. The president of the Wilber House stood at the microphone. "I would like now to say a few words about the man of the hour. Victor Dillon has been a generous supporter of our youth here in Winchester County. The list of all of his financial contributions would be too long for me to enumerate in the time we have allotted."

Which was why those contributions had been listed on the inside of the program. *Direct them to the inside of the program,* Dillon silently urged. But the woman did not. The crowd had gathered at the Wilber House on the spacious grounds of the Black Oak Winery, in which Dillon had a 35 percent stake, to pay him homage and to open their checkbooks.

"Still, I would be remiss if I did not touch upon his extraordinary gifts to promote opportunity for youth through his sizable donations to the Winchester county school system, to fund the expansion of the Winchester County library, and to construct the Fresh Start Youth Training Facility."

Dillon gave a humble smile. *Why was she leaving out the amounts of his generosity?* And yet the woman continued to do just that, noting the contributions, but not the dollar amounts then abruptly concluding.

"Ladies and gentlemen, I give you the man of this hour and so many others here in Winchester County, Victor Dillon."

The applause was adequate but not thunderous. Frankly, Dillon had expected more, but the woman had no sense of timing or how to build up a crowd. He met the president at the podium, shaking hands while the photographers reassembled. When Dillon felt the woman's hand pulling away he gripped it to allow the photographers adequate time to get their shots. He knew applause was contagious, and his publicist had ensured that several well-placed guests would stand. When they did, so did everyone else, and the applause increased in volume. Only when every butt had left its seat did Dillon let the president's hand drop and take the podium for himself.

"I want to thank President Andrzejewski for that very kind introduction. It is very humbling and I am deeply moved," he said. "As many of you know this is not my forte, speaking in public, especially when the subject I am asked to speak about is, well, me."

The audience laughed. Dillon had been unsure of the line but was now glad he had not deleted it.

"While some of you may consider these acts to be acts of charity, I consider them to be acts of necessity, a prudent investment in the future of Winchester County and a vote of confidence in our youth."

He paused, a cue for the applause. After it subsided, he continued.

"Opportunity cannot be bought, but it can be provided. I learned this in my youth. A child without opportunity is a child without hope, and a child without hope is a desperate child, and desperate children do desperate things. I did. Born to a single mother in a poor neighborhood not far from here in Stockton,

I spent my formative years between the ages of thirteen and eighteen incarcerated in the juvenile justice system. I was not a dumb kid. I don't believe I was a bad kid. I was a kid without opportunity. I was a kid without hope. I was a desperate kid." Dillon paused.

"My crimes were borne of that desperation. The institutions in which I was placed did not offer me opportunity. They did not offer me hope, only despair. I was fortunate to have been given opportunity by someone who saw potential in me. Without that opportunity I would not be here today. I would likely be in jail. I used that opportunity to succeed, and when I had, I turned to helping others, to giving them that same opportunity. I believe we can do better for our youth. The Fresh Start Youth Training Facility has proven that here in Winchester County we have done better."

The screen behind him filled with the smiling images of three young boys, white, black, and Hispanic. The next slide showed boys engaged in a game of basketball, another depicted students in a classroom, one boy with his hand raised, an eager look on his face. They'd used the photographs in the brochures.

"Fresh Start offers our young people opportunity to improve their minds and their bodies so they can improve their self-esteem and, dare I say, begin to hope for a better future. They can turn desperation into innovation, and they can use their street skills to make something of their lives. But they cannot do this without hope, without the kind of opportunity each one of us in this room can provide. Their future is up to each of us."

The applause resounded, the room back on its feet. Dillon waved and nodded as the president retook her place at the podium. This time Dillon did not cede it. He remained standing by her side. He needed to close the deal. The president held up a small white envelope, like the kind found at the end of pews in houses of worship, just long enough to insert cash or a check, and printed with a place on the inside flap to provide a credit card number.

"Your table captains have ten envelopes, one for each of you, and I would urge you to make a charitable donation to Victor Dillon's nonprofit, Fresh Start," she said. "I am going to ask you all to take a moment with me and fill out these envelopes, or to enclose your contributions and hand them to your table captains, as I am doing." She slid a check into the envelope and licked the back flap, sealing it before handing it to Dillon.

Between the amounts each table paid to attend the breakfast, and the amount to be collected in the envelopes, Victor Dillon had just made back his $30,000 charitable contribution several times over, proving once again that philanthropy was not a bad way to make a living.

FRESH START YOUTH TRAINING FACILITY
SIERRA NEVADA MOUNTAINS

Jake could barely keep from turning around and running for the bathroom; his mind imagining what horrors the man-child could inflict. But he knew if he turned again the guard would become suspicious and follow him. So he willed himself forward, one step after the next. When he reached the footpath leading to the horse stables he'd reached a point of no return. He turned. The guard had left.

He started back to the bathhouse, staying along the path behind the dorms so he would be approaching from behind the block wall where T-Mac stood sentry. He had no idea what he would say to get past him, and while he liked his odds against T-Mac when healthy, he was less certain of his chances in his current weakened condition. Without time for further planning he took a deep breath and stepped around the corner.

"Bathroom's closed," T-Mac said. "They're cleaning it."

Jake didn't stop. "I don't see a sign."

T-Mac stepped between Jake and the entrance. "I'm the sign. And I say it's closed."

They stood toe-to-toe and eye-to-eye, T-Mac thicker through the chest. Still, wrestling had given Jake certain skills, and he had taken down opponents bigger than T-Mac when he wrestled up in weight class.

"I'm in no mood, T-Mac. I have to pee. Move or I'm going to piss on your shoes."

The shove to Jake's chest was quick and violent. It knocked Jake on his back. Every muscle in his body cried out in pain, reminding him, again, that he was in no shape to fight. T-Mac stepped forward and delivered a kick intended for Jake's side but that Jake partially blocked with his forearm. Then T-Mac reached for the zipper on his coveralls. "Maybe I'll piss on you."

Jake slid backward. "Okay, fine. Fine." He got to his feet. "I'll find a tree."

He went around the back of the building and pressed against the block wall, thinking. Then he heard T.J.'s pleas.

"No. Stop. Stop."

Jake turned and looked up. The voice filtered through open windows over Jake's head, but the glimmering hope of climbing in one faded when he saw they were hinged at the bottom. The top flipped out only three to four inches. No way to climb in.

Big Baby's girlish giggle and lisp followed T.J.'s plea. "You're going to suck it," he said. "Or you're going to drown."

"No. Hel . . ." T.J.'s voice faded. The toilet flushed.

Jake looked about and picked up a rock the size of his hand. The problem was he'd lost the element of surprise with T-Mac, and if T-Mac dodged the blow Jake would only be providing him a weapon. Still, he had to do something. About to step from the side of the building, Jake saw Bee Dee walking across the yard to the bathroom. Nearing, Bee Dee gave Jake a furtive glance, enough to let Jake know Bee Dee had somehow assessed the situation and had come to help. Unfortunately, Bee Dee was significantly smaller than T-Mac.

As Bee Dee stepped to the entrance Jake heard T-Mac issue his command.

"Bathroom's closed for cleaning."

"Get out of the way, T-Mac. I got to go."

"Pick a fucking tree, Bee Dee."

"I got to take a shit."

"Then pick a log. Just don't wipe your ass with poison oak."

"You know, T-Mac, I used to think you were tough, but without Big Baby around I think you're just a big pussy."

"What did you call me?"

Jake watched Bee Dee step back, T-Mac following, and realized Bee Dee was luring T-Mac from the entrance.

Bee Dee retreated another step. "What are you, deaf and dumb? I said without Big Baby around you're nothing but a big pussy."

"I'm gonna kick your ass, nigger."

Bee Dee scoffed. "That's original, T-Mac. I've never heard that before. What's the 'T' stand for anyway, 'tiny'? Like the size of your dick?"

Bee Dee took two quick steps backward to evade T-Mac's lunge. Sensing his opportunity, Jake stepped around the corner, but then T-Mac spun and grabbed Bee Dee and Jake had no choice but to veer his course and help. He struck T-Mac in the back of the head with the rock. The boy crumpled.

For a moment neither one of them moved, then Bee Dee bent and grabbed T-Mac under the arms. When Jake bent to grab T-Mac's legs Bee Dee shook his head.

"Go!" he said.

WINCHESTER COUNTY COURTHOUSE
WINCHESTER, CALIFORNIA

It was not unusual for Earl Boykin to work on a Saturday, usually after watching one or more of his granddaughter's soccer games. What was unusual was for him to have a visitor in his office. He used his weekends to catch up on his work and had come to enjoy the serenity, when the phone wasn't ringing and his court staff was not present. But his visitor this Saturday could not come to the courthouse during regular business hours, even using the back staircase into Boykin's office. He couldn't take the chance.

"David Sloane is digging into things he should not be digging into," Boykin said. "And he seems intent on trying to challenge my authority."

"Do you want me to pay him a visit?" Atkins asked.

Boykin shook his head. "I'm thinking of a more measured response. At the moment Sloane thinks he is playing with a full house. He thinks he has nothing to lose by pushing this."

"What did you have in mind?"

"I want him to consider how his actions may impact on others."

"The kid?"

"I want him to understand there are consequences, but not anything so severe that it could serve instead as additional motivation."

"A warning of some kind."

"Something that will let him know his hand is not as good as he might think. That the longer he continues to play it, the greater the likelihood I'll call his bluff. Has the kid done anything that might warrant a longer incarceration?"

"If that's what it takes."

OLD TOWN
WINCHESTER, CALIFORNIA

Sloane and Molia walked back to their car in silence. Rizek provided more information than either had expected, and what she had offered was both informative and sobering. They already suspected Fresh Start was not the summer camp the parent liaison had portrayed, but Rizek had confirmed Jake and T.J. were in serious trouble. The problem was Sloane had no way to speed up the legal process, which only reminded him again of Father Allen's admonition that helping Jake was not a problem he would be able to solve by outsmarting everyone in a courtroom. And Molia's course of action, to dig into the lives of those involved and try to find some evidence of wrongdoing, would similarly take time; Rizek had spent six weeks digging and had been unable to find any hard evidence to confirm her suspicions that incarcerating kids at Fresh Start was making money for someone.

What Sloane needed was to find some way to bring the issue to a head sooner rather than later, and he expressed this to Tom Molia as they walked to the parking lot.

"What if we just tracked down Victor Dillon and asked him if having kids sentenced to Fresh Start without trials and without the assistance of counsel is his idea of helping? Put his feet to the fire. Rizek says he's meticulous about maintaining his image. What if we threaten to put a black mark on it?"

Molia stopped on the incline in the shade of several trees, shadows falling across half his face. "The problem with that idea is if Dillon and Judge Earl are in this together, we only alert them that we're on target, and that gives them the chance to cover their tracks."

"You really think that could be the case? Or are we just seeing what we want to see?"

"Okay, let's put bias aside for a second and look at the evidence objectively. What do we have?" Molia asked.

Sloane stepped into the shade so that Molia was not looking into the bright sun.

"Rizek says that places like Fresh Start are only profitable if full," Molia said.

"So we have an incentive," Sloane agreed.

"And who has control over whether Fresh Start remains full?" Molia asked.

"Judge Earl."

"And Judge Earl just so happens to be sentencing kids at an unusually high rate and for abnormally longer periods than any of his peers," Molia said. "Not to mention rushing them through the system without legal counsel or parental input that might impede the process. Why? People rarely do something for nothing, David."

Sloane played devil's advocate. "Ego. Remember what Barnes said? Judge Earl fancies himself after his lineage, the last of the hanging judges."

"Maybe, but in my thirty years I've never met anyone who valued ego more than cold, hard cash. Ego doesn't pay the bills. Money does. And if Judge Earl is profiting from this, who's his likely financier?"

"Dillon," Sloane agreed.

Molia walked the rest of the distance to the parking lot. "So let's see what Alex digs up on Earl's finances. But as they say in Denmark, something is rotten in Winchester."

Sloane's cell phone rang, a number he did not recognize.

"Mr. Sloane? This is Lynne Buchman, the parent facilitator in the juvenile justice department in Winchester."

"What can I do for you, Ms. Buchman?"

"I hate to be the bearer of bad news," she said.

SIXTEEN

Sloane felt as if he'd taken a blow to the stomach.

"What is it?" Molia asked. "What's wrong?"

Sloane disconnected the call. "They've extended Jake's sentence two months."

"What? Why?"

"They said he tried to escape while on a supervised hike. The administrator at Fresh Start made the recommendation, and Boykin granted it. They're punishing him for the motion," Sloane said.

"We don't know that," Molia said, but without much conviction.

"Of course they are. It's just like Rizek said. I'm just making it worse for him, and for T.J."

Molia seemed to consider the implications. "Listen, another couple months is irrelevant to what we're trying to do," he said. "We don't intend for either of them to carry out their sentences any longer than it takes us to get them out."

"But until we can—"

"Until we can we've just got to be smarter about what we're doing."

Sloane's phone rang again. He was relieved to see Alex's name and number on the screen. "Are you someplace you can talk?" she asked.

Sloane looked around the parking lot to ensure they were alone. "Let me put you on speaker so Tom can hear, too." He pressed the button.

"I think you might be on to something, Tom," Alex said. "Judge Earl's had an interesting past two years financially."

"Interesting how?" Sloane asked.

"According to his income tax returns and judicial accounting records he borrowed eight hundred and fifty thousand dollars to remodel his house. Two months later he took out another one point five million to buy a commercial office building in downtown Winchester. Both loans came from a local bank, Winchester First Street."

"What'd he use for collateral?" Sloane asked.

"I don't know. The bank is stalling my request for further information."

Sloane felt a twinge of anxiety because of the prior phone call. "Who did you tell them you were?"

"I found the name of Judge Earl's accountant and personal financial adviser from his income taxes and said I worked in the office and needed the information to determine potential tax ramifications for the judge and his wife. The bank officer said he'd dig up the paperwork and send it over."

"What if he does? Where are you going to have him send it?"

"Relax. I set up a fake e-mail account and used the financial adviser's Web site to fashion a phony tag line. Pfishers on the Internet do it all the time."

"Fishers?" Molia asked.

"Spelled wth a 'P,' " she said. "It's like copying a company's stationery and putting your name on it. I copied the company's e-mail format."

"What if he calls instead?" Sloane asked.

"Same thing. I created a phone number with the proper area code that will ring through to my computer. What's got you spooked, David? I can hear it in your voice."

"They've extended Jake's sentence. I'm worried it could be punishment for us pushing too hard on this. We just met with a reporter who said Judge Earl's sentences are harsher and longer than any of his contemporaries and the only way these mountain boot camps are profitable is to keep them full."

"You think he's taking kickbacks?"

"Seems the logical conclusion, doesn't it? See if you can find whether the judge has any ties to Victor Dillon. Forget the press release stuff and look into Dillon's background. I want to know how he came into his money. And take a closer look at this bank. Let's find out who sits on the board of directors and when it was started. But keep this all as quiet as possible. Do as much as you can through back doors, just in case."

FRESH START YOUTH TRAINING FACILITY
SIERRA NEVADA MOUNTAINS

The block wall prevented the sunlight from entering the bathhouse, and the small windows high above the shower stalls faced west, admitting only dull gray light. The contrast with the bright sunshine outside made the room appear dark as dusk as Jake stepped in.

He did not see T.J. or Big Baby.

The air remained sodden from the morning showers and smelled of the damp towels in the cloth bins, and urine. He checked the shower stalls, five vertical tiled coffins with opaque curtains that allowed the guards to maintain their constant vigilance.

Not there.

He stepped around the edge of the toilet stalls holding the rock at his side and stopped when he remembered the camera in the upper corner of the room. A towel had been draped over the machine, blocking the lens.

"Suck it. Suck it or you're going to drown."

Big Baby's voice came from one of the stalls. Jake took a deep breath and peered around the edge, seeing a pair of red coveralls in a heap on the floor. Hunched over, Big Baby's backside stuck out the last stall, a hideous patch of tufts of hair amid red welts and pimples that ran the length of his back and thighs and brought to mind the image of a warthog. What followed was a hideous cackle, Big Baby sounding like a child becoming more and more animated. "Suck it! Suck it!"

"No!" T.J. spoke in between gasps for air, a drowning man struggling to breathe. "Leave . . . Leave me . . . alone."

Jake stepped closer and watched as Big Baby shoved T.J.'s head into the toilet, using his other hand to flush the handle. When the toilet emitted a gurgling rush of water Jake recognized his chance, using the sound to cover his attack. He raised the rock, but as he lowered it to strike, Big Baby turned and the rock struck him across the forehead, above the temple, a glancing blow. His legs buckled and he stumbled, but he did not fall and before Jake could strike again Big Baby lunged, grabbing Jake by the throat and shoving him backward against the block wall.

"I'm going to kill you," he said, spit hissing between the gaps in teeth too small for his mouth. A trickle of blood flowed down the side of his face. He pulled back his arm, as an archer might the bow of an arrow and balled his hand into a massive fist. Jake braced for the blow, but the arm did not shoot forward. It lingered, as if Big Baby was having second thoughts. Then it dropped. So too did the hand gripping Jake's throat and Big Baby's eyes rolled back in his head, two hideous white orbs. He teetered, pitched sideways, and dropped like a felled tree, the side of his head hitting the concrete floor with a sickening crack.

THE SUTTER BUILDING
WINCHESTER, CALIFORNIA

The address of Judge Boykin's commercial office building was near the new Winchester business district, though the two-story stone structure would have blended nicely into Old Town. As Molia and Sloane approached the glass front doors they noticed a plaque on one of the stones indicating why the building had not been torn down to make way for the more modern glass-and-stucco buildings surrounding it. A historical landmark, the Sutter Building had been constructed in 1851 with rock from a local quarry and had served as the first supply store in Winchester, catering to miners seeking their fortunes.

When Sloane pulled on the handle the glass doors rattled, which drew the attention of a security guard seated behind a desk in the small lobby. Molia waved and smiled.

"Closed," the guard said, loud enough to be heard but not bothering to get up from his desk or to put down the novel he'd been reading.

Molia held up a finger to indicate he had a question while speaking to Sloane under his breath. "Put the book down, skippy. Three steps won't kill you."

The guard gave a noticeable sigh and reluctantly set down his book, fanned open to mark his location. He was not the stereotypical overweight security guard that walked the shopping malls with an oversize flashlight. The muscles of this guy's arms pressed taut the short sleeves of his white shirt and his broad shoulders tapered to the utility belt at his waist. He used a key attached to a ring on his belt to unlock the dead bolt and pushed open the door just enough to talk.

"Sorry to bother you," Molia said. "I'm looking for West Coast Cutlery."

The guard scowled, annoyed. "Never heard of it."

Molia reached into his pocket and pulled out the receipt from the coffee at the Shanghai Ale House, as if to read the address of the building, which was stenciled above the glass doors. "Fifteen oh one Church Street."

"That's this address," the guard said. "But I've never heard of that business."

"Are you sure? The woman on the phone repeated it twice."

"I'm sure." He started to close the door.

"Is there another Church Street?"

The guard sighed. "Not that I'm aware of."

Molia rubbed the stubble of his chin. "Could I maybe come in and check the register of businesses?"

"The building is closed."

"Maybe you could check it for me?"

Becoming more frustrated and less friendly the man said, "No reason to. There's only one name on the register, Trinity Investments. Like I said, I've never heard of West Coast Cutlery. It isn't here. You got the wrong address. You sure she said Winchester?"

"Boy, I thought so," Molia said sounding less sure and already stepping away from the door. "But with my hearing who knows?" He flashed that disarming smile again, chuckling as he spoke. "I don't imagine Trinity makes mail-order cooking utensils."

The guard did not return the smile. "I don't imagine they do," he said.

"She'll be upset when I don't come home with those knives she ordered, but it won't be the first time I disappointed her. Thanks for your time."

The guard closed the door without further comment and they walked off to the sound of the guard reapplying the dead bolt.

"Nicely done," Sloane said, already pulling out his cell phone to call Alex.

"While she's at it, ask her to look up 'On-Guard Security.'"

Sloane glanced at him. "Why?"

"Does it strike you as odd that a closed and locked building in this town would require an armed security guard to sit in the lobby?"

FRESH START YOUTH TRAINING FACILITY
SIERRA NEVADA MOUNTAINS

T.J.'s coveralls were soaked to his waist. Beads of toilet water continued to drip down his face. He stared down at Big Baby with a distant, vacuous gaze, the rock still in his hand. The sound of shoes on concrete broke the silence. Bee Dee came to an abrupt halt where Big Baby lay facedown on the concrete floor, head twisted to the side, blood flowing from the wound. What Jake had thought to be acne scars on Big Baby's grotesque backside he now realized were something far more horrific, burn marks, dozens of them. Big Baby had not always been the torturer.

Bee Dee looked up at the camera covered by the towel then knelt and put two fingers to Big Baby's neck.

"Is he dead?" T.J. asked.

Bee Dee stood. "No. He's not dead. And neither is T-Mac."

"What do we do now?" Jake asked.

"We get the hell out of here. Where are you supposed to be?" Bee Dee directed the question to T.J.

"The garden."

"Then you go to the garden." Bee Dee grabbed him by the collar. "You don't say anything to anybody. You understand? You tell no one. They'll ask everyone. Captain will hold an inquiry. You do not tell anyone no matter what. You understand? You don't say anything."

"I won't," T.J. said.

"This is just another day. Can you act like this is just another day?"

"I will."

"Go."

T.J. bolted for the door.

"Walk," Bee Dee barked at him.

T.J. slowed. At the door he turned back to Jake. "Thanks," he said.

"Go!" Bee Dee urged. He turned to Jake. "We need to get to the horse stables." He picked up the bloodied rock, stepped to one of the metal sinks and rinsed it quickly, shaking off the water. "Anyone asks why we're late we'll say you twisted your ankle last night and now you're having trouble walking. I'll say I stayed back to help you." He shoved the rock into one of the pockets of his coveralls, keeping his hand in place so the bulge would be less noticeable.

Outside, they stepped around the back of the building where T-Mac lay unconscious, partially concealed in plants, and walked down the path leading to the amphitheater.

"You think he'll say anything?" Bee Dee asked.

"T.J.?" Jake shook his head. "I don't think so," he said, though in truth he didn't know. "I think he's pretty scared though."

"That makes two of us." Bee Dee removed the rock and tossed it toward underbrush but it hit the ground with a thud and tumbled short of the foliage. Before either of them could kick it farther they heard footsteps coming up the path. A guard rounded the corner.

"Where are you two headed?"

"Horse stables," Bee Dee said without hesitation.

"You're late. Where have you been?"

"He twisted his ankle; he's having trouble walking."

The guard, one Jake had not yet seen, glared at them. "Well, boo-fucking-hoo. Who are you, Florence Nightingale?"

"No, sir, I'm Bee Dee Wells. This is—"

"What do you think, you're funny? I don't give a shit who you are. What I care about is where you are. Get your ass to the horse stables before I think of something else for the two of you to do. And you, if you can't work, I'll find something else for you. Atkins told me to keep a close eye on you."

"No, sir, I can work," Jake said.

The guard leaned into them. "Then move."

Henry looked up as Jake and Bee Dee approached. He held a pitchfork. Sweat dripped down his face.

"What's the deal? I've been here by myself."

"Jake twisted his ankle," Bee Dee said.

"Hey." A stocky Hispanic man emerged from the barn leading a white mare. He handed the rope to Henry, who dropped his pitchfork, which made the horse snap back its head and neck, mane quivering in protest.

"You're late," the man said, voice heavily accented. "You want for me to call the guards?"

"He hurt his ankle."

The man made clucking and clicking noises with his tongue and slapped the horse's back end to get it to move out of the way. Henry led it to where another horse and a mule had been tied to a zip line strung between two trees.

The man turned his attention to Jake. "Who're you?"

"Jake."

"Okay, Yake, you come with me."

"No, it's Jake."

"That's what I say, Yake."

"Jake," he said, emphasizing the "J."

"You make the fun of De la Cruz? You want for me to call the guards?"

"No, sir."

Jake followed the man into the barn. The stalls were empty but for one containing a donkey. As they passed the animal stuck its head over its stall door and brayed, causing Jake to jump backward. He turned and looked out the barn door, half expecting to see guards thundering down the footpath like an angry mob.

"Hey? What's with the standing around?" De la Cruz waited by an open door just past the last stall on the left. Stepping inside the room Jake saw pitchforks and shovels neatly arranged on the wall along with ropes and halters. Saddles straddled sawhorses and two wheelbarrows were leaned up against the wall. Each showed patches of rust.

"You ever clean horseshit, Yake?"

"No, sir."

De la Cruz rolled his eyes and gave a dramatic sigh, speaking in Spanish. Jake couldn't understand the words, but the gestures were clear enough. "Come on. Come on," he said. "You grab a pitch-fork."

Jake took one from the wall, grimacing when the wooden handle pressed against his palm.

De la Cruz noticed. "*Aqui, aqui,*" he said indicating he wanted to see the palms of Jake's hands.

Jake shook his head, not wanting the man to send him back to the Administration Building. "It's all right."

But De la Cruz insisted, and when Jake opened his fingers the man grimaced and shook his head. This resulted in another flurry of gestures and a string of Spanish and ended with De la Cruz motioning for Jake to follow him. At the back of the room the man lifted the lid on a green tin and scooped out a gob of copper-colored gel with his index and middle fingers.

"Give me your hands." Jake resisted. "Give me your hands, Yake."

Jake reluctantly held out his left hand and De la Cruz slathered the goo across his palm. Whatever it was, it had an antiseptic smell and accompanying burn that made Jake grimace in pain. De la Cruz had no sympathy for him, scooping out another gob.

Jake shook his head. "No. No way."

"You want the infection, Yake? Huh? You want the fever? You working with horseshit here."

Jake held out his other hand and De la Cruz smothered it, bringing the same stinging pain. As Jake paced the room, grimacing and grunting, De la Cruz replaced the top on the tin and pulled large hunks of cotton off of blue backing. He used tape to wrap Jake's hands. Then he gave Jake gardening gloves. "Now you clean the shit."

For the next twenty minutes Jake and Bee Dee used the pitchforks to scoop urine-saturated hay and sawdust, and green-and-black clumps of horseshit into the wheelbarrows. The bandages and gloves helped but did not completely ease the pain. Neither Jake nor Bee Dee said much, but Henry spoke enough for all three of them, jabbering on with an incessant chatter. Jake would occasionally catch Bee Dee's eyes wandering to the footpath and his eyes, too, were drawn to it.

When they had filled their wheelbarrows Jake and Bee Dee pushed them to a massive compost pile buzzing with flies.

"What do they do with all this shit anyway?" Jake asked as they upended the wheelbarrows.

"I think they mix it with the compost and make fertilizer."

"For what?"

Henry shrugged. "The garden, I guess."

After dumping the wheelbarrows they filled them with clean sawdust from a large mound kept in a lean-to behind the barn and spread the flakes in the stalls.

"When do we get to ride the horses?" Jake asked, spreading the sawdust in one of the stalls.

Henry laughed. "What, did you see that in one of the brochures or something? We don't. Only the guards ride them."

"What do the guards need horses for around here?"

"Not for around here," but before Henry could finish his answer a siren blared, causing the horses to spook and the donkey to bray.

Bee Dee looked to Jake. The guards had found T-Mac and Big Baby.

* * *

In a wide-brimmed hat, sunglasses, and his khaki shirt and shorts Captain Overbay looked like a weekend hiker. He tilted back his head as he pulled a red bandanna from his back pocket, wiping the back of his neck and brow and dabbing at his chest.

"No one saw a thing." He smiled, gave a sort of chuckle. "I find that absolutely remarkable."

Jake and the other inmates, twenty-three in all, stood in silence. The guards had directed them into three rows, two rows of eight and one row of seven. In their red coveralls Jake imagined they looked like a captured British regiment in the American Revolution. It very much felt like a firing squad, and Jake kept waiting for someone to point him out as the perpetrator of the horrific crimes that had broken the captain's precious rules. He doubted the captain gave a rat's ass about Big Baby or T-Mac and suspected that what was really bothering him was that someone had broken one of those rules. "A violent act against another inmate is grounds for punishment," he'd said, but only if the captain could identify the perpetrator, and he couldn't do that with no one saying they'd seen anything. Jake sensed beneath the calm exterior the captain was doing a slow burn.

"Inmate Stand-up?"

The first bullet struck. "Yes, Captain."

"Step forward."

Jake did as instructed. The captain approached, close enough for Jake to detect the bitter smell of coffee on the man's breath. "Officer Babcock tells me he saw you and Inmate Wells walking down the trail to the stables this morning at a peculiar time. He said you were late."

"Yes, Captain."

"Yes, Captain what?"

"Yes, Captain, sir."

A few standing in line snickered but if the captain heard it he did a good job ignoring it. He removed his glasses and vigorously cleaned the lenses with the red bandanna, holding them up to the sun for further inspection. "I meant, Inmate Stand-up, is it true that you and Inmate Wells were late getting to your assigned chores?"

"Oh. Yes, Captain, I was. We were."

Overbay leaned in. As unnerving as it was to see himself in the reflection of the captain's glasses, Jake found it worse to be staring into the man's beady, almost translucent blue eyes. "And why is that?"

"I hurt my ankle, sir."

"And you wouldn't know anything about the assault on inmates McCarthy or Shelton?"

"Who, sir?"

"T-Mac and Big Baby."

"Someone assaulted them, sir?"

Overbay pursed his lips. "So you know nothing about it?"

"No, sir, Captain. Maybe it was one of the guards."

Overbay made a noise, air pressing between the gap in his two front teeth. His tongue ran along his uppers as one might after a good polishing at the dentist's office. "Watch your mouth, boy."

"Yes, sir, Captain."

"Step back."

Jake did and Overbay stepped down the line. "Interesting." He stopped in front of Bee Dee. "And you, Inmate Wells, you have no information on this assault either?"

"No, sir, Captain."

"And the reason *you* were tardy?"

"I was helping Jake," he said.

Overbay replaced his glasses. As he did, the front gates parted and two ambulances pulled into the yard, the sun reflecting sharply off their windshields and causing everyone to raise an arm to deflect the glare. They stopped in front of the Administration Building, which also housed the Fresh Start hospital, a generous word for a room with a first aid kit. The blinding sun made it hard to even see the vehicles but they all watched as paramedics exited and removed gurneys from the back, setting them on the ground and snapping them up before wheeling them through a side door of the building.

"As of this moment," Overbay said, dwarfed between two guards, "all weekend privileges are suspended." Overbay turned to the guard who had accosted Jake and Bee Dee on the trail. "Officer

Babcock, I believe that exercise is good for the soul, that it stimu-
lates the mind and the memory. See if a good run might jog any of
their recollections."

"Yes, sir, Captain Overbay."

"Upon your return you shall complete your chores," Overbay
said. "Then you shall remain in your dormitories. The cafeteria
will be closed for lunch. If I receive no further information on the
assault it shall remain closed for dinner. However, should any of
you recall something while on your run, perhaps decide you did see
something and decide to come forward, I may reconsider my decision." Overbay spun and strode across the yard.

"Fall in line, single file." The guard led them past the ambulances to the front gate where two other guards took up positions,
one on each side of the line. As they waited for the gates to reopen,
Jake watched the paramedics wheel out the first of the gurney. Big
Baby had his eyes closed, a bloodied bandage about his head. As
Jake suspected, Overbay passed without even a pause to consider
Big Baby's condition. The paramedics pushed the gurney into the
back of the ambulance, the legs collapsing automatically. T-Mac
followed on the second stretcher, in much the same condition.
Once loaded, the two ambulances departed the yard together and
as they left Jake noticed smiles on the faces of the inmates standing in line, everyone but Bee Dee and T.J. They knew better than
to smile, or to feel any sense of relief. Big Baby and T-Mac would
be back, sometime, and there would be no place for them to run
or to hide.

KNOCK-ME-STIFF RANCH
GOLD CREEK, CALIFORNIA

Sloane spent the better part of the afternoon at the table in the
bunkhouse, reading through the stacks of articles provided by Alex.
Victor Dillon had, as Rizek stated, spent his formative years in the
California Juvenile Detention System and likely would have continued on to the California Penal System but for a local real estate
developer who saw potential in the boy.

"He worked at a company called PFI, Property Foreclosures, Inc.," Sloane said. Molia sat across the table, reviewing other documents and Alex was live on Sloane's computer screen. Bennett, who was turning out to be a jack-of-all-trades, had hooked up a camera that allowed them to see Alex on Camano Island while talking to her over the Internet on a Skype line. "It says here," Sloane said, reading from an article, "that he showed an adept skill at buying foreclosed properties in depressed areas, fixing them up, and flipping them for a profit. At some point he made enough money for a down payment to buy the Gold Rush Brewery, turning what had been a declining business into one of the larger and more profitable microbreweries in the United States."

The article indicated that rather than compete with the mass-market breweries like Coors and Budweiser, Dillon took advantage of the growing popularity of microbrews and brought in a brewmaster to create the brewery's signature cask ale, Gold Rush Pale Ale. It did well enough that Dillon produced six other lagers by the end of the 1980s. As the business succeeded he began buying property to plant and grow the brewery's own hops, which were used to create Gold Rush's signature ales and sold and distributed around the world.

"He owns a web of limited liability companies in a wide array of businesses," Alex said. Her picture was slightly distorted, and there seemed to be a delay between when her lips moved and when her voice came through the computer speaker, like a Japanese B-movie. "Most are related to his brewery: commercial trucking lines, a beer distribution company, a company for his hops operations. He also has a real estate company that's taking advantage of California's financial crises, buying large chunks of land from the government, most in the general area around Fresh Start."

"What's he doing with it?" Molia asked.

"Growing his hops, apparently. From what I read it's the right climate and latitude—lots of sun, dry soil, temperature in the 80s and 90s in the summer and plenty of water from nearby streams and rivers."

"So he's a true rags-to-riches story?" Sloane asked.

"That's certainly the facade," she said. "Almost seems too good to be true, doesn't it?"

"Sort of like Truluck," Molia said.

"Something set off your radar?" Sloane asked.

"Nothing major," Alex said. "But I got ahold of PFI's corporate tax returns and I'm a bit confused. The business reported substantial losses during the four years *prior* to Dillon's purchasing the brewery."

"Wouldn't be the first time a company cooked the books to reduce its income on paper and reduce its tax exposure," Sloane said.

"Maybe. Except the company was taking tax write-offs for selling the homes it purchased in foreclosure."

"I thought the articles I read said he flipped the houses for a profit?"

"They do, but the returns don't bear that out."

"Which raises the question," Molia said, "where did he get the money for the down payment to buy the brewery?"

A light went on for Sloane. "Let me guess. Dillon took out a loan."

"Nearly two million dollars," Alex said, smiling.

"And the loan came from none other than Winchester First Street Bank."

"Bingo."

"Awful cozy," Molia said.

Sloane considered the information. "Have you found out anything more about it?"

"I'm working on it," she said. "The bank manager is being pissy."

Molia leaned in so that his face would be in front of the camera. "What about On-Guard? Did you find anything on them?"

"I'll send you the paperwork in a minute, but I think you're going to like this answer, too. It's a complicated setup, sophisticated, but when you cut through all the layers On-Guard is another one of Victor Dillon's limited liability companies."

"So Victor Dillon's security company is guarding a building that's owned by Judge Earl," Molia said. "This just keeps getting more and more incestuous, doesn't it?" He grabbed his windbreaker and started for the door.

"Where are you going?" Sloane asked.

"To borrow Bennett's truck and a video camera with a zoom lens."

"What for?"

"I get antsy reading this much. My puny brain can't handle all these numbers. I'm going to do what I do best, and leave the two of you to do what you do best."

FRESH START YOUTH TRAINING FACILITY

SIERRA NEVADA MOUNTAINS

After returning from their forced run, a distance Jake estimated to be three miles, the guards confined them to their dormitories. Jake went with Bee Dee, T.J., and Henry to their dorm, and the guard didn't do anything to stop him. Once inside he expected the others to begin moaning and groaning about the unfair turn of events, but to his surprise they lay down on their beds smiling and looking relaxed for the first time since he had arrived. And that's when he realized it.

Nobody was going to say a word.

As upset as they might have been about the run and the loss of their weekend privileges, and the canceled meals, it was worth it to them to have a weekend free of T-Mac and Big Baby. But it was more than that. Jake suspected they were taking silent pleasure in the knowledge that someone had given both a big dose of their own medicine, knocked them out cold.

And that realization spawned another. The others had to know Jake did it. They didn't *know* it, know it—not in a sense that they had personally seen or heard anything, but they knew it. Captain Overbay had pretty much confirmed it for them when he called Jake out of line. That was the reason for their wry smiles and subtle nods, and why no one asked him any questions. If they didn't *know* anything, even if they really did, then they couldn't be forced to say anything, no matter what further punishment the captain might have in store. They were protecting Jake.

Their revelry lasted exactly two hours before the siren sounded and Overbay had the guards reassemble them. Overbay asked if anyone would like to come forward with any information, telling them there was still time to open the cafeteria for dinner. When no one did, he ordered them to spend the remainder of the afternoon working in the hot sun. Before dismissing them, however, he called out the names of three inmates and asked that the guards bring them to the Administration Building.

So would begin the Grand Inquisition.

The guards led the rest of them to a rectangular patch of dirt staked out near the camp garden, handed them garden hoes, pickaxes, and wheelbarrows and informed them that their job was to rid the soil of rocks, some as big as basketballs when they were finally unearthed. Throughout the afternoon, the guards continued to pull inmates off the project, presumably to be interrogated.

Bee Dee and Jake worked as a team, loading the unearthed rocks into wheelbarrows and dumping them on an accumulating pile. Jake kept an eye on the guards, waiting until they became disengaged, as bored with the task as the inmates. Then he asked Bee Dee the question that had been bothering him most since he heard the siren signaling that the guards had found T-Mac and Big Baby.

"Why haven't they said anything? Do you think maybe they don't remember?"

Bee Dee continued to toss rocks into the wheelbarrow, each hitting the metal sides with a clang. "They remember. They remember exactly what happened."

Jake wiped the sweat from his brow with his sleeve. "Maybe they're afraid we'll turn them in for what they were trying to do to T.J."

Bee Dee used a pickax to unearth a reluctant rock. "I told you, Big Baby is a psychopath and T-Mac isn't far behind. They're not afraid of us saying anything about that because they're not afraid of being caught. Their minds don't work that way. They don't have that thing, that, whatever it's called that makes people not do stuff."

"What?" Jake asked.

"That thing that makes us not do certain things."

"A governor," Jake said.

Bee Dee scowled. "A what?"

David used the term. He said everyone had a governor, that tiny voice that told us right from wrong. "A conscience."

Bee Dee nodded. "Right."

"Okay, but that still doesn't explain why they aren't saying anything?"

Bee Dee stopped digging. The visible portion of the rock indicated it to be at least the size of a small coconut. "Because if they said something, Overbay would have to ship you and me and T.J. out of here, that's why. That's the rule; you assault another inmate and you're gone. Captain wouldn't have a choice. He can't hide this one. Why do you think it took so long for the ambulances to get here?"

Jake hadn't thought about it. "I don't know."

"Because once they had to call the paramedics, get others from outside involved, they couldn't make up some bullshit story like they usually do—'Oh, he just fell down and hit his head.' Maybe one fell. But two? The doctors would know; they'd know someone hit them both in the head with a rock. They can tell those things. So the captain had to tell it for real. That means enforcing the rules *if* he finds out who did it. He'd have to ship us out." Bee Dee began picking at the ground again. "Big Baby's a psycho, but he isn't stupid."

Jake felt his knees go weak with the implication.

"Big Baby's coming back," Bee Dee said, voicing it. "He's coming back eventually, and when he does, he intends to handle this on his own."

The guards called out three more names, including Bee Dee's. Bee Dee handed Jake the pickax and Jake watched him leave, disappearing up the path.

"Get back to work," one of the guards said.

Jake took a whack at the rock Bee Dee had been unearthing. Every swing made the blisters on his palms burn. Blood showed through the cotton and the tape strips. He straddled the rock and took a hard swipe, the pointed end of the pick digging underneath the rock. Since he couldn't use his hands to apply pressure, he leaned into the handle with his shoulder and drove forward with his legs, trying to free it. The handle flexed, then gave way and Jake sprawled onto the dirt.

"What are you doing?" a guard asked.

The handle had come out of the slot forged in the metal pick, which remained wedged beneath the boulder. "The handle broke."

"Get another one and get that out," the guard said.

Jake walked to a metal shed. Inside he found pallets of Miracle-Gro fertilizer, Epsom salts, and boxes of insect spray. Farther in he found boxes of rat poison, dozens of rolled-up black garden hoses and balls of brown coarse string, but no gardening tools. Exiting, he walked to the entrance of an adjacent glass building. A padlock hung open in the hook. Jake pushed the door in and entered, and came to a stop.

"Whoa." Row after row of plants in different stages of growth, from seedlings to a foot tall sprouted in rich dark soil.

"What are you doing in here?" Jake wheeled at the question. A guard stood at the entrance, hands on hips. "I asked, what do you think you're doing in here?"

Jake held up the pick handle. "It broke. I was told to get a new one."

"You're not allowed in here. You need another tool, you ask for one."

"I did." Jake caught himself. "I'm sorry, sir. I didn't know."

The guard stepped closer. "You better learn to respect the rules around here," he said. "Now get the hell out."

SEVENTEEN

T om Molia sipped at the cold remnants of his coffee. When he had bought it, at the crack of dawn, he'd damn near burned his lips with the first sip, and he was still spitting pieces of dead skin peeling off the roof of his mouth. He'd maintained his vigil all night, taking breaks only to relieve his bladder and to get the cup of coffee when daylight slowly crept up the street, pushing back the shadows and the morning chill.

The security guard on duty when Molia had arrived at the Sutter Building was relieved at midnight, confirming twenty-four-hour security. If the guards worked eight-hour shifts, the graveyard would end in roughly fewer than seven minutes. Molia only had to wait two minutes to confirm his deduction. A car turned into the parking lot adjacent to the building, parked next to the car the guard drove in at midnight, and the relief guard got out.

"I love it when I'm right," Molia said, waiting for the guard to walk toward the entrance before exiting Dave Bennett's truck.

The temperature had warmed with the rising sun, but Molia still felt a chill in his bones from sitting through the night. He wasn't as young as he'd been when he'd started his career. Back then he could do a ten hour shift, get off duty, lift weights for two more hours, and get home to make love to Maggie after she got the kids out the door to school. The thought of her made him melancholy, but he pushed those feelings aside, slowing his pace to time his approach with the relief guard's arrival at the front door. He didn't try to hide Bennett's video camera. To the contrary, he brought it up and flipped open the side panel, stopping to film the stone building, which caused the guard to stop and consider him.

Molia lowered the camera. "Is it okay? I just love these old buildings; you don't see many like this where I'm from."

"Knock yourself out." The relief guard tapped a key on the glass and waited for the guard in the lobby to gather his things.

Molia panned up and down the building, zooming in and out, catching the guard looking back over his shoulder. "If you really like old buildings you should drive into Old Town." The man pointed. "Just down the bottom of the hill."

"I read about it in the brochure," Molia said. "That's where I was headed when I saw the placard and figured I'd stop and have a look-see."

"That's the original Winchester," the man said. "They got all kinds of old buildings down there."

"Well I am itching to see them, too," Molia said.

The guard arched his eyebrow as the guard inside unlocked the door. He considered Molia before handing his relief the key, just as the first guard had done when he'd arrived at midnight.

By the time Molia returned to Dave Bennett's truck the relief guard had taken up his spot at the desk, where he would remain for the next eight hours. He would get up to stretch the boredom and fatigue from his muscles and maybe once or twice to use the bathroom around the corner from the elevator doors that never opened, but he would not use the elevator. He would not open the door to the stairwell to the second floor. He'd never make rounds inside or outside the building. There was no need. The lack of cars in the parking lot was the final bit of information Molia needed to confirm that, on a Monday morning, nobody was coming to work in the Sutter Building.

Whatever line of business Trinity Investments was in, it didn't require manual labor.

WINCHESTER COUNTY COURTHOUSE
CLERK'S OFFICE
WINCHESTER, CALIFORNIA

Sloane had Dave Bennett call Eileen Harper to give her a heads-up, not wanting to startle her. Still he had to give Harper credit for her acting skills. Though Harper had to be nervous, she didn't show it when Sloane walked into the clerk's office bright and early Monday morning. She just continued going on about her work. The morning light from one of three arched windows spilled across her desk, though it did not yet reach the counter where Sloane awaited assistance.

Sloane had debated the consequences of what he was about to do. It wasn't exactly subtle, as he and Molia discussed, but subtle wasn't his nature. He wanted Boykin, and whoever else was involved, to know that if they messed with Jake, Sloane would push even harder to find out all their dirty little secrets. And he hoped that would draw their attention from Jake to him.

As with every other county in the state, and likely the country, the Winchester County Courthouse records and files were accessible online; the legislatures required it, and the courthouses, even the historic ones, were obligated to comply. Sloane had gone online first thing that morning, printed the request slips, and filled in the case numbers for the files he wanted to review, and he had a hunch it would set off a few alarms, no matter how quietly he went about it. Evelyn Newcomber met him across the polished oak counter. In her midfifties, Newcomber looked to have a flare for the dramatic with long painted fingernails, purple this morning with a blue crescent moon, and colorful bead necklaces. "Mr. Sloane, you're back," she said, a touch of surprise in her voice.

Sloane acknowledged the smile. "Actually, I never left; stayed the whole weekend right here in Winchester County."

She glanced at the sheets of paper. "Are you filing something this morning?"

"Not this morning. This morning I'm looking to review a couple of files." He handed her the request forms, and she separated them on the counter.

"These are closed files. They'll be in storage. It could take some time for me to have them pulled."

"I'll wait," Sloane said.

"Might take some time," she repeated. "Why don't you leave a number and I'll call when they're ready."

"I have no place else I need to be," Sloane said.

"I can get them." Eileen Harper approached the counter, her voice even. "I'm not busy this morning; I can pull them for you."

Newcomber's smile soured, but with Sloane waiting she couldn't very well tell Harper to mind her own business. "Thank you, Eileen." She handed Harper the request slips without further comment. "You can take a seat," she said to Sloane, pointing to a wood-slat bench against a wall lined with a series of black-and-white period photographs depicting the clerk's office through the years. Sloane considered them, though the photographs weren't his interest. The light through the arched windows reflected in the glass covering the photographs in such a way that he could see the workspace behind the counter. Newcomber made busywork for a bit, moving a few piles around her desk as if attending to matters. Then she picked up the phone, turning her back to Sloane. It wasn't long after she'd hung up that Archibald Pike walked in, glanced in Newcomber's direction, and approached where Sloane waited.

"Mr. Sloane." Pike tried to act surprised, but he was not nearly as competent an actor as Eileen Harper. "Are you filing additional pleadings?"

Sloane shook his head. "Not here," he said, the implication being something would be filed that morning with the Third District Court of Appeal in Sacramento. Sloane offered nothing further, which allowed for an awkward pause. Silence unnerved most people, especially people seeking information. Pike hadn't come to shoot the breeze.

"So then what brings you back?" Pike asked.

"Just interested in reviewing a couple of files." The paddle fans rotated slowly overhead.

Pike waited. When Sloane didn't add anything he said, "A couple of files?"

Sloane nodded. "That's right."

Pike cleared his throat. "I've, uh, been here a long time. Perhaps I can help. Is there some file in particular you're interested in."

"Small town?" Sloane said.

"Small town," Pike agreed.

Sloane waited, as if giving the offer due consideration. "I don't want to trouble you."

"No trouble."

"It's probably a more appropriate discussion to have with the city attorney anyway. They're civil matters."

"Not much passes through here I don't know about," Pike reiterated. "Civil and criminal."

"Well, since you offered. I'm interested in a lawsuit filed by a contractor." Sloane opened a folder and pretended to search for the name. "Tom Goode Construction. He sued the county over the build-out of the Fresh Start facility."

"That's right. What's your interest in that case?"

"You're familiar with it?"

"Some."

"I read an article in the archives that Goode sued the county for cost overruns and received one point five million dollars, I believe."

"I don't recall the dollar amount," Pike said.

"I'm looking for the city attorney's motion to disqualify Judge Boykin."

The arrow hit its mark. Pike flinched. "Why, why would the city attorney have sought to disqualify Judge Boykin?"

"So it was Judge Boykin who tried that case? The article didn't say."

Pike pinched his lips.

"Tom Goode Construction was the contractor on the remodel of the judge's home." Sloane had started his morning at the Winchester County Building Department.

Pike smiled but disbelief crept into his voice. "Remodel? The judge's house?"

"Goode's name is on the set of construction drawings at the building department. I didn't see any permits actually pulled for that work, though. Did the judge have his home remodeled?"

Pike shaded red. "I really wouldn't know."

"No? Small town and all?"

"He may have. I think he started the process. I don't know."

"Well, I would think that would be a conflict, wouldn't you?"

"Unless the city attorney didn't see it that way, as a conflict I mean; he might not have. Judge Boykin knows a lot of people. If he was challenged each time he knew a party or witness he'd be sitting on the sidelines more than on the bench."

"But he wasn't on the sidelines for the lawsuit by the Estate of John Wainwright." Pike looked like he was shitting a brick. "He did sit on that case, didn't he?" Sloane asked.

"I'm afraid I'm not following you; what is it about *that* file you're interested in?"

"Same thing, motion to disqualify."

"And the basis for a disqualification in that case would have been what?"

"The defendant was Winchester First Street Bank."

"I understand that."

"Judge Boykin sits on the bank's board of directors." Sloane paused to allow for the figurative "thud." *Thank you, Alex.*

Pike started to reply, but Eileen Harper returned carrying two bulging files. She put them on the counter, calm and professional as ever. "You can't remove them but I can provide you with a desk while you review them," she said.

Sloane hadn't taken his eyes off Archibald Pike. "That's okay," he said. "I think I have all the answers I need. The prosecutor might want to review them, though."

FRESH START YOUTH TRAINING FACILITY
SIERRA NEVADA MOUNTAINS

Jake set his tray down and sat across from Bee Dee, Henry, and T.J., all of whom were moving slowly and looked a bit worse for wear this morning. Dirt caked their hands and forearms, and blackened their fingernails. With the morning light at their backs they looked like construction workers getting ready to start their shift. The guards had worked them until ten minutes before lights-out Saturday night, got them up early Sunday, and continued the labor camp. They gave them little to eat and did not allow them to shower or to brush their teeth, at night. They marched them straight to their dorms. Henry told him Overbay couldn't work them Monday because of the teachers and counselors.

Now they all sat trying to wake up. Only Henry was eating, stabbing at his pancakes and making short work of sausage links.

"What do you know about the greenhouse?" Jake asked as Henry shoved a large wedge of pancake dripping with maple syrup into his mouth.

"It's restricted. You can't go in," he mumbled, jaws working overtime.

"I did."

Henry stopped chewing. "They lock it," he said, which came out sounding like, "They wock it."

"The door was unlocked. I broke my pick and was looking for another one."

Henry drank milk and swallowed with effort. "What's in there?"

Jake shrugged. "Plants. Lots of them."

T.J. shrugged fatigue from his shoulders and joined the conversation. "So why do they lock it?"

"That's that I'm wondering," Jake said.

Henry used the final wedge of pancake to mop up what was left of the syrup. "I don't know." He stabbed his fork at the second of T.J.'s pancakes. "Are you going to eat that?" T.J. slid his plate to the side.

"They have a bunch of string, too."

Henry nodded. "They use it for the hops," he said, rolling the pancake into a burrito and eating it with his hands.

"What are hops?" Jake asked.

"It's a plant. They use them to make beer. I've seen 'em before. They grow on the string like a vine. They grow them up in the mountains. They make us work up there."

"When do they do that?" Jake asked.

"They plant in April or May and go through the summer. That's when they cut down the vines, like August or September. The brewery uses the hops to make its beer. The guards pick kids out and take them up there. It's in the brochures. They call it outdoor education and make it look like you're learning all these cool survival skills, but it's all bullshit. The kids in the brochures are actors. They make us work."

"Have you ever been?" Jake asked.

"Once. And it sucked big time."

"Is that what they use the horses and donkeys for?" Jake asked.

Henry nodded. "They have to pack everything in. They drive you in the bus as far as they can. Then they make you hike the rest of the way. That sucks big time, too. They fit you with these heavy packs and it's steep as hell."

The first bell rang, signaling the end of breakfast. They had fifteen minutes to get their rooms straightened for inspection and to brush their teeth before the second bell, a five-minute warning to get to class. Henry folded the remainder of T.J.'s pancake around another sausage link and shoved it in his mouth in two bites.

When Jake stood to clean his plate T.J. asked, "Have you heard anything?" T.J. had asked him the same question five times over the weekend. Jake hadn't told him what Bee Dee had said, that Big Baby and T-Mac had likely kept their mouths shut because they wanted an opportunity to get even.

"Nothing." Jake put his tray with plate and utensils on the conveyor belt, and it rolled through the window into the washroom.

"So we're good then," T.J. said, following Jake and Bee Dee to the exit. "If nobody has said anything by now, they're probably not going to, don't you think?"

"Probably not," Jake said, glancing back to reassure him and nearly running into the back side of Bee Dee, who had come to an abrupt halt just outside the mess hall.

Atkins had stepped into their path. "Well, look what we have here. Inmate Stand-up, have you made yourself some friends over the weekend?"

Jake didn't answer.

Atkins leaned forward. "I heard about what happened." The smile vanished. "Don't think for a minute I don't know who was behind it."

"I don't know what you're talking about, sir."

Atkins smiled. "That's what I heard everyone was saying this weekend. But you do . . . You know."

"No, sir."

"We're going to find out. Tomorrow we're going hiking again, and this time it's not going to be just a day hike. We're going overnight, Stand-up. And we're taking your newfound friends with us. I think you're going to really enjoy it. You might even remember some of those things you seem to have forgotten."

WINCHESTER SUPERIOR COURT
JUDGE EARL BOYKIN'S CHAMBERS

Archibald Pike did the unthinkable. Then again, he wasn't really thinking. He flung open the door to Judge Boykin's chambers and entered without even a courtesy knock. Carl Wade sat in one of the chairs across from Judge Boykin's desk. Hands in his lap, his wide-brimmed hat teetered on the edge of the judge's desk. Wade looked as relaxed as a southern gentleman whittling wood on a hot summer day.

"Where's Judge Earl?" Pike asked.

Wade pointed a finger from his lap. "Still on the bench, I guess."

Pike considered his pocket watch, snapped it shut. An awkward silence ensued. "Do you have a meeting with the judge?" he asked.

Wade shrugged. "Judge asked me to be here at eleven. So here I sit. Something wrong? You look like you saw the courthouse ghost."

"No, nothing."

"You going to close the door?"

Pike shut the door and stepped farther in. Four generations of Boykins stared at him with eyes as dark as a crow's. The black-and-white portraits hung in succession, starting with great-grandfather Earl, and they always gave Pike the willies. The family resemblance was truly remarkable, especially the eyes, cold and dark. Pike wandered to the second chair, pulled out his pocket watch, and reconsidered it.

"Something on your mind, Archie?"

Pike did not appreciate the nickname, but he'd given up reminding Wade. "I need to talk to the judge."

"What about?"

"Private matter; you wouldn't be interested."

The interior door opened. Judge Earl bounded to his desk, black robe unzipped, pausing when he saw Pike. Boykin dropped a file with a thud, shrugged from his robe, and flung it onto his chair. The robe hid much of the man's girth. Without it, his barrel chest and belly were on full display beneath a white, short-sleeve shirt and paisley tie.

"Did we have an appointment?" Boykin asked.

Pike looked to Wade. Boykin raised a hand, motioning for him to get on with it while keeping busy at his desk. Wade smiled.

"Sloane came back. He was in the clerk's office this morning. Evelyn let me know."

"Filing more pleadings was he?" Boykin asked, sounding unconcerned.

"Having files pulled." Pike again looked to Wade, but Boykin offered no further explanation for Wade's presence, and the severe look on his face, like the faces in the pictures on the wall, did not invite further inquiry.

"He asked for the Tom Goode file, the one for the cost overruns at Fresh Start. He said he wanted to see the motion to disqualify filed by the city attorney."

"There was no motion," Boykin said, sifting through papers.

"That was his point."

Boykin stopped moving the pile. "What else did he say?"

"He said Goode did a remodel of your home, that he'd checked the plans at the building department. Did you remodel your home?"

Boykin ran a finger across his lips. The window at his back created a rectangle of light on the carpet. "What other files did he ask to see?"

"The Wainwright file. For the same reason, to see whether the city attorney had filed a motion to disqualify you because you sit on First Street's board of directors."

Boykin cleared his throat. "Thank you for the information, Archibald. If you hear anything else, keep me advised."

Pike didn't move at first, then realized he'd been dismissed. After Pike had closed the door Boykin directed his comments to Wade. "Carrie at the bank called yesterday afternoon. She said a bank examiner has been asking for some of my loan documentation."

"You think it's Sloane?" Wade asked.

"She said it was a woman; probably someone working for Sloane though. Too big a coincidence."

Wade asked, "How do you want to handle it?"

"It appears that Mr. Sloane is having a hard time getting the message."

"You want me to get ahold of Atkins again?"

"We need to send Mr. Sloane a more direct message. One that ensures he knows there are consequences to his actions."

"What did you have in mind?"

"I don't have anything in mind. Let Dillon know. That's his arena. But tell him I want this handled in a way that does not come back to bite me in the ass. Tell him that if it does, I'm going to take a much bigger chunk out of his ass. Tell him I want it made clear to Mr. Sloane, and to the detective, that I don't appreciate people looking into my private matters, that their two boys aren't the only ones who might find themselves in a dung heap of trouble."

KNOCK-ME-STIFF RANCH
GOLD CREEK, CALIFORNIA

Monday night Dave Bennett brought Molia and Sloane Tupperware filled with diced chicken sauteed with onions and peppers in a mole sauce, rice, beans, and warmed tortillas. Molia had taken an afternoon nap after his all-night vigil at the Sutter Building, but awoke at the smell of food. He sat at the table looking half asleep, dark bags under his eyes, hair unkempt. Sloane was glad the bunkhouse didn't have a mirror. He knew he didn't look much better. The stress was wearing on both of them physically as well as mentally.

Molia filled one of the tortillas and rolled it like a cigar, eating it with his hands as gusts of wind continued to shake the bunkhouse and whistle through the unfilled cracks in the knotted pine. The windows rattled so hard Sloane half expected them to blow out, frame and all. "This whole place might explode if we don't open the doors and give the wind a place to pass through," Molia said, only half joking.

The gusts had begun late in the afternoon, rolling over the hills and across the valley, at times sounding like a high-speed train. Sloane had papers strewn across the worktable, reading with the aid of the two camp lights.

"What did I miss?" Molia asked.

Sloane picked up his legal pad, reviewing his notes. He'd written the names of Judge Earl Boykin and Victor Dillon on the page along with First Street, and the Sutter Building and drew lines between them each time he found an interconnecting thread.

"Boykin takes a loan from the bank on whose board he sits as a director, ostensibly to remodel his home. He even goes so far as to get a set of construction drawings drawn up, though the contractor never pulled any permits and the work never actually happens."

"So he pockets the eight hundred and fifty thousand?" Molia asked, wiping the corners of his mouth with a napkin. "How does the bank reconcile that?"

"Federal regulators frown on banks giving away money," Sloane agreed.

"So what? Boykin takes out the one-point-five-million-dollar loan to cover the eight hundred and fifty thousand? He's got the same problem, only bigger."

"Which Alex thinks means Judge Earl has to have another income stream he's using to pay off the loans."

"He's playing a shell game."

"In essence."

"Dillon?"

"Seems the logical choice, doesn't it? Or maybe it's this guy Tom Goode." Sloane flipped the notepad so Molia could see as he spoke. "Goode got the contract to build out Fresh Start and was paid with county funds. That wasn't a coincidence. After he finishes he manufactures two point five million in cost overruns and bills the city. When the city balks, Goode takes them to court, Judge Earl gets the case assigned to him and eventually negotiates a settlement, which just so happens to be one point five million. Only maybe the money doesn't go to Goode," Sloane said drawing a line between $1.5 million and Boykin. "Maybe it goes to Judge Earl to use to repay the loans to the bank."

"He's washing the money?"

Sloane didn't know. "Alex can't say yet. But if Judge Earl is willing to fix a case, what's to keep him from ensuring Fresh Start remains full?"

"So maybe we're not as dumb as we look," Molia said. "So then what's Dillon's motivation? All indications are he has more money than God."

"Maybe he doesn't have the money he acts like he has. Maybe it's one of those paper tiger things. Maybe the image is a facade. Maybe he needs a steady income stream from Fresh Start to keep the brewery afloat."

"Which brings us to Trinity Investments," Molia said.

Sloane moved one of the camp lights from a stack of papers Alex had sent that afternoon. What she'd found out about Trinity added to the intrigue. "Trinity was set up as an offshore investment company in Aruba."

"Aruba, the banking capital of the world," Molia joked.

"It's for people trying to hide assets," Sloane said. "And Trinity has assets. She said its portfolio is nearly half a billion dollars."

Molia whistled. "Did you say half a *billion*?"

"Unfortunately the members of the limited liability company weren't identified on any documents she was able to find."

"So Dillon could be running one of those big Bernie Madoff ponzi schemes, and Judge Earl is in on it."

"It wouldn't surprise me if Judge Earl had his fingers in just about every pie in town," Sloane said.

Molia smiled. "Maybe that's what they're guarding in that building. Maybe that's where they keep the records of the investors and accounts."

"You might be right," Sloane said.

"Whatever is in there, it's on the second floor," Molia said.

"But as far as you can tell the security guards don't have a key?"

"Not to the elevator or to the stairwell," Molia said. "They share a single key to the front door."

"So even if we could get into the building somehow, there's no way to get up to the second floor."

"There's always a way," Molia said.

"Yeah? You gonna keep that canary in your mouth or share it?"

"I'll tell you when I get back from the head. But I'll give you a hint. You can get arrested for yelling it in a crowded theater."

Molia took one of the lanterns with him. He had to lean his shoulder into the back door to open it in the wind then hold it tight to keep it from slamming shut. He lowered his head, walking in the knee-high grass as it whipped and swayed. Despite the wind, the temperature had not dropped and Molia likened it to the inside of a convection oven.

The outhouse was built from the same blackened, knotted pine siding as the bunkhouse and sat atop two skids. Bennett had explained that when the Knock-Me-Stiff had been a functioning cattle ranch the building had to be moved when the hole in the ground reached capacity. Since no one had used the facility in years, that was no longer a problem. Still, Molia had visions of sitting down to do his business and having the wind propel the entire structure backward, like a runaway sled, with him inside.

The door opened outward, the only way it could given the dimensions inside the structure, perhaps three feet square with most of that taken up by an elevated box on which the toilet seat had been attached—Bennett called it "the shitter." It prevented the door from opening inward. Bennett had instructed them to add a scoop of lime from a sealed plastic container every other trip to aid the decomposition and keep the smell and flies down.

Molia held the edge of the door against the battering wind and used the lantern to check for spiders along the roof and walls and around the toilet seat. He didn't want to be sitting in the dark, thinking about things crawling up his leg or dropping on his head. When satisfied he wasn't about to sit on a tarantula, he maneuvered inside, pulled the door shut, and flipped the rectangular piece of wood that acted as both the handle and the lock.

Harper had fixed up the interior as best she could, hanging red and white curtains above the lone window on the back wall and putting a small vase of fake flowers on the shelf below it, beside extra rolls of toilet paper and an air freshener. Molia thought it like that old adage about putting lipstick on a pig. The moon, full but low in the sky, looked blurred through the old silica glass. Molia dropped his drawers and mooned the moon, smiling at the thought of it.

Sitting, he had little room between his knees and the door, so he set the lantern behind him on the shitter. The "rules" to the outhouse, typed up and slipped inside a piece of plastic, hung from a nail on the door. Being a guy and having brought nothing else to read, Molia read and reread the rules.

1. Use only as much toilet paper as you need.
2. When finished, apply one scoop of lime into the hole.
3. Make sure to reseal lime bag, as it will absorb moisture.
4. Lower the toilet seat lid.
5. Make sure handel to door to outhouse is turned to the left to keep door from blowing open and banging in wind.

The third time through he noticed the misspelled word.

"Handel," he said out loud.

The door rattled—a particularly strong gust followed by an odd thump, and for a moment Molia thought his premonition about being propelled backward across the yard might come true. Then he noticed the door had bowed inward an inch or two. When it did not self-correct he reached out, turned the rectangular piece of wood, and pushed. The door flexed but did not fly open, as he would have expected, given the howling wind. He leaned forward and shoved harder, feeling the resistance.

Standing, he pressed his shoulder against the wood but the door still did not budge.

That's when he smelled gasoline.

EIGHTEEN

True to his sadistic word, Atkins met them as they walked out of the building after their last class of the day. The other inmates gave the guard a wide berth. No such luck for Jake, T.J., Bee Dee, and Henry. Atkins wore his usual sunglasses and shit-eating grin, but the wide-brimmed cowboy hat was new.

"Time to load up, boys. Daylights burning, and we have miles to go before we sleep," he said.

Jake thought Atkins misquoting the American poet Robert Frost had to be a coincidence. He'd studied Frost that year in school, though it now seemed a lifetime ago. He couldn't imagine Atkins had ever cracked a book in his life, let alone read a poem.

Atkins accompanied them to their dorm and handed each a small sack, watching as they packed extra pairs of undershorts and T-shirts as well as their toothbrushes.

Outside, he escorted them down the footpath to the horse stables. De la Cruz had loaded two of the horses and was in the process of loading the obstinate donkey into the back of a white, four-horse trailer showing signs of rust. De la Cruz cursed the beast in Spanish when it failed to cooperate, and it stuck out its head and brayed its displeasure. As if in answer, the second donkey, still in the barn, brayed back. Atkins slapped the donkey hard on the ass and it trotted up the ramp and inside the trailer, its metal shoes thumping like someone beating the inside of a metal drum.

"Sometimes all a dumb animal knows is brute force," Atkins said, looking directly at Jake.

Atkins directed T.J. and Henry to get two bales of hay and two bales of straw from the barn and handed Jake and Bee Dee two long hooks with wood handles and instructed them to get on top of the horse trailer. When T.J. and Henry returned he instructed them to load the hay atop the trailer and they attempted to comply. They lifted the bales overhead, teetering off balance before righting. They dropped the first bale twice—before Atkins shoved them out of the way and lifted the bale overhead by himself, high enough for Jake and Bee Dee to reach over the side of the trailer and sink their hooks beneath the wires holding the bales in shape. Even then it was difficult to hoist the bale up onto the roof. When they had the second bale in place they secured both with netting.

After they had climbed down, De la Cruz instructed them to load the straw in the empty fourth stall inside the trailer. The horses continued stomping, and the donkey continued to bray. When they had finished De la Cruz closed the gate with a thud and flipped the handle but did not lock it. He climbed into the cab, and the engine started with a sputter of burned diesel before settling into a steady knocking.

Atkins directed them to follow the truck down a dirt road parallel to the back fence. They jogged to keep up, covering their mouths to keep from breathing the cloud of dust kicked up by the truck and trailer. De la Cruz parked beside the metal shed near the garden and Atkins put them to work hauling out supplies—stuff Jake had seen on his unauthorized visit—black gardening hoses and bags of fertilizer, boxes of insecticide and rat poison, the balls of string, and shovels and pickaxes. They loaded everything in the fourth stall with the bales of straw. When they had finished, shadows had inched up the sides of the mountains to the east, though the tops remained bathed in golden light. Atkins considered his watch but issued no further instructions. Bee Dee, T.J., and Henry stood in a line, holding their small bags, looking like runaways who'd reconsidered their decisions to leave home. After several minutes they all turned their heads to the familiar sound of gears grinding and an engine revving. The yellow bus came around a corner and made its way up the hill, spewing dust. It came to a stop behind the horse trailer. The doors folded back, opening, and T.J. started to step up, then lowered his leg and stepped away. Big Baby stepped down, filling the doorframe, shoulders so wide he had to turn sideways to fit. A white bandage remained wrapped around his head. He looked down at them with a strange sneer then jumped at them, causing all four to fall back, afraid.

"Look who's back," Atkins said with a big, phony grin. "You all remember Big Baby?" When no one responded Atkins said, "No? Because I'm certain Big Baby remembers all of you, don't you, Big Baby?"

"Yes, sir," Big Baby said, looking them over with his queer smile. "We're good friends."

Jake looked for T-Mac, but the bus was empty and he wondered if T-Mac's head injury had been more severe. Then again, Big Baby likely had less brains to injure.

"Well that's fine," Atkins said, looking at Jake. "Because when you boys get back I've arranged for all of you to spend a lot of time together. Day and night."

KNOCK-ME-STIFF RANCH
GOLD CREEK, CALIFORNIA

Sloane moved the lantern closer to the documents Alex had found on Trinity Investments. The light spilled over the pages and off the edge of the table but not far. The bunk beds in the corner remained in the shadows, like wooden beds in the bowel of a ship. He continued making notes, connecting threads and trying to find others. Victor Dillon's security company guarded the Sutter Building, which was owned, at least on paper, by the judge and his wife. Trinity Investments was an offshore investment company Dillon had some connection to, but what kind of investments remained a mystery. Judge Boykin had been instrumental in Dillon's limited liability company receiving the land grant to build the Fresh Start facility, then sat in judgment on the case brought by the contractor to recover the cost overruns, a tidy sum that just so happened to be the same amount as the loan Boykin took out from Winchester First Street Bank to purchase the Sutter Building. Boykin had also taken out a loan to have that same contractor remodel his home, which did not appear to have ever happened, and he was in a unique position to ensure that regular and long-term-paying occupants filled Fresh Start. The conflicts of interest were rampant, and it was all very interesting, but also all circumstantial. Sloane had tried enough cases to know circumstantial evidence wouldn't get him far in court and likely wouldn't frighten anyone, and it did absolutely nothing to get him any closer to rescuing Jake and T.J.

The thought of the boys made him think of Lisa Lynch and he decided to give his eyes a break and find out about the appeal.

Lynch answered on the third ring. "Your ears must have been burning. I was just about to call you. We got it filed late this afternoon, along with a motion that the hearing be expedited. We added an argument to have Jake and T.J. transferred to facilities closer to their homes as a fallback."

Sloane heard a tone in Lynch's voice he had not heard before, a lyrical flow to the words. "You sound almost optimistic?"

"I don't want to get your hopes up, but we may have actually caught our first break."

"Please, get my hopes up," he said. "I could use getting my hopes up."

"One of our newbies here, fresh out of McGeorge, did some of the research," she said. Sloane knew McGeorge to be the law school at the University of the Pacific in Stockton. "Her law school roommate got a judicial clerkship with the Third Circuit in Sacramento. She's going to see what she can do for us, try to get this a little extra attention."

"Hey, I'll take it," Sloane said as a shadow danced across the pages on the table.

"Can't hurt, right?"

"Can't hurt," he agreed. The shadows danced again. Distracted, Sloane turned to determine the source. He was about to turn back when the tip of a reddish orange flame snapped like the tail of a whip just outside the window.

Sloane dropped the phone and rushed over to see the outhouse engulfed in flames. Running, he pushed open the back door and started across the field, but as he approached a blast of heat caused him to retreat. Flames leapt into the sky, crackling and hissing and whipping in a demonic dance. Sloane could not get near the outhouse. He dashed back inside, pulled the sleeping bag off his bunk bed, and draped it over his head, trying again. Nearing the flames he saw a post propped up against the outhouse door, the other end wedged in the ground, but each time he took a step forward the flames forced him back.

Catching movement in the dark, Sloane turned to see Bennett and Harper rushing from the main house. Bennett carried two shovels and tossed one to Sloane, then commenced digging at the ground, uprooting the grass and tossing clods of dirt onto the fire. Sloane, too, dug in, the shovel blade grinding against the hard dirt and rocks, but when he tossed the first shovelful, the wind mocked him, catching the soil and blowing it back. He moved to the opposite side, digging and throwing at a frantic pace, advancing until close enough to kick the end of the post and knock it down. Too late. Flames had engulfed the entire structure, a virtual tinderbox. Bennett looked to have conceded the building, digging a semicircle to act as a firebreak to keep the flames from spreading.

Sloane grabbed his shoulder and shouted over the wind and roaring flames. "Molia's in there!" He pointed at the outhouse. "He's in there!"

Bennett's eyes widened and he dropped his shovel and took off, running back to the main house. Sloane recommenced digging, shoveling one scoop after the next, digging, shoveling, digging. His shoulders and forearms strained, and sweat cascaded down his face.

He heard an engine and looked up to see two cones of light bouncing violently across the field. Bennett slowed at the fire and used the blade on the front of the truck to advance. When the blade hit the outhouse, the structure collapsed like a house of cards. Bennett backed the truck up and advanced again, this time getting the edge of the blade under pieces of the burning wood pile and pushing it away from the hole. With the structure collapsed and the flames reduced Sloane moved closer, still shoveling dirt. Bennett continued to lift and push pieces of the pile until Sloane reached the only part of the outhouse that remained, the smoldering elevated shitter atop the skids, its toilet seat melted and deformed.

Molia was not there.

Unmarked Dirt Road

Sierra Nevada Mountains

Jake felt a moment of relief when Atkins instructed Big Baby to get back to his dorm and the man-child lumbered off, like a bear disappearing into the woods. Jake had feared Big Baby was going to be joining them in the woods, free to bugger and torture them. But his relief was short-lived. Atkins loaded them onto the bus and applied the handcuffs, but then he walked back down the aisle a second time and systematically slipped black hoods over their heads.

Claustrophobic, Jake felt an initial rush of anxiety and thought he might suffocate, but the masks were thin enough to breathe through, if not to see through, and he found a rhythm to his breathing, sat back, and tried to relax. The darkness was disorienting, but Jake did his best to again keep track of the time, counting the minutes and listening intently to the way Bradley continued to grind the gears. They were climbing a grade. He'd counted thirty-two minutes when he leaned far to his left, assuming the bus was taking another switchback. Instead it came to a stop. If they'd been traveling an average of twenty-five miles an hour they had only traveled between ten and fifteen miles, but because the road had been so winding, it was likely less.

Moments after stopping Atkins plucked the masks from their heads. With the engine off, the only sound was the metallic clink of the key against the cuffs and Atkins ordered that they get off the bus, form a single line, keep their mouths shut, and await further instructions. The sun had faded farther behind the mountain tops. It wasn't cold, but compared to the searing heat of the day, Jake got goose bumps on his arms. Bradley had parked the bus in what appeared to be a man-made turnabout at the end of a dirt road. Three large boulders, too perfectly spaced and bigger than any others nearby to have been left by nature, blocked a footpath that continued up the hill and disappeared into the shadows of the trees.

As De la Cruz unloaded the horses Atkins barked orders at them to remove the supplies from the back of the trailer. He produced military-style backpacks and gave them orders on how to load them, the coiled, black plastic hoses first; the bags of insecticide, poison, fertilizer, and string. He ordered T.J. to turn around and extend his arms and loaded the first pack on his back. T.J.'s knees bent under the weight. Atkins tied a shovel across the top, horizontal with T.J.'s shoulders. Finished, he shoved T.J. out of the way. T.J. stumbled and fell to his knee. Jake helped him up.

Atkins set up Bee Dee and Henry with similar packs, saving Jake for last. When he fit the pack on Jake's shoulders, Jake estimated the weight to be fifty pounds. He didn't know how long they were expected to hike, but he was beginning to feel no matter how far, he could handle it.

"You're a strong boy, aren't you, Stand-up? A regular hero."

Jake felt Atkins open up his pack. He couldn't see what the guard shoved inside, but he could feel it, and whatever it was, it made the pack significantly heavier.

"Time to hike," Atkins said.

KNOCK-ME-STIFF RANCH
GOLD CREEK, CALIFORNIA

Bennett jumped down from the cab, grabbed his shovel from Harper, and rejoined Sloane. In the distance the wind carried the wail of sirens and Sloane lifted his head long enough to see red lights shimmering through the leaves of the darkened oak trees, advancing down the road. Harper left, rushing to unlock the gate.

Sloane and Bennett used the shovels to lift and toss the pile—a wall, portions of the roof, the door. With each red-hot piece Sloane expected to find some part of Molia's blackened body beneath it, but when they moved the final, biggest section they saw nothing but blackened and smoldering ground.

Sloane looked at Bennett, the wind whipping his hair back off his face. "Where the hell is he?"

Bennett shook his head. "Maybe he got out."

"The door was wedged shut." Sloane yelled into the wind. "Tom? Tom!"

Bennett too began to yell, but the approaching sirens and the howling wind swallowed their words.

"Wait! Wait!" Sloane raised a hand, listening. He walked in a circle, hands cupped behind each ear. "Tom! Tom!"

He heard the sound again. Someone coughing, then a voice calling his name.

Bennett stopped beside the shitter and pounded on the wood with his fist. "Tom! Tom!"

"Here!"

Bennett grabbed at the closed lid and just as quickly pulled back his hand, wincing in pain. Sloane picked up his shovel and shoved the blade under the melted plastic, prying it off. He and Bennett stepped up to look down in the darkened hole. Tom Molia stood at the bottom, four feet deep, bare chested, coughing spasmodically into his shirt, which he pressed tightly over his nose and mouth.

Inside the bunkhouse Molia sat at the table being treated by paramedics, a sleeping bag draping his shoulders. He continued to cough, but now it came in short bursts and not nearly as harsh as when Sloane and Bennett first pulled him from the hole. He had immediately fallen to his knees, back arching and body retching. Sloane feared the detective had seared his lungs, but one of the firefighters said the use of his shirt had likely saved Molia from a lifelong affliction.

Harper had taken Molia's clothes to the house to be cleaned. In between coughs, Molia thanked her, and Sloane knew his friend would be okay when Molia added, "You can burn those."

While the paramedics attended to Molia, Sloane and Bennett stepped outside to talk with Sheriff Matt Barnes, who arrived not long after the fire engines. They left the two lanterns inside and stood at the edge of the wedge of light that spilled out onto the darkened porch. The wind had finally died down, now a low howl, like the sound of distant, baying wolves.

"Could it have been an ember from an old burn pile, Dave?" Barnes asked. "With the wind whipping around—"

"He smelled gasoline," Sloane interjected. "I smelled it, too. And I don't care how hard the wind was blowing, Sheriff. You're not going to convince me it was the wind that blew a post up against the door."

Barnes's face pinched and his eyes narrowed, giving Sloane a hard stare. "I don't suppose you know why?"

"Oh I know why. You're damn right I know why. Because we're pushing buttons that some people don't want pushed."

"Judge Earl?"

"He'd be one. Victor Dillon. Probably Archibald Pike and a few others."

"Pike? What's he got to do with this?"

"I paid a visit to the courthouse this morning. I was just laying out some cheese to see which rat scurried from his hole. Pike came first."

"What were you doing at the courthouse?"

"Did you know Sam Goode sued the county for cost overruns building out Fresh Start, and that the Estate of John Wainwright sued the county for gifting the land to Victor Dillon."

"I think I recall reading about both those cases. What do they have to do with anything?" Barnes asked.

"Goode is also the contractor of record on a set of construction drawings to remodel the judge's home."

Barnes scoffed. "Remodel? Judge Earl wouldn't change an inch of that house. It was built by his great-grandfather. It's like a museum."

"Then what did he do with the eight-hundred-and-fifty-thousand-dollar loan he took out from Winchester First Street Bank?"

Barnes's face pinched again.

"Here's the thing, Sheriff. The judge also took out a one-point-five-million-dollar loan to buy the Sutter Building. That's the exact amount he awarded to Goode in his suit against the county. And do you know whose security guards sit in the lobby of that building twenty-four-seven guarding it like it was Fort Knox?"

Barnes shook his head.

"Victor Dillon's. Dillon also has some connection to a limited liability company called Trinity Investments that has half a billion dollars in assets in an offshore financial center in Aruba set up under a web of other limited liability companies, and I can tell you that whoever set it up knew what they were doing. Guess the mailing address for Trinity?"

"The Sutter Building?" Barnes said. Sloane didn't comment further. "Pardon me for asking, Mr. Sloane, but what does any of this have to do with your two boys?"

"Fresh Start remains profitable if it remains full. Judge Earl keeps it full."

"Wait a minute. What are you suggesting? Judge Earl is taking money to put kids away? What evidence do you have to support something like that?"

"What evidence? His sentences are completely out of whack with any other county in the state and he rushes kids through the system before they ever have the chance for an attorney or for their parents to protest. Why? Being a mean SOB is one thing. Being a mean and stupid SOB is another. Judge Earl doesn't strike me as stupid, Sheriff."

"No he isn't. Some say he's brilliant."

"So then why would he do it? Why do something so blatantly wrong?"

"It doesn't mean he's taking bribes."

"Maybe not, but it's another thread to Victor Dillon, and when you have enough threads you have a web."

Barnes ran a hand over his face and mouth. "Mind sharing where you're getting all this information?"

"Not at the moment."

Barnes simmered. "Then let me say that what you have, in my humble opinion, is just that, threads. Can you tie any of these threads together?"

"I'm working on it." Sloane looked back inside the bunkhouse to where the detective remained seated. The paramedics had begun to put away their equipment. "But what happened tonight tells me we're getting closer."

"Closer to getting yourselves killed," Barnes said. "And that's *my* business, Mr. Sloane. This is my job. This is my county. I don't want to believe something like what you're suggesting could be, and I'm saying *could be,* going on under my nose, but that doesn't mean I'm disinterested either. I would have appreciated a phone call giving me some notice. I might have been able to prevent what happened tonight, posted one of my deputies to keep an eye on the place. Next time you might not be so lucky."

"We didn't know what we had, Sheriff. We'll keep you advised going forward."

"Do." Barnes shook Bennett's hand. "I'll keep a patrol car at the gate," he said and walked off the porch into the dark.

ELDORADO NATIONAL FOREST
SIERRA NEVADA MOUNTAINS

The initial grade was a wicked struggle. Jake's thighs and calves burned. He heard the others huffing and puffing and the occasional sound of a shoe slipping in the loose rock. Bradley rode the horse at the front of the line with a lead line attached to the donkey, the animal laden with two big packs. Atkins brought up the rear, tall in the saddle, the butt of a rifle protruding from a scabbard.

Jake noticed T.J. faltering and offered encouragement. "Keep your head down," he whispered. "Try to focus only on your next step. Don't look up."

After a half hour they crested the top of the mountain. The trees thinned. Scrub and boulders prevailed. Jake caught his wind as they started down the back side, but going downhill wasn't any easier than climbing up. The weight of the pack felt like someone pushing him from behind and forced him to plant each step to keep from stumbling into T.J. His knees ached from the pounding. Atkins showed no sign of easing the pace.

Jake did his best to continue to keep track of the time and their direction, but night began to fall, and soon they were hiking in moonlight. The temperature dropped, cold enough that the animals' breath marked the air. Jake, covered with sweat and hollow with hunger, felt chilled.

T.J. had the unfortunate luck of being directly behind the donkey, which was farting a horrific ammonia smell. After one blast, T.J. turned his head, stumbled on a partially hidden root, and went down. The line came to an abrupt stop.

"Get up," Atkins said from his saddle.

T.J. didn't respond. He just knelt there, head down.

"I said, get up."

T.J. was crying. Jake reached down to help him.

"Leave him alone, Stand-up."

Jake ignored Atkins and grabbed T.J.'s shoulder. "Come on, T.J., get up."

Atkins climbed off his horse and shoved Jake out of the way, the weight of his backpack causing him to fall back against the hillside. "I said leave him alone." He stood over T.J. "I gave you an order. Get up." He emphasized each word.

T.J. did not move.

For a moment Jake thought Atkins might pull T.J. to his feet, but that would have been too humane. Instead he walked to the horse and grabbed the rifle from the scabbard. Then he squatted on his haunches in front of T.J. "Look at me."

T.J. did not.

"I said, look at me." T.J. raised his head, their faces less than an inch apart. "You get up and get moving. You understand?"

"I can't," T.J. said, his voice soft, meek.

"You can and you will."

"I hurt my ankle." It sounded like the excuse that it was.

Atkins stood and stepped back. "Do you know what we do to a horse that goes lame?"

Jake's heart hammered in his chest.

"We shoot it, in the head, and leave it for the other animals to rip open and pull its flesh from its bones."

Jake took a step forward. "T.J., get up—"

Atkins whipped the rifle at him. "Stand-up, you shut your mouth or so help me God I'll drop you where you stand."

Jake took a step back. Bee Dee and Henry looked on, eyes wide with fear.

Atkins turned again to T.J. "We have no place to leave you. So I'm going to give you to the count of three to get up and get moving. I won't reach four. You can't walk; the other three are going to start digging a hole."

Jake couldn't swallow. Even in the dark he could see Henry had gone pale. Bee Dee was looking from T.J. to Atkins, as if about to do something.

"One." Atkins cocked the rifle. T.J. did not move.

"Two." Atkins shouldered the rifle and took a step closer, lowering the barrel inches from the top of T.J.'s head.

Jake felt his knees go weak. *Get up. Get up, T.J., God damn you. Get up.*

The forest became devoid of all sound. Blood pulsed inside his head, ringing in his ears. Whether or not Atkins paused a split second longer between two and three, Jake would never know, but the moment felt like an hour. He watched Atkins finger the trigger, noticed Bee Dee about to step forward.

T.J. moved.

He slid his second leg beneath him, slowly rising to his feet.

Bee Dee stepped back. Jake exhaled.

Atkins used the barrel to raise T.J.'s chin. "Next time I don't wait 'til three." He threw the reins over the horse's ears and returned the rifle to the scabbard. "Move out." Bradley set off as Atkins swung back up into his saddle, waiting for the path to clear.

They walked into the encroaching darkness, the forest thickening, the moon filtering through the branches in slats of light. The horses' metal shoes scraped rock and shale and every so often they heard the occasional hoot of an owl. After another twenty minutes, Jake spotted a light in the distance, too bright to be the moon. The light grew in intensity and size as they approached, a lantern hanging from a tree branch.

Bradley stopped and dismounted. Only then did Jake see another person standing in the dark, backlit by the lantern's glow. He carried a gun, but it was not a rifle. A magazine protruded out the bottom, the kind of gun carried by soldiers. He appeared young, perhaps in his early twenties, with the start of a wispy beard. He said something in Spanish, and a second man materialized from the dark. He looked older but not by much. His white tank-top T-shirt was stained and dirty and his camouflage pants sagged, revealing the blue ink of a tattoo across his stomach. He clenched a cigarette between his teeth as he took the reins and led the horses and donkey farther up the trail.

"Move," Atkins said to the four of them.

They followed the animals into a small garbage-strewn camp. A camouflage plastic tarp, its four corners tied with rope to the trunks of trees, hung shoulder high above the ground to create a lean-to. Plastic bags and tin cans littered the ground, along with empty jugs of what looked like juice, propane tanks. Nearby, logs had been set on end, a small camp stove on one, a few pots and pans on another. Clothing hung from ropes strung between trees.

"Welcome to Shangri-la, boys," Atkins said.

KNOCK-ME-STIFF RANCH
GOLD CREEK, CALIFORNIA

The smell of coffee only partially masked the lingering odor of charred wood left after the fire. Eileen Harper filled two of the three mugs. Molia put a hand over the third. "I'll pass on anything else hot tonight," he said. His coughing had lessened but now, when it came, it came in bursts. The paramedics had wanted to take him to the hospital. Molia refused.

Bennett suggested Sloane and Molia move to the main house, but Sloane declined.

"You've been generous enough. Nobody's coming back tonight." The real question was, what did Bennett and Eileen want to do? The stakes had been raised, and by a considerable amount. Sloane didn't want to put either of them in further danger. "This might be a good time to take a couple days of vacation," he suggested.

Bennett looked to Harper, some unspoken message between them; Sloane thought for sure he and Molia would be packing. "It's like Sheriff Barnes said. This is my home, too. Our home," Bennett said. "We don't like thinking that what you're suggesting is taking place right under our noses, but I'm not leaving my home."

Sloane looked to Harper. "Tommy's still in that place," she said. A few minutes later she and Bennett left Sloane and Molia alone.

"I guess we're on the right track," Sloane said.

"That might be the understatement of the week, given that someone just tried to roast my nuts," Molia said, anger seeping into his voice.

"But Barnes is right." Sloane said. "What we have are threads, and I'm not exactly sure where the hell to go from here."

"I am," Molia said. "The second floor of the fucking Sutter Building."

In the commotion and aftermath of the fire Sloane had forgotten that just before walking out the door Molia had left him a riddle about how they might get into the second floor. He'd said it was a word you couldn't yell in a crowded movie theater. Every constitutional law professor posed the same question to his first-year law students as a means to explore the degree of free speech accorded by the First Amendment. *What about yelling "fire" in a crowded theater? Is that protected speech?*

"Fire," Sloane said. "What you can't yell in a crowded theater."

Molia smiled. "I would have picked a different riddle if I'd have known it was going to prove prophetic." He fought back another coughing fit and sipped water. "Here's the question. The security guards don't have a key to access the second floor. So in the event of a fire, how does the fire department gain access?"

"I don't know," Sloane said. "I suppose they'd break it down."

Molia shook his head. "Then they'd have property damage, and the county would get the bill. And you can't expect the fire department to stand around waiting for a building owner to show up with the key while the building, and possibly others around it, burn."

"So what then?" Sloane asked.

"Every building has to have what's called a Knox-Box on the outside. It's a county ordinance in Virginia, and I noticed that Bennett has one on the post by the front gate. If he's not home and the fire department needs access to his property or to get back into the hills to fight a fire, the box has a key to the gate."

"And there's a Knox-Box on the side of the Sutter Building?" Sloane asked.

"You can see it on the videotape I shot. And I'm betting that inside is a key not only to that front door, but also to the second floor."

"Okay, but even if we get the Knox-Box open tell me how we get to the second floor with the security guards sitting at their desk every minute of every day? I don't think they're going to believe you and I are the cleaning service."

"They won't believe you and I are anything. I'm going to do this on my own." This time the coughing became violent. Molia bent in pain.

"The only thing you're doing is taking a trip to the hospital."

"Not a chance," he said. "They upped the ante. We need to counter."

"Then whatever your plan is, I'll do it."

"You can't; if you get caught we strike out twice. Who retries the case?"

"I don't intend on getting caught."

"You going to guarantee that?"

"We're both tired, okay? And I'm just as pissed as you. But that's all the more reason to think this through. Whatever your plan, you can't do it in your condition. If I get caught, then Lisa Lynch retries the case. But before I sign off on this, maybe you better tell me what you have in mind."

"First, get Alex on the computer. I need to ask her a few questions. Is she as good at this computer stuff as she appears to be?"

"Better."

Molia nodded. "Then all we need to find out is just how well Eileen can sew."

NINETEEN

Blue-gray moonlight trickled through the canopy in uneven streaks. The guards moved the only lantern from the hanging branch to beneath the camouflage tarp, and the hissing propane reminded Jake of Big Baby's pronounced lisp, which made him shudder at the man-child's pledge to be waiting for them back at Fresh Start.

After they had unpacked the contents of their backpacks and the mule packs, Atkins had instructed them to load the garbage into their packs. He tied everything onto the mule and he and Bradley packed it out. Jake knew it was only a short reprieve, but the thought of not having to worry about Atkins, even if only for a few hours, actually brightened his mood.

After feeding them beans out of a tin can, the guards spent the rest of the night trying to scare them, talking in broken English about bears being able to smell a human from miles away.

"You fuck around," the younger of the two said, revealing stained teeth, "and we put the chocolate bar in your pants and tie you to a tree."

The second man, who Jake considered the "cook," because he had attended to the beans, sat on a plastic bucket drinking tequila from a small bottle and scraping the blade of a machete over a stone. When it came time to bed down the guard took their shoes and had them lay shoulder to shoulder on their backs. He snapped a leg iron on their right legs and ran a heavy chain through rings welded onto the shackles. The chain moved and clinked like a metal snake across the ground. No one would be making a run for it in the night. The guard wrapped the excess around a tree trunk, snapping a padlock through two links. The temperature continued to drop, and Jake spent a fitful night on a piece of plastic over hard ground with only a thin green blanket for warmth. When he finally dozed off it felt like he'd been asleep minutes when the guard kicked his socked feet, unlocked the padlock, and pulled the chain through the irons.

"Get up," he said.

Jake's body protested. His back ached, and he had a kink in his neck that ran down his right shoulder. The others, T.J., Bee Dee, and Henry, moaned and yawned in similar discomfort. None looked to have slept much. The cook sat on his upturned plastic bucket, stirring the contents of a steaming pot over a camp stove's blue flame. He'd lined up four metal mugs on a tree stump, the handles of spoons sticking out.

The guard tossed them their boots to sort through. Jake slipped his on and checked out their surroundings. The camp looked worse in daylight, even with the garbage gone. The tarp strung over their heads hung catawampus beneath a canopy of branches and scrub. Logs of varying lengths lying end-to-end formed a crude perimeter, and Jake deduced from the dripping sap along the bark that the logs had been recently cut.

The guard motioned for them to sit on the tree stumps. They watched with revulsion as the cook, a cigarette hanging from the side of his mouth, spooned a gray, lumpy substance into the four cups, scraping the remnants into the cup in front of Bee Dee.

"Eat," he said, turning to wash out the pot with water from a plastic jug.

When Jake lifted the spoon the porridge clung to it.

"Eat." This time the order came from the guard, squatted on his haunches at the edge of the camp, automatic weapon slung over his shoulder, also smoking a cigarette.

Jake brought the spoon to his mouth and stuck out his tongue. The porridge had little taste; the texture like paste, with a gritty consistency. Jake doubted they had any brown sugar to sweeten it, but he also knew there wouldn't be a second choice or a second helping, and that it was important he eat as much as he could to continue to regain his strength. He took a spoonful and forced it down, then turned to T.J., who sat on the stump next to him looking miserable.

"Hey, you got to eat," Jake said. "Remember what I told you." He looked from the guard to the cook, who had turned his back to them, wiping out the pot with a rag and eventually tying the handle to a string hanging between two trees. "Our dads are still trying to get us out."

T.J. sighed. "It doesn't matter. Big Baby and T-Mac are going to kill us when we get back, if *they* don't kill us here."

"We'll worry about Big Baby when we have to," Jake said. "But now you have to eat everything they give us."

"Jake's right," Bee Dee said, leaning in to join the conversation. "Eat it all."

"Try to just let it slide down your throat without tasting it," Henry said. "It's easier that way."

T.J. sighed, picked up the spoon, and touched it to his lips, like a little kid. He recoiled at the first taste and gagged but managed not to throw up. After another minute they were all shoveling the porridge lumps into their mouths until the clink of the metal spoons alerted the cook they had finished. He retrieved the cups and commenced cleaning them. The guard dropped his cigarette and crushed it with the ball of his shoe. "We go."

He directed them to retrieve the shovels and the pickaxes as well as bags of fertilizer, several lengths of the coiled black hoses, and balls of the twine. The cook exchanged his utensils for a second automatic weapon, and the two men, the cook at the front and the guard in the rear, led them out of the camp along what did not appear to be a designated trail, pushing back tree limbs and stepping over fallen logs and boulders. Occasionally the cook would lower his weapon and use the machete to hack through the undergrowth or at a low-hanging branch.

Fifteen minutes into their excursion, Jake heard the sound of babbling water, a nearby stream or a creek. The cook pushed through brush, and they stepped into an area perhaps twenty feet square that looked to have been partially cleared of the immature trees, the ground dimpled with stumps. It seemed an irregular pattern; some of the smaller trees remained. The taller pines created a broad canopy but still allowed streams of sunlight.

The guard instructed that their job would be to dig up rocks and throw them in a pile as they had done working in the garden. Within minutes Jake felt sweat trickling from his temples. As the temperature warmed, the guards let them lower their coveralls to their waists and remove their T-shirts. Bee Dee showed them how to fashion their shirts around their heads like turbans and said it would help them keep cool. The work was hard, but Jake actually found it refreshing not to be under Atkins's thumb, and the guards allowed them to talk freely, something Atkins never would have allowed. The sound of their voices mixed with the sound of the pickaxes and shovels digging in the ground and the occasional ping indicating they'd struck another rock.

When the sun crossed high in the sky they broke for lunch— hard bread, a hunk of cheese, and water. The food was bad enough to make Jake miss the Fresh Start cafeteria. While they ate, the guard and cook stood off to the side smoking and speaking Spanish. After lunch, the guard instructed Jake and Bee Dee to load some of the unearthed rocks into one of the backpacks along with several of the hoses. When they had, he indicated they were to follow him. Jake slipped back on his coveralls and hoisted the backpack on his shoulders. It was heavier than the night before and the dense foliage through which the guard led them tugged at his coveralls and left scratches on his arms. They walked perhaps fifty yards, until coming to the stream Jake had heard earlier. The guard took a deflated plastic water container, the kind that when filled held five gallons, and waded out into the knee-deep stream, instructing Jake and Bee Dee to follow carrying the hoses and pack with the rocks. As hot as Jake had been, the stream offered immediate relief, but within minutes his feet were going numb. The guard directed them to dump the rocks and use them to create a crude dam along the bank beneath a crop of bushes, the branches of which hung out over the water. As they built the dam the water began to pond deeper. The guard used a knife to cut a hole in the top of the plastic container and submerged it, wedging it with rocks to keep it at the bottom. In the shadows created by the over-hanging branches, among the speckled rocks, the clear container was nearly undetectable.

Next, the guard directed Jake and Bee Dee to give him a hose, and he wedged a threaded end between two rocks but did not screw it to the spout of the plastic container. He showed them how to lay the hose along the bottom and use rocks to keep it in place. Again, with the flickering shadows and varied colors, the black hose could not be detected. They proceeded downriver, unfurling hose as they went and threading lengths together when necessary. Jake could no longer feel his fingers or toes. His knuckles ached when he flexed them and he was relieved when they stepped back onto the bank. They pushed through brush and found T.J. and Henry still digging in the soil, the cook spreading fertilizer. The guard handed Jake and Bee Dee two of the pickaxes. Jake didn't have to be told what to do next. He'd figured out the purpose of their excursion. They were creating a crude irrigation system. He and Bee Dee dug a shallow trench to bury the hose that would bring the river water from the stream to the ground. The question was why? Jake no longer believed this was all part of a hops-growing operation for some brewery. Businesses didn't operate this way. From the moment Atkins slipped black hoods over their heads, to hiking in the dark, the number one priority seemed to be secrecy. And if two Mexican guards and four juveniles working for free were the best employees a brewery could afford, it had some real problems. It only confirmed the urgency of what Jake had been plotting from the moment he watched Big Baby descend the bus stairs and announce his return.

He and T.J. could not go back to Fresh Start. That was no lon-ger an option. They needed to escape when they had the chance, here in the mountains. And now, Jake thought, he might just know how.

THE SUTTER BUILDING
WINCHESTER, CALIFORNIA

In the end, Sloane had prevailed, which was to say common sense won out. Now he, not Tom Molia, sat in the cab of Bennett's truck, talking to Alex and watching the entrance to the Sutter Building. He'd parked up the street from the orange glow cast by an overhead streetlamp, but close enough to observe the glass door entrance to the building. Tom Molia's plan had a simplicity to it that Sloane liked, but it would also require some high-tech help from Alex to pull it off.

"Okay," Alex said. "Ed Means has received a call at home advising him that his shift has been canceled." She was referring to the security guard scheduled to relieve the guard at the desk in the lobby at midnight. She'd hacked On-Guard's computer system to find the schedule, names, and employee information, calling their fire wall *juvenile*. "Let me make a call to the lobby now."

Sloane watched the guard inside the glass doors while continuing to listen to Alex on his phone. The guard had his feet propped on the corner of the desk, chair tilted back, reading. He glanced at the phone, as if uncertain it had actually rung, which further confirmed it didn't ring often, if at all. Which could be good or bad. Sloane felt a nervous twinge. If the guard became suspicious he was likely to call On-Guard to confirm. When it rang a third time he lowered his leg and sat forward, picking up the receiver. Alex must have had the call on a speaker because Sloane could hear the guard through his cell phone.

"Sutter Building, Montoya."

"This is dispatch. Your relief has called in sick," Alex said.

"Ed's sick?"

Uh-oh, Sloane thought; they hadn't figured the two guards could be friends.

"Said he caught a bug and was shutting off his phone to get some sleep. Didn't want to be disturbed." She was good. Quick.

"Does this mean I'm working a double shift?" Montoya did not sound happy about the prospect, and Sloane couldn't blame him, given that the guards did nothing more than watch the time pass for eight hours.

"We're sending a standby. He's new. Go over the ground rules with him when he gets there."

"Will do," Montoya said, sounding relieved. He hung up the phone and looked up to consider the clock on the wall, he hesitated, and looked back to the phone, but whatever thought crossed his mind passed and he leaned back and recommenced reading.

"Show time," Alex said.

Sloane backed the truck into a parking space beside what he assumed to be Montoya's Toyota Corolla, snowplow facing out in case he needed to quickly exit. He stepped from the cab and adjusted his shirt. It wasn't an exact copy of the security guard's uniforms, but Eileen Harper had a full day to replicate it with the aid of Molia's video and had done a credible job. Sloane didn't have the utility belt, but he wore a blue windbreaker to conceal that omission, adjusting it as he walked around the corner of the building, backpack slung over his shoulder, and approached the glass doors. Montoya remained in deep concentration. When Sloane tapped his keys on the glass the guard looked up, nodded, and slid a bookmark between the pages before shutting the book. Sloane glanced to the side as Montoya approached and unlocked the dead bolt with several twists of the key, pushing the door open. Sloane stepped in.

"You must be my replacement."

Sloane shook the man's hand. "Steve Venditti," he said.

"So you're new, huh?"

"Just a couple weeks."

"Where've they had you working?"

"All over," Sloane said. "Mostly as a replacement."

Montoya patted his shoulder. "Well you're in for a treat tonight."

"How's that?"

Montoya laughed. Bushy eyebrows knitted together. "Let's just say I hope you brought a good book with you."

"Yeah, I figured this time of night it would likely get pretty boring?"

"Paint drying is more interesting. I've been asking off this detail for weeks. Another month and I may hang myself just to break the monotony."

"So nobody ever comes by?"

Montoya walked to the desk and held up a clipboard. The blank document contained signature lines for anyone entering and exiting the building along with a space for the date and time. "All we do is sit."

"What about rounds? Do I need to keep a log?"

"You want to walk around outside, be my guest, but this square patch of tile is pretty much it."

"What's upstairs?"

Montoya shook his head. "Don't know."

"We don't go up to do rounds?"

"We don't even have a key."

"The elevator?"

"Turned off. Don't have a key for that either."

Sloane tried to look surprised. "So, no idea what's up there, huh?"

"Nobody knows." He showed Sloane where the bathroom was, behind the elevator, then picked up his backpack. "Have fun. I'm going home." He started for the door, turned back. "Almost forgot." He took the key off the ring and tossed it to Sloane. "You have to lock me out. When your relief comes, you give him the key. Nobody else gets in."

Sloane shut the door behind Montoya and locked it. Then he went behind the desk, waiting for the sound of a car engine. A minute later the blue Corolla drove past the front entrance, the sound of its engine fading as it sped off down the street. Sloane pulled out his cell phone and called Alex. "I'm in. Any traffic?"

She continued to monitor the calls into and out of On-Guard's security center. "We're good."

Sloane unzipped his backpack and pulled out the cigarette lighter and the chunk of tar shingle that had been atop the roof of the outhouse. He held the flame to the tar until it began to smoke, knelt, and slid it halfway under the door that presumably opened to a staircase to the second floor. He left it to smolder and went back to the desk, calling the Winchester County Volunteer Fire Department. He gave the woman who answered the building address and said he smelled smoke in the stairwell. She asked Sloane to put his palm on the door and feel for heat. Sloane didn't.

"I'm not sure," he said. "It might be warm, but it's hard to tell. I'd open it but I don't have a key. The smell is pretty strong, though."

The woman said they'd send out a truck. Sloane hung up and spoke into his cell. "We still good?"

"Still good," Alex said.

Sloane ditched the tar shingle along the back of the building. The fire department arrived in good time, thankfully different men than those who'd responded to the fire at Dave Bennett's ranch the prior evening. He held the glass doors open as they pulled the truck to the curb and exited in full apparatus.

"I can smell it in the stairwell," Sloane said to the one who appeared in charge.

The firefighter put his hand on the exterior of the door, feeling for heat.

"Can you smell it?" Sloane asked.

The man would have to have the mother of all colds not to be able to smell the burned tar. He sniffed at the door then dropped to a knee. "Yeah, definitely. Did you call the owner?"

"My first night," Sloane said. "Not really the way I want to get started, you know? I thought I'd call you guys first and see if it's anything to be concerned about."

"You don't have a key to this door?" The firefighter sounded incredulous.

"Just the front door, but I think I saw a Knox-Box on the side of the building."

The firefighter directed another one of the responders to check the Knox-Box before turning back to Sloane. "Why don't they give you a key?"

Sloane shrugged. "Like I said, my first night."

When the second responder returned with a ring containing three keys, Sloane felt a great sense of relief. Molia's intuition had been correct. The firefighter felt the door again before slowly opening it. When no flames leaped out he stepped into the stairwell. Sloane followed, feeling the weight of the metal reinforced door. They proceeded to a second door at the top of the stairs. The lead firefighter again placed his palm flat against it before he inserted the key. The lock did not turn. Sloane felt a twinge of anxiety, but the firefighter flipped the ring to the third key, inserted it, and the handle turned.

Sloane wasn't sure what he expected to find. He wouldn't have been surprised if the second floor had been completely empty. But it wasn't empty. Blue light glowed from a dozen computer screens aligned along folding tables. And that was it for furniture. Sloane saw no chairs, no telephones, no desk lamps, garbage cans, pens or pencils, staplers, no pieces of paper. In fact, there were no keyboards on the tables, just the computers and the monitors and black electrical cords snaking out the backs.

The firefighter looked equally perplexed. "What kind of business is this?"

Sloane shrugged. "I'm not sure."

The man pulled open a closet door, revealing the blinking and glowing lights of a computer server. "Well, at least there's no fire," he said.

"Yeah," Sloane said. "I guess that's good."

"Ordinarily we'd check to make sure nothing was smoldering, but . . ."

"I'll lock up," Sloane said. "I don't want to waste anymore of your time. Sorry to have bothered you."

The firefighters departed, boots echoing as they descended the stairwell. Sloane stepped to the windows facing the street. They were treated with a film to prevent anyone from seeing in, but he could see out. He waited until the fire truck drove off before going back to the computer screens. Each displayed two columns of numbers, a series of nine-digit numbers rolled from the bottom to the top of the screen in one column, and ten-digit numbers did the same in a second column. The digits were all different.

He pulled out his cell phone, about to call Alex, when it vibrated in his hand to indicate he'd received a text message.

> Fire department called Boykin. Boykin called On-Guard.
> Car dispatched. Move!

Sloane had a camera in the backpack, but there'd be no time for that now. He called Alex as he went back to the first computer monitor.

"How much time do I have?"

"Minutes."

"I'm going to take a few pictures on my cell and send them to you."

"No time. Just leave."

"Have to. I'll explain later. If I don't get out, at least you'll have them."

He hung up before she could respond and took a picture of the first screen, fumbled with the apps, attached the photo to an e-mail, and sent it.

He called. "First photo is on its way. Let me know when you get it."

"Just get the hell of there, David."

"Just let me know."

He went to the windows, looking down at the deserted street. "Okay, it came through. I'm opening it now." Seconds passed. "Got it," she said.

"Can you use it?"

"What is it?"

"Computer screen. I'll explain more later. Can you read the numbers?"

"Hold on, I'm playing with it. Yeah. Yeah I can use it. I can read them. Now get out. Go!"

"I'm going to send more."

"Shit! No! Leave!"

He hung up and took a picture of the second screen, attached and sent it, silently urging it to finish. When it did, he repeated the process at the third and fourth screens, realized he was pushing his luck and started for the door. He heard a car engine. Back at the windows he watched a black SUV stop out front of the building and a man and a woman step out, both in On-Guard uniforms, both armed. They talked on the sidewalk, gesticulating before the SUV drove around the side of the building and turned in to the parking lot. At least three, Sloane thought. Not good odds.

He started toward the door at the top of the stairs, about to close it when he realized he couldn't lock it from the inside. The dead bolt was on the outside. He considered the rest of the office but found little to work with. He circumvented the room, looking out the building windows and found what he was hoping for on the east side, a fire escape. He snapped free the lock atop the window frame, tried to slide it up, and momentarily panicked when the window stuck. With greater effort he was able to raise it enough to slide his hands beneath the frame and used brute force to pull it up. About to step out onto the landing, he saw the padlock secured to the release mechanism that would have otherwise dropped the ladder.

Dead end.

Footsteps in the stairwell. Sloane was out of time and options.

Sloane watched the man enter the second floor and sweep his gun left. The woman followed behind him and swept the room in the opposite direction. These were not your ordinary security guards. They paused, eyes scanning the room, listening. The man gave a hand signal that he would move to the closet.

Look to the window. Look to the window.

The woman turned her head. Bingo. She'd seen the open window. She gave her partner some nonverbal signal and he changed course, stepping quietly away from the closet. Sloane let out a held breath. He lost sight of them from his hiding place inside the closet but kept listening. In his mind he imagined the woman leaning out the open window and noticing the lock preventing escape to the street. He hoped it would cause her to look up, as it had Sloane, and when she did she would see the piece of shirt he'd ripped and stuck in one of the rungs leading to the roof. He heard the fire escape rattle and emerged from behind the computer server in the closet. He watched through the gap between the closet door and the doorjamb. The woman stood on the fire escape landing looking up. The man climbed up the rungs ahead of her. Then she followed. Sloane hurried across the room, checked the stairwell, saw no one at the bottom, and closed the door to the room and applied the dead bolt. He heard footsteps walking on the roof. He had contemplated the roof but realized it presented the same problem as a means of escape as locking the door; it might have bought him some time, but he'd only have been cornering himself. That left the closet as his only place to hide, which also made it his pursuer's first choice to search. Opening the window to the fire escape, he'd hoped, would give them a different choice, or at least one that would keep them from focusing too intently on the closet. He had left the closet door open for the same reason, hoping it would persuade them not to consider it too closely.

At the bottom of the stairs he checked the lobby. Empty. The driver had likely stayed with the SUV. That would be a problem, but only if Sloane could get to Bennett's truck. One problem at a time.

He closed the door at the bottom of the landing, locked it, and moved quickly to the front door, pausing to ensure the street was empty before exiting in the opposite direction of the parking lot. He had devised his plan in the closet, but he was, to a large extent, just taking the path of least resistance.

At the east corner of the building he stepped from the sidewalk into the shadows and pressed his back against the rock wall, looking up and watching the fire escape, waiting. The fire escape rattled, the woman stepping over the roof ledge and descending. The man followed her down. When both had slipped in the window Sloane continued along the side of the building to the back where he had ditched the burning piece of tar. He continued to the corner abutting the parking lot and heard the chatter of hushed voices. The guard in the parking lot was monitoring his colleagues' progress through the building on a hand-held radio. The woman's voice came through loud and clear.

"Doors locked. Shit, he locked the damn door."

The man's voice, "We're locked on the second floor. Repeat. We're locked on the second floor."

Sloane dropped to a knee and peered around the corner. The third guard rushed from the parking lot in the direction of the front entrance, unconcerned with leaving his post because he had parked the SUV perpendicular to the front of Bennett's truck, thinking he had blocked it in place.

Sloane stepped from his hiding place but did not immediately climb into the cab of Bennett's truck. He walked to the driver's side of the SUV, ducked under the dash, and pulled at any wire he could find, hoping at least one would prevent the car from starting.

He slid into Bennett's truck cab, started the engine, and pressed hard on both the brake and the accelerator. With the engine revved he dropped the truck into drive and slid his foot off the brake. The truck shot forward, the plow crashing into the side of the SUV with a horrific metallic crunch, pushing the front end across the asphalt, its tires protesting. He quickly reversed to give himself a running start, shifted into low, and again punched the accelerator. The plow hit the SUV with greater momentum and force, freeing more than enough room for the truck to get out and not with a moment to spare.

As the truck's tires bounced over the curb into the street the third guard returned, gun in hand, and took a shooter's stance. Sloane swerved and drove directly at him, punching the accelerator.

THE SUTTER BUILDING
WINCHESTER, CALIFORNIA

The front door to the building remained open, one of Dillon's security guards waiting in the lobby, his shirt torn and dirty. He had abrasions on his forearms and forehead.

"Where are the others?" Boykin asked.

"He locked them upstairs."

Boykin felt a rush of panic. "What are you talking about? No one is to go upstairs."

"That's where he was, apparently."

"Who?"

"The guy driving the truck."

"What are you talking about? What truck?"

"The one that nearly ran me over."

Boykin flushed. "You let him get away?"

"The truck was parked in the lot. I pinned it against the wall."

"Then how the hell did he get away?"

"It had a snow blade on the front. He pushed his way out."

"I mean how did he get into the truck with you watching it?"

The man began to stutter. "I waited with the car. They radioed and said he locked the door to the second floor. They couldn't get out."

"He locked the door? How did he get a God damned key?" Boykin asked. None of the guards had keys. Then he remembered the call at home. The fire. "Was there any evidence of a fire?"

"Not that I saw."

Boykin stepped back outside. The Knox-Box was unlocked, the keys inside missing. "Son of a bitch."

He pulled out his cell phone, shouting to the guard in the lobby as he made the call. "You. Come here." He spoke into the phone. "One of them got into the second floor. He called in a God damned fire and used the key in the Knox-Box. I don't know exactly how he did it. No, they let him get away."

The guard approached. Boykin questioned him. "What kind of truck was it?"

"Chevy," he said. "Older model. Beat up. It had a snow blade on the front. I wrote down the license number."

Wade had told Boykin that the truck parked in front of the Sutter Building had a snow blade. Boykin took the piece of paper and relayed the information into the phone as he handed the guard his set of keys. "Get the other two out and relock the door. Wait for me in the lobby." Speaking back into the phone he said, "If it was Sloane or the detective they're likely headed back to Gold Creek. Get something set up. I don't know what, God damn it. Just do what you have to do."

HIGHWAY 89

WINCHESTER COUNTY, CALIFORNIA

Sloane felt his adrenaline rush subsiding, but he continued to check the rear and side mirrors for headlights. When satisfied he had not been followed he turned his cell back on. He'd shut it off when he stepped into the closet. As he waited for it to power up he could feel his body continuing to decompress, like a balloon leaking helium.

He used the center dashes to anticipate the curves beyond the reach of the truck's dull headlights, waiting until he came to a relatively straight stretch of road before he called Alex.

She answered on the first ring. "Shit, where are you?"

"I'm fine, I'm out. You have the photographs?"

"I'm going through them now. I'm just cleaning up the images a bit so I can read the numbers better. Tell me what happened?"

"What do you think they are?"

"I'm not sure at this point. Maybe account numbers, maybe phone numbers. I want to run them past a friend in the morning. How far are you from where you're going?"

"Another twenty minutes."

"Call me when you get there."

"Will do."

"I mean it, David. Call me so I know you're all right."

He assured her he would call, disconnected, and eased into the turns. About to call Tom Molia, a light reflected sharply in the rearview mirror, momentarily blinding him. He flipped the mirror to cut the glare, then had to brake hard and pull the wheel to the right to keep from skidding off the road. The car had come out of nowhere, and at a high rate of speed. Sloane considered it in the side mirror. What had descended was not a car but a truck, the body raised high above oversize off-road tires. Floodlights across a roll bar over the roof of the cab lit up the inside of Bennett's truck.

The adrenaline kicked back in, tires squealing, Sloane accelerated and decelerated in and out of turns, straddling the center stripe, trying to keep away from the edge, but he could not get the truck off his bumper. Twice the truck pulled out, as if to pass, but had to slide back when Sloane turned hard to the left. Sloane came out of a turn and saw a straight patch of asphalt, but before he could react the truck had swerved to the left, the engine roared, and the cab was alongside him. The driver knew the road, and Bennett's old truck was not built for speed.

Sloane braced for the impact. When it did not come he glanced to his left, expecting to see guns. Instead he saw a shirtless man hanging out the passenger window, hair whipping in the wind. Two more stood in the truck's bed, holding on to the roll bar. They yelled and taunted him over loud music blaring from speakers. The man hanging out the window threw a beer can that bounced off the windshield, splattering beer. Sloane braked, and the truck blew past. One of the men in back launched another can at him; the second flipped Sloane a one-finger salute.

Sloane's chest and shoulders heaved. He slapped the wheel. Four punk kids. He hoped Bennett kept a bottle of Scotch somewhere in the house because he was going to need a strong drink. He watched the truck's red taillights disappear then reappear around a bend in the road, and slowed to put more road between him and the truck. Coming out of the next turn he caught another glimpse of the red taillights. This time, rather than disappear, they suddenly moved vertically, as if the back end had hit a speed bump. A string of four loud pops followed, and the lights moved violently left and right, the driver fighting to maintain control of the truck, overcorrecting. Its center of gravity altered, the truck flipped. Sloane watched, horrified. The two men flew from the bed as if they'd been roped from behind and yanked out. The truck flipped a second time then a third, a horrific screech of metal emitting orange and red sparks. Fixated on the truck, Sloane almost didn't see the body now lying in the road. He hit the brakes and pulled the wheel hard to the right, managing to avoid the body, but the front right tire dropped off the asphalt edge. The rear tire followed before he could correct, and the truck listed hard to the right, leaving the road completely. Bushes and tree limbs whipped against the windshield. Then the truck rolled. Sloane's head hit the ceiling hard. His shoulder crashed against the door. The truck flipped a second time, continuing down an embankment.

The roll ended with a splash, Sloane upside down in the cab, conscious but dazed and disoriented. Blackened water poured into the cab. In pain, Sloane released the seat belt and dropped into numbing, waist-deep water. With the truck upside down he couldn't immediately get his bearings but managed to find the armrest, reaching along it for the door handle. The truck shifted again, pushed and shoved by the current. When it stopped, Sloane pulled the door handle and pushed on the door. It didn't budge. Thinking it locked, he took a breath and submerged, feeling for the knob, pulling it up. When he surfaced the water had risen to his chest. He pulled the handle and pushed again, but the door still did not budge. Sloane leaned back, held the steering wheel to get leverage, and kicked at the window.

The truck shifted again, this time more violently, metal grinding against the rocks, as if tearing the cab apart. The cab spun 360 degrees, picking up speed and smashed against another boulder. Water continued to rush in, the sound deafening. Sloane gathered himself and kicked again at the door and window. His body began to go numb, his remaining strength ebbing. The water rose to his chin. He took a breath and submerged, kicking blindly. When he could no longer hold his breath he breached the surface, gasping for air. The water had risen to just inches from the floor of the truck, now its roof. He tilted his head and sucked in another breath, submerged, and drove his shoulder into the door again and again.

The truck spun, like a teacup on a carnival ride. Sloane surfaced, sucked in more oxygen, submerged. This time when he lunged against the door it moved, the current having freed it from the obstruction, but only enough for Sloane to get his head and shoulders out. He pushed and pulled but couldn't squeeze through the opening. Fearing he would get stuck, and running out of oxygen, he pulled himself back inside the cab and rose for one final breath of air, searching for the pocket.

It wasn't there.

TWENTY

T om Molia coughed and doubled over as the pain radiated across his chest, so intense it felt as though his sternum might split open. He'd acquiesced. He'd let Sloane go to the Sutter Building. The cough had left him no choice. The lozenges Eileen Harper provided had helped, but not enough to pull off a convincing act as a security guard.

He didn't know if he'd seared his lungs or cooked them as black as a hamburger patty forgotten on the Fourth of July barbecue. The paramedics said he'd likely suffered some smoke inhalation. They wanted to take him to the hospital, but upon further questioning they also admitted there wasn't much that could be done. Steroids would reduce the swelling of his bronchiole and help him breathe more easily, if that became a problem. They also said that tying the shirt around his face had been smart thinking, significantly reducing the crap he otherwise would have sucked into his lungs.

He checked his watch. Sloane should have been back. Molia had been adding up the minutes it should have taken Sloane to get to the Sutter Building, convince the guard on duty to leave, wait for the fire department, search the second floor, take some pictures, and get the hell out and back to the ranch. He calculated two hours, two and a half at most. Sloane had been gone more than three.

Still, he fought the urge to call. He and Sloane had agreed they couldn't take the chance that the call might come at an inopportune moment and decided that Sloane would call Molia when he was safe, or he wouldn't call him at all.

When Molia's cell phone rang he nearly hit the wrong button fumbling to answer it.

"Hello? David?"

"It's Alex."

"Did David call you?"

"Yeah, I talked to him about a half—an—"

"He's all right? He made it out okay?" Molia asked.

"Isn't he back yet?"

Molia's relief turned to foreboding. "No. Where did he say he was when he called?"

"He said he was twenty minutes out at the most. That was thirty minutes ago. He was supposed to call me when he got there."

Molia picked up the keys to the rental car. "Did he say where he was?"

"Just driving back."

"I'm going out to look for him; if he calls you, call me."

As he drove back toward Winchester, Molia dialed Sloane's number twice. The calls went immediately to voice mail, indicating Sloane likely had the phone turned off. But Alex said she'd spoken to him, which meant Sloane had had his phone on at one point. So why hadn't he also called Molia? And why wasn't he answering the phone now?

Molia drove slowly, scanning the road for any signs of tire tread marks or broken foliage. Fifteen minutes into the process he came around a bend and saw flashing lights atop a sheriff's vehicle parked at an angle, blocking further progress. A deputy sheriff flicked a flashlight at him, arm outstretched.

Molia felt sick.

He lowered the window and drove alongside the deputy.

"Traffic accident up ahead, sir. I'm afraid I'm going to have to reroute you."

"What kind of car?" Molia asked.

"I need to reroute you, sir; where are you headed?"

Molia flashed his identification. "I'm a cop. I need to know the make of car."

"Not a car, a truck."

Molia's heart sank. "I think I might know the driver. I was expecting him half an hour ago. How bad is it?"

"It's bad. We have bodies all over the road."

"Bodies, as in more than one?"

"Several."

"I need to get up there. You can let me through or call your sheriff, Matt Barnes, and tell him my name."

The deputy handed Molia's identification back through the window. "Sheriff Barnes is up at the site." He pointed. "Couple hundred yards. Drive slow."

Molia gripped the steering wheel so hard his knuckles turned white. As he approached the accident scene there were so many lights atop the vehicles that it looked like the circus was in town. He parked in the middle of the road and stepped out. Another deputy stopped him, but Molia badged him as well. "Looking for Sheriff Barnes."

The deputy directed him down the road, to what remained of a large truck that had been altered with oversize tires, shocks, and a roll bar. It lay on its side, banged and smashed and completely crumpled. Bits of glass was everywhere. Paramedics worked on one of two bodies in the cab. A young man. Blood streaked the windshield and the dash. As Molia passed he made the sign of the cross. He'd seen his share of traffic accidents and most this bad involved more than one vehicle, but he saw no other vehicle in the road. He walked to the edge and looked down the bank, but saw only darkness, though he could hear the rush of the river surging past. He turned to further consider the scene, noting cans of beer strewn about the asphalt and thinking the accident could have been the reason for Sloane's delay—they sent him on a detour, but even as Molia had the thought, he quickly dismissed it—the scenario still didn't explain why Sloane had not called, or why he wasn't answering his phone now. The apprehension settled back over him like a heavy tarp.

At the rear of the truck he noticed that the tire hanging in the air was flat, which by itself was not unexpected given the severity of the crash, but so was the tire on the ground. Examining them more closely Molia detected multiple puncture marks. He walked to the front and found both those tires had also been punctured.

"Detective Molia?" Sheriff Barnes approached. "What are you doing here?"

"I'm looking for David," he said.

Barnes squinted. "Sloane? Why would you be looking for him here?"

Molia looked over his shoulder at the truck. "Stop stick," he said. Every police vehicle in West Virginia carried one in its trunk. The stick, with protruding metal spikes, was tossed across a road, a sure-fire way to stop a vehicle that didn't want to be stopped.

Barnes stepped past him and put his hand on the puncture wounds in the tires. Then he looked again to Molia. "This was intended for Sloane, wasn't it?"

HIGHWAY 89
WINCHESTER COUNTY, CALIFORNIA

It felt like a dream, and he was floating. Sloane saw no white light and felt no comforting warmth. Immersed in darkness he felt only bitter, bitter cold.

And then the ground came back, though not beneath his feet. He felt it against his chest and his cheekbone, as if he had fallen from the sky and landed on his stomach, arms spread wide. Opening his eyes he saw a brilliant white light and in it someone or something. The light eclipsed the shadow of a body. But then the shadow disappeared, if it had ever been there at all.

Sloane coughed, water spilling from his mouth. He lifted his head. He lay on the bank of the swollen creek. The sky at the top of the steep incline pulsed red and white. He managed to turn over onto his back and felt a stabbing pain run like an electric current through his body. His right wrist throbbed. His feet felt numb. He realized that his legs, from the knees down, remained in the water. He scooted farther up the bank and fought to get his bearings. He remembered the truck flipping in front of him, seeing a ball of yellow sparks, the two men in the back flying out. He remembered seeing a body in the street, swerving to avoid it, branches whipping against the windshield, being upside down in the cab, the water rushing in, rising, struggling to free himself from the seat belt, to get out.

But he hadn't gotten out. He couldn't get the door open.

He'd drowned.

Yet here he sat, by all accounts still very much alive.

He looked again to the light into which the person in his dream had walked but saw no one. He got to his knees and made it to his feet, his body protesting, stiff and sore and shivering from the cold. He continued to collect the bits of information and tried to meld them into some coherent whole. He started up the incline but couldn't let the thought go and walked back to the river, to the muddy bank. Kneeling, he touched the mud with his fingers, adjusting his body to allow the light to better illuminate the ground, searching.

And he saw it, prominently cast in the mud.

Tom Molia said nothing.

"So then it begs the question," Barnes said, unwilling to let it go. "If *they* hit the stick, where is Sloane?"

Molia didn't know the answer to that question either. He walked to the edge of the road and looked down the bank, then continued down the road to where the asphalt curved and disappeared around the bend. He kept to the edge, looking for any sign that another car could have gone over the side, skid marks, pieces of tire, disturbed brush, broken branches, bits of plastic or glass. As he concentrated he heard Barnes's voice behind him.

"Holy mother of God."

Molia looked to where Barnes stood, but the sheriff's gaze was fixed farther down the road, past Molia, his eyes wide and disbelieving. Molia turned and saw the figure limping forward. Dripping wet, his arms wrapped across him, body shivering violently, Sloane marched up the road.

TWENTY-ONE

They kept Sloane overnight at the hospital for observation. He had a deep gash on the back of his head that required six stitches. He'd also broken his right wrist, now fitted with a cast. The doctor on call said he was fortunate not to have broken any other bones. Sloane didn't feel fortunate; he felt battered and bruised and sore as hell.

"And you'll feel worse tomorrow," the doctor promised.

They called Alex from the hospital after agreeing to tell her that Sloane had been delayed because of a traffic accident and hadn't called because his phone lost reception. Neither was an outright lie. There had been an accident and Sloane couldn't get reception, not with his phone somewhere at the bottom of the river, unlikely ever to be found again.

Molia had spent the night at the hospital, not wanting to leave Sloane, and taking the opportunity to get himself examined. His lungs had not been seriously damaged, but the smoke and chemicals from the outhouse fire had irritated his throat lining, as the paramedics had surmised. It had made for an interesting conversation, trying to explain to the emergency room doctor how one man could be suffering from smoke inhalation from a fire while the other brought in with him had nearly drowned and was hypothermic. The doctor prescribed steroids, as the ambulance driver had predicted.

Barnes had asked difficult questions, like why Sloane was dressed in what looked like a security guard's uniform, and whether the two of them had anything to do with a report of a fire and break-in at the Sutter Building earlier in the evening. But the sheriff relented and ceased his interrogation when the doctor gave Sloane something for his pain that made him drowsy. Before drifting to sleep Sloane had one question for Barnes.

"Did anyone die in the crash?"

Barnes shook his head. "Miraculously, no."

The following morning, as they drove back to the ranch, Molia's coughing had diminished but not his anger. "It was a stop stick," he said. "And it was meant for you."

"So they know about the Sutter Building," Sloane said. "Well, whatever those numbers are, they're worth killing to keep a secret."

"We need weapons, David. I talked to Bennett this morning. He has some shotguns and a couple handguns."

"Something strange happened last night," he said.

"No shit."

"No, I mean something while I was in the water. I couldn't get out, Tom. I couldn't get out of the cab. Someone had to have pulled me out."

"Could you have imagined it? You took quite a bump on the head."

"This was real."

"There was no one else around, David."

"I didn't get out by myself."

"A guardian angel?"

"Don't laugh," Sloane said. "The thought crossed my mind. But . . ."

Molia looked over at him. "But what?"

"Guardian angels don't leave footprints. Whoever pulled me out of the truck did. I checked."

"You're sure it wasn't one of yours?"

"I'm sure."

"So maybe a good Samaritan? Someone helped you, didn't want

to get involved, and moved on." Molia didn't sound convinced as he said it.

Neither was Sloane. "At that hour of the morning? I didn't see another car in either direction until that truck came up behind me. Like you said, there was nobody else."

"So it had to be someone already there."

Sloane nodded. "Somebody waiting around the bend."

"But that doesn't make any sense."

"I know. If they were waiting for me, why would they save me?"

Molia shook his head. "Nothing in this county makes much sense."

When they entered the bunkhouse and powered up the computer the Skype call from Alex was nearly instantaneous.

"I think I might have something," she said. "Remember I told you Trinity Investments was a limited liability company out of Aruba and that I thought it could be an investment company, a place for people to park money made out of the country to avoid Uncle Sam."

"You no longer think that to be the case?" Sloane asked.

"The first column of numbers on the computer screens is a routing number, the second column are numbers for foreign bank accounts, likely in multiple offshore financial centers. I'm still wading through it all, but there are at least half a dozen."

"I'm not the most polished spoon in the silverware drawer, but that sounds exactly like people trying to hide their money," Molia said.

"It is, but I don't think it's investment money, and I don't think it's thousands of investors. One of the numbers in the left column repeats. Want to guess to which bank it belongs?"

"Winchester First Street," Sloane said.

"I called in a friend who does this kind of stuff. She says whoever set this up knew what they were doing. It's complex, sophisticated stuff, but in essence they built a computer program that divides Trinity's so-called investment money into amounts well below any federal reporting requirements and makes deposits into dozens, maybe hundreds, of different bank accounts.

That's the second column of numbers. Only the money doesn't stay in those accounts long, just a matter of seconds. Trinity is just a shell corporation, without any assets, and Winchester First Street is just a holding place for Trinity's money to pass through."

"Pass through to where?" Molia asked.

"The computer transfers the money out of the country to confidential offshore financial centers in the places we discussed like Aruba, Gibraltar, the Bahamas, Liberia, tax havens that allow for complete confidentiality and secrecy. Once the money is offshore, another computer program gathers all the accounts and issues transfer instructions. The money is consolidated into fewer accounts, likely somewhere in Switzerland. It's laundered, good to go, and pretty much untraceable."

"You said so-called investment money, that Trinity is just a shell. What does that mean?" Sloane asked.

"It means there aren't any investors. The bank accounts are fictitious."

"So then where is all the money coming from if there aren't any investors?" Sloane asked.

"That's the five-hundred-million-dollar question, isn't it?"

GOLD RUSH BREWERY
HOPS PROCESSING PLANT
TRULUCK, CALIFORNIA

Dressed in a long-sleeve blue shirt, Wrangler jeans, and his well-worn, camel-colored Carhartt boots, Victor Dillon looked more like a country farmer than the CEO of one of the most well-known microbreweries in the country, which was his intent. Dillon escorted his three potential customers through the nutrient rich, deep brown soil, cultivated to perfection after twenty years in business. They strolled casually beneath a canopy created by the twenty-foot-tall telephone poles pounded into the ground at a slight angle and the spiderweb of wires crisscrossing overhead from pole to pole to discourage birds and to tie the vertical strands of coarse string up which the hop vines grew. The three men walked in shin-high black rubber boots. They had come for this business meeting in designer shoes to match their hand-tailored shirts and suits, attire hardly fitting for a tour through farmland. Dillon kept half a dozen pairs of the rubber boots just outside his office door. He had also encouraged the men to remove their suit jackets and ties and roll up their shirtsleeves, advising them that the heat of midday sun also made such attire impractical. Nothing made men more uptight than neckties. Wearing one demanded formality. Discarding it did wonders to help that man to relax, and Dillon liked his prospective business partners to be relaxed. He always started his business meetings with a tour of the Gold Rush Brewery plant and hops-growing operation. The suggestion of a tour usually caught his prospective buyers off guard, hence the improper attire. But Dillon believed a walk through the dark soil amid the plants evidenced he was much more than a wealthy CEO. It evidenced that he was knowledgeable about, and intimately involved in, every aspect of the growing process, unafraid to get his hands and his shoes dirty. He believed the impression translated into confidence in the quality of his product, which of course helped when it came time to negotiate the price.

Dillon stopped in the shade of one of the plants to pull a bud from the stalk. "Each vine is grown from a seedling," he continued to explain. "Each must be hand-trained to grow up the string. These plants are currently about nine feet in height, indicating they are growing on schedule. In this heat, you can almost see the vines growing before your very eyes. In two months, just before harvesting, the plants will reach seventeen feet. Some will reach the wires overhead." He let that thought germinate. "The plants are harvested as they were planted—by hand. Workers drive the fields in a truck with a boom and cut the stalk at the base and the string at the top and the plant falls gently into the back of the truck."

Dillon invited the three men to mimic him as he crushed the bud between his thumb and index finger and brought it to his nose. "To the ordinary person it smells like grass," he said. "But the trained nose can detect hints of citrus, berry, perhaps even garlic, depending on the hybrid."

This was a part of the tour Dillon favored, watching the three men pull their fingers away, surprised by the pungent odor of the oil within each bud. They smiled and laughed, speaking in Spanish, a language in which Dillon had become fluent. "Growing hops is an art, gentlemen. It requires attention to detail and experimentation to create the very best hybrids for the particular climate and soil. The heartier the plants, the more abundant the buds. This is of utmost importance in a labor-intensive industry. A man must maximize his profits through a quality product and an efficient manufacturing process."

Dillon discarded the bud and wiped the residue on his jeans. "Come," he said. "Let us continue our tour."

Dillon led the men into one of several metal-framed warehouses at his factory. This one was empty at the moment but for the various machinery. In two months the warehouse would be filled with the itinerant farmworkers Dillon hired each harvesting season, as well as his regular employees who operated the equipment and oversaw the process. He believed it important for his buyers to see the full operation and explained to these men that the workers hung the harvested plants on the overhead cable that acted as a conveyor belt which took the plants to the machine that stripped the buds from the stalks. "Once harvested, it is a twenty-four-hour, seven-day-a-week operation, my friends. We work quickly to process the product and move it out. These machines are never turned off."

Dillon proceeded to the kilns and described how the buds were then spread evenly and dried at temperatures of 130 to 140 degrees. From there Dillon brought the men into another warehouse, this one containing two-hundred-pound bales wrapped in burlap sacks. The building was decidedly cooler and Dillon watched as the men reacted to the bitter aroma of the packaged hops. "It is strong, isn't it?" he said, raising his voice to be heard over the sound of the heavy equipment at work. "That's the oils in the buds you're smelling. It's one of the reasons we have to keep the warehouse at thirty-eight degrees. Hops have been known to spontaneously combust." The men looked at one another. "Boom!" Dillon said, using his hands for emphasis, which drew understanding expressions. "Cold storage in metal buildings," he said.

Dillon walked the men to where a worker stood emptying the contents of an opened burlap bale into a machine. "The hops can be processed in a leaf form," he said, pulling apart a portion of the green bale and rubbing the leafy plants vigorously between his palms before holding it to his nose. "But I would like to show you the end product of this machine," Dillon said.

He led them to the other side of the machine, the pipes and temperature gauges white with a frost. "Liquid nitrogen," he explained. Then he pointed to where the machine spit out the end product he hoped would seal the deal. The leafy hops had been processed into pellets that resembled rabbit food. Dillon grabbed a handful and showed them to his customers. Their eyebrows arched with interest. "The pellets make it much easier to transport the product. It can be weighed to the minute ounce and packaged in various sizes. Come."

The men's curiosity sufficiently piqued, Dillon took them on the final leg of his tour, leading them into another of the metal warehouses. Here, three women and four men stood in a processing line weighing out various portions of the pellets and sliding the precise quantities into sealable bags specially made and emblazoned with the logo for the Gold Rush Brewery, as well as the particular brand of hop, the aroma it produced, and the typical beer style best suited for the brand, in this case lagers, pilsners, or wheat. He held up one of the bags. "One ounce. Twenty-eight point four grams and not a gram more," he said. He tossed several packs to his customers. "We like to accommodate not just the large brewers, but also the home brewer," Dillon said. "And to ensure the freshness of our product each bag is vacuum-sealed so that it emits no detectable odor. In the unlikely event any odor were to escape, say a bag was to be punctured, I assure you the smell of the hops, whatever the brand, would dominate." Dillon smiled. *"Comprender, mi amigos?"*

Alex continued to explain what she had learned, "It took some doing, but I finally got my hands on a copy of Victor Dillon's juvenile records from San Joaquin County. Dillon was arrested multiple times for dealing marijuana, and it was a fairly large operation for a kid."

"He's selling pot?" Molia asked.

"I dug a little deeper into that company he worked for, PFI. It might have stood for Property Foreclosures, Inc.," she said, "but it could have just as easily stood for Peter Finch, Inc."

"Who's Peter Finch?" Sloane asked.

"Finch was at one time suspected to be one of the biggest pot distributors in California, which made him one of the biggest dealers in the world during the 1980s. He was a big fish. It explains the company tax returns showing losses. PFI wasn't buying the homes in depressed markets. It was acting as a hard money lender, financing them to fictitious buyers. Every six months or so PFI would repossess the note on the home when the fictitious 'buyer' failed to make the mortgage payments, then lend the money to another fictitious buyer or sell the home outright."

"They were using the business to launder the proceeds of the illegal drug sales," Sloane said.

"In part. PFI would lend the money to a fictitious buyer who would 'buy' the home. They would then go in and set up grow operations. It takes roughly six months to grow a mature marijuana plant," Alex said. "After six months, maybe a year, they'd pull up stakes, reclaim the home, and sell it outright."

"They kept their operation mobile," Molia said. "If the police ever raided a house they'd find a trail leading to a fictitious owner and PFI could plead ignorance, saying they were simply a hard money lender. Brilliant. So what happened to this guy Finch? An untimely death?"

"An untimely disappearance. My friend says the ATF and FBI had a joint operation under way, but that Finch must have got wind of it. He fled the country to parts unknown. Never again to be heard from."

"Which left a gaping hole for a young Victor Dillon to step in and fill," Sloane said.

"The brewery would be the perfect cover," Molia added. "Shit, Dillon has his entire distribution set up with the truck lines and hop processing plants."

"What he would need is cheap land to grow his crops," Alex said.

"And there's no shortage in the Sierra Mountains," Sloane said. "Especially in California's current economic climate." He left the table and returned with the map Lisa Lynch had provided depicting the location of Fresh Start, unrolled it, and laid it out on the table, placing the lamps on each end to hold it open. Fresh Start bordered the Eldorado National Forest. "We know that Dillon is buying up land around the Fresh Start facility, right?"

"I have the records here," Alex said. "I know what you want. Let me get the parcel numbers and I'll map them out in relation to Fresh Start."

"So Fresh Start becomes the excuse Dillon needs to get the supplies he needs for his grow operations into the mountains without attracting attention?" Molia asked

Sloane said, "He's got hundreds of thousands of acres surrounding him. Remember what that parent liaison said about Fresh Start owning the surrounding land to keep out inadvertent hikers."

"And the hops growing is not only a perfect figurative cover, it's a literal cover," Alex said. "Hops are planted in the early spring and harvested between mid-August to September, which is very close to the gestation period for an outdoor marijuana grow. Plus the hop vines grow on string and can get upward of twenty feet, which would act as a further canopy to protect against aerial surveillance."

"I thought they used infrared now," Molia said.

"They do, but cedar and pine trees give off readings similar to marijuana plants. So do hops. It would make the pot plants damn near impossible to detect."

"And there's a ready supply of water from streams and creeks," Alex said. "Dillon could be preparing multiple grow sites and at the same time be harvesting others. It's just like the homes, a mobile operation he keeps moving. And since they're on public land, if someone does stumble onto one and reports it, the authorities can't link it to him."

"How lucrative is it?" Molia asked.

"Lucrative enough that Mexican drug cartels have moved their operations over the border to avoid the hassle of smuggling product across it," Alex said. "My friend said the serious growers prefer the outdoor grows because they produce bigger plants with more usable buds, and outdoor grow operations can produce a lot of plants in a compact area. They've found grow sites as big as forty thousand plants."

Molia whistled.

"What does that amount to in dollars?" Sloane asked.

"He says it depends on the variety of the plant and how they're cared for and harvested, but a sophisticated grow operation in business for as long as we suspect Dillon's to have been would likely have produced its own hybrid that grows best in that climate. Somebody who knows what they're doing can get up to fifteen pounds from each plant, with every pound having a street value of up to fifteen hundred dollars. And the way Dillon has it set up his costs are at a minimum."

"Hell, he's passing those costs on to the county and to the families who are paying Fresh Start to incarcerate their kids," Sloane said.

"Who watches the grows?" Molia asked. "Somebody has to tend the plants. On-Guard?"

"Unlikely. They would be too easily linked to Dillon. My friend says they usually use illegals smuggled across the border from Mexico. They'd have no idea who they're working for and, according to my friend, they're scared into believing that if they say anything their families back in Mexico will be killed."

"Outdoor education," Molia said.

"What?" Sloane asked.

"You remember Lynne Buchman telling us about the inmates at Fresh Start having outdoor education, going out on survival hikes." He searched through papers strewn across the table until he found one of the Fresh Start brochures and flipped it open. "They take them up into the mountains for outdoor adventures, some as long as a week."

"They could get a lot of work done in a week," Alex said.

Sloane studied the map. "Get me the parcel numbers, Alex. If we can pinpoint a likely grow area and find one, we'll have something concrete to take to Barnes to shut down Dillon, and if we do that, we shut down Fresh Start. And that gets Jake and T.J. out of that place."

Three hours later, with the heat of the day turning the bunkhouse into a sweatbox, Sloane and Molia had colored in the parcel numbers of the plots of land purchased by Dillon on the map and were showing it to Sheriff Matt Barnes. The area they'd colored created a red, crescent moon shape above the Fresh Start facility that extended into the Eldorado National Forest. The information had helped to narrow the acreage of likely grow sites, but as Molia said, "That's like saying removing a pinch of the hay pile made it easier to find the hidden needle."

The gross acreage of the Eldorado National Forest was some 787,000 acres, of which nearly 200,000 were privately owned, and that included Dillon's significant chunk. Sloane didn't know any of these facts, but Barnes was giving him and Molia a crash course on reality. Dillon's acreage would not only provide grow sites, but also a buffer to keep out those pesky hikers and backpackers who might ostensibly stumble into Fresh Start, but which Sloane now thought really was intended to keep them from inadvertently finding one of Dillon's homegrown forests of hallucinogenic plants.

"If it was that easy ATF and Fish and Wildlife would be finding grows by the hundreds every year," Barnes said. "Hell, if they find ten thousand plants there's likely another million they don't find.

And if what you're saying is even remotely true, this is a sophisticated operation set up to *not* be easily found."

"You wanted hard evidence, Sheriff," Sloane said. "Those routing numbers are hard evidence. Dillon's laundering tens of millions of dollars through a bank on which Judge Boykin sits as a director. And he isn't pulling that money out of his brewery. The guy has a long history of knowing how to grow pot, and he's put that knowledge to good use and developed a hell of a good cover."

"It ain't hard evidence until we find a grow," Barnes countered, keeping his temper out of his voice, though not his complexion, which was as red as the crescent moon on the map. "Even then we have to tie the grow to Dillon," Barnes continued, "and you yourself said that if the grow is on public land it's unlikely we'll be able to do that."

"So we go to one of Dillon's warehouses and see if hops is all he's distributing." Molia said.

Barnes shook his head. "They harvest end of August, early September. So its unlikely we'd find anything this time of year. I suspect, if what you say is true, that the pot doesn't stay in the warehouse long. Besides, do you think Judge Earl is going to sign a warrant for me to storm Dillon's warehouse?"

The more time Sloane spent with Barnes the more he viewed him as one of those types who was like a simmering kettle on the stove, always on the verge of blowing if someone turned up the fire under him. Sloane had done just that with the evidence of the routing numbers.

"So we find a grow and cross that bridge of proving it's Dillon's when we come to it," Molia said, becoming animated. "We get the evidence. We let the lawyers fight over what it all means, but it starts with the evidence." He jabbed a finger at the colored map.

Sloane stepped back from the table. The heat was getting to all of them. He pulled cold drinks from the cooler and handed one to Barnes and one to Molia.

"If we're right, if Dillon is using Fresh Start as a home base for his grows, then he's running the supplies through it and using the kids as labor to prepare the sites." Sloane ran a pencil on the map. "That means he's likely growing his plants on the lands he's purchased or on land close to it. Even on horses there's a limited distance they could trek to carry in those supplies from the accessible roads. It significantly reduces the acreage."

Barnes rolled his eyes. "Do you know how many marked and unmarked trails there are up there?"

Sloane knew Barnes was playing devil's advocate and didn't mind. The questions were helping to focus their thinking, and that would help to centralize the most likely grow areas. "But they have to trailer the horses." Sloane paused to allow that thought to sink in. "They have to start someplace where they can drive a trailer and unload the horses. That should narrow it further, shouldn't it?" Sloane said. "The grows also need a ready water source. We can talk to Fish and Wildlife."

Barnes sat down on the bench. "Hell, Mr. Sloane, there's as many streams and creeks and rivers up there as there are trails. Look, I'm not trying to throw cold water on your fire, but there could be thousands of potential locations."

"We just need to find one, Sheriff," Sloane said. "Just one."

Barnes ran a hand over a tired face and shut his eyes, grimacing. Most people would have gone on talking, trying to convince him of the validity of their position. Sloane saw young attorneys do it to judges but he knew better. So did Tom Molia. They'd made their best pitch. Saying it twice wasn't going to make it any better. So they waited, listening to the buzz of insects and smelling the charred remains of the outhouse on what little breeze blew through the open door.

"All right," Barnes said, eyeing them both. Sloane knew the sheriff wasn't completely convinced but he was throwing them a bone. "A full-scale operation with Fish and Wildlife and ATF, DEA would take a lot of time to pull together, even if we could convince them. Given your predicament I don't suggest we wait to do that. This is a small town, as you two are finding out quick. Word travels fast. I don't suggest you mention what we're about to do to anyone. Not even Bennett. After the stunt you pulled at the Sutter Building last night, you may have already scared off the prey. Dillon may have pulled up stakes—if he ever planted any to begin with."

Sloane shook his head. "I don't think so, Sheriff. They haven't harvested yet. Like you said, Dillon's not going to leave hundreds of millions on the table and he likely has orders to fill or find himself in real trouble. That's a month, maybe two away. It's cheaper to kill us, which is why they've been trying so hard to do just that."

"And nearly succeeding, I might add."

"We're not trying to be heroes here, Sheriff." Sloane nodded to Molia. "We both know this is a double-edged sword. We both know that pushing this might put our boys in greater jeopardy, but my son let me know he was in peril the first day he called. So I have just one more request."

Barnes nodded.

"If we go up there and we do find a grow, or evidence of a grow, you have to assure me our next stop is Fresh Start, that you'll take custody of Jake and T.J. I don't care if you lock them in your jail until we get them a new trial. You just make sure you get them out of that place."

ELDORADO NATIONAL FOREST
SIERRA NEVADA MOUNTAINS

Jake had made sure to lie down beside T.J. before the guards applied their leg irons. He was dog tired after working all day but fought to stay awake, keeping his mind occupied until he heard one of the guards snoring, likely the cook, who had drunk a lot of tequila during the night.

When he was satisfied both guards were asleep he rolled to his left, whispering, "T.J.?"

When T.J. did not answer Jake poked his shoulder. "T.J.?"

T.J. startled. "Huh? What?"

Jake clasped a hand over his mouth to prevent him from waking the guards. "It's me."

An owl hooted, and the wind caused the branches overhead to creak and moan, and rustled the plastic tarp over their heads.

"What's the matter, what's wrong?"

"I've been thinking."

"About what?"

"About what you said, about how we can't go back to Fresh Start."

Jake had not been able to shake the vision of Big Baby, the hatred in his eyes when he pulled back his fist to decapitate him in the bathhouse. Big Baby would kill them when they got back to Fresh Start. Jake didn't doubt it.

A pan rattled and clanged. Jake lay back, holding his breath, heart racing. He heard rustling near the camp stove. In the pitch-black, he couldn't see but decided it was likely the gray squirrel they'd seen scurrying around the camp earlier that evening. When he heard the rhythm of the guards' breathing return to normal he rolled over again.

"T.J.?"

"What are we going to do?" he asked, fear in his voice.

"We have to get away; we have to run."

"What? Where?"

"Our dads are still here. If we can get to a town and use a phone we can call them."

"How? We don't even know where we are; Atkins blindfolded us."

"I've been keeping track. We're not that far from Fresh Start, so we're not that far from the towns below it. We have to follow the streams. Water runs downhill. That's where the towns will be. They set them up that way for the gold. We find a town, we find a phone."

For a while T.J. didn't speak. Jake knew he was likely doubting him, thinking about what had happened the last time he'd followed one of Jake's plans. T.J. might have also been weighing their chances of actually succeeding and getting away, which Jake had already decided on his own to not be very good, but didn't want to say out loud.

"If Atkins catches us, he'll kill us and bury us up here."

Jake knew Atkins was a sadistic bastard, but up until the moment he pointed the rifle at T.J.'s head and nearly pulled the trigger, he'd never thought he'd actually kill any of them. He'd thought the threats were just another way to scare them, make them think twice about escaping or breaking a rule. But he'd looked into the man's eyes that night when he tried to intervene, and he'd seen more than a sadist. He'd seen something much darker. It was the same thing he'd seen in the eyes of Anthony Stenopolis the night Stenopolis killed his mother then pointed the gun at Jake's face. The same thing he'd seen in Big Baby's eyes. Atkins was a killer, and there was no amount of logic or reason that would keep him from killing. What to do with the body? What to do with the other three witnesses? How to explain to a parent their child was missing? Atkins wasn't considering any of those questions. A killer didn't think that way. That's what Bee Dee meant about Big Baby being a psychopath, acting without any governor. People like that, like Stenopolis and Atkins, would kill and worry about the consequences later. Maybe Atkins already had killed and gotten away with it. Maybe there were bodies decomposing in shallow graves all over the mountains.

"No, he won't," he said, and it wasn't a complete lie. "He can't. He doesn't want anyone snooping around up here. Think about it, why would he cover our faces with masks? Why did he pack out the garbage? Why are they so careful at night with the camp light? They don't want anyone to find this place. That means they're doing something illegal. They're growing pot, T.J. I know it. I've seen it done. If Atkins shoots us and buries us, our dads will have these mountains crawling with people. Atkins can't risk that."

"I don't know."

"He can't. But if Big Baby does it for him, kills us, then Big Baby goes off to prison, and he's going there anyway. Atkins gets rid of us."

"When would we go?" T.J. sounded scared, which meant Jake had to be brave for both of them, confident.

"Remember when Atkins dropped us off? He said three days. That means he's coming back tomorrow, probably in the afternoon, so they can get a full day's work out of us and bring us back to Fresh Start at night. We have to go before that."

"How?"

"I have a plan. I saw it in a movie."

"What!"

"Shhh! We need to get a roll of that string. In the morning I'll create a distraction to get the guards' attention. You drop it down your coveralls. It's over by the shovels. We need to take it with us when they take us to work. You follow my lead." T.J. did not speak. Jake persisted. "Can you do it?"

"Yeah," he said. "I can do it."

"So then, tomorrow. We go tomorrow. First we escape. Then we find our dads."

TWENTY-TWO

Sheriff Barnes returned before dawn and brought with him three men from the Department of Fish and Wildlife. They wore camouflage pants and shirts and floppy hats and brought extra sets for Sloane and Molia. After introductions, the men waited outside on the porch while Barnes gave Sloane and Molia the lay of the land.

"Here's the deal," he said. "This isn't an official investigation. So they're not in uniform, and neither am I. This is their day off and I called in sick so we're *not* on official business. As far as we're all concerned we're going hunting, looking to tag a deer or two, and we're bringing you two along out of the goodness of our hearts. Capiche?"

Sloane nodded as he buttoned the shirt. "Understood."

"For the same reason, if we do happen to find something, we aren't going in guns-a-blazing. We mark it on the map, slip out quiet, and report what we've found. Then we come back with the cavalry. I've known these guys a long time and I'm not looking to get any of them shot. They'll tell you the people guarding these grows can set up sophisticated booby traps and be heavily armed. They'll tell you about a joint ATF and Fish and Wildlife raid in Washington State where the camp residents opened up with grenade launchers." Barnes punctuated the remark with a furrowed brow.

"We understand," Sloane said. "We're not looking to get ourselves or anyone else killed."

Barnes seemed to soften. "They're good men, dedicated. Greg's a marine, so he can be a bit of a cowboy when the adrenaline starts pumping, but he's steady. Dean and Leonard are more subdued but just as passionate about what they do. We're in good hands, gentlemen. If something were to kick-start, I'd go to battle with these guys."

Barnes turned to the door and called for the three to enter. He unrolled the map across the table. He'd already gone over it with Dean, the shortest of the three and likely the oldest, at least from the amount of gray in his hair. Sloane noticed new pencil marks and notations on the map.

"Dean knows this area as well as anyone," Barnes said. "I'm going to let him handle this."

Dean set down a lidded cup of coffee and picked up a pencil, which looked small in his meaty hand. "There's a forest service road here." He pointed with the lead pencil tip at an area not far from Fresh Start. "It would be easily accessible from the facility and maintained well enough to drive a truck with an attached horse rig to about here. That's where the road ends." Again he indicated with the pencil. "There's a trailhead, but it isn't open to the public. Some hikers still use it, but it isn't well defined or traveled. If someone wanted to get up around the back of the facility, it would be a good way to travel." He shook his head. "From there it's anybody's guess, but there are a couple of streams that run through this area and feed the lakes. Growers like to set up their grows within a quarter mile of the water source and run irrigation lines downstream to the site, again to minimize the chances of a hiker or fisherman stumbling onto it."

"Seems well reasoned to me," Sloane said. "It's as good a place as any to start."

Dean laughed. "You're an optimist. That's rugged country up there, even for us. We have our work cut out for us today. The two of you sure you're up for it?" He asked the question while looking at the cast on Sloane's wrist. Sloane also still had the bandage on his head, and as the emergency room doctor predicted, he'd awakened even more sore than when he'd finally crashed for a fitful few hours of sleep. His lower back ached.

"Lead the way," Sloane said. "I'll be all right." In truth he hoped the six ibuprofren would kick in because he didn't want to take the Vicodin.

Dean didn't look as convinced when he turned to Molia. "I might be big, but I'm slow," Molia said, which got a laugh out of the group. "Don't let the size fool you. I won't slow you down."

"I'm not worried about the size; what about that cough?" Dean asked. "You start hacking you're liable to give us away. We need to go in stealth."

The steroids had brought a marked improvement in Molia's breathing and his coughing had been far less frequent, though it still persisted at times. Molia pulled his hand out of his pocket clutching a fistful of throat lozenges. "I'm loaded for bear," he said. Then he got serious. "This isn't my first rodeo, boys. I'm not about to do anything I thought might put any of us in jeopardy."

Just after six, the sun not yet up, they loaded into Greg's SUV, an older model Suburban that looked to have been driven its fair share of hard miles, dinged and dented and rusted in patches, but also big enough with the third bench seat for the six men to ride comfortably and to store their rifles and supplies in the back.

"It's never failed me," Greg said, spitting through the hole in the plastic lid of his cup. His bottom lip bulged with a pinch of chew. He smiled in the rearview mirror at Sloane, seated beside Dean in the middle seat. Molia and the third man, Leonard, sat in the back. Barnes sat in the passenger seat. "And I've taken it places I never should have," which Sloane deduced to be the reason for the winch and cable mounted to the front bumper.

After that, nobody spoke much. In their camouflage uniforms they looked like a military unit, and the gravity of what they were about to do weighed on them. They could pretend they were just six men out hunting for deer, but if they stumbled into the wrong area they might have a hard time convincing people stationed to guard the site of that, and might not even get the chance to explain before someone started shooting or one of them had a leg blown off stepping on one of those booby traps Barnes had mentioned.

Greg turned off the county road onto dirt and gravel, the SUV continuing to ascend, its tires crunching and spitting up rocks with a ping beneath the chassis. Out the back window a cloud of dust spewed, and occasionally the car pitched and rocked when Greg failed to avoid a pothole. They hadn't seen another car on the county road, and Sloane didn't expect they would now that they were on the dirt and gravel. The sun began to shine, but only on the peaks. They drove in the shadows.

Almost two hours from the time they had packed into the car, Greg came to a stop. He didn't have much choice since the road came to an end at a turnabout. Large boulders, which looked to have been strategically placed around the edge of the road, acted as a further impediment to a vehicle proceeding any further.

"This is where the trailhead starts," Dean said as they exited and stretched the ride from their muscles. "It's a steep pitch out of the chute, but fifteen minutes or so into it, the grade levels out a bit."

Greg lowered the back window and started handing out rifles with shoulder straps as well as backpacks loaded with water, protein bars, and ammunition. Dean had walked off toward the trailhead. When he came back he held pieces of hay and straw. Barnes considered it before glancing in Sloane's direction.

"Horse manure also," Dean said. "Someone cleaned it up, but not perfect. And hoofprints." He looked to Sloane. "You may very well be on to something."

Greg continued handing out the supplies, distributing them equally in the backpacks. In between he spit a coffee-colored stream into the dirt. They slung the rifles over their shoulders and fashioned sidearms on their hips. Greg pulled an eight-inch serrated knife from a sheath.

"What do you use a knife like that for?" he asked Dean.

"Huntin'," Dean answered, deepening the tone of his voice.

"Hunting? What do you hunt with a knife like that?"

"Name it," all three said in unison, smiling.

First Blood." Greg explained to Sloane and Molia they were quoting lines from the movie. Sloane had watched it with Jake.

"Still Sylvester Stallone's best movie," Greg said fashioning the knife in its sheath against his thigh.

"We have to carry our own personal weapons since this isn't part of our official duties," Barnes said. He handed Molia a rifle. "Detective, I assume you're familiar with a Remington?"

Molia took the gun and considered it. "Model seven, bolt action, twenty-inch barrel, three-oh-eight caliber." He smiled. "I've shot a few deer in my time, Sheriff."

Greg pulled out another rifle, started to hand it to Sloane, then hesitated. With the cast on his wrist, there was no way Sloane would be able to shoot anything.

"I can carry it for somebody," Sloane said. "In case we need it." He slid the strap over his shoulder.

Greg handed Dean and Leonard backpacks, adjusted his to fit, slid on wraparound sunglasses, spit another wad of liquid, and gave Sloane a stained-teeth smile. "Time to hunt," he said.

ELDORADO NATIONAL FOREST
SIERRA NEVADA MOUNTAINS

Jake did his best to eat his oatmeal, but his nerves made his stomach upset and his taste buds screamed in protest. T.J. also sat stirring the pasty substance with his spoon, but not otherwise bringing it anywhere close to his mouth. Bee Dee had his head up, eyes shifting between Jake and T.J., as if he knew they were up to something. Only Henry ate, head down, shoveling it in and swallowing with a look of disgust.

The other guard was somewhere in the bushes, taking care of his morning business, but the cook stood watching them with eyes so bloodshot they were more red than white. He scowled, indicating he was not too pleased with their reaction to the food. He looked from Jake to T.J. and apparently decided he'd waited long enough. He said something in Spanish Jake didn't understand but interpreted to mean, "Fuck you, you don't want to eat," and knocked the cup out of T.J.'s hand. The spoon went with it and landed on the ground beside the upturned cup. But not a bit of the gooey substance had come out, not even when the cook snatched it from the ground. The oatmeal clung inside like glue.

The cook eyed them, as if daring them to say a word, knowing exactly what they were all thinking. "You think it funny," he said in his broken English. "You don't eat nothing!" He grabbed the cup from Jake's hand. "You see how funny." He continued eyeing them as he walked back to his makeshift kitchen and popped the lid on a plastic container then attempted to shake out the contents. When it still didn't budge he shook more aggressively, and a small amount flew out, only it didn't drop, it flew up and struck the cook in the face. It was like a fart in church. Bee Dee burst first, and that set the rest of them off. Henry laughed so hard he lost his balance, toppling off the stump backward, which only made everything funnier. Tears streamed down Jake's cheeks. The cook threw the cups hard into the bucket, water splashing. Then he grabbed his sharpened machete and took three quick strides toward Bee Dee, shouting in Spanish, machete raised. Jake thought for certain the next thing he'd see was Bee Dee's head rolling on the ground.

He shot to his feet. "No!"

The cook, thinking it an attack, turned and swept the machete through the air. Jake bent his knees and leaned back, like a man stooping beneath a limbo bar. He felt the wind from the blade against his neck and tumbled over, falling onto his back. The cook advanced, whipped the blade through the air, and brought it high overhead like a snake coiled to strike.

A shot rang out.

The cook froze, the shot reverberating. The guard, who had been in the bushes, walked slowly back into camp with the rifle pointed at the sky. The button of his pants still undone, zipper down, and his stained white tank-top T-shirt inched up his stomach to reveal more of the blue ink of his tattoo, some demonic-looking snake. His eyes took them in, then shifted to the cook. He spoke in Spanish. The man, still breathing hard, glared at Jake and Bee Dee before turning his back to them and returning to his kitchen.

"Work," the guard said.

He directed them to the shovels and pickaxes and told them to bring the last of the black hoses. Henry got up off the ground looking pale, and Jake expected T.J. to look even whiter, but T.J. gave him a small smile and glanced down at his chest. Jake noticed the small bulge in the coveralls.

T.J. had the ball of string.

ELDORADO NATIONAL FOREST
SIERRA MOUNTAINS

Dean had not lied. The first half hour was rough, a steep ascent on a trail that wound back and forth with endless curves and switchbacks, but it was the only way up the steep pitch. Dean stopped occasionally to put his fingers in the dirt and trace the faint outline of a horse's hoof, or to check his topographical map. Sloane was grateful for each respite. His muscles and joints, still remembering the accident, hurt worse than he thought they would, and the exertion had caused his wrist and the cut on the back of his head to throb. He knew the others were keeping a close eye on him, and he didn't want to give them any excuse to leave him behind. Barnes handed him a water bottle at each stop and asked how he was holding up.

Molia had also been true to his word. He hadn't slowed them down. Though the detective was a big man, he moved with them step for step and had only infrequently coughed. He looked to be in deep concentration. Sloane deduced it was sheer willpower and mental determination pulling Molia up that mountain more so than physical prowess.

When they reached the summit Sloane looked out over an incredible, panoramic view. The rolling sea of green seemed to reach all the way to the rust haze on the horizon, an expansive carpet that was both awe inspiring and disheartening. He knew now what Barnes had been trying to tell him, a picture in this case definitely being worth a thousand words. Finding a grow site wouldn't be like finding the needle in the haystack. It would be harder. The haystack might take time to cull through, but at least you could pick your way through each piece to a logical end. As if reading Sloane's mind, Barnes walked over and handed him a fresh water bottle and a protein bar. Thankfully, he didn't say "I told you so."

Sloane took a seat on a nearby rock, drinking water and eating the protein bar. Molia had found his own rock, rifle across his lap, seemingly considering the landscape and becoming just as depressed. Dean and Greg stood off to the side, using a flat boulder to lay out their topo map and presumably decide the group's next path. Dean said he could continue to track the horses and believed that would be their best bet. Other than their two voices, Sloane didn't hear another sound. The air was thin and cooler at the summit, but they had little shade from the sun, and though it remained early, not yet nine, it beat down harshly.

After another minute, Greg and Dean had reached some consensus. Dean folded the map and slipped it into a waterproof bag, then inserted it inside a pocket of his shirt. Sloane and Molia stood and followed Greg and Dean down the backside of the mountain. Sloane's body felt as if it had finally awakened. The pain in his muscles had lessened, as had the pounding of his wrist and head. Another hour into their hike, mostly a descent, they were back walking beneath an expansive canopy and pushing through thick brush.

The gunshot sounded like a cannon blast, causing them all to instantly drop to a knee.

Sloane noticed that every head had snapped to the left, the direction of the initial sound, though the retort echoed across the mountaintop before dissipating. Sloane was no expert, but the shot did not sound far off. Greg looked back at Dean, and they both looked to Barnes. Without a word, Greg gave way to Dean, and he made a hard left and pushed on, quickening their pace. They hiked another ten minutes when Dean dropped again to a knee and raised a hand. The others mimicked his movements. Dean turned to Greg and pointed two fingers at his own eyes then pointed to the left. Greg produced a small pair of binoculars from his backpack and scanned in the direction Dean had pointed, he lowered the binoculars and nodded to Dean, then to Barnes.

Barnes slid forward, taking the binoculars. After a minute of viewing, he lowered them and motioned for Sloane and Molia to advance. They took a knee.

"There's a spot ahead where the light filters through the trees in an irregular pattern," he whispered. "Could be where someone cut them down to clear land, or it could just be a patch where the trees died from disease or drought, or even a fire. But it's also where those hoofprints lead and the direction of that gunshot we heard."

Greg slid the binoculars inside the backpack and removed two handheld walkie-talkies, turning a knob at the top on both and handing one to Barnes. Barnes turned to Molia. "Detective, you go with Dean and Greg to get a closer look. We'll wait here until Greg gives us the word. You see anyone you come back; remember we're not here to engage. If it is a camp, and it's empty, that doesn't mean they're gone. That shot could have been a warning from a look-out who saw us coming telling everyone to scatter, which means they're still somewhere around here in the woods, and we already know they're armed."

Molia crept forward with Dean and Greg. Well trained, they kept low to the ground and moved silently despite the brush and trees. Every so often Greg would stop and he and Dean would give each other nods and finger signals before inching their way forward. Molia could see the clearing where the sunlight reflected differently through the trees. With greater effort he could see the trappings of men—cut logs in an unnatural layout to create a crude border, an article of clothing hanging from rope strung between trees.

Molia felt the adrenaline pumping, senses on full alert as they watched the camp, waiting until convinced no one was present. Greg finally broke the surveillance and circled to the right. Dean motioned that he would move to the left. Molia was to move straight ahead. Molia pulled back the bolt and checked again to ensure the gun was loaded, snapped the bolt back, and crept forward, keeping low to the ground.

They reached the camp at about the same time, Greg slightly before Molia and Dean. Molia knew immediately this was not a day hiker's camp. The logs surrounding the camp and the propane tanks indicated the occupants intended a longer stay. The provisions had been trekked in, likely on the horses. Further examination revealed fertilizer, pesticides, and rat poison. Greg walked to a camp stove, bent, and touched it. Then he walked to a plastic bucket and pulled out a cup dripping water and a gray goo.

"They haven't been gone long," he said, keeping his voice low. "Could be off for the day to a grow site or they fled." He looked at Molia. "Guess we got lucky." He raised the walkie-talkie to call Barnes.

Molia raised the rifle. "Don't."

Greg and Dean looked at him.

"A little too lucky," Molia said.

Many things had bothered him, and it had started with the truck accident the night before, when he examined the tires and concluded that the puncture marks had been from the use of a stop stick. While stop sticks certainly could be purchased, they weren't readily available, and there was nothing more convenient than having one in the back of a police vehicle.

And Barnes seemed to be ever present.

That morning, Molia's suspicion heightened when everything had come together just a little too neat and clean, finding the evidence of horses, the hoofprints, and ultimately the camp on a first try, as if they had known where to look all along. They'd been good actors, using the topographical map, Dean dropping to a knee like he was an Indian tracker, but in the end it was just common sense. You didn't reach into the hay pile and pull out the needle on the first try. The question was motivation. Why would Barnes do it? But Barnes had also given Sloane and Molia that answer when they first met, back at the Winchester County Jail. It was about money, sure, but this went beyond money. This was about entitlement.

Greg grinned. He didn't try to dissuade Molia or tell him he was being paranoid. "What are you going to do, Detective? Shoot us?"

"Give me a reason."

Greg took a step toward him, the grin inching into a smile. "Go ahead, pull the trigger."

"It's loaded, Greg. I wasn't born yesterday."

"Maybe the day before yesterday?" Greg turned to Dean, who stood with his rifle at his side, butt on the ground, unconcerned. They shared a smile. Then Dean lifted a bottle of water to his lips and drank. Greg raised the handheld. Molia took aim.

Greg's smile broadened. "Go ahead, Detective, pull the trigger."

Molia did. The trigger clicked, but the gun did not fire.

Greg put a hand to his chest. "Oh, you got me," he said, mocking him.

Dean stepped up and pulled the rifle from Molia's hands. "Slight modification to the safety."

At the same time two men dressed in khaki emerged from the brush to Molia's right. Carl Wade entered the camp from the left.

"Morning, Detective." Wade checked his watch. "You boys made good time, though I'm told my watch is a few minutes fast."

Sloane remained on one knee, waiting and thinking of the conversation he'd have with Barnes if it turned out they'd located a grow site. The deal was they would drive to Fresh Start and get Jake and T.J. He didn't think Barnes was the kind of man who'd renege on a promise, but Barnes might also come to realize the difficulty of the task—coming up with some reason to justify removing T.J. and Jake without giving away that they'd found out Victor Dillon's dirty enterprise. Sloane had a ready-made lie for him. All Barnes had to say was the court of appeals granted a hearing on the appeal and he was to take custody of T.J. and Jake. A phone call from Fresh Start to Judge Boykin's chambers could reveal that lie, but if it was after five they might not be able to reach Boykin or the court of appeals for confirmation, and by that time they would have T.J. and Jake out the front gate. Sloane didn't care what happened next. It was like that old saying, "Better to ask forgiveness than permission."

He heard static over the hand-held, then Greg gave an "all clear."

Barnes pushed to his feet, nodded to Leonard, and the two men walked from the brush and started down the slope. "What does 'all clear' mean?" Sloane asked, catching up. "Did they find a camp?"

"They did," Barnes said.

"So why are we going in? I thought we were going to confirm and get out, get back down the hill."

"I like the detective's idea better. We need evidence of the camp."

"We have evidence. We have eyewitnesses."

"Might not be good enough," Barnes said.

Even before he pushed through the brush and entered the camp, Sloane had a sinking feeling something had gone terribly wrong. Tom Molia sat on the ground, hands behind his back. Greg and Dean stood with two men dressed in khaki, and Carl Wade stood, smiling his shit-eating grin.

TWENTY-THREE

The guards hiked them to a different site than the one they'd worked the first two days, farther out from the camp, just under forty-five minutes. Jake feared the change in location had just ruined his plan of escape, but then he saw that only the place had changed; the procedure remained the same. Gray scrub brush six to eight feet tall had been fortified to further conceal a patch of land. Someone had hacked and stacked branches to make the brush even more impenetrable—likely the cook with his beloved machete.

The man remained agitated. He spun the machete by a leather strap wrapped around his wrist, and it rotated like the blade of a fan cutting through the air. Occasionally he'd hack at a limb of a branch or the trunk of a tree, but mostly he just spun the blade, looking angry. Bee Dee and Henry lowered their coveralls to their waists but left their T-shirts on, a chill still prevalent with the sun not yet high enough to warm the patch of dirt in which they toiled. Jake kept his coveralls over his shoulders. He didn't want to arouse suspicion when T.J. did not lower his.

After an hour the guard stood from his squat. "You, Yake." He handed Jake a three-foot saw blade with severely jagged teeth, wood handles at each end.

"You cut. You and him," he said, pointing to Bee Dee.

The guard directed them to cut down certain of the thinner trees and drag the trunks and lay them in the brush. Jake became concerned they'd spend the entire day working to clear and till the patch of dirt, much the way it was apparent the prior crew had hacked at and stacked the brush, but following a water break the guard directed him to grab a coil of hose. Before the guard could give the second coil to Bee Dee, Jake took it and tossed it to T.J. Bee Dee noticed. So did the guard. The man hesitated, but Jake was counting on the man's indifference being stronger than his curiosity. Indifference won out. What did he care who did what task as long as the work got done? The guard turned and started off into the brush. Jake and T.J. followed.

EL DORADO NATIONAL FOREST
SIERRA NEVADA MOUNTAINS

"Here's the terrible thing about these camps," Barnes said. "They're hidden so well, sometimes a man stumbles into one before he ever sees it. Ordinarily that's not a big deal. Most campers are friendly types and welcome the brief interruption, but in this instance, it can be deadly."

Sloane sat beside the detective. They had fashioned two zip ties together to fit around the cast on his arm and used a third to bind it to his other wrist behind his back. The sun shone over Barnes's left shoulder and caused Sloane to squint until Barnes moved to block the light. It seemed an odd gesture of courtesy given the circumstances. The others, Dean, Leonard, Greg, and now Wade and the two guards who Barnes called Atkins and Bradley, formed a sort of semicircle around them.

"That's why I warned the two of you not to take matters into your own hands and come up here," Barnes continued, "which is the last time anyone ever saw you. You stumble into a camp like this with armed men and the consequences can be dire. Plus they have all this acreage to bury your bodies, or the animals get you."

"So you work for Dillon," Sloane said, thinking Barnes might be a good sheriff, but he was one hell of an actor.

"Everyone works for Dillon to some extent," Barnes said. "And everything was just fine until you two came along."

"Fine? Is that how you rationalize turning your back on a sworn oath to uphold the law?" Molia asked. "You tell yourself everything around here is 'fine'?"

"I wasn't the one who turned my back, Detective. The State of California turned its back on me. Thirty plus years of service, and they tell me they're phasing me out. 'Sorry, budget cuts you know.' The suits down in Sacramento can't manage the budget to save their lives, so everyone's got to pay. Only everyone isn't paying. Mostly it's those of us who put our asses on the line every day who are paying. They tell me I can't retire at fifty-five, that the pension is billions in the red, so they want to take another ten years out of my hide. Oh I can go ahead and retire, just like me and my wife planned, but now we're going to have to do it on a lot less, as well."

"So you became your own private police force and went to work for Dillon," Molia said.

Barnes shrugged. "Pay is better. And I'm only asking for what I'm entitled to, Detective. You of all people should know what I'm talking about."

Molia shook his head. "Don't lump me in with you or your band of mercenaries. You justify it any way you want, but you know that don't make it right."

"Be that as it may, I did warn you not to push things. You can't say I didn't."

"Yeah, well I'm a stubborn son of a bitch," Molia said. He eyed the others. "You all think this is over? You can't keep something like this hidden forever. Eventually you'll all get caught. Every one of you."

"Maybe so," Wade said. "But you won't be there to see it."

The others smiled. Barnes looked more resigned. "Nothing is forever," he agreed. "And I'm not greedy; just want what I earned, what I have coming to me. Another year, when the State cuts Winchester from its budget, I'll retire willingly. The difference between me and every other public servant getting screwed is I won't worry about not receiving my full pension. The wife and I can do just as we planned, maybe even a little more. She deserves it more than I do, waiting up nights, worrying about me. She deserves to go see all those places we've talked about. I can take her just about anywhere in the world and disappear."

"Not going to happen, Matt," Molia said. "Pipe dreams never do."

Barnes turned to Atkins. "Where are they?"

"Grow site sixteen, about a quarter mile east."

"You see, we even moved your sons up here to make it appear this was a rescue mission while they were out of the facility that went horribly wrong," Barnes said.

Sloane gave Molia a quick glance. Jake and T.J. were here, close. A burst of hope shot through him, but just as quickly that burst faded with the circumstances.

"Get them back to Fresh Start," Barnes told Atkins and Bradley. "There will be people up here searching when I report these two have disappeared. Leave the camp as evidence. And the site. I'll tell Dillon we have to abandon it. Who shot the gun?"

Each in the group looked to the other. "Heard it, don't know who shot it," Atkins said.

Barnes sighed. To Sloane he looked and sounded worn down. "Find out. See that it doesn't happen again." Barnes turned to Wade. "You can handle it?"

Wade nodded. "Looking forward to it."

Barnes seemed to give this due consideration. He looked to his three men. "Leonard, you go with him."

A radio crackled. The intrusion interrupted Barnes's train of thought. The radio had come from where the horses had been tied up. Atkins left in that direction.

"All right," Barnes said, recovering. "Let's move out." Greg and Dean lifted Sloane and Molia from beneath their armpits to their feet. The back of Sloane's legs felt weak, and not from a lack of circulation. "I'm sorry it had to come to this, gentlemen. I genuinely liked the both of you."

Wade motioned with the barrel of a semiautomatic for Sloane and Molia to start walking when Atkins returned with the handheld. He looked a shade or two redder than when he'd left. "We have a problem." He ripped the sunglasses from his face and looked at Sloane, eyes burning. "Like father like God damn son," he said. He spoke to Barnes. "They're running. Both of them."

"How?" Barnes asked.

"Hell if I know. Fucking Mexicans. I ought to shoot those two worthless bastards."

Barnes turned to his men. "Leonard, you go with the two of them," he said, meaning Atkins and Bradley. "Bradley, you get the rest back to the bus. Stay in radio contact." Then he directed his gaze to Atkins. "You find the two runners, and you get them back to Fresh Start. Understood? Nothing happens to them until you get them back or we'll have a whole God damn posse crawling around up here. You keep your temper in check."

ELDORADO NATIONAL FOREST
GROW SITE SIXTEEN

When they reached the creek Jake grabbed the deflated plastic water container from the guard, intending to wade out and sink it. The guard smiled when Jake held out his hand for the knife. He shook his head, saying something in Spanish that Jake translated to be, "You think I'm stupid?"

The guard flipped the blade open, took back the container, cut the hole, folded the blade, and stuck it back in the pouch on his belt. He handed Jake the container. Otherwise, he was all too happy to squat at the creek's edge, smoking his cigarettes and keeping his boots dry. Jake handed the coil of hose to T.J., and they waded out into the stream to submerge the container. He showed T.J. how to use the stones from the river to hide it and keep it submerged. Then he took a length of the tubing and reached down, shoving it between two rocks where it would eventually be twisted onto the spout of the container.

As they uncoiled the hose, sinking it along the shore, Jake kept a close eye on the guard. The man remained in his squat, gun slung over his shoulder, tossing pebbles into the water and blowing smoke into the air or squinting up at the sun. Twenty yards downstream, Jake stepped from the stream onto the shore. He grabbed the pickaxes and shovels from where the guard had dropped them. The guard stood and followed him for a few yards, but the brush hung out over the creek and prevented him from continuing along the bank. He did not appear interested in wading into the stream and getting his shoes and socks wet.

Jake stepped from the bank into the calf-high water, sloshed downstream, and ducked into the thicket where he'd left T.J. He handed him the pickax. They were concealed from the guard but Jake knew he'd be listening. "Give me the string and start shaking the branches and picking at the ground like you're in here working," he whispered.

T.J. unzipped his coveralls and handed Jake the string. He looked apprehensive, scared.

"Relax," Jake whispered, "and just keep shaking that bush and picking at the ground like we're digging."

The string was coarse, and strong. He tied an end around a thick branch, wrapping it several times, then threaded it around additional branches, unspooling the string up the eventual path where they would lay the hose and tying it around a third branch. He tested the line, tugging on it. All three branches shook. "Okay," he said to T.J., "back in the water, stick close to the bank, and head downstream."

"Where'd you learn this?" T.J. asked.

"*Cool Hand Luke.* My uncle loves that movie. Go."

Jake followed T.J. into the water, walking backward downstream, unspooling string as he went and tugging on the line to make the branches shake. He didn't know how much string he had, but it kept unspooling and he kept it taut, shaking as he went. The farther away they got the faster they moved. After he'd let out half the string, what Jake estimated to be a hundred yards, he dropped it, pulled T.J. to the bank, and ran.

ELDORADO NATIONAL FOREST
SIERRA NEVADA MOUNTAINS

Carl Wade kept a safe distance behind Sloane and Molia. Sloane contemplated turning and telling Wade he wasn't going to walk another step, that if Wade wanted to drop their bodies in some ravine he would have to carry their dead weight to it, but then he thought of Jake and T.J. on the run, maybe close. The only thing that mattered was staying alive as long as possible with the slim hope that somehow they might survive and find their sons.

As they marched on, hands tied behind their backs, Sloane began to hear a distant, dull roar. It grew in volume as they continued up a footpath, a persistent grade, a light mist wet his face and arms. After five minutes they rounded another bend to where the path came to a fork that looked down on white water gushing through a chute of boulders, no doubt carved by some ancient glacier.

"Stay to the right." Wade had to shout over the sound of the water. He indicated for them to take the path that inclined more sharply. It was mostly loose shale. With their hands behind their backs and their center of gravity off, Sloane and Molia bent forward at the waist, like two old men whose bodies had seen better days, but still their feet slipped on the loose rock. Sloane nearly fell more than once and without the ability to pump his arms, his legs had to work even harder. His thighs soon burned. They ascended until they stood atop a bald slab of stone that looked out over the swollen river, the white water surging through a canyon of boulders and jagged rocks and out over a precipice as if shot from an enormous fire hose tumbling into the canyon. The rushing river and fire hose created its own wind, the spray drenching the boulder and the three men atop it. On the horizon Sloane noticed billowing clouds gathering, thunderheads moving in their direction.

Sloane understood now why Wade and Barnes had not just shot them at the camp. The deafening roar of the waterfall would conceal the sound of the gunshots in case anyone happened to be in the area, and the ravine would likely prevent their bodies from ever being discovered.

Six feet away, the rifle slung over his shoulder, Wade held a handgun at his side. The heavy mist had dampened his hair. Water dripped down his face.

"Okay, boys, who'd like to go first?" he yelled over the rush of the water. When neither Sloane nor Molia answered he said, "Doesn't matter to me. Both of you turn around."

Sloane shook his head. It might have been the final futile act of defiance of a condemned man, but he didn't care. He was going to make Wade look him in the face.

"You'd like that wouldn't you," he yelled, "to shoot us in the back. Jesus, you're a coward, Wade. You don't even have the courage to look a man in the face when you kill him."

Wade stepped forward, gun outstretched, barrel less than a foot from Sloane's face. "You're wrong," he shouted back.

Atkins swung down from his saddle, brought the reins over the horse's ears, and handed them to Bradley. Bee Dee and Henry sat on the ground. The cook with the machete stood beside them, looking genuinely frightened.

"Tie their hands," Atkins said. Bradley pulled zip ties from one of the horse's packs and proceeded to fasten them around the boys' wrists.

Atkins approached the cook, holding out his hand. The cook gave up the machete without protest. Atkins hacked through the brush. In no time he'd cleared a path to the river, ignoring the scratches on his arms where the jagged ends of branches cut across his skin. The second Mexican guard stood at the bank, holding the stock of the rifle, one boot in the water. He, too, looked frightened. He held up string, tugging on it, causing the branch to shake. Atkins took it and shoved the man out of his way, into the stream. Atkins let the string slide through his hand, stepping into the water and following it ten to fifteen feet downstream before walking back.

"Where were you?"

"*Aqui,*" the guard said.

"*Aqui?*" Atkins asked, eyebrows raised. He pushed back the hat from his forehead and glanced up, the sun reflected in each lens of his glasses.

"*Sí, pardon. Aqui.*"

Atkins nodded, lips pursed, seeming to give the answer due consideration. He turned as if to walk downstream, pivoted, and thrust back his elbow, quick and violent. The man's nose broke with a sickening snap and a gush of blood. He fell backward into the brush with an anguished cry. Atkins picked up the automatic rifle and tossed it to Bradley, who snatched it from the air. Then Atkins grabbed the Mexican by the collar, holding the machete under his nose.

"*Aqui?*" he shouted. "*Aqui?* If you were *aqui*, where the hell are they? Huh? *Donde están los niños?*"

"No. Pardon, no." Blood flowed down the man's chin and neck, staining his shirt. "I find. I find."

"*Sí*," Atkins said, pulling the man close. "*Sí*, you find. You find, or . . ." He flicked the machete across the tip of the man's nose, taking a piece of the skin, drawing more blood.

The Mexican pleaded. "*Sí*, pardon. *Sí*. I find. I find."

Atkins shoved the man back into the brush and returned to Bradley. "You and Leonard take those two back down the hill," he said. "When you get to the bus you radio in and tell the captain we may need the dogs."

"Aren't you going to take a horse?" Bradley asked.

Atkins shook his head. "Terrain's too rough, we'll go on foot, me and my two compadres."

Leonard, who Barnes had insisted accompany Atkins, looked up when shadows fell over them. "Send one of the Mexicans back with him. I'm going with you. You heard Barnes."

Atkins looked ready to argue, but Leonard again glanced at the sky. "Storm clouds are moving in fast," he said. "We're wasting time."

T.J. stumbled and fell. Jake stopped, bent at the waist, hands on thighs. "Come on," he said offering his hand. "Get up."

"Wait," T.J. pleaded in between breaths. "Wait. I just need to catch my breath." The final phrase came in a rush of words.

Jake paced in a circle, hands on his waist. He had been urging T.J. forward for the last ten minutes. "We can't stop. We have to keep going. You can do it."

T.J. looked over his shoulder. "I need—I need water."

They'd followed the stream, staying on land when the brush thinned and wading in the water when the brush got too thick to make progress. Jake hoped if they brought the dogs it would throw off their scent, but an hour into their escape the stream had merged into a wider and deeper river, the water rushing over rocks and boulders and cascading into pools of white foam. The bank had steepened, and the increased drop to the river now prevented them from using the water as an escape, or from quenching their thirst.

"We can't get down there; the bank's too steep. We have to keep moving. Come on, T.J. We're almost there."

"Almost where?" T.J. shouted. Sweat trickled down his neck. "We don't even know where we are!" T.J. was fighting back tears.

Jake saw no reason to lie. "No, we don't. But we know we can't go back. So we have to just keep going forward, right? Come on, we have to just keep going forward. Follow the river."

"You go," T.J. said. "I'm just slowing you down."

Jake grabbed the front of T.J.'s coveralls and leaned down, pulling him close, eye to eye. "I'm not leaving without you. You understand me? Either we go together or we go back and face Big Baby together. You decide. What do you want to do?"

T.J. took deep breaths and wiped his eyes. After a minute he said, "I'm okay, now. Let's go."

Jake started off, trying to do a better job controlling the pace while ducking under branches and fighting through scrub. He kept the river on his right, not always able to see it but able to hear it. They found a rhythm to their footsteps, T.J. keeping up, huffing and puffing, but not quitting. At times they had to backtrack, and with each step Jake felt as if he were leading them into the lion's mouth. He followed the paths of least resistance, though not always certain which way the river turned. The ground sloped down then inclined again and finally came to a stone edifice.

"Let's climb up and see if we can get a better view," Jake suggested.

They climbed, using foot and finger holds, pulling themselves to the top. Jake reached the top first and came to a sudden stop. He helped T.J. to his feet, holding onto him so he wouldn't fall. The drop was unnerving.

"Whoa," T.J. said.

The bank had become a cliff, the river fifty feet or more below, heaving through a ravine of rock and stone, twisting and crashing against the sides of the canyon, rebounding and careening downhill through the gorge until both seemed to come to an abrupt end, as if vanishing in midair.

"Waterfall," Jake said. White foam and spray shot out over the precipice and tumbled out of site. Dead end. He searched but saw no way across the ravine and knew that to go around meant hiking miles across the side of the mountain, time they did not have to waste. Disheartened, he did his best to hide it. He wiped the sweat from his brow and turned from the ledge, trying to sound positive. "At least we know we can't get down this way."

"What do we do?" T.J. asked.

"We go back down, find a way around it."

"We can't get around that!"

"Then neither can anyone following us; they have to go around, too."

"What about following the river? How will we know we're going the right way?"

"I don't know," Jake said, trying not to sound like he, too, was losing hope. "I don't know. We'll keep listening for it. Come on, go back down." He took a step when T.J. grabbed his coveralls. "Jake."

"We got to keep moving, T.J."

"Look. Look!"

T.J. was pointing. Far below them, in the valley, something appeared from around a large boulder, the head and shoulders of a man, then the rest of his body. A second man followed, both ascending a steep incline, the path hugging the side of a cliff. Bent over, the two men appeared to have their hands behind their backs. Hikers, Jake thought, but also maybe guards. He crouched to his belly but T.J. remained standing and started yelling and waving his arms.

"Hey. Hey!"

Jake pulled him down. "Be quiet. It could be guards."

"No," he said. "It's them. It's them."

"Who?"

"It's our dads."

Jake's initial thought was that T.J. had lost it. Then he slid forward and looked again to the two men ascending the slope. A third man appeared behind them, the three marching to the summit of the barren dome of rock.

Jake wondered if the fatigue and hunger were playing tricks with his mind, but if they were, T.J. was having the same hallucination. It *was* them, Jake was also certain of it.

"Dad!" T.J. screamed, getting to his knees and waving his arms. "Dad!"

Jake again pulled him down. "He can't hear you," Jake said. "The waterfall is too loud. Besides, whose the third guy?"

The distance was too far for him to clearly make out facial features, and he was uncertain he would know the man even if he could. But something seemed odd.

"What's he doing?" T.J. asked. "Why are they standing like that?"

Their fathers stood as if at attention, their backs to the cliff, hands clasped behind them, facing the man. Jake squinted, inching closer to the edge, and realized why they had been bent over, why their hands remained behind them. "Their hands are tied," he said. And that realization brought another even more horrifying one— why they stood at the edge. "Oh shit!"

"What?" T.J. asked. "What!"

Jake got quickly to his feet and frantically considered his surroundings, seeing nothing he might use.

"Jake, what's wrong?"

Panicked, Jake picked up a piece of shale, throwing it as far and hard as he could, nearly losing his balance. The stone plummeted harmlessly into the gorge.

"What is it?" T.J. asked again, on his feet and now panicked.

"He's going to kill them," Jake said. "He's going to shoot them."

"What? No. No." T.J. waved his arms furiously, shouting. "Dad!—DAD! What do we do, Jake? What do we do?"

Jake didn't know. The man stepped forward, arm outstretched, gun in hand. "Oh God." His legs collapsed. He fell to his knees. T.J. dropped beside him, sobbing. "Dad. No. Dad."

For a brief moment nothing happened. Time froze. Then David and Tom Molia turned and faced the edge and the man took another step forward, arm outstretched.

"No. NO!"

The barrel emitted a tiny spark. David's legs folded and he dropped to his knees, teetered, and tumbled over the edge.

The man took a single step to his right, redirected his aim, and fired the second shot into the back of Tom Molia's head.

TWENTY-FOUR

They moved quickly down the mountain, Barnes following Greg and Dean. They took a detour to a clearing with a view of the valley, the Mokelumne River having over centuries carved a path through the wilderness.

"Give me the binoculars." Barnes sighted along the ridge, focusing. It was a way off, but he knew the mountains well. He found the canyon and followed it until he saw the drop-off. Though he could not see the falls from their particular angle he could see the spray of white water. From there he focused on the ledge before the falls, where he knew Wade intended to take Sloane and Molia. Within minutes the two men came into view, climbing the trail, Wade behind them. "You see them?" Greg asked.

"Yeah I got 'em."

Sloane and Molia stood at the edge. For a moment nothing appeared to be happening. Then Wade raised his arm and advanced a step closer.

"What the hell is he doing?" Barnes said aloud. Then he realized exactly what Wade was doing, brandishing the weapon. "God damn him. He's taunting them."

"Wade's a sick bastard," Greg said, "I've always thought it."

Just as Barnes's anger had nearly peaked, Sloane and Molia turned their backs and faced the ridge. Still, Wade did not immediately shoot. "God damn him," Barnes said. The muzzle of the handgun flared a small white flash. Sloane dropped, listed, and his body tumbled over the side. Seconds later, Molia met the same fate.

Barnes started to lower the binoculars then caught sight of something else, on another ridge, perhaps upstream. The red stuck out amid the forest's natural colors. "Give me the handheld." Greg handed him one of the radios and Barnes depressed the call button. "Leonard, you there? Over."

Leonard answered, his voice indistinct amid the static. "I'm here. Over."

"I got a bead on your two runaways," Barnes said, "stand by."

Greg had taken out the topographical map, running his finger along the different quadrants. "Got it," Greg said.

Barnes provided Leonard the coordinates, having to repeat them twice.

"We're not far," Leonard said.

"Get it done," Barnes said. "And make sure that sociopath Atkins keeps that temper of his in check."

Barnes handed the binoculars and walkie-talkie back to Greg. The sky continued to rapidly change, billowing thunderheads gathering, growing dark and menacing.

"I don't like the looks of this," Barnes said. "Let's get the hell off this mountain."

Atop the boulder, still on their knees, Jake and T.J. remained utterly paralyzed. The echo of their cries had long since dissipated, but Jake felt no desire to move. T.J. too remained slumped, head bowed. A raindrop hit Jake in the neck. He looked up. The sky had turned an ominous black. Raindrops ticked on the rock all about them. It brought another recollection, of another sky. He and David had taken out the boat on the Puget Sound to fish for salmon and had been so engrossed in the sport and conversation they had not noticed that the sky had turned dark and foreboding. As the storm hit they tried to outrace it back to shore but the waters soon turned violent, and the wind blew fiercely, tossing the boat like a cork in the ocean. Sloane had difficulty steering, the propeller coming out of the water with each big wave. And just when it seemed it couldn't get worse, it did. A wave struck just as Jake stood to help and tossed him from the boat and into the frigid water. Even in a life jacket the waves engulfed him as he watched the boat get smaller and smaller, disappearing in the valleys between the crests. He thought there was no way David could save him, and yet somehow David had managed to get the boat turned around, throw him the ski rope, and pull Jake back into the boat. Then he'd somehow managed to get them back to shore. Neither seemed possible, but David had done it.

Later that night they sat by the fire with his mom and talked about what had happened. Sloane told Jake he too had been afraid—not for his own death, but for Jake's.

"But you didn't die," Sloane said. "Because we didn't lose our heads. It would have been easy to panic in that situation, but we didn't. There's nothing stronger than the will to survive, Jake, except the will to save your child. I want you to know that I will never give up, no matter what. So you can't either, not ever. You never give up. You understand? No matter how bad things ever get, you never give up. You fight until your very last breath."

Jake got to his feet and pulled on T.J.'s coveralls. "Get up."

T.J. looked up at him, face smeared with dirt from tears and rain.

"We need to go, T.J. Now. Get up."

"Where?" he asked, voice a whisper. "Where are we going to go? Who are we going to call now?"

"We'll call my dad."

T.J. raised his head and his voice. "Your dad's dead. So is mine."

"My other dad. Frank. I have two. I have one left."

"I don't."

"No, but you have a mother." He knelt. "We can't give up. Our dads wouldn't want us to. We have to get home. You need to get home, for your mom. Come on, there's nothing we can do. Get up!" He reached down and grabbed T.J. by the collar, helping him to his feet.

T.J. could not keep the tears from streaming down his face, and Jake knew they were as much tears of despair as they were grief, because Jake had cried those same tears for months after his mother died. T.J. did not believe they were going to be okay. Jake didn't know one way or the other but he had learned that crying didn't bring his mother back and it wouldn't bring back David or Tom Molia. The rain would come and it would go. The sun would rise and set. The world would go on, and so would Atkins. The guard was still out there, still coming for them. And he wasn't going to give up until he found them and killed them or handed them over to Big Baby. Jake didn't know which one it would be, but he knew one thing for certain. He'd do as David had taught him, as he had promised. He'd fight for both him and T.J. He'd fight until his final breath.

Because now there was no one left to save him. So he'd either kill Big Baby, or he'd die trying.

TWENTY-FIVE

Wade advanced. "You're wrong," he said. "About everything."

Then he winked.

For a moment Sloane thought Wade was trying to clear the water from his eyes, but then Wade said, "They're watching." He waved the handgun, as if giving Sloane and Molia nonverbal directions. "I need you to turn around. I'm going to fire by your left ear. It will be loud as hell. When you hear it, you'll flinch. Don't fight it. Just drop to your knees and roll forward over the edge. The footpath continues about nine feet below. Don't go over the footpath or you really will be bear food. I've hidden a backpack in the rocks. In it you'll find a knife to cut the ties, supplies, and a weapon. They're out looking for your sons. When they find them, they'll take them back to Fresh Start. There's a topographical map inside the backpack. Can you read it?"

Neither Sloane nor Molia responded.

"Stay with me gentlemen! I don't have a lot of time here to explain. Can you read it?"

"I can read it," Molia said.

"Good. I've marked the spot where the bus picks up the kids. It's where they parked the SUV. Get there before they do."

"Who are you?" Sloane asked.

Wade brandished the gun again. He grimaced and spoke through clenched teeth. "Details later. I've been undercover three years. We have a task force in place to take down Victor Dillon, but we hadn't planned to move for another two months, after the harvest. You've forced our hand a bit." He stepped back and raised the gun. "Okay, Mr. Sloane, you're first. Make it look good. Drop to your knees, fall to your side, and roll."

"You were the guardian angel; you pulled me from the car."

Wade nodded. "I tried to get the detective here to pull over to talk, but he launched a milkshake grenade at me instead. Sorry it's come this far. Okay, we can't delay this much longer. Turn."

Sloane looked to Molia. He wasn't sure what to believe. Molia's shrug said what Sloane was thinking. *What choice do we have?*

Sloane turned, closed his eyes, and prayed.

The gun exploded, a deafening blast. Sloane flinched, fell and rolled to his side and over the ledge. With his hands zip-tied behind him he couldn't protect his face and as he rolled the weight of his body crashed down on his casted wrist. The pain nearly made him cry out, but he clenched his teeth and swallowed the agony. He hit what he assumed to be the footpath, jamming his shoulder. His momentum carried him one more roll, and he came to a stop on his stomach, one leg dangling over the edge, the disturbed rock and dirt continuing to cascade down on top of him. He lay motionless, grimacing in pain, ears ringing. He heard the second shot but, though tempted, he did not open his eyes or otherwise move. More rock and dirt cascaded down the hill. Tom Molia landed with an audible grunt.

Sloane lay perfectly still, resisting the urge to speak. Minutes passed. When he could not wait any longer, Sloane opened his eyes and lifted his head. "Hey," he said.

Molia too lifted his head. Sloane looked to his right, over the edge, a thirty-foot fall above jagged rocks and boulders. He pulled back his leg and scooted against the hillside. His wrist felt like it was on fire, the pain shooting through him.

Molia got to his knees and pushed to his feet. His lips moved, but Sloane could not hear him over the ringing in his ears and the rush of the waterfall. The detective stepped closer.

"You all right," he yelled.

Sloane nodded. "My wrist. Just give me a second."

Molia walked to where a strap protruded from beneath rock and shale. The backpack Wade had buried. It was hard maneuvering but he was able to lower enough to grasp the strap. He pulled it from the rock, set it on the ground, and used his teeth to get the zipper open, spitting out dust. Then he turned around and felt inside the pack, pulling out the knife. Molia leaned closer, yelling in Sloane's ear. "I don't know what the hell just happened. Maybe you really do have a guardian angel."

He managed to pull the blade open, hearing it snap in place. "Turn around," Molia said. "Let's get these off."

They stood back to back, Molia holding the knife. Sloane looked over his shoulder and pressed the plastic tie against the blade, moving up and down until the tie snapped. Then he took the knife and cut Molia lose.

The detective rummaged through the pack and pulled out two water bottles, handing one to Sloane. He also found iodine tablets, protein bars, a loaded pistol, and the topographical map inside a sealed plastic bag. Wade had marked the location where they had left Greg's SUV with a red star and their present location at the base of the rock with a green triangle and traced a path between the two in red. It was not a significantly long distance, but they already knew the terrain to be rugged.

Molia folded the map so he could read it inside the plastic sheath and slipped it into his pocket. "Let's go get our sons," he said.

Something moved.

Below the rock from which they had fallen, Jake thought he saw something move, but now he was not certain.

"What is it?" T.J. asked. "What are you looking at?"

It was probably only more of the loose stone tumbling down the side. "Nothing," he said. The rain had increased, darkening the rock. "Come on, let's go."

He started down.

"Jake!" T.J. still faced the rock. "Look."

Jake went back to the ledge and felt his knees go weak. It had not been loose rock. Sloane emerged on a footpath below the rock, the detective behind him, a backpack slung over his shoulder. Their hands were free. "They're alive?" T.J. said. "How?"

"I don't know," Jake said, overwhelmed with relief. "I don't know." For a moment he could not move, confused and uncertain. Then joy and instinct kicked in and he quickly got to his feet. "Come on. We have to get down there"

He climbed down off the rock, running off balance, nearly falling. This time T.J. did not lag behind, each of them fueled by hope and adrenaline. Their arms pumped. Their legs churned. Jake followed the path he hoped led to the ravine. Below them the bend in the river crashed off the wall and continued parallel to it. If they could get around the bend they could climb down to their dads' elevation, perhaps get close enough to call out.

The sky opened, heavy drops of rain beating through the canopy. Thunder rumbled in the distance and the forest lit up with the first bursts of blue light. Jake and T.J. kept moving, running at times, slowing to get over rocks or downed trees, pushing through branches, running again. The forest had turned dark as night and the rain became fierce, a deluge of water that made it difficult to see. Jake ducked beneath the overhang of a boulder that looked to have been sheared in half. Out of the rain, they both struggled to catch their breath.

"When this passes we'll start again," Jake said, blowing on his hands to warm them, his breath marking the air. Water trickled over the edge of the overhang and puddled at their feet.

T.J. wiped his eyes. "Do you think we can find them?"

"We need to find a way down. We're too high. But they were headed east." He motioned vaguely with his arm. "We'll head that same way."

T.J. shook his head. "That guy shot them," he said. "Didn't he?"

"Hell if I know," Jake said. "I have no idea what happened." He stuck his head out from under the ledge. The downpour had eased, though rain continued to fall and the thunder rumbled closer. "Let's go."

Jake led them what he thought to be east, though with the cloud cover, unable to see the sun, he couldn't be sure. What he did know is that they needed to get around the bend in the river and then find a way down. His initial joy had been tempered with the realization that it remained a long shot they would actually be able to find their fathers, but the odds were certainly better than before. They were alive, and they were out there, closer than ever. That's all that mattered. And even if they didn't catch up to them, at least he and T.J. were moving again in the right direction, downstream. Maybe they'd find footprints or some trail to follow, if the rain didn't wash them away. Maybe they'd find a house and be able to make a phone call. They had to try.

The trees thinned. Then they stopped altogether and he and T.J. stepped out onto a large domed rock without any foliage but for patches of low-lying scrub. They'd reached the bend in the river and looked down perhaps a hundred feet onto the foaming water as it crashed against the face of the sheer cliff.

The forest lit up again, this time a huge flash of lightning that made the hair on Jake's arms stand on end. Thunder exploded immediately, a deafening blast that shook the ground.

"Get down!" he said. "Get down!"

They retreated back beneath the canopy and pressed their backs against a large pine tree. Another burst of light lit the area in a blue light. Jake felt a tingling sensation in his arms and legs as the sky exploded. He looked back at the boulder they had to cross and estimated it to be the length of a football field.

"Should we wait?" T.J. asked.

Jake shook his head. "We can't."

"But the lightning?"

Jake couldn't help but laugh. "Really? After everything we've been through? Come on."

They left the shelter of the trees and scrambled up the side of the rock, feet slipping on the slickened surface, sliding backward. Jake dropped to all fours and bear crawled to the top, then turned and offered T.J. his hand, helping him. The lightning struck again, and this time Jake heard a crackling noise in the forest. Thunder boomed, louder than the others.

"Run," he shouted.

They took off in a dead sprint, picking their spots, trying not to stumble. Three-quarters of the way across, the rock sloped down. The footing became treacherous. Jake slowed and dropped onto his butt, scooting the final yards, sliding off. The drop was farther than it appeared, and he landed hard in the dirt. T.J. fell beside him.

Jake helped him to his feet. "We did it," he said. "We're almost there, T.J."

The lightning struck again, illuminating T.J.'s face a brilliant blue. When it faded the color did not return to his face. He had gone pale.

The voice came from behind, and it made the hairs on Jake's neck stand as straight as the lightning had.

"I hope you boys had a nice hike, because I guarantee you it will be your last," Atkins said.

TWENTY-SIX

Tom Molia pulled out the map and considered it in between sips of water. Soaked through, his clothes felt weighted. The rims of their floppy hats sagged like wilted flowers. They'd found cover beneath the branches of two trees, enough at least to consider the map and the compass that unscrewed from the bottom of the handle of the knife.

"Are we still going in the right direction?" Sloane asked, looking over Molia's shoulder.

"I sure as hell hope so," Molia said.

"You hope so?"

"We are. We are," he said. "But we got a couple more miles to cover." He showed Sloane the route on the map. "When we came up the mountain with Barnes we took this route. We're heading perpendicular to that now and should intersect it about here, above the drop-off location. It should afford us a good view to determine if anyone beats us there."

"Then let's get moving," Sloane said.

Atkins grabbed Jake by the throat and shoved him against the trunk of a pine. "You've caused me problems for the last time."

The two Mexicans stood to the side, looking exhausted. The guard Jake and T.J. had tricked had blood down the front of his water-soaked shirt, a split lip, and an open wound at the tip of his nose.

A second man leveled a gun at Atkins's head. "Let it go, Atkins. You heard Sheriff Barnes; we get them back to Fresh Start." Atkins shot the man a look, enraged. "What happens to them there is your concern. But it's like Barnes said, we can't afford to have more people searching for anymore bodies up here, and I'm not carrying them back down the mountain. So chill out and let's get moving."

Jake looked to T.J., an unspoken thought passing between them. They think they're dead. They think our dads are dead.

Atkins loosened his grip, but leaned in close. "I'm going to feed you to Big Baby," he said.

He spun Jake around, pulled his arms behind his back, and secured his wrists with a zip tie so tight the edge of the plastic cut into Jake's flesh. He secured T.J.'s wrists in a similar fashion, shoving them from behind. "Move."

They kept a blistering pace, despite the rain, which eventually eased to a drizzle, the clouds giving way to pockets of blue sky. Jake and T.J. stumbled ahead. If they fell Atkins kicked at them or hit them with the butt of a rifle. T.J. got up each time, no doubt thinking, as Jake was, that Sloane or Molia would materialize from around a tree at any moment. But the longer they pushed on, the more Jake realized they were not heading east to where the bus had dropped them off, the direction their fathers had taken. They were heading due south, down the mountain. That meant Atkins was hiking them directly back to Fresh Start, as he and Overbay had done the first day, when they took Jake hunting.

Molia knelt. They were looking down over the horseshoe cul-de-sac at the end of the dirt road. The Suburban was gone. He scanned to the edge of the trail, looking between the swaying branches and shimmering pine needles and saw something red. Upon closer examination he saw the faces of two boys. They sat with their hands tied behind their backs. Neither was Jake or T.J. The second guard, Barnes had called him "Bradley," stood watching them. Two horses and a donkey had been tied to the trees.

"They're not here," Molia whispered. "But the others are."

"Could mean they haven't found Jake and T.J. yet," Sloane said.

"Or they have and haven't arrived yet."

Molia pulled out the map. "Fresh Start isn't far from here. They could have decided to take them directly there instead."

"What do we do now? Should we wait. See if they arrive?"

"Can't wait." Molia pointed. Far down the hill Sloane spotted a glint of yellow, the Fresh Start bus ascending the hill.

"I'm open to ideas," Sloan said.

Molia turned to Sloane then looked back to the bus. "How well do you know your Greek mythology?"

Half an hour later, Jake looked down at the rectangular plot of dirt and the metal roofs of the buildings reflecting the light of the reemerging sun. Fresh Start. He didn't get much time to admire the view. Atkins shoved him, and they continued down the mountain, every step one step closer to the inevitable confrontation with Big Baby.

They approached Fresh Start's back fence. The gate pulled apart, and Atkins and the man in camouflage escorted them and the two Mexicans inside. The other inmates working in the field and the garden stopped and stared, as if uncertain what they were witnessing. Atkins marched Jake and T.J. past the dormitories and the mess hall directly to the Administration Building. Inside he instructed the civilian at the front desk to open the Plexiglas safety door. Captain Overbay met the party in the lobby with three other men Jake had never seen.

Overbay stepped forward, inches from Jake, his breath acidic and sour. "Some who come here, simply can't be helped," he said. "It is an unfortunate reality of our society that some are incorrigible. They cannot follow rules. They cannot live by rules. It is innate in their nature to break the rules, to break the law. They are beyond redemption. They are beyond rehabilitation. They are beyond saving."

"If this is being saved, you can shove it up your ass," Jake said.

Overbay raised a hand to strike him but one of the men grabbed it. "They're not to be touched," he said. "Put them in the holding cell and keep them in isolation. Nothing happens to them until we get the rest of this sorted out." Then the man motioned to the others and they departed, taking the Mexican guards with them.

Atkins stepped closer. "Oh, we'll get this sorted out, Stand-up. You bet your ass we will."

Molia came down the hill behind where the guard stood watching the road, no doubt for the approaching bus. Sloane waited in the brush near the trailhead. They didn't have much time. When Molia was in position, Sloane stood and Bradley took notice. He reached for his weapon at the same time Molia steppe up behind him and pressed the gun Wade left in the backpack behind the guard's ear.

"Don't," Molia said. "Take your hand away from the gun." Bradley complied.

Molia disarmed him and ordered him to kneel with his fingers laced, hands behind his head.

Sloane cut the ties binding the two kids' wrists. The black kid moved quickly to the horses. "They keep the zip ties in the saddle," he said, returning with a handful. Molia took one, bound Bradley's hands behind his back, then dragged him back into the brush.

"Where are Jake and T.J., do you know?" Sloane asked.

"They're taking them back to Fresh Start," the black kid said. "Big Baby is going to kill them."

Sloane felt his pulse quicken. "Who's Big Baby, one of the guards?"

"He's worse than a guard. He's an inmate. He's a certified psychopath."

Sloane heard the whine of the bus engine. "Okay, time for a little acting, boys. Sit down and put your hands behind your backs."

TWENTY-SEVEN

Atkins locked Jake and T.J. in separate isolation cells.

He would abide by Sheriff Barnes's edict; he'd leave them be until the problem with the two fathers blew over, but once it did, Atkins would hand them over to Big Baby to play with until he tired and killed them. When he did, they'd ship his ass off to Pelican Bay or some other hellhole to live out the rest of his life.

Atkins returned to the guard locker room, which included a break room with a television, two leather couches, Ping Pong table, and kitchen. He was alone. He set the AR-15 rifle in the corner and sat on one of the couches still trying to decompress. His arms were scraped and scratched, his clothes still damp from the afternoon thunderstorm. He'd shower and change as soon as he calmed down.

The radio in the room that monitored all of the individual guards' radios crackled. Atkins recognized the voice of the guard at the front gate. "This is the front gate, over."

"This is transport inbound with two prisoners. Approaching front gate. Over."

That would be Bradley, bringing in Bee Dee and Henry. Atkins hadn't yet decided what to do with the two of them, but he envisioned each on the obstacle course. "Ten-four. Gate will be open. Over."

He stood to meet the bus but the radio crackled again, this time a different voice, heavily accented.

"Hey, this is De la Cruz."

Atkins shook his head. No matter how many times he told the fucking Mexican, he still didn't understand the concept of saying "over" to signal he had finished speaking.

The civilian at the front desk responded. "This is base, over."

"I come to get the horses, but they no here."

A pause ensued, no doubt the civilian waiting for Cruz to say "over." When he didn't, the man said, "Repeat De la Cruz. Over."

"I say, I come to get the horses, but they no horses here. No one here."

Another pause. Atkins picked up the receiver in the break room and broke into the conversation. "De la Cruz, this is Atkins. What do you mean, 'no one there'? Over."

De la Cruz's voice became more animated. "I mean no one here, man. They all gone. The mule, she come back when she hear the truck, but the horses I no find. And no peoples either. Just the mule."

Atkins thought of the inbound bus. "Hang on." He switched frequencies. "This is base, over."

"This is the front gate, over."

"Do not . . ." Atkins let his voice trail.

The guard at the front gate said, "Base I lost you. Did not hear transmission. Over."

"Nothing. Never mind. This is base, out."

He changed frequencies again. "De la Cruz?"

"Yeah this still De la Cruz."

"Find the horses," he said. He set down the receiver, retrieved the rifle from the corner, checked the magazine, and pulled open the door to greet the bus.

The guard at the front gate looked up at the sound of the approaching bus, gears grinding, engine revving. The radio inside the bus crackled.

"This is the front gate. Over."

"This is transport inbound with two prisoners. Approaching front gate. Over."

"Gate will be open. Over."

Sloane sat behind the wheel, Bee Dee kneeling at his side, speaking into the radio. Bee Dee dropped to his stomach as the gate swung inward. As Sloane drove past, he raised his left hand in mock salute to further shade his face. Not that it mattered. The guard in the booth paid little attention, giving a perfunctory wave.

"Drive to the side of the Administration Building," Bee Dee instructed. "It's the first one, right there. Park with the sun at our backs. It's wicked this time of day." With that Bee Dee got off the floor and sat in the second seat, in case anyone watched their approach. They'd expect him to be seated, hands cuffed to the bar across the seat. Henry sat across the aisle, hands also propped up on the bar. The guard, Bradley, and the bus driver lay in their underwear, shackled to the floor at the back of the bus, Molia's Trojan horse. It had been their best chance to get inside Fresh Start. They weren't leaving without Jake and T.J.

After surprising the bus driver, Molia took his and Bradley's uniforms. He cut up one of their T-shirts to gag them. Then he slipped the black hoods intended for the boys over their heads and zip tied them to the floor.

"Where is everyone?" Sloane asked, looking out the bus window at the barren yard.

"Lockdown," Bee Dee said. "They've locked everyone in the dorms. That means Jake and T.J. are back."

"Tell me about the guards again," Molia said.

"One to each dorm. Those three buildings over there. One at the front gate. That leaves Atkins and the captain," Bee Dee said. He looked out the window. "Shit, that's him. That's Atkins."

"I thought you said they don't carry guns," Molia said. "That's an automatic rifle."

"Something's wrong," Bee Dee said. "Atkins knows."

"Maybe it's just because of the lockdown," Molia suggested.

Bee Dee shook his head. "The guards never carry guns unless they're outside the perimeter." He looked and sounded worried. "Something's not right. Atkins knows something."

"How?" Sloane asked.

"I don't know, but he knows."

* * *

Atkins watched the bus slow at the gate, turn, and enter the compound. The afternoon sun, low in the sky and radiant after the rain, reflected sharply behind the bus. Atkins raised his hand to deflect the glare, but even with sunglasses he could not completely shield the shimmering light. He stepped to the side to see at an angle, but it only partially deflected the glare and he could not see inside the windshield. Everything appeared as it should.

Except for the horses.

Bradley would not have left the horses and mule unattended. He would have waited for De la Cruz. At the very least he would have tied them securely to prevent their running off. Horses were pack animals, and the ones at Fresh Start knew when they were returning to their stable and what awaited them. They always stepped a bit quicker on the trail down the mountain, trained to expect fresh hay and a bucket of oats in the trailer on the drive back to the stables. So even if the horses had gotten loose somehow, they would not have wandered far, and they would have come back, as the mule had, at the distinct sound of the diesel truck's engine.

Something wasn't right.

The bus door opened. Atkins couldn't be certain who stepped off first. It could have been Babcock, who had signed out as the bus driver, but he turned his back, facing the bus door. Atkins lowered his right hand to the stock of the rifle as Bee Dee stepped down off the bus, belly belt in place, hands cuffed. Henry followed. Bradley stepped down last. At least he looked to be the right size, similar build. But he had his head turned watching the inmates and Atkins couldn't be certain.

Bee Dee and Henry shuffled forward, directly toward him.

"How'd it go?" Atkins called out, seeking to engage. "Any problems?"

The guard in the back waved a dismissive hand. As he did, the chain fell from Henry's hand and he stumbled over it, falling to the ground. He wasn't cuffed.

Atkins swung the rifle up. "Freeze! Freeze!"

The line halted. Atkins stepped forward, cautious, gun under his chin, locked and loaded. He aimed at the man at the front of the line. He wore a guard's uniform but now, closer, without the sun blinding him, Atkins could see that the man was older. Heavier through the chest. "Drop your weapon. Now."

The man dropped the weapon and raised his head. "Take it easy."

"Son of a bitch," Atkins said, momentarily stunned. He recovered and used the gun to motion the detective to the side. "You, in the back, step up, slowly. Keep your hands where I can see them."

Sloane stepped forward, hands raised.

Atkins shook his head, disbelieving. "I'll be God damned." Then, as if struck by a thought, he said, "Wade."

He stepped back, gun still aimed, and motioned for Molia and Sloane to cross in front of him. When they did, he turned his head, disregarding Bee Dee and Henry.

The kick was both sudden and violent.

Overbay kept an intercom on his desk to monitor the transmissions throughout the day. At the moment he was listening to the chatter between the bus driver and Atkins, as well as the transmission with De la Cruz. Something was amiss. He heard it in Atkins's voice.

He unlocked the top drawer of his oak desk, removed his master set of keys, and started from his office, stopping to consider the locked gun safe. He opened the safe and chose his hunting rifle. Halfway down the hall he peered through the wire-reinforced windows into the isolation cells. Jake paced in his cell, like an animal in a cage at the zoo. T.J. sat on the edge of the metal framed bed bolted to the wall, head in his hand, his gaze directed at the floor. Overbay would deal with them in due course. Continuing down the hall he pushed open the Plexiglas door, then stepped out the heavy metal exterior door. He stopped when he saw Atkins aiming an automatic weapon at two men. Atkins motioned the two men forward, turning to follow as they complied.

That's when Bee Dee sprang.

A blur of red, so fast Overbay almost couldn't process what he was witnessing, Bee Dee struck with a vicious kick. Atkins's leg crumpled and he dropped with an anguished cry of pain. Just as quickly, one of the men relieved him of his rifle, swinging the butt and striking Atkins hard under the chin.

Overbay raised his rifle but as he did a shadow crossed the ground. He looked up expecting it to be one of his guards. Big Baby had stepped from the foliage onto the path.

"What are you doing out of your dorm? There is a lockdown in effect. Return immediately."

Big Baby shook his head, smiling his queer smile.

"You listen to me, Clarence. If you want things to continue as they are, you will get back to your—"

The hand gripped Overbay about the throat with such force it buckled his knees. Big Baby relieved him of his rifle, tossing it in the bushes. "I don't like to be called Clarence," he said.

He applied greater pressure, choking and dragging Overbay farther off the path. Black and white spots blurred Overbay's vision. When the pressure eased Overbay collapsed to his knees, gasping and choking.

"You listen to me," he said, trying to catch his breath. "As of this moment your privileges have been revoked. If you don't return immediately to your dorm I will see that you are shipped out of here to—"

Big Baby had stepped behind him, his massive hands gripping him about the head. "No more punishment," Big Baby said. "No more rules," he said and snapped Overbay's head hard to the left.

Bee Dee sprung, boot raised. Atkins turned, but not quickly enough. Bee Dee's boot struck the side of Atkins's left knee, as if breaking a stick propped against a curb, and Atkins's leg caved inward with a sickening pop. He folded, screaming in agony. Just as quick, Molia knocked the barrel of the rifle into the air, ripped it from Atkins's hands, and swung the butt up under his chin, snapping back Atkins's head and drawing blood from the guard's chin and mouth.

Bee Dee removed the handgun from inside his uniform and pressed it against Atkins's temple. "You got him?" Molia asked.

"I got him."

"Which dorm?" Sloane asked.

"I know." Henry snatched the key ring from Atkins's belt and raced across the yard, Molia and Sloane following.

Atkins grimaced in pain, spitting blood. He looked to have bitten his tongue. He looked up at Bee Dee, eyes enraged, jaw clenched, blood dripping down his neck from the gash in his chin, staining his uniform.

"Surprise," Bee Dee said.

"Give me the gun, Bee Dee, and I'll say they forced you into this."

"I don't think so."

"You're going to jail for the rest of your life. You know that, don't you?"

Bee Dee smiled. "Funny, I was just about to say the same thing to you, you sadistic son of a bitch."

Atkins chuckled. "You can't win, Bee Dee. Overbay's probably already taking them out the back. You're too late."

Bee Dee looked to where Sloane, Molia and Henry had run, realizing his mistake. Jake and T.J. wouldn't be in their dorm. They'd be in the isolation cells. And Henry had taken Atkins's keys.

Atkins laughed. "You can't beat me," he said. "I told you, you're too fucking stupid."

Bee Dee smashed the gun against the side of Atkins's head, knocking him to the ground. "Wrong." He pulled a zip tie from the pocket of his coveralls and bound Atkin's hands behind his back, then he bound the guard's feet. With the way they had positioned the bus, the guard at the front gate could not see what had happened and would not come to Atkins's aid.

Bee Dee ran for the Administration Building, hoping he wasn't too late.

Sloane followed Henry across the yard to one of the cement block buildings. Mike Tyson, the boxer, had once said everyone had a plan until they got punched in the mouth. Then the plan went out the window. Molia had a plan, and his Trojan horse had worked. It got them into the facility, but Atkins approaching the bus carrying an assault rifle had been the punch in the mouth that destroyed the rest of the plan. Fortunately, Bee Dee had countered.

Bee Dee had explained on the bus that his real name was Daniel Neuzil. A DEA agent out of Iowa, Neuzil had worked undercover narcotics in local high schools because he could pass for sixteen, though he was actually twenty-eight. The DEA had grossly underestimated the scope of the corruption in Winchester County when it sent Carl Wade undercover to gain information on what it suspected to be a sophisticated marijuana operation. It took more than a year for Wade to work his way into Victor Dillon's inner circle, but when he did, what he found had appalled and horrified him.

"He put in an immediate request to get a DEA agent inserted into the facility as a guard," Neuzil explained, "but with law enforcement jobs scarce in a bankrupt state the list of correctional officer applicants was daunting. It was faster to get an inmate inside."

Neuzil explained that it had not been difficult. "They created a fictitious crime, the theft of an automobile, and the Department of Justice had a judge in Sacramento sign an order incarcerating me along with a request for a transfer to Fresh Start. Winchester County was more than willing to take Sacramento's money."

When Neuzil had seen Atkins advancing toward the bus and carrying the gun, he advised Sloane and Molia to stick with the plan, but with two exceptions. First, he told Henry to drop the chain when Molia waved his hand and to hit the ground so he would be out of harm's way. He said Atkins would believe Henry had dropped the chain by accident, giving away their ruse. Once Atkins's had disarmed them, he'd believe he was back in control, not realizing the real surprise was not that Sloane and Molia remained alive, or that Bee Dee and Henry were never handcuffed. The real surprise was that Bee Dee had the ability to dislocate Atkins's knee in under a second.

When Sloane reached the dorm he slipped back on the reflector sunglasses and followed Henry inside. By the time the unarmed guard figured out what was happening, Sloane and Molia had their guns trained on him. He offered no resistance.

Sloane looked about the room. T.J. and Jake were not there.

"Where's T.J. and Jake?" Henry asked the group.

"Captain locked them in isolation," a Hispanic boy said.

Molia instructed the guard to get on his knees and used zip ties to bind his hands behind his back.

"Where's isolation?" Sloane asked Henry.

"Administration Building. Take the path by the woods."

"Stay here," Molia said to the boys in the room. "And stay away from the windows."

Sloane followed Molia along a wooded path, running until they came to unnatural markings in the dirt trail, as if an animal had dragged a carcass across the path. They didn't have to go far. The man lay on his back, eyes open but vacant, lifeless. His hairpiece had fallen cockeyed on his head, revealing a hideous red scar. Stitched over the breast pocket of the man's shirt were two words. CAPTAIN OVERBAY.

Bee Dee stepped through the exterior door into the Administration Building. The civilian who worked in the front office reached for the radio. Bee Dee leveled the gun and aimed through the Plexiglas. He had no idea if it was bulletproof or not. "Don't."

The man put the radio transmitter back on the desk.

"Open the door."

The Plexiglas door buzzed. Bee Dee pulled it open and stepped inside. The man rose from his desk, hands raised, backing away. "I just work here," he stammered.

Bee Dee didn't buy the excuse. In his mind every guard and civilian had been complicit in the mistreatment of the inmates, but he had more pressing concerns. "So there's no reason for you to do something stupid," he said. He walked over and killed the switch to the radio.

"Please. I have a wife and kids."

"Put your arms down; I'm not going to shoot you. I'm a federal agent." He walked the man down the hall, stepping to the men's room. "Get in and lock the door. Lay on the floor until someone comes and gets you."

The man was eager to oblige.

As Bee Dee continued down the hall he heard a siren and went to the windows, looking out into the yard where the bus remained parked. Beyond it a stream of cars approached the front gates, lights flashing. "Better late than never, fellas."

He hurried down the hall to Overbay's office, finding it empty. He rummaged through the desk but did not find a set of keys. Rushing from the office he turned the corner at the end of the hall to the corridor with the solitary confinement cells. Big Baby stood in the corridor pulling open one of the doors. He had a set of keys.

Bee Dee raised the hand gun and called out as he moved forward. "Big Baby! Don't!" But the man-child simply grinned and shook his head, stepping inside the room and shutting the door.

Jake stood at the sound of the key in the lock, took a step toward the door, then stopped. Big Baby filled the frame, grinning down at him, bandages still wrapped around his head.

Someone shouted from down the hall, "Big Baby! Don't!"

Big Baby's smile broadened and he let out a thin squeal, as if this were a game. Then he stepped into the room and pulled shut the door.

Jake retreated but there was no place to go. "I don't know what happened to you," he said. "I don't know what someone did to you, but the guards are using you."

Big Baby's smile became a sneer, his lips pulling back to reveal those too small teeth. Jake was no match for him. He knew it, but he also wasn't going down without a fight. As a junior he'd wrestled the state champ, Isaac Markacus. Markacus had breezed through his season undefeated. He had a reputation for being a psycho and perpetrated it by shaving his head in a nohawk. Most opponents were so intimidated they lost before the referee blew the whistle. The day of the match, Jake received some advice. Markacus, he was told, had a temper and would lose focus when made angry. Jake held his own in the first two periods and sensed the boy tiring, never having had to wrestle past the first period. In the third period Jake taunted him. Markacus got angry and charged, and that was all Jake needed to flip him and pin him.

"They're using you," Jake said again. "Are you that stupid that you don't realize it or so stupid you realize it and are letting them do it anyway?"

That did it. Big Baby bull rushed forward.

Jake dodged to the side, ducked, and rolled. He kicked out with his legs, catching Big Baby in midstride, tripping him. Big Baby stumbled off balance. Unable to stop his momentum his shoulder and head impacted the wall. He fell to a knee. Jake would have no other chance. He leapt onto Big Baby's back, wrapping his left forearm about his throat, and gripping his left wrist with his right hand, choking him. At the same time he wrapped his legs about his body and locked his ankles. This had ended the match with Isaac Markacus but not Big Baby. He got to his feet, stumbling backward, turning in a circle. He pulled at Jake's arm and reached overhead, trying to grab and claw Jake's face. Jake buried his head against the base of Big Baby's neck and squeezed with every ounce of strength, holding on like a rider on a raging bull released from its chute. Big Baby propelled himself backward and slammed Jake into the door with tremendous force. Pain exploded up his spine.

Still he hung on.

The man-child continued to stumble across the room, pinballing from one wall to another. Jake grimaced with each impact, but fear and adrenaline continued to fuel him. He maintained his grip and sensed Big Baby tiring. He stumbled again. This time he did not reach a wall. He teetered in the center of the room, a drunken man on the deck of a moving ship. Then he fell to a knee and dropped to one hand. His attempts to reach back and grab Jake became less purposeful. Gurgling sounds, like water backing up a pipe, escaped from his throat. Jake tightened his grip.

The other leg gave out. Big Baby fell to both knees and rolled onto his side.

Sloane pulled open the door to the Administration Building and came to the locked Plexiglas door. He pulled out the key ring.

"Stand back," Molia said. He squeezed the trigger. The assault rifle emitted a thunderous roar. Molia kicked in what remained of the door. They moved quickly through the empty front office. Cars and SUVs sped into the facility, spinning lights reflecting in the windows and lighting up the yard. Sloane and Molia hurried down a hall, running blindly, not knowing the lay of the land. They reached an empty office, scattered papers strewn across the desk and floor. Someone had gone through it in a hurry. A placard, faceup on the floor, read, CAPTAIN OVERBAY.

They stepped from the office and heard someone shout. "Big Baby! Don't!"

Running toward the sound of Bee Dee's voice, they turned at the end of the hall and saw him standing outside a door, looking through the glass. At the sound of their approach Bee Dee turned his head.

"Keys!"

Sloane tossed the keys. Bee Dee snatched them from midair, fumbling with the lock.

Sloane looked through the glass, seeing the backside of the hulking figure in red, Jake atop him, gripping him about the neck. They crashed from one wall to the next.

Bee Dee inserted the key, but the lock did not turn. He swore and inserted a second key. Inside the room Big Baby dropped to a knee then fell forward to a hand. The lock turned.

Big Baby rolled over onto his back, his face turning blue.

Bee Dee pulled open the door, and Sloane rushed in, kneeling beside Jake, trying to get the boy's attention. His eyes were black spheres, fully dilated. "Jake! Jake!"

At first Jake did not react, his face a mask of rage and anger, teeth bared, spittle flying. "Jake! Jake! It's okay, son. It's okay."

Jake turned his head, eyes finding him. "It's me, Jake. It's David." He lowered his voice. "It's going to be okay. Everything is going to be okay now. Let him go. Let him go, Jake."

Jake's pupils shrank. The blue color returned to his iris. His grip lessened, and he released his wrist, falling backward onto the floor, physically and emotionally spent. Big Baby let out a huge gasp, gagging and wheezing. Sloane pulled Jake out from under the boy's body and lifted him to his feet, hugging him.

"It's going to be okay," Sloane said, holding him. "Everything is going to be okay."

TWENTY-EIGHT

T he sun had faded. Shadows crept across the yard. The lights atop the bevy of SUVs and other government-issued vehicles continued to pulse against a spectacular purple-and-orange-colored sky.

The bells at Fresh Start continued to ring at their programmed intervals, but the inmates were not in the mess hall, or showering, or waiting in their dorms to be released for one of their scheduled activities. They weren't following any schedule at all. They milled freely about the yard, their newfound freedom etched on their smiling faces as they watched the flurry of activity with both interest and trepidation. In the center of the yard, seated atop one of the wood tables, Jake and Bee Dee held court, Bee Dee explaining to the others as best he could what had happened, and what was likely to transpire now.

Carl Wade, federal agent Don Wicks, stood with Sloane and Molia in front of the Administration Building, filling them in on what he could only briefly allude to atop the rock beside the waterfall.

"When we started this operation three years ago we thought we were investigating a significant grow operation with ties to a Mexican drug cartel. The deeper I got the more I began to realize we had something far more than that."

Wicks explained that the DEA would eventually be working in tandem with thirty-six federal and state law enforcement agencies throughout the United States and thirteen foreign countries.

"My job was to infiltrate and learn as much as I could," he said. "We had no idea the size of the hornets' nest we'd dug up, the extent of the corruption. Then the county opened Fresh Start." He shook his head. "By that time I was too deep, and we'd uncovered too much about the extent of Dillon's operation for me to blow it up. That was the hardest part, standing by and watching Judge Earl abuse those kids. But we'd invested too much in the operation. They tried to get a guard in. When that failed they got Neuzil inside as an inmate. It was a compromise. It was by no means perfect. We agreed to move this harvest season."

Wicks's phone rang, and he excused himself to take the call. Word continued to filter in from various police agencies around the world that the operation had gone off like clockwork at more than seventy-five of Dillon's distributorships, including the team that descended upon Dillon's brewery and home.

When he wasn't taking phone calls and explaining things to Sloane and Molia, Wicks directed the army of federal agents and attorneys from the Department of Justice who descended upon Fresh Start with subpoenas signed by a federal judge authorizing them to seize computer records and files and take immediate control of the facility. Sloane thought Wicks looked like a man who had just finished a good meal in a fine restaurant. There remained much to be done, but that would predominantly be the work of the attorneys.

"He did his job," Molia said, explaining that he knew exactly how Wicks felt. "He found the evidence. Now it's the lawyers' job to make it stick."

Wicks returned to explain that reports indicated thousands of pounds of marijuana had been seized along with caches of weapons, and that hundreds of millions of dollars had been frozen in bank accounts around the world. Wicks said that by seven o'clock Pacific standard time more than 1,500 people had been taken into custody worldwide and that the number was expected to increase.

"What about Barnes and his men?" Molia asked.

"We picked them up driving down the mountain," he said. "He won't be living out his golden years on any beaches, that's for sure."

"Well, I can't say I feel sorry for him," Molia said. "But I can empathize. Doesn't seem right the State can unilaterally take away what's been earned."

"No, it doesn't," Wicks agreed. "No, it doesn't." He explained that the Fresh Start guards, who had been handcuffed and loaded onto the bus, would be transported to the Sacramento County Jail, where they would be booked and processed. It would take time to sort out each man's crimes. Atkins had been handcuffed and placed in the back of an ambulance. "He'll go to county general to get his knee repaired and chin stitched before joining the party at the county jail," Wicks said. The two Mexican guards in the car with Barnes would be processed through INS, their fate less certain. Captain Overbay wouldn't be processed anywhere. His remains were on their way to the coroner's office, having been killed by what he had created, his own Frankenstein.

The door to the Administration Building opened and Sloane watched multiple federal officers lead a lumbering and shackled Big Baby across the yard. The boy towered above them, looking confused and disoriented, feet shuffling. Sloane felt sorry for the kid, in many ways as much a victim as the others. "What will happen to him?"

"They'll book him, charge him with Overbay's murder. I imagine that will be the first of a litany of charges they'll eventually file," Wicks said.

"He needs help. He needs a psychological evaluation," Sloane said.

"He'll get one." Wicks sighed. "Like I said, it's going to take some time to sort this all out." Wicks turned his attention to the ambulance and they watched the paramedics slide Atkins, lying on a stretcher, into the back and slam shut the doors. "Won't be good, wherever he ends up. Word gets around they have a former correctional officer in their midst and it's usually just a matter of time."

Sloane's immediate concern was much more focused. "What will happen to all the boys?"

"We're notifying family members. That will also take some time to process. The Justice Department has a team of attorneys in place to go through the files and sort out what's what. Those wrongly accused and convicted will be set free and their records expunged, but it won't happen overnight. They'll remain here tonight, under the custody of federal correctional officers."

"That just leaves Judge Earl," Sloane said.

Wicks grimaced. "I'm afraid you're not going to like this answer too much. The Justice Department will be talking to Judge Earl's lawyers about cutting a deal."

"What? Why?"

"Judge Earl set up most of Dillon's enterprise, all the limited liability companies, the accounts offshore, everything. It started when he was in private practice, before he was elected to the bench. That's how he got his fingernails into Dillon in the first place. He really does have a brilliant legal mind. He created a labyrinth of companies we might never untangle without his cooperation."

"He knows where the bodies are," Molia said, sounding disgusted and discouraged.

"He knows where the money is," Wicks said. "Without him Justice doesn't think it can tie everything together. Oh, they'll get Dillon just fine, but they want the entire operation, and they want the money. There's too much at stake to ignore."

"So he's going to walk?" Sloan asked.

"We've had to make tough calls throughout this investigation," Wicks said. "Watching kids be sentenced to a place like this, knowing the conditions. It made me sick to my stomach to be a part of it. But Victor Dillon has always been the target. He's always been the goal. We take him down and we dismantle a huge criminal enterprise. Justice thinks Boykin can get us there."

Sloane seethed. "He didn't just betray all these kids, Agent Wicks; he betrayed the entire justice system. Every time he put on that black robe he swore to uphold the legal system. Then he abused it. He abused these kids, and he took advantage of their families. He abused his power and he abused their trust, and he did it for his own financial gain."

"You're preaching to the choir, David. I empathize. I really do. But that decision is being made by people a whole lot higher up the food chain than me. Is it fair? Hell no. Frustrating? You bet. Is there anything I can do about it?" He shrugged.

Another man in a blue windbreaker approached. "Agent Wicks? I have a call for you."

Wicks excused himself.

"Unbelievable," Sloane said.

"Sometimes law enforcement sucks," Molia said. "But he did his job. You can't blame him. But yeah, we're going to be spitting out a very bitter taste for a very long time."

Molia's phone rang. He almost didn't answer it. "Hello?"

It was Lisa Lynch. She said she had been unable to reach Sloane.

"That's because his phone is at the bottom of a river," Molia said. "Hang on. I'll let him explain."

Molia handed the phone to Sloane. He told her he'd fill her in on everything later but that they were at Fresh Start and had Jake and T.J. "It's a long story," he said.

"And I thought I had good news." Lynch said. "The court of appeals granted our motion for a new trial." Sloane didn't immediately respond. He turned and found Wicks standing in the fading light, the bruise-colored sky at his back. "David?" Lynch said.

"Sorry, Lisa. There's a lot going on at the moment. Let me call you back." He hung up and walked across the yard. Jake sat with the other inmates. "Can I talk to you for a minute?"

Jake slid off the table, and they walked off to the side. Sloane explained to him the situation with Judge Boykin.

"That's not right," Jake said, becoming agitated. "He sent us here. He sent us all here."

"I know," Sloane said. "And I think I might be able to do something about it, but I can't do it alone. Even if I can get all of these people around here to buy my idea, I'm going to need your help. It's a lot to ask, Jake, and I want you to think about it before you answer."

Sloane explained what he had in mind. When he'd finished, Jake broke out in a smile. "I don't have to think about it. Hell, yeah, I'll do it," he said.

Sloane left him to talk to Wicks, arriving as Wicks concluded his call. "Has Justice spoken with Boykin's attorney?"

"What?" Wicks asked.

"Has any deal been struck with Judge Earl?"

Wicks shook his head. "Doubtful anything's happened yet; we're in the preliminary stages. I just thought I'd give you a heads-up—"

"Can you get me a meeting with the person at Justice making that decision?"

Wicks didn't immediately answer. Then he said, "I suppose so. Mind telling me why?"

"What if I told you I had someone who could unravel Victor Dillon's operation for Justice, that she could find all the limited liability companies, all the accounts, all the money?"

"I'd say I'm listening." Wicks smiled. "But I'm also getting a sense you'd like something in return."

"I want Boykin."

"Mind sharing how you're going to do that?"

"I need to talk with whoever it is at Justice who's going to be making the deal with Boykin. They need to agree not to put him on administrative leave or remove him from the bench."

"Two minutes ago you were fuming that Boykin wasn't going to jail; now you want to keep him on the bench?"

"What's a guy like Boykin value more than anything?"

"That's easy. Being a judge. It's his legacy—his entire family's legacy in Winchester County."

"Exactly. So you know he's going to at least try to negotiate a deal in which he gets to stay on the bench."

"That ain't going to fly. Once this story breaks, the public outrage will compel that he be removed."

Sloane put up a hand. "Not if Justice pitches to Boykin that in exchange for his cooperation they'll protect his reputation, paint him in the press and the media as having been a part of the undercover operation, that he was working to take down Victor Dillon's criminal enterprise and clean up Winchester County."

"Why the hell would they ever do that?"

Sloane smiled. "Those kids went into Boykin's courtroom thinking they'd receive justice and found injustice. Why not do to Boykin the same thing he did to those kids."

"Like I said, I'm listening."

"First things first, Justice needs to represent that in exchange for Boykin's cooperation he gets to remain on the bench. Pike, too. He keeps his job."

"Pike? Why Pike?"

"Because I want him to think he dodged a bullet also." Sloane looked across the yard to where Jake and T.J. sat. Even in the dark Sloane could see Jake continuing to smile. "I think it only fitting that Judge Earl get to preside over one last trial right here in Winchester County. And I guarantee you it will be remembered long after he leaves the bench."

Two dozen boys circled Jake and Bee Dee, eyes wide with curiosity and awe. They asked questions with a tone of reverence, wanting to know what had happened and what was to happen, hanging on each and every word. T.J. stood to the side, at the back of the group, in the shadows that continued to steal the last remnants of light.

"We all knew it was you," Rafe said to Jake. "We knew it was you who kicked Big Baby's ass."

"How'd you do it, man?" Jose asked.

The others chimed in. "Yeah, tell us how you did it?"

Jake started to answer, stopped, and looked to where T.J. stood. What Jake had got, he deserved. He'd been a major shit. T.J. was guilty of nothing more than trying to befriend him, and he had paid dearly for it. "It wasn't me," he said. "It was T.J."

"T.J.?" the boys said in near unison.

T.J.'s eyes widened. Heads turned in disbelief.

"T.J. took Big Baby down, twice," Jake said. "He saved me in the bathroom, knocked Big Baby out, and he saved me in that isolation cell. T.J. did it. If it wasn't for him, I'd be dead."

T.J. stared at him, eyes searching, wondering what was the catch. He was about to deflect the accolade, but Jake nodded, a silent acknowledgment that there had only been the two of them present in the bathhouse and nobody but Bee Dee knew what had happened in the isolation cell. The truth was whatever they chose to make it. "Go ahead," he said. "You deserve to tell it."

As the crowd drifted to T.J., Jake slipped off the table and walked off, to an empty spot in the yard, alternately watching the commotion continuing to unfold and staring up at a pale moon and the first faint stars in a sky still awash with the colors of the passing storm. Physically he hurt all over, his body battered and bruised. He'd lost weight, how much he couldn't be certain, and he was exhausted and hungry. He'd been running on adrenaline, and now, with the end of their ordeal actually in sight, his body was giving in to the fatigue. He thought of his mother up there among the stars. She'd raised him Catholic, and said his faith was a gift but also that he wouldn't realize it until he got older. She told him to always trust in God, to believe that everything happened for a reason. She said we didn't know God's ways but we had to have faith that everything was part of his plan. Jake couldn't fully accept that her death was part of any plan, but he was starting to at least understand what she had meant. Maybe he'd never get the answer he sought most—why she had to die at so young an age. Maybe he just had to accept that was the way it was, and believe that he'd somehow be okay. He realized that his inability to accept her death had led to his frustration and his frustration had become the anger that had poisoned him. Anger, as much as anything, was the reason he had ended up in Fresh Start.

He heard the sound of approaching footsteps.

"You all right?" Bee Dee asked.

Jake nodded.

Neuzil motioned to where T.J. had become the center of attention. "That was a nice thing you did."

Jake shook his head. "I got a lot to make up for. What's going to happen to everyone? Do you know?"

"All the cases will get reviewed. They have an organization in place to go through every one of the files. They'll shut this place down."

"Too bad," Jake said.

Neuzil frowned, confused. "How do you figure?"

Jake shrugged. For the first time since his arrival he saw the beauty of the mountains. "You take away the guards, and this is a beautiful place. They should turn it into a camp or something."

Neuzil nodded. "Maybe they'll do that." He stuck out his hand, and Jake shook it. "You got the rest of your life ahead of you, Jake. Don't waste it on drugs and alcohol. I've seen too much of that in my life, too many good kids dying and ending up in places like this, or worse. It takes a lifetime to build a life. It only takes a second to ruin it. Do something great with your life. You have it in you." Neuzil walked in the direction of the bevy of SUVs and unmarked police vehicles.

"Hey, Daniel."

Neuzil turned.

"You never told me what Bee Dee stands for."

Neuzil smiled. "What, you don't believe it stands for 'big dick'?"

Jake laughed.

Neuzil walked back to him. "This is between you and me; I've never told anybody this story, but I think you'll appreciate it. When I was a kid I was picked on because of my size, bullied by the bigger kids, you know, the usual childhood problems. On days when it got particularly bad, my mother would hold me and rest my head against her chest. It was the best feeling in the world. I'd sit there and she'd say, 'Don't you fret about it, Daniel. You have better days ahead of you.' Eventually she shortened it. She'd just say 'better days.'"

"Sounds like my mom," Jake said. "She used to say 'everything happens for a reason,' that I had to have faith."

"My mom died when I was thirteen," Neuzil said. "They diagnosed her with a rare blood cancer, and she died fifty-four days later. The night before she died I went into her room to kiss her good night and she opened her eyes and looked at me. She was too weak to sit up by then or to talk much, but I heard her. It was a whisper, something between just the two of us. She said, 'Better days.'" He looked off for a moment before looking back. "Your mother's right. Everything does happen for a reason. If I wasn't so small and hadn't got picked on she might never have enrolled me in martial arts and then I would never have had the skills I needed today. If I didn't look immature for my age, I couldn't do what I've been doing, could never have been here. No one would believe I was sixteen. I've put away a lot of people who hurt kids with drugs. I like to believe I've saved a few lives doing it. I'm hoping yours is one of them." He put a hand on Jake's shoulder. Then he walked off.

"Better days, Daniel," Jake whispered. He hadn't intended to speak the words aloud, but they carried on the still night air and Neuzil stopped, turned.

"Better days, Jake."

TWENTY-NINE

Judge Earl Boykin took the bench looking very much like a man who believed he remained in control. "Call the next case," he instructed the clerk sitting in the space normally reserved for his regular clerk, Melissa Valdez. Valdez could not be in the courtroom. She sat in the hall outside, along with the other witnesses for the prosecution.

The clerk stood and did as instructed. "The People of the State of California versus Jake Andrew Carter."

The charges against T.J. had been dismissed. Jake had testified before the review board tasked with going through the hundreds of juvenile cases Boykin had presided over and told them he was responsible, that T.J. had been an innocent bystander who unsuccessfully tried to stop him. The board overturned T.J.'s conviction, and the arrest was expunged from his record.

At the request of the Department of Justice, however, the board agreed to let Jake's conviction stand so that the appeals court ruling would mandate he received a new trial. They advised Sloane that Jake had a right to have his case heard by an impartial judge, as did all those juveniles whose cases would be reheard. Sloane declined. In fact, he specifically asked that the matter remain assigned to Judge Earl Boykin. The review board, though confused by the Justice Department's mandate that Earl Boykin remain on the bench, and by Sloane's request that Jake's retrial remain assigned to him, had granted the request.

Most judges would have smelled a trap. Most would have recused themselves and put as much space between themselves and Sloane as possible. Most in Judge Boykin's position, with his attorneys seemingly in heated discussions to negotiate an immunity agreement with the Department of Justice, would have stepped aside, acknowledged they had dodged a bullet, retired, and moved on, grateful not to be spending their glory years in a federal penitentiary. But Judge Earl was not most judges. When the Justice Department dangled the carrot that he would not only receive immunity but also remain on the bench, his family legacy intact and preserved, he could not resist the temptation, and now his ego would not allow him to walk away from what he considered a direct challenge to his authority. He had already justified his actions to himself, as unbelievable as that seemed. Men like Boykin could rationalize just about anything. In his mind he still had a score to settle with David Sloane, the attorney who does not lose, and he was not about to allow that opportunity to pass.

The first thing Sloane did was file a motion to have Jake's confession thrown out. Boykin took that bait as well, denying the motion and holding that the State had the right to prove in the retrial that Jake had admitted his guilt, ruling that it went to Jake's credibility now that he had recanted his in-court confession.

The die cast and the stage set, Sloane and Archibald Pike stood and stated their names for the record. Pike looked nervous and drawn, dark bags beneath his eyes, gaunt through the cheeks, a man who had not slept or eaten much. Pike was not like Boykin. He likely would have preferred to have been anywhere but in court that morning, standing opposite Sloane, but his fate was dictated by others. His sickly appearance also could have been attributable to nerves. This morning Pike was not playing to an empty house and reading from a well-rehearsed script. This morning the gallery was full, every seat taken front to back with overflow spectators seated in the jury box and standing along the back wall. And there was no script. This was live theater. Anything could happen, and Sloane suspected from the buzz of the audience that they felt the same.

Tom Molia sat in the front row behind Sloane, T.J. and Maggie beside him. T.J. had wanted to be present for Jake and Maggie said she wasn't about to take any chances leaving the two of them alone again. Dave Bennett was in the gallery, along with Frank Carter and Tamara Rizek, the reporter who had met with Sloane and Molia at the Shanghai Ale House. The news of the arrest of Victor Dillon and of his marijuana ring had initially drawn the attention of hundreds of reporters and media outlets. They had descended on Winchester County and Truluck in a horde. Their nightly reports had been splashed all over the world news. This morning, two weeks after the bust, only half a dozen of those reporters remained, either curious or talented enough to smell something more was about to happen. They, too, sat in the gallery, along with Winchester County's citizens.

Boykin nodded to Pike's side of the table. "Mr. Pike, the State may proceed."

Pike called the owner of the general store first, and the tall, lean man loped to the stand, raised his right hand, and swore to tell the truth, the whole truth, and nothing but the truth. Pike ran him through the preliminaries before getting to the meat of his testimony, establishing that Jake had attempted to buy beer and cigarettes and had produced a fake ID. The man testified that he confiscated it, which led to a confrontation. When Pike sat, Sloane stood and approached.

"Did you suspect the defendant to be underage?" he asked.

"I did."

"How old did you suspect him to be?"

"I don't know. Sixteen or seventeen."

"Did you question his age before you asked for his ID?"

"I believe I did."

"And what did he say?"

"He said he was twenty-one."

"So he lied."

"You bet."

"He didn't confess to being underage, did he?"

"No, he did not. He lied to my face."

Sloane thanked the store owner and excused him.

Pike followed with one of the arresting officers. He again led the man through each step up to his arriving at the general store and eventually arresting Jake and T.J. in the foothills above Truluck. He said they were both intoxicated and in possession of a loaded firearm. Again, Sloane's cross was brief.

"You took the defendant into custody?"

The officer confirmed he had.

"Did he confess to you, blurt out that he was guilty of breaking into the store, stealing the alcohol and the gun?"

"No, he did not."

Sloane dismissed the man, hoping his strategy was becoming clear to both Pike and Boykin.

Pike stood. "Your Honor, the State would like to move on to proving that Mr. Carter confessed to his crimes."

Boykin nodded. "Proceed."

With that Pike called Melissa Valdez. The clerk entered the courtroom in a simple blue dress. As expected, she testified exactly to what Pike said, that Jake confessed and waived counsel.

Sloane dismissed her without asking a question.

The final witness for the State was the clerk of the court, Evelyn Newcomber. She entered in a black and white knit sweater and black skirt. This morning her fingernails and necklace were red. Pike again walked her through the preliminaries, looking and sounding more confident. Then he asked her to explain the procedure employed when her office received a recording of a court hearing. At this point Newcomber began to look uncomfortable.

"We put a copy of the disc in the file," she said.

"Did you place a copy of the disc used to record the hearing on June twentieth, two thousand and twelve, involving the defendant Jake Andrew Carter in his file.

"Yes, I did," she said.

"Now, sometime later, was your office directed to transcribe that hearing?"

Newcomber kept her focus on the right side of the courtroom, away from Sloane and Jake. "We were."

"Would you explain those circumstances?"

"We received a motion from Mr. Sloane asking that the hearing be transcribed. Later that day Judge Boykin granted the motion."

"And did your office transcribe the audio recording of that hearing?"

"We did not."

"Why not?"

"When I went to the file I found the disc was blank. I don't know how it happened, if it was erased accidentally, or perhaps never recorded, which can happen." The last sentence sounded rushed, and Newcomber grimaced, as if she'd like to snatch back her words.

"So there is no record of the hearing that morning?"

"There is not."

Pike thanked her and turned to Sloane. "Your witness, Counselor."

Sloane stood. "Ms. Newcomber, you said that a recording can, from time to time, not be recorded. Would that be due to human error?"

"I suppose it could be."

"Maybe a technical glitch of some sort as well?"

Pike stood. "He's asking this witness to speculate."

Boykin sustained the objection.

"How long have you been the clerk here at Winchester County Superior Court, Ms. Newcomber?"

"Fourteen years."

"And during that time, have you ever had a proceeding meant to be recorded not be recorded, for any reason that you're aware of?"

Sloane didn't like to ask questions to which he did not know the answer, but he didn't care too much what Newcomber's answer would be. He just wanted to make her even more cautious in how she answered his questions, knowing that he would pounce on any misstep, overstatement, or outright lie. The fact that Newcomber didn't immediately respond seemed to indicate his strategy was working.

"No," she said finally.

"So we can say that this is not a usual occurrence here in Winchester County Superior Court, is it?"

"No, it isn't."

"In fact, it is unheard of, isn't it?"

"Yes, I suppose you could say that as well."

"Were you concerned that a hearing was not recorded?"

"As I said, I don't know if it was not recorded or if it was recorded and somehow got erased."

"Let's assume it was not recorded; would that concern you?"

"Yes it would."

"One of the functions of the clerk's office is to be the custodian of the court record, is it not?"

"It is."

"And you are in charge of that office; the buck stops with you, so to speak."

"I suppose it does, yes."

"You take responsibility."

A pause. "Yes."

"You certainly wouldn't want this to happen again, would you?"

"No."

"I'm sorry, Ms. Newcomber. I'm having trouble hearing your answers. Could you perhaps lean forward and speak into the microphone?" There was nothing wrong with Sloane's hearing.

Newcomber shifted in her seat and leaned closer to the microphone. "I said, 'No.'"

"But as concerned as you were you never sought to determine what actually happened?"

She blanched. "No."

Sloane walked back to counsel table and picked up his notes, letting her answer, and its implications, linger. He carried the papers with him to the witness stand and flipped through them, as if searching for something. "And what if the alternative had been true? What if the lack of a record was not because the hearing was not recorded; what if it had been recorded and subsequently erased? Would that alarm you?"

"Of course."

"Because that would indicate someone had tampered with an official court record, wouldn't it?"

Pike was on his feet to object that the question called for speculation, but not before Newcomber answered.

"Well, no, not necessarily."

"Really? Can you explain that to me?"

Pike remained standing, now uncertain whether to object or not. "Well, it might have been a mistake. Someone, someone might have erased it by mistake," she stammered.

Sloane nodded, as if understanding. He turned to look at Pike. "And a mistake would be an accident, as opposed to a premeditated and deliberate act. Is that what you're saying?"

"Yes."

"So which was it in this instance—a mistake or a premeditated act?"

This time, Pike got his objection in. "Speculation."

Boykin agreed. "Sustained."

"You don't know?" Sloane asked.

"I don't know," Newcomber agreed. Pike sat.

"Because you never investigated it."

She did not answer.

"Or because you already knew this was no accident?"

Pike shot from his chair. "Objection, Your Honor." He fumbled a bit. "No foundation. This witness has testified she did not investigate the incident. Therefore she can't possibly know if the erasure was by accident or an intentional act."

"Sustained," Boykin said. "Your question is bordering on harassing the witness, Counselor."

"My apologies, Your Honor. Let me try to lay a foundation. Ms. Newcomber, do you have personal knowledge whether the disc recording the proceeding on June twentieth was erased by accident or by a deliberate act?"

Pike had remained standing. "Your Honor, it's the same question. Same objection."

Before Boykin could respond Sloane spoke. "I beg to differ. It is not the same question. I'm asking this witness, sworn by oath to tell the truth, whether she knows, without having undertaken an investigation, if the disc was erased accidentally or intentionally."

Newcomber reached for the glass of water on a table to the side of the witness chair. Her hands trembled as she sipped. Sloane waited. So, too, did Pike. The rest of the courtroom, as well as Boykin, leaned a little farther forward in their seats.

Newcomber appeared to swallow with difficulty.

Boykin stepped in, as Sloane knew he would. "I think it's the same question and I'll instruct the witness that she need not answer it."

Pike rested the State's case. He looked tired but relieved. The State's case had gone in relatively smoothly. It looked, for all intents and purposes, like Jake would be convicted. They broke for lunch and returned at one thirty, Judge Boykin advising he needed an extra half an hour to attend to a personal matter. Sloane suspected he was talking to his attorneys, trying to ascertain what type of deal the Justice Department had offered.

When they resumed, Sloane stood. "Your Honor, the defense calls Ms. Eileen Harper."

Sloane had to provide Pike and Boykin with a list identifying each witness he intended to call in his case in chief. Harper's name was on that list, so his calling her did not come as a surprise, though what she might testify about surely intrigued them. Harper took the stand in a navy blue skirt and jacket and white blouse, swore to tell the truth, and spelled her name for the record.

"Where do you work?" Sloane asked.

"I work in the Winchester County Superior Court clerk's office."

"What do you do as a clerk of the court?"

"We manage the court's files, accept pleadings, file them, make sure they are kept in the proper files, and provide copies to the Judge's chambers."

"And that would include juvenile proceedings?"

"It would," she said.

"Is every juvenile proceeding recorded?"

"It's supposed to be." Harper explained the system the court employed to record each proceeding.

"So normal procedure would have been that the proceeding involving my client would have been recorded?"

"Yes."

"And you would have put a disc of that recording in his file."

"Yes."

"Did you put a disc in his file?"

"Yes." The answer caught the room off guard, though not Sloane, who had purposely decided not to cross-examine New-comber on this fact so as not to give her a chance to correct herself.

"You did? It wasn't Ms. Newcomber?"

"No, I did it."

"And did you also go to get the disc upon receiving Judge Boykin's order that it be transcribed?"

"No. Ms. Newcomber did that."

"Were you present working that day?"

"I was."

"And even though you had been the one in the office to file the disc, you weren't the one to retrieve it. Did Ms. Newcomber ask you to get it?"

"No. She never did."

"And did she come to you later and tell you that the disc had been erased?"

"No."

"She never told you?"

"No."

"Did she ask you if you knew what could have possibly hap-pened, since it was you who filed the disc?"

"She never told me about it. Never asked me any questions."

"Did you subsequently learn the disc had been erased?"

"Yes. I heard from another person that the disc was erased."

Pike stood. "Objection, Your Honor. No foundation this witness has any personal knowledge whether the disc was 'erased.' Further, if it was a statement made by another, it's hearsay."

"Sustained," Boykin said. "You will contain your answers only to what you personally know, Ms. Harper. Do I make myself clear?"

Harper smiled up at him. "Very clear."

Sloane nodded. "Let me ask you, Ms. Harper. Do *you* have any personal knowledge whether the disc was *erased*?"

"Yes."

Pike shot Boykin a glance. The judge shifted in his seat, leaning forward, about to speak. Sloane beat him to it.

"How could you possibly know the proceeding was erased? Maybe, as the prosecutor and Ms. Newcomber suggest, the hearing was never recorded?"

"Because when I heard that the disc was blank I pulled the disc of the same hearing from the other defendant's file, Thomas James Molia, and I checked that disc, and the hearing was recorded on that disc."

A murmur spread through the gallery. Tamara Rizek smiled. When Sloane invited her to attend the hearing he said it would provide context to the contents of the package he had delivered earlier in the week. He said if she did attend he'd also make sure she finished the story she began years earlier about Judge Boykin, that she would have more Fresh Start inmates and parents to talk to than she could have ever imagined. He also said he would give her the inside track on a federal drug investigation that would implicate a superior court judge, and make front-page news across the country.

Pike's face went blank. Boykin paled. Sloane faced Harper, so he did not see Newcomber's reaction, but he could guess that she, too, looked sickened, sitting in the gallery.

"Did you put that disc back in Thomas James Molia's file?" Sloane asked.

Harper shook her head. "I put a blank disc back in the file in case someone had intentionally erased the other one. I didn't want that to happen again. I kept the original to protect its contents." She opened her purse and held up the disc.

Boykin banged his gavel. "Bailiff, seize that disc. That is court property. You had no business taking that from the file. Bailiff, you will confiscate that piece of evidence."

The bailiff did as instructed. Harper handed it over willingly. The courtroom stirred ever louder.

"I will take custody of that," Boykin said, reaching down and seizing the disc from the bailiff.

"Ms. Harper, you must be relieved to know that the court now has possession of that disc," Sloane said.

"I am," she said, smiling up at Judge Earl. "I wouldn't want anything to happen to it."

"Your Honor," Sloane said, "I'd like to play the disc. Its contents are clearly relevant to the issues before this court as to whether my client confessed to his crimes or waived his right to counsel, as well as the credibility of Ms. Valdez, Officer Langston, and the court clerk."

"Your request is denied, Mr. Sloane. The court will review the disc to ensure there is nothing inadmissible."

"Then I would request an immediate recess to allow the defense an opportunity to file an interlocutory appeal with the Third Circuit Court of Appeals to have this matter resolved forthwith. It greatly prejudices my client's ability to effectively cross-examine the witnesses the State has proffered here today. Furthermore, Your Honor, the contents of that disc may very well be grounds for Your Honor's immediate recusal."

Boykin's eyes blazed.

"To the extent that disc reveals Your Honor has subordinated perjury," Sloane said, adding the final brush that painted Judge Boykin into the proverbial corner. If Boykin denied Sloane's request to play the disc, it would be suspected by all present that Boykin had subordinated perjury. And if he granted the request, the entire courtroom, including Tamara Rizek and her cohorts in the media, would hear for themselves that Boykin had done just that. They'd also hear how Boykin sentenced Jake and T.J. by having T.J. count the number of pigeons on the courthouse window ledge.

It was largely unnecessary, for reasons that would unfold in a moment, but Sloane had followed courtroom procedure because, at the very least, when he did return to Seattle and had the chance to sit down and have a beer with Father Allen at The Tin Room, he wanted to be able to look the priest in the eye and tell him that for once Allen had been wrong. Sloane had resolved the matter in a court of law. The system, while imperfect, could still work. But, just in case, Sloane had covered his bets.

On cue, the courtroom doors opened. One by one, those boys Boykin had wrongfully sentenced to Fresh Start filed in, accompanied by one or more parent. They were dressed in long shirts and pants. Some wore jackets and ties. Assembled in the back they looked like the Vienna Boys Choir. Sloane had not placed them on his witness list for his case in chief, and court rules did not require he list his rebuttal witnesses. Now he intended to call each and every one to rebut the State's position that Jake had willingly and intelligently confessed to his crimes. Their testimony would show that the State engaged in a pattern of intimidation and trickery to elicit confessions and that they had not been given intelligently.

Boykin, having figured this out, though too late, slammed his gavel. "We'll take a recess. I'd like an opportunity to listen to this disc in chambers and decide whether there is inadmissible material that must be deleted before its introduction." The judge retreated quickly from the bench. The gallery stood, and those present no longer tried to suppress their voices. Questions and conversation filled the room.

Sloane wasn't concerned with what Judge Boykin would do to the disc. Harper had made a dozen copies. One was in the packet Sloane had given to Rizek.

The last person to enter the courtroom after the families was Don Wicks, known to Judge Boykin as Carl Wade. Wicks stepped through the railing to where Molia had met Sloane. "Ready?"

"As a newlywed on his wedding night," Molia said.

Wicks led them to the door leading to the judge's chambers. The court correctional officer stood guard. Wicks badged him. "Step aside or I will have you arrested for interfering in a federal investigation."

The murmur in the room lowered to a hushed silence. The officer stepped aside.

They proceeded through the anteroom. Wicks pushed open the door to Boykin's chambers. Several federal agents were already inside the office, waiting. Judge Boykin had his back to them, staring out the window, gazing down upon the roofs of the buildings in Winchester's Old Town. He did not acknowledge their presence; his ego would not allow it. Sloane knew Boykin was not just considering the town, he was also considering his heritage, and his legacy, which he had disgraced. No shortage of people would want to write about the four generations of Boykins and their abuse of power in Winchester County. They would not speak glowingly of Earl J. Boykin or his ancestors. That's how it was with history, forever at the mercy of modern-day historians. Sloane had no pity or sympathy for a man who made a sport out of abusing young men for financial gain.

"While you're standing there," Sloane said, "you might want to count the number of pigeons on the ledge, and multiply that number by ten."

EPILOGUE

Outside the courthouse, beneath a still blazing summer sun, Sloane said good-bye to Dave Bennett and Eileen Harper, as well as her son, Tommy. After they departed, Sloane and Jake said their final good-byes to Tom Molia and to T.J.

"Well, I don't think I'll forget this vacation anytime soon," Molia said.

"That makes two of us," Maggie added, squeezing her husband's hand.

"I'm really sorry," Jake said, "for everything. And I'm not just saying it. I really am sorry."

Molia stepped forward and embraced him in a bear hug. "You know what? I believe you," he said. When the detective released his grip Jake stepped to T.J., and the two walked off for a private moment. Molia looked at Sloane and just shook his head. "It's always an adventure with you, I'll give you that. Maybe one day we can actually have that quiet vacation in the mountains."

Sloane smiled. "I hope so."

Maggie gave Sloane a hug and kissed him. "Thank you, David."

"Don't thank me," he said. "Thank your husband. If it wasn't for him we would have never found the evidence we needed to do what we did today. He's a good police officer, but he's a better man."

"I know," she said. She stepped back and wiped away tears. "I plan on keeping him." Then she turned to her son. "T.J., we have a plane to catch."

Sloane watched the two boys shake hands and say a few more words before walking back.

"All set?" Molia asked T.J.

"All set," he said. "Jake's going to come out and visit. Maybe next summer."

"You're always welcome," Molia said.

They said their final good-byes before departing for Sacramento to catch a plane back to West Virginia.

Sloane turned to Jake. "You still have to complete your substance abuse program, and grief counseling," he said.

"I know. I will."

"And you know that I'm always here for you, even if we're not together. I mean it. I'll never abandon you again. All you have to do is make a call and I'm on the next plane. You know that, right?"

"I know it. Same with me."

"I'll hold you to it," Sloane said. There was an awkward pause. Then Jake stepped forward and hugged him fiercely. "I love you, Dad."

"Make her proud," he whispered. "Make your mother proud."

"I will. I promise."

"I love you, too, son."

Sloane waved to Frank, wo waited across the parking lot. Then he turned quickly to his car, getting in the driver's side. Once inside he turned his head and watched Jake pull open the door to Frank's Mercedes. He looked away, fighting his emotions, taking another deep breath. He put the key in the ignition and reached to buckle the seat belt. Jake stood at the passenger-side window, his backpack on his shoulder.

Confused, Sloane turned the key and lowered the window. "What's wrong? Did you forget something?"

"Just my backpack." Jake opened the back door, threw his backpack across the backseat, and slid into the front seat.

"I don't understand," Sloane said.

"You did say I was spending the summer with you in Seattle, didn't you?"

"Yeah."

"Well, summer's not over, is it? Besides, I already started the grief counseling with Father Allen and you're always telling me to finish what I begin, aren't you?"

Sloane looked out the window. "What about Frank?"

Jake shrugged. "He's cool with it. He said we can discuss things at the end of summer."

"You sure you won't be bored?"

"I'm looking forward to being bored."

Sloane backed out of the spot and drove to where Frank stood, lowering the window. "You did it once," Frank said, and Sloane knew Frank was referring to that day in court when Sloane gave up custody of Jake to Frank. "I figured I could, too."

The two of them shook hands. "I'll take good care of him, Frank."

"I know."

As they exited the parking lot Jake sat back in his seat.

"You going to listen to your music?" Sloane asked.

Jake shook his head. "No. I was thinking maybe we could talk and that when we get home maybe we could take the boat out. The salmon run this time of year."

ACKNOWLEDGMENTS

As usual, there are many to thank.

During my youth, a good friend and I would take trips to Yosemite Valley. After several days Chris and I would return, taking the back roads through California's gold country, stopping in all the old mining towns. I remember those drives fondly, despite the hot weather and the occasional slow driver who would make the excursion to the next town on the one-lane roads seem to take an eternity. Never in my wildest imagination did I anticipate using that experience as the backdrop for a book. Last summer, however, I spent two days touring some of those old towns. While I could not re-create the experience of my youth, the trip once again helped me to recall those places and why I found them so fascinating. The problem was that everyone I met and spoke to—from the woman at the visitors' center just outside Auburn to those people in the chambers of commerce of each town I visited—were each so darn friendly and helpful. I couldn't find a nasty town in which to place Judge Earl and Carl Wade and Victor Dillon. So I made one up: Truluck, California. I also made up the county, Winchester. Since some of you loyal readers e-mail me and tell me you've gone looking for some of the places I've used as settings in my books, fair warning: you won't find either.

I also want to thank the correctional officer at the Auburn Courthouse who was kind enough to provide me with a tour of that historic building, including the historic courtrooms on the third floor: Though I can't find your business card to acknowledge your generosity properly, know that I am grateful. If you are up that way, it is worth stopping for a look. You don't see that craftsmanship in today's buildings, and those courtrooms on the third floor are a step back in time. The courthouse and courtroom became home to Judge Earl Boykin. Judge Earl is fictional, made up, and not based on any judge in particular. There is not a judge in the country at all like him, to my knowledge.

I also want to thank my friend Jim Russi, who owns the Piety Flats Winery and store in Yakima. Jim and I met on a trip back from Mazatlán to Seattle. I was standing at the airport curb with my daughter and seven thousand pounds of luggage, along with two boogie boards my kids insisted we drag all that way and back . . . and never used . . . when Jim greeted me. He held a briefcase and proceeded to tell me that his boogie board could fit inside it. After a very long day, tired, and waiting for my wife and son, who had gone to get the car, I don't think Jim realized how close to death he really was. We laughed and exchanged information. He didn't for a minute believe I was a writer and I didn't for a minute believe he'd call. But he went home and looked me up on the computer. The next day he e-mailed me and asked if I wanted to speak to the Yakima Rotary, something I have now been blessed to do twice. On the first trip, two years ago, Jim gave my son, his two cousins and me a tour of the many hops fields in Yakima. I noted the type of plant and how it grew, its buds and smell to the untrained nose. I said I thought it the perfect cover for an illegal marijuana operation. Again, I had no idea this would become the premise for a book.

This last trip Jim arranged a tour of a hops-manufacturing factory. Gary McGrath was kind enough to give me an hour of his time and a tour of his facility. Gary was gracious with his information and the experience was a fascinating one. Again, Victor Dillon and his illegal operation were fabricated out of whole cloth and the idea of a hops grower using his business to cover for a marijuana operation is, to my knowledge, completely fictional.

I also want to thank Meg Peavey, a very bright young woman who helped me significantly by researching not only the history of juvenile boot camps, but also outdoor marijuana grows in the Sierra Nevada Mountains. Her research was terrific and thorough and I was blessed to have it. Any similarities to any actual boot camps is pure coincidence. Fresh Start does not exist. And any mistakes in this novel are not the product of the research, but belong to me. Thanks, Meg. I couldn't have written the novel without your help.

I want to thank Dave Bennett and Lisa Lynch for lending me their names for this manuscript. Congratulations on winning the Character in a Book contest. I also want to thank Don Wicks for his generous contribution to the La Conner Rotary in exchange for becoming a character in this novel. Rotarians do good work across the United States and I am fortunate to be able to help their causes, even in a small way.

Could the premise for this novel—widespread corruption that allowed juveniles to be sentenced to a privately owned, for-profit facility—actually occur? If you doubt it, you might want to google "jailing kids for cash" and see what pops up.

Thanks to Meg Ruley of the Jane Rotrosen Agency, my stellar agent. Meg remains my champion and I am thankful for all that she continues to do for my career. Thanks also to the rest of the Rotrosen team who read my drafts and offer suggestions. I do appreciate all of your support. I couldn't do it without you.

Thanks to Tami Taylor, who runs my Web site and does a fantastic job doing it. Thanks to the cold readers who labor through my early drafts and help make my manuscripts better. Thanks to Pam Binder and the Pacific Northwest Writers Association for their tremendous support of my work and all those other conferences who invite me to teach and speak.

Thanks to Touchstone/Simon & Schuster for believing in *The Conviction* and in David Sloane. This includes publisher Stacy Creamer, Sally Kim, Marcia Burch, David Falk, Meredith Kernan, art director Cherlynne Li, production editor Josh Karpf, production manager Alicia Brancato, and interior designer Renata Di Biase.

And the biggest round of applause to Lauren Spiegel, my editor. You made this manuscript better and remain a joy to work with. Thanks for your support, your attention to detail, and prompt responses to my inquiries. I'm glad to have you.

I'm also glad to have Jessica Roth. If there is a better publicist out there, you'll have to prove it to me. Like Lauren, Jessica does her often difficult job with a jovial personality that makes her a joy to work with. Here's hoping the canceled flights and storms are a minimum this year and the publicity and marketing of *The Conviction* are smooth sailing. And if it is not, I'm glad you're captaining this ship.

To Louise Burke, Pocket Books publisher, and Pocket Books associate publisher Anthony Ziccardi as well as editor Abby Zidle for great insight and support. And thanks to all on the Touchstone and Pocket Books sales forces. I wouldn't be writing this without you.

Thank you also to you loyal readers who e-mail me to tell me how much you enjoy my books, raise questions, and await the next. I look forward to those e-mails and read every one. You are the reason I keep looking for the next David Sloane adventure, and beyond.

I've dedicated this book to my two kids, Joe and Catherine. I am blessed to have not one but two great kids. They make me proud in everything they do, from football to basketball and baseball and how they perform in the classroom. But I am most proud of the way they conduct their lives, generous and kind. For this I owe my wife, Cristina. She is such a good person, far better than I deserve, and a lot of that goodness has rubbed off on our kids. As always, thanks for standing beside me. Since I'm an old movie buff, and turned fifty this year and thus am officially an "old guy," I'll finish with this plagiarized and corny line a young guy could never get away with saying. "Here's looking at you, kid."

Quick, e-mail me and name the movie.

Bob Dugoni,
June 2012